I0841088

THE LAST WILL

THE LAST KNOWN WILL

Lou Ann Jasinski Book 2

By

Tanya Goodwin

This is a work of fiction. Names, characters, places, and incidents are the product of the author's imagination. Any resemblance to persons, events, or locales is entirely coincidental.

ISBN-13: 979-8-218-17477-4

Dedication

I dedicate THE LAST WILL, a sequel to THE LAST KNOWN SURVIVOR, to all the rescued victims of sex trafficking and their families who together must piece together life after a nightmare. And for those families who hang onto the hope that their loved ones are alive and may some day and somehow return home.

I would like to thank my editor, Faith Freewoman, who has been steadfast by my side, as well as Rae Monet, my cover artist.

Also by Tanya Goodwin

Suspense /Crime Fiction Novels

The Last Known Survivor-Book-Lou Jasinski Book 1

If Memory Serves- Dr. Tara Ross- Vol 1

The Embalmer- Dr. Tara Ross - Vol 2

Brush With Death- Dr. Tara Ross -Vol 3

Code Pink- Dr. Tara Ross-Vol 4

Cold Case- Dr. Tara Ross-Vol 5

Do Not Disturb

Hidden Obsession

Christmas Novellas

An Evergreen Christmas

An Evergreen Wedding

An Evergreen Baby

An Evergreen Holiday- Boxed Set

The First Star-Dr. Tara Ross Christmas Edition

Snowfall

Contemporary Medical Romance

Roxanne

Fang Hospital- Dr. Gabriella Van Court Book 1

Fang Baby- Dr. Gabriella Van Court Book 2

Fang Vacation- Dr. Gabriela Van Court Book 3

Fang Wedding- Dr. Gabriella Van Court Book 4

ABOUT THE AUTHOR

Tanya Goodwin writes suspense, police procedurals, and crime fiction. Her experiences as a physician are reflected in her characters and in her stories, and her life as a doctor allows her to switch from stethoscope to keyboard. A former New Yorker, she now resides in Florida. Tanya is a member of Sisters in Crime and Mystery Writers of America.

You can reach Tanya Goodwin at:

http://www.tanyagoodwin.com
www.facebook.com/tanyagoodwinauthor
Twitter: @TanyaGoodwinDoc
Instagram tanyagoodwinwrites

1

Kaylee dropped her suitcase in the middle of Lou Ann's living room. Because they'd so abruptly left Greece, she'd only packed one suitcase, leaving the rest of her belongings Demetrios gave her in Greece. Those treasures remained at his mansion that was hers now, but without Demetrios. She twisted the ruby ring he bought for her on their day in Athens when she revealed her true identity to him. Now he was dead and she was once again alone.

She looked around the strange place that was to be her new home where she would live with an aunt whom she didn't know and what's more, had no intention of acknowledging her as her family. Her parents were dead, and her so called aunt now claimed Joanna, an imposter, as her blood.

Kaylee took a deep breath.

But this wasn't Joanna's fault. Both she and Joanna were victims of Newell, may he rot in hell, along with that cretin partner of his, Otto, who she killed with a simple plastic fork to the eye. She grinned just thinking about it. Even Joanna gave her a kudos for a job well done. They both suffered at the same hands.

Lou Ann approached Kaylee and picked up her suitcase.

"You can stay with Joanna for tonight until we figure out another arrangement," Lou Ann said.

Kaylee shrugged and followed her aunt.

Calling her "aunt" felt forced, and she'd had enough of being forced to last her a lifetime. She decided to call her Lou Ann, for the moment.

Kaylee's eyebrows shot up when she walked into Joanna's cramped bedroom. She quickly lowered them, not wanting to seem ungrateful, but the bedroom was one quarter the size of her walk-in closet in Greece. She'd been free of Newell for only days when she could finally demolish the prison cell he'd kept her in. Her new bed in Greece was sweetly soft, and so was the awakening of her heart.

But Newell once again shattered her dreams and any hope of a life with Demetrios. She had kissed Demetrios on his forehead as he lay in his blood while whispering his last words to her. His body hadn't even cooled before she was hustled out of Greece and to Clearwater, Florida, and not even to her former home in Miami. Not that there was anything left there but a few of her possessions. Her real home was in Ekali, Greece.

Joanna sat on her queen-sized bed and patted the sheets on the mattress.

"Um, which side would you like?" Joanna asked.

"Doesn't really matter."

That was an understatement.

"Okay. I usually sleep on the right," Joanna said.

"Then I'll take the left."

Joanna got up and went to the dresser and began to empty two drawers.

"You can put your things here." She turned to face Kaylee. "I know it might be a little tight in here but it's nothing like…"

Joanna went pale.

Kaylee knew exactly why. They'd both been imprisoned in that cell in the house of horrors by the same monsters, just at different times.

It was until they were in Greece and on Demetrios's mansion's front lawn that they first met face-to-face after Joanna beat the shit out of Margo, Newel's other partner and official "groomer" of the girls sold into slavery.

Joanna nearly killed the bitch. Too bad she didn't. Now they'd surely end up testifying at Margo's trial. How ironic that Margo was now locked in a cell smaller than that room that she and Newell had the keys to. But this time Margo didn't have any keys at all.

Kaylee and Joanna stared attach other. It was like looking into a mirror. No wonder they were mistaken for one another.

"I'll let you get settled."

Joanna left the bedroom.

Kaylee didn't mean to chase Joanna away.

Sanctuary meant everything.

Kaylee plopped her suitcase on the bed and opened it.

There it was, the white sundress with tiny red roses, the one she wore on that last and only outing to Athens with Demetrios. He bought her the ruby ring to match the roses. The dress was the first thing she packed. She needed it.

She brought the dress to her nose and inhaled his scent.

Tears trickled down her cheeks, but she didn't bother to wipe them away.

She heard Lou Ann clear her throat from the bedroom doorway behind her. So much for privacy. Joanna didn't close the door on her way out.

"Can I help you, um, with anything?" she asked.

Kaylee didn't turn around. She refused to let the woman see her cry.

Kaylee quickly swallowed her grief. There was no point in attaching herself to her aunt because the minute Margo's trial was over and that woman was in prison, Kaylee would return to Greece, for good. But then the will would be finalized, and she'd have the money to fly back and claim what Demetrios wanted her to have. The only one to stand in her way was Adam Sakalis, Demetrios's estranged nephew. He was about as close to Demetrios as she was to Lou Ann.

But she'd fight to the finish because she was a survivor.

Kaylee turned around and looked at Lou Ann.

"No thank you. I've got it," she said.

Lou Ann sat next to Joanna on the couch in the den and sighed.

"Give her time to adjust. This isn't her home in Miami or in Greece. She's completely confused just as I still am. I just happen to have gotten a head start, a bizarre one at that. Plus, she's grieving, not to mention the post-traumatic stress we have in common."

Guilt grabbed Lou Ann and shook her hard. She wanted the old Kaylee back. But that's what happens when time stands still, fourteen years of it. And whose fault was that? Hers and her brother, Lyle. Dead brother, that is.

It was Joanna who attended Kaylee's parents' funeral. Not Kaylee. Kaylee couldn't keep anyone she loved to stay alive, not even a wealthy Greek man who paid for her, thinking she was Joanna.

Monsters had twisted the two girls' lives together. Now it was up to Lou Ann to untwist them while doing as little damage as possible. Tall order.

Kaylee walked into the den and stood near the open door, avoiding sitting next to Lou Ann or Joanna. Instead she walked over to a recliner in the corner and sat.

The disconnect among the three of them resonated in the silence. The only sound in the room was the squeak-squeak of the rocking recliner.

Damn. Harry never fixed that. Probably, like with Kaylee, it eventually was the sound separating him and Lou Ann, and gave them an excuse to not talk to each other. Lou Ann made a mental note to get rid of that squeak, tomorrow. It was too important to make sure nothing got in the way of them communicating with each other. But it would take much more than getting rid of the squeaks to even begin to heal what ailed the three of them.

Lou Ann stood.

"I'll go start dinner."

Joanna pushed up off the couch.

"I'll help you."

Kaylee said nothing, looking straight ahead while continuing to rock in the recliner, faster and faster.

Lou Ann left Kaylee to her chair and calmly walked out of the den. But she refused to walk out of Kaylee's life, again.

Harry rang the doorbell and hugged the casserole dish while waiting for Lou Ann to let him in the house they once shared. Ever since he and Lou Ann risked their lives while freeing Kaylee and Joanna from the horrors of sexual slavery, their once-dead relationship had been resurrected, and going forward, he'd do whatever it took to keep it that way. And that included respecting lingering boundaries.

Lou Ann opened the door.

"Harry! Come in! You're just in time."

She kissed his cheek.

She'd given him a quick kiss on the mouth during the plane ride back from Greece, but any kiss gave him hope that she'd forgiven his past indiscretion.

"Here, let me take that. You didn't need to bring anything, and you didn't need to ring the bell.

Yes, and yes I did.

Harry nodded."Okay," he said.

He followed her into the kitchen, where Joanna and Kaylee sat at the table facing each other.

"Hey, girls."

Secretly he still wanted to refer to Joanna as Kaylee. He and Joanna, and Joanna as Kaylee, had a relationship, but he still was working on one with the real Kaylee. Calling them "girls" prevented him from mixing up the two. Lou Ann had confided to him that she struggled with the same.

Joanna leaped up from her chair and hugged Harry while Kaylee remained in her seat.

"Hello, Harry," she said with excruciating politeness.

"Hi, Kaylee."

Kaylee blinked at him.

But it was after a pause. He'd have to work at gaining her trust.

Lou Ann brought platters of grilled chicken breast, roasted red potatoes, and Harry's favorite, her green bean casserole.

Joanna clapped. "Wow! Mac and cheese!"

"It's only from a box," Harry admitted.

It was the only kind he could make. Maybe next time he could figure out how to make it from scratch.

"My favorite kind," Joanna said.

Kaylee stared at the yellow noodles but offered no comment. Her stone face said it all.

Lou Ann forced a grin and sat down next to Harry.

"Let's eat," she said.

Everyone loaded their plate with all the dinner offerings except Kaylee, who skimped on everything and bypassed Harry's mac and cheese.

Harry accepted Kaylee's rejection. Boxed mac and cheese wasn't for everyone.

Kaylee stood from the table.

"Excuse me," she said, and then walked away.

"Hey! Where did she go?" Joanna asked.

Lou Ann's eyes went big.

It's all right. Let her be. Keep eating," he said.

A minute later both he and Lou Ann got up from the table.

"Okay. Which one of you is going to check on her?" Joanna asked.

"I'll go. It was my mac and cheese," Harry said.

Kaylee sat on the front stoop, face buried in her hands. Her shoulders shook while she wailed and hot tears filled her palms.

Someone sat quietly beside her.

The last thing she wanted was to address Lou Ann and her needs, so she remained cocooned in her own grief.

"Leave me in peace, Lou Ann. Please," she blubbered.

"Not Lou Ann."

Kaylee sniffled.

"Harry?"

"Yes, it's me. I can leave if you want. It's okay."

Kaylee lowered the fortress of her hands.

"No. You can stay, but I don't want to ruin your dinner or anyone else's."

"I can heat mine up. It won't be the first time. And last I checked, the rest are eating, or that's what I told them to do."

"I'm sorry."

"Okay. Apology accepted."

"Are they mad at me?"

"No. Maybe more like confused and hurting for you."

"Why?"

"Because they're your family and that's what families do."

Kaylee whipped her head to face Harry.

"They're not my family! Both my families are dead!"

Harry remained silent.

"Where are my mom and dad?"

"They're buried in Miami."

"So you were there?"

"Yes. Me, your Aunt Lou Ann, and Joanna, who we thought was you. I'm so sorry."

"Hardly as sorry and angry as I am. The last time I saw them was in that car. It was all Dad's fault. Mom and I begged him to slow down, but he had to pass that truck on a slick road. He killed Mom and me. Or might as well have killed me, because what happened to me afterward killed a part of me forever."

Kaylee burrowed her face into Harry's chest.

"God forgive me. I didn't mean that."

Harry hugged her tight.

"I know you didn't."

Harry's embrace slowed the hot rage waiting to spring out again. But she was tired now.

Kaylee pushed away from Harry.

"I'm ready to go back inside."

They stood from the stoop, and Harry offered his hand to her. Kaylee accepted it, just like she did when Demetrios offered his hand the moment he met her upon her arrival in Athens. Kaylee inwardly grinned recalling the constipated looks on Newell's and Margo's faces when Demetrios whisked her away.

But Harry's hand was one of genuine concern, while Demetrios's was one of genuine love.

"You don't have to eat my mac and cheese," Harry teased her.

"I'll try it, but don't tell Lou Ann that I hate green beans."

"It will be our secret for now, and I'll eat your share."

"Deal."

* * *

Lou Ann tapped her finger on the kitchen table. She hadn't taken a bite since Kaylee got up and left so abruptly. She wanted to go after her, but Harry beat her to it.

Joanna preferred Harry to her at first. Now Kaylee probably did too.

Just what was wrong with her?

Lou Ann looked at Joanna, who was scooping a second helping of Harry's mac and cheese onto her plate while plenty of Lou Ann's green bean casserole remained.

Figures.

"Why did you like Harry first?" she asked Joanna.

It was such a grade-school question.

Joanna sucked in a deep breath. "Because he was less complicated, and safe. You tried a little too hard at first."

She could understand that Harry was less complicated than she was. He couldn't cook, much less buy new underwear, unless he was forced to. Her heart beats in aching waves.

She was always daddy's girl, and her deputy partners were all male. Was this a female thing?

"How about now?"

She needed to know.

Joanna grinned between forkfuls of mac and cheese and green bean casserole.

Then she winked.

"I love you both, but I'm admittedly partial to you."

Lou Ann's heart returned to a steady beat.

Kaylee returned to the kitchen with Harry.

She went over to Lou Ann and gave her a quick hug.

"Sorry I left like that," Kaylee said.

"We all have days like that."

Kaylee nodded and returned to her seat.

She didn't take any green beans, but that hug, and the fact that she returned, were progress.

2

Kaylee and Joanna left the den and left Lou Ann and Harry canoodling on the couch while they were enthralled with some lame superhero movie.

Kaylee never liked those movies, but she and Jimmy, her high school boyfriend, watched them because he did. She couldn't follow all the sequels. He'd seen every one of them.

But she'd left Jimmy behind. He was a boy, and Demetrios was a man, and Jimmy now trailed hopelessly behind. Their status was irretrievable on her part. She'd moved way past him. Not that she planned it—it just happened.

Kaylee stretched and yawned. "I'm beat."

"So am I," Joanna admitted.

Kaylee opened a drawer and took out a pale pink negligée.

Joanna arched her brows.

"Wow!'

"It's from Greece."

"He really showered you with gifts."

"He did."

"Too bad he thought he was giving it to me. You know all that was meant for me. I was the one he paid for."

That was a bridge way too far.

Kaylee narrowed her eyes and threw the negligée at Joanna.

"Here! Take what *belongs* to you!"

Joanna threw it back.

"I don't want it. It's used."

"What do you mean by that? That I'm *used*? Look who's talking!" Kaylee shot back.

"I didn't grow up with a silver spoon in my mouth. More like a plastic one."

Kaylee began to laugh.

"What's so funny?"

"I didn't grow up poor, but not silver-spoon rich. But I can't help but laugh at that plastic fork that I jabbed into Otto's eye after I slashed up his face with the same razor Margo used during the humiliating shave session."

"I couldn't have done that because I was way too sick—so sick that Newell was sure I was dead. I only wished I was."

Kaylee sat on the bed.

"I'm sorry."

"Me too."

"Even in his stinking grave, Newell wins when we fight," Kaylee said.

"You're right. Let's not attack each other."

Kaylee slipped into her nightie while Joanna pulled out one of the ones Lou Ann bought her.

"That's nice," Kaylee commented.

"Aunt Lou Ann bought it. At first I refused to wear it because I wasn't sure what was happening to me and was sure they'd find out I'm an imposter and would take everything away. Plus I didn't think I deserved it."

"I know exactly what you mean, because it was the same for me when everyone thought that I was you."

"So we have that in common," Joanna said.

"Yes we do."

Kaylee rubbed her arms.

"It's chilly in here."

"Yeah. Lou Ann always runs the AC on high. There's a comforter in that closet."

Kaylee approached the bedroom closet.

"Wait!" Joanna yelled. She rushed to the closet. "I'll get it."

Joanna's strange overreaction only convinced Kaylee to open the closet door.

Kaylee gasped.

"I can explain."

Kaylee turned to face Joanna, whose face had tightened like a child caught in a lie.

"Start," Kaylee demanded.

A truce had started between them…and now this.

"I went with Lou Ann and Harry to Miami to get some of your belongings before the funeral so that we could leave right after. I, who had to pretend I was you, went through your things and boxed the ones I admittedly wanted. I took some of your clothes, shoes that fit me, your comforter,…"

Kaylee picked up the white teddy bear.

"How *could* you?"

She didn't care about the comforter, or even the clothes or the shoes—it was the invasion—but the white teddy bear that Joanna stole was the bear in the center of the dozen pink roses Mom and Dad presented to her after her ballet performance. The roses dried up, but the little white bear was forever.

Kaylee grabbed the bear out of the closet and hugged it.

"You can have anything else but not *my* bear."

Joanna sniffled.

"I did take care of the bear until his owner came back for him. Honest. I didn't want to leave it there."

"Why did you hide this from me?"

"I didn't intend to. We just got back. I wasn't thinking. Everything is yours and the bear was always yours."

Kaylee handed the coral comforter with tiny white polka dots to Joanna.

"Put this on the bed."

"Okay,"Joanna replied, softly, and then spread the comforter across the bed.

Then they lay silent on the bed they would have to share, at least for tonight.

Kaylee clutched the white teddy bear to her chest.

Joanna flung off her half of the comforter and went back to the closet, opened the door, and knelt.

"What are you doing?" Kaylee asked.

She'd had enough surprises for the night.

But Joanna continued to dig into the closet and finally pulled out a box, and then carried it to the bed.

"There's one more important thing I need to give you."

"I told you, you can have it all."

"Not this."

Joanna opened the box.

Kaylee's heart suddenly felt too heavy for her chest.

She looked away from the framed photo of her and her parents that once happily hung on the hallway gallery among other photos. It was the last photo taken of the three of them.

"Lou Ann took it off the wall and insisted I have it as a keepsake."

Joanna rested her palm on Kaylee's shoulder.

"It's important that you have this." Joanna paused. "Although I was dumped in the same car with them, I didn't remember them. I had no idea what these people looked like until I saw them in this photo with you. I went to their funeral. It was closed casket, but when I approached their caskets, I knew what they looked like, so suddenly it wasn't so fake. To my surprise, I felt connected to them and wished that they were my real parents. I had a lousy mother and no father."

Kaylee swiped the tears off her cheeks with the back of her hand and again studied the framed photo. She'd passed that photo a million times and never really looked at it that closely. Now it held every memory of her wonderful life with her parents.

She brought the photo closer and kissed the glass.

"Thank you. I'm sure they would have really liked you."

"I would have wanted them to—desperately."

Kaylee set the photo on the nightstand and they both climbed back into bed.

Kaylee positioned the teddy bear between her and Joanna.

"Until tomorrow," Kaylee said.

Joanna patted the bear. "You can count on that."

3

Lou Ann stood over the burner and flipped the pancakes ate the first sign of them bubbling. Two pancakes didn't make the timed flip and ended in an irregular half curl.

"Shit!"

She tried to salvage the rogue pancakes but failed to redeem them as recognizable flapjacks.

Lou Ann whacked the spatula against the frying pan. She should've stuck to toasted bagels.

She glared at her attempt to serve the girls' first breakfast in their new home together.

"Arghh!"

She was trying too hard again.

Kaylee and Joanna entered the kitchen.

Joanna winced. "Ooh! Something's burning!"

Lou Ann sucked in a deep breath.

"That would be, or would've been, breakfast," Lou Ann said between gritted teeth.

"Are those supposed to be pancakes?" Kaylee teased.

"Yes!"

"My dad used to make the best kind."

Lou Ann bowed her head and turned off the burner.

"How about cereal this morning?" she asked.

"Cereal would be great," Joanna said.

Kaylee nodded. "Fine by me."

"Cereal it is."

It was something all three of them could agree on.

Besides, she'd wasted enough time on an unrealistic breakfast. She had thirty minutes to get ready to return her sheriff's duties.

Her vacation didn't turn out as planned. Plus, with the trip to Greece to search for Kaylee, and so she could nab the perpetrators who'd sold both Kaylee and Joanna, and countless other girls, into slavery, she had requested and was approved for extended time off.

But it was time to return to normalcy.

"Girls, I have to go back to work. I have a twelve hour shift ahead of me, and then depending on what goes down, I may have to stay longer to fill out forms. I may not get back until 8 or 9 pm at the latest."

Damn, that sounded so bleak.

"I'll call Harry and see if he can come over and stay with you."

Kaylee rolled her eyes and Joanna frowned.

They'd just arrived and hadn't anytime to adjust to their new living arrangement, their new family. She especially worried about Kaylee, who seemed determined to call this home temporary.

Lou Ann tapped Harry's contact number in her cell. How ironic that just over a month ago, she'd been dodging his persistent calls and texts.

But they'd begun a new peace, a nice slow one to rebuild what they once had. They had grown to trust one another again during the takedown of Newell, and that filtered to their own renewed status.

Harry answered on the second ring.

"Hey, good morning!" Harry greeted her.

"Good morning!"

It was only hours since their smooth night at home, and based on the lilt in his voice, apparently he had a good time too.

"I'm about to head out for my first shift back on the job."

"It will be challenging to get back into a routine, but you know what they say, it's like riding a bike."

"Yeah, let's hope. By the way, I need to ask you a favor."

"Shoot. No pun intended."

"I know it's a lot to ask, but can you spend the day here with Kaylee and Joanna?"

"I'd love to, but I can't. I got a call early this morning to do an interrogation. I should be back in a day. I was about to call you so you wouldn't think I sneaked away because it's not true."

"I know."

They both paused at the admission that their relationship was once deemed irreconcilable.

"They're seventeen and don't ned a babysitter. Girls that age and younger babysit all the time. Are you worried about leaving them alone?"

Lou Ann looked at Kaylee and Joanna as if they knew what Harry was saying.

"Lou Ann, where do you think they're going to go?"

"Point taken."

"You gave them cell phones, right?"

"Yep."

"Okay. Go worry the whole day, or not. Tell you what, I'll call to see what they're up to in between my bouts of grilling some scum. It'll be a pleasant break for me. Between the two of us they'll be busy answering our calls. By the end of today they'll be sick of us."

Lou Ann chuckled. "Absolutely. Thank you, Harry."

"Don't mention it. Now get going or you'll be late for your first day back."

"Okay."

"They'll be fine. Bye."

"Bye, Harry."

"I take it that you were wrangling Harry to babysit us?" Kaylee asked sarcastically.

"I've been on my own," Joanna added.

That's exactly what concerned Lou Ann.

Families were difficult. Instant families were on a whole different level.

"I just thought you guys and Harry could have a good time together. Perhaps he could've taken you out for a bit."

Who would've guessed a year ago that she'd trust anyone, human or animal, to Harry?

"Well, we'll miss him, and you," Joanna said.

"Go on. We'll hang here," Kaylee reassured Lou Ann.

"All right. I put my cell contact in both your phones."

"And we appreciate that, and we also want you to know how grateful we are for the cell phones," Joanna added.

Lou Ann hurried to her bedroom, put on her sheriff's khaki uniform, and pulled her hair back into a sleek ponytail. She checked herself out in the mirror and took a deep breath. She needed to be alert and on point today. Being distracted could not only be deadly for her, but also for her partners, not to mention potential perpetrators. The last shots she fired were in Greece. She was sure that the multiple shots fired at Newell came from her gun, but the one fired at Peter, Demetrios's white-haired right hand man and Kaylee's friend and protector, was an instinctive and in that case, a wrong reaction. Lou Ann's mouth suddenly went dry. She'd injured an innocent man. That could never happen again.

Nothing came of the incident, other than her tortured conscience. Lou

Ann was positive that Kaylee would never forgive her for shooting Peter. But it was Peter who had forgiven her. He never revealed what happened in that garden that day, the day Newell and Demetrios died.

Lou Ann put on her Kevlar vest, strapped on her gunbelt, and walked out of the bedroom.

Kaylee's and Joanna's eyes went big.

Neither had seen her in her uniform before.

"How can you run, or walk, with all that?" Kaylee asked.

"You get used to it. You adapt," Lou Ann said.

But after weeks of running "bare" the belt seemed extra-heavy.

Lou Ann tapped her taser and her pistol.

"The fridge is stocked up, Isabelle's food is in the cupboard, and I filled her water bowl. It's going to be a hot day, so you may need to refill it. She eats twice a day, and her leash is by the door. The extra key to the house is on top of the living room credenza. Keep the doors locked, and make sure you lock up if you take Isabelle for a walk. Otherwise, enjoy the patio and stay well-hydrated."

"Yes, Aunt Lou Ann," Kaylee and Joanna sing-longed at the same time.

"Okay. I get it," Lou Ann responded.

Lou Ann leaned over and petted Isabelle.

"You be good."

Isabelle barked.

Turn around and just go. They'll be fine.

Then she walked out the door and tested to see if the front door was locked.

Check.

She climbed into her police cruiser and looked in the rearview mirror before driving away.

"She's gone," Kaylee said.

Now she could check her email without Lou Ann sneaking up behind her.

Kaylee entered her username and password to her email account into the cell Lou Ann provided her.

Bingo! She was in.

She scrolled though the hundreds of emails accumulated on her phone.

Back in that cell, she had no clock or calendar or any idea how long she had been gone. She didn't consider an email in Greece because there was no point in connecting with anyone in her past. She was planning to set up a whole new email account in Greece, but everything changed after Demetrios was murdered.

At least Kaylee had managed to give Peter her email before she was ripped away from her new home.

She licked her lips while continuing to scroll through the countless messages.

She halted at her best friend, Shawna's email.

Hey! I tried to text you like hundreds of times and you never texted back so I resorted to antiquated email. How was your college road trip with your parents?

Tears streamed down Kaylee's cheeks.

So what are your top picks? I pray you stay in Miami because I just got my acceptance letter to FIU. Jimmy is still waiting to hear. Wouldn't it be way awesome if the three of us could remain together?

Well, off to soccer practice.

Text me when you can.

Miss you, "Leggie"

Love ya,

Shawna

Kaylee set the phone down and stared at the email date. It was sent three months ago.

She picked the phone back up and was poised to send Shawna a reply, but stopped when she realized the absurdity of it. What was left of her personal friendships now belonged to Joanna. That's who they saw. Kaylee didn't know them anymore, and Shawna didn't know the whole truth. It was for the best for everyone to let go of what was. And after what happened to her, she was't the same anymore. She'd buried the old Kaylee. She needed to.

Kaylee scrolled past Shawna's email without looking back.

She scrolled and scrolled, but there was nothing from Peter.

Her heart beat hard and her fingers trembled against the cell's keyboard. Her stay at the mansion with Demetrios had been brief, but so intense and passionate that it felt much longer. But they'd all forgotten her, as if she'd never existed, or they didn't want to remember the pain she'd brought with her to Greece. It was over. She'd lost another family, another home.

Joanna put her hand on Kaylee's shoulder.

"What's wrong? Why are you crying?"

"Nothing," she lied, badly.

"I don't believe that."

Kaylee rested her forehead in her palm.

"I shouldn't have checked my emails."

She didn't want to discuss Shawna, because there wasn't anything that she could or should do about it. But it was the silence from Peter that gutted her.

"I was looking for, or more like hoping for, an email from Peter. Do you remember Peter from Greece? He was the one Lou Ann shot by accident."

"Yeah, I remember him. I didn't know him, but I know how much you liked him, and I know he felt the same."

"I gave him my email so we could correspond until I returned."

"Have you checked your junk mail? Not to say Peter is junk,"Joanna qualified.

Why didn't she think of that?

Kaylee tapped into her junk mail, and there it was—Peter's email.

Grinning, she did a little bounce on her bed and she clicked on his email.

It was mostly in English, but with a smattering of Greek words.

"What's he say? What's he say?!"

Even Joanna was excited.

Kaylee read through the email out loud, skipping over the Greek words. But his correspondence was enough for her to understand.

"He says that they miss me terribly. Vasaliki cries all day. Come soon and be with attorney so we live with you good. I saved some money. I send you so you may come. With much respect, Peter."

"Wow!"

"I need to go back."

4

Lou Ann stopped at a red light. Her stomach protested with a loud growl.

Thankfully things were quiet during her first shift back, allowing her to peacefully transition back into her duties as Deputy Sheriff.

After the morning's breakfast fiasco, she could really go for a hearty lunch.

She made a left at the next light and headed to Java and More, a grill frequented by deputy sheriffs and police officers alike.

With all the negativity and verbal and physical abuse law enforcement members had to endure, this place was a true oasis for them. Being in law enforcement was at a particularly precarious time, and they all needed to remain steady and extra-vigilant.

Up until now, it was just her and at times Harry, an FBI Special Agent. They both accepted the risks of the job. Now she had a family to consider. But she was in it for the long haul, professionally and personally. And so was Harry.

Lou Ann entered the restaurant and took her regular seat by the window with her back to the wall where she could see anything or anyone untoward coming at her. Plus, it was an easy exit to her cruiser.

"Good afternoon," Margie, her favorite waitress said with a big smile.

"Hey, Margie."

"How are things going?" Margie asked.

"Uh…okay."

"The usual?"

"Yep," Lou Ann confirmed.

"Okay, cheeseburger, fries, and a coke, coming right up."

Lou Ann grinned, remembering how she, Joanna and Harry stopped at a diner after Joanna—or Kaylee as they all thought—was discharged from the hospital, and Harry teased Joanna about ordering cheeseburgers with "mondo fries!" Joanna's eyes got so big! He'd made up the funny name on the spot and they all had a much-needed laugh. Harry could be such a jokester!

Margie returned with the cheeseburger deluxe platter and a coke.

"Can I get you anything else?" Margie asked.

"Oh, no. This is plenty. I had to skip out early and didn't have much of a breakfast because I didn't want to be late."

"I know what you mean. I'm trying to train my new puppy to do her business outside, and that takes most of my morning."

"I got lucky with my Isabelle. She caught on fast. Yours will too, eventually. It takes patience and consistency."

The advice just rolled off her tongue. She'd surprised herself with her own advice regarding Joanna and Kaylee. Especially since she had this lingering sense in that this wasn't going to work out—that she was in over her head. But she couldn't abandon Kaylee again, and Joanna never had any stability.

Patience and consistency she repeated to herself.

She decided to call home from the restaurant.

Hmmm. Home.

Lou Ann whipped out her personal cell and started to tap in Joanna's cell, sure that Joanna would readily answer while Kaylee would probably be passive aggressive and let her call go to voice mail.

But before she could call home, her earpiece that was connected to her shoulder police radio buzzed.

Dispatch: *Hostage situation at a bank.*

Lou Ann bolted out the booth.

"Gotta go, Margie," she called.

She tossed a twenty on the table and rushed out of Java and More.

Lou Ann cut the siren two blocks before arriving at the bank and eased her cruiser to in front of the bank where she parked. The last thing she wanted to do was heighten an already tense situation.

She calmly exited the vehicle—or at least acted like she was calm—because her heartbeat was hammering in crisis mode.

Fine first shift back.

The dispatcher warned that the robber was armed and informed her that a throng of backup and SWAT were on the way.

Lou Ann assessed the crisis through the bank's glass doors.

A woman who appeared to be in her late thirties to early forties was waving a gun from teller to teller, and then spinning around to point it at customers who crouched against a wall. It was a teller who had pressed the emergency button under her counter.

The woman had not fired any shots, and Lou Ann wanted to keep it that way.

Lou Ann saw that the woman's hands were shaking while she waved the pistol, haphazardly pointing it around.

She could sense right away, that based on her long experience, this woman wasn't the standard criminal, and more so, that the woman had no idea what she was doing, which told Lou Ann she was dealing with an amateur—an unsteady one at that.

This woman was angry—vengeful. Something or someone set her off. Was she a disgruntled ex-employee?

Lou Ann slowly reached for the glass door's handle while nodding at the woman.

The door readily opened and she bucked protocol, entering the situation alone instead of waiting for the parade of lights to arrive.

Lou Ann prepared to grab her taser and firearm if necessary, but she was pretty sure that the woman wasn't going to shoot anyone.

But "pretty sure" could get others hurt or killed, herself and the woman included.

She proceeded anyway.

"It's all right," Lou Ann said to the woman. "I know you don't want to hurt anyone."

The woman waved her pistol and began to blubber.

"No. I d-d-don't."

"Good. No one wants to hurt you, either."

The woman's cries shifted to painful wails.

"Hey, what's going on?" Lou Ann softly asked.

The woman lowered her gun to her side.

Progress.

"He took everything from me including all the money from our account. That cheating bastard! But I got his gun before he did. All I want is my money back. They just handed it to him. No questions. He took off with that bimbo! I just need my money. Just enough to exist. But no one here understands."

Okay. She got it now. A broken heart gone wild. She could relate to the woman to some small degree.

The woman sniffled.

"I have to go with you, right?"

Lou Ann hesitated. This could end deadly.

"Yes , but I understand how you must feel. Most any woman would."

The woman laid down her gun.

"Thank you," Lou Ann said.

Lou Ann had gained the distraught woman's confidence.

She slowly approached the woman and reached for the handcuffs on her belt.

"I'm going to have to do this."

The woman sniffled."I understand."

"I do need you to put your hands behind your back and turn around. Policy."

The woman did as Lou Ann instructed.

A collective sigh followed.

Sirens screamed and a cavalcade of sheriff's vehicles skidded, taking up the whole street in front of the bank. SWAT in their tactical gear rushed Lou Ann and the cuffed woman.

She'd radioed that the situation was under control and that the sole perpetrator was compliant and cuffed.

But she knew they were all going to descend on the bank. She would. She'd studied hostage negation and how to keep the lines of communication open. She'd eventually have to answer about the way she chose to handle this to her superiors. There went her promotion.

However, in her defense, she was the closest to the bank, and the incident was in her territory. And she got the call and then she correctly assessed what was happening. Although her superiors might not see it that way, it didn't hurt that the Glenda Martinez, the Chief Deputy Sheriff of Lou Ann's division of the Pinellas County Sheriff's Department, had sided with her on multiple occasions, including granting Lou Ann extended time to search for Kaylee in Greece. Sure they'd say it was a "woman" thing, but everyone knew Glenda meant business. She was even-handed and collected facts before reacting, and her words matched her judgment.

May Lou Ann be judged fairly.

Lieutenant Dan Mathews, one of her superiors, who actually had less time on the job than she did, pointed his finger at her.

Lou Ann met his annoyed look.

Dan Mathews then lowered his hand, sighed, and walked away.

SWAT narrowed their eyes at her while they passed by her.

The show was over for everyone except for the woman and Lou Ann.

<h1 style="text-align:center">5</h1>

"So what's the plan?" Joanna asked Kaylee.

"What plan?"

"The plan for us to go to Greece."

"We?"

Joanna's home was clearly here. Joanna had no business going to Greece. But Kaylee clearly did. She promised Peter and Vasiliki and everyone that she'd return.

But there was a problem. Her real passport was somewhere in her house in Miami. All she had to do was find it.

The problem mushroomed.

How was she going to get to Miami? She had no money and no car.

Kaylee pressed her lips together and sighed.

"What's wrong?" Joanna asked.

"I have to figure out how to get to Miami…and to Greece. My passport is somewhere in Miami, along with my driver's license."

Newell had used Joanna's passport to get Kaylee into Greece.

She and Joanna had looked so scarily alike that no one questioned its authenticity.

"Do you still have that passport that Lou Ann and Harry had got you?" Kaylee asked.

"Yes, but Lou Ann put it away somewhere. You had my passport—the passport Newell got for me to go to Greece, but that he forced you to use —was still on file. So that's how I got a new replacement one so I could go to Greece to search for you and Newell and Margo."

No. She couldn't use Joanna's passport. It wasn't right then and it wasn't right now.

Joanna rubbed her cheek with her finger. "Hmmm. I just thought of something. When I left the hospital, they gave me a plastic bag with the belongings they found in the car."

"They found stuff?"

"Yeah. Some clothes."

Kaylee forgot about the change of clothes she had on the back seat.

"And maybe your wallet with your ID. They must have thought it belonged to me, along with the itinerary they found in your mom's purse."

Kaylee's soul sagged remembering how excited she was to be going on that college road trip. Mom was always so organized.

"Do you know where that bag of *my* belongings is?"

"Probably somewhere in Lou Ann's room."

"Come on. Let's go check! " Kaylee urged while leading the way to Lou Ann's bedroom.

Why would Lou Ann have kept her or rather "Joanna's belongings as her," away from her? She must want to keep her captive here. There was no other explanation. Well, she'd show her!

Kaylee ripped open dresser drawer after dresser drawer searching for what rightfully belonged to her. She rummaged through every one of them. No wallet.

She stuffed Lou Ann's things back in the drawers and slammed each one shut. She didn't care. She'd been once again betrayed!

Kaylee looked over at Joanna, who was kneeling deep inside Lou Ann's closet. Joanna had tossed out every item that was in her way.

Good!

"Found it!" Joanna called.

Joanna pulled out a white plastic bag that had Good Samaritan Hospital Patient Belongings stamped across the front.

Kaylee held out her hand. "Give it to me! Give it to me!"

"Here."

Kaylee ripped the bag open.

And there it was—her pink wallet. And inside of it was a warped twenty dollar bill and her Florida driver's license, which was still safely sealed in its protective sleeve.

Bingo!

Lou Ann assisted the cuffed woman from the back seat of the sheriff's cruiser while protectively ducking the woman's head. It was a standard move, to not only protect the victim, but also the sheriff's department from future claims that the arrestee had been physically abused or injured.

Lou Ann was now convinced the woman hadn't intended to shoot anyone. Possessing a gun—that was a whole different problem.

The woman's gun had been confiscated as evidence, and now she sat in the back seat of Lou Ann's vehicle with her head bowed, while they waited for the prison van to arrive to haul the silent woman to the Pinellas County Sheriff's Department Jail.

Lou Ann turned and looked at her arrestee in the back of her cruiser—her charge for now.

"What's your name?" Lou Ann asked.

"Diedre. Diedre Kramer."

Lou Ann searched for Diedre Kramer on her cruiser's laptop and came up with *nada*. Diedre Kramer never even had a speeding ticket or anything else. She had no priors up until now. That might be in her favor, but that was between Diedre, her appointed attorney, and the judge.

The prison transport van arrived.

This was where they would be parted.

Diedre sniffled.

"Thank you for being kind under the circumstances," Diedre said.

And then Diedre Kramer was led away to be processed.

All that was left was for Lou Ann to do was to enter a complete report from start to finish.

Lou Ann stretched in her desk chair with her hands behind her head.

Filing reports—the bane of every officer's existence.

No use procrastinating. It had to be done. She was determined to finish the report today. Not tonight. Not tomorrow.

The crisis-induced adrenaline finally faded.

Now all that was left to do was to describe what had happened today.

Lou Ann rested her fingers on her keyboard...but that was as far as she got.

She'd better call the girls and let them know she'd be late.

After years of only having to take care of herself, and at first Harry, she never needed to call anyone about when she'd return home. Isabelle was the sole being she'd ever needed to apologize for being extra tardy... up until now. But things had changed dramatically for her, and Kaylee, and Joanna. Not to mention between her and Harry.

Lou Ann picked up her cell and called Joanna.

The phone rang and rang and then she heard the prompt that the voicemail had not been set up.

Damn!

Her head spun in panicked circles.

The phone rang five times, plenty of time for Joanna to answer. It was already 5 pm. Where were they?

She called again.

Again, no answer.

Harry wasn't available to go check on them, and it was her first shift back and she wasn't nearly finished with her report.

Her stomach knotted and she rested her hand on her stomach in hopes to calm it.

It looked like a late, late dinner at this point.

She'd try calling home again.

Joanna answered on the second ring.

Thank God!

"Oh, hi, Aunt Lou Ann," Joanna chirped while Kaylee rolled her eyes.

"Is everything all right?" Lou Ann asked. "I tried calling twice, but you didn't answer."

"Everything's fine. Kaylee and I were in the backyard with Isabelle so she could go potty. We left the phones inside. Sorry to have worried you. We'll take them with us next time."

"I'm glad everything's going well. Have you guys had lunch and dinner?"

"Yeah, we had sandwiches for lunch and are planning on leftovers for dinner."

She left out that they'd ransacked her bedroom in her absence.

"Go ahead and eat. I'll be home about 7:30."

"We'll save you a plate."

"Thanks."

"You're welcome. See you then."

"You sounded convincing," Kaylee said.

"I wasn't acting," Joanna emphasized.

Perhaps she wouldn't go to Greece with Kaylee. Her attitude was becoming really annoying. But she'd keep Kaylee's plans a secret. With Kaylee gone, she'd have her room back and be able to live peacefully with Lou Ann, and hopefully soon, with Harry.

Kaylee did belong in Greece. She'd be happier there.

Joanna waved her cell at Kaylee. "Shit! We've got twelve hours to clean up the mess in Lou Ann's room, walk and feed Isabelle, and get our and Lou Ann's dinners ready."

"Geez. Calm down," Kaylee said. "I got what I needed, so let's cover our tracks and get on with it."

Kaylee headed toward Lou Ann's bedroom.

Covering tracks. Yeah, Joanna had done that most of her life. When Lou Ann entered her life, she'd put a distance between her and the aunt who'd come to claim her. And she recalled how she'd decided that if she didn't like Lou Ann, she'd hitchhike out of Florida to wherever life's circumstances took her. It took time and concerted effort, but eventually it all worked after all the deceit she put Lou Ann and Harry through and the last thing she wanted was to jeopardize that. She'd grown fond of Lou Ann and Harry. Isabelle was the easiest to love.

May Newell sit next to Otto while they burn in hell!

"Come on, Isabelle. Let's go clean up the mess."

Kaylee studied the mess she instigated. But to be fair, it was Lou Ann who crossed the line.

Kaylee paused.

Maybe Lou Ann wasn't aware of what was in that hospital bag. That was possible. She was so eager to blame the aunt who just walked away years ago. But it was her dad's fault too. Would any of this happened if she had the guts to call Lou Ann's cell while they were visiting the college campus in Tampa? Clearwater was just around the corner. Had she done that perhaps Lou Ann and Dad could have finally worked things out, and Dad wouldn't have been so angry and eager to leave Tampa, and that fatal accident wouldn't have happened.

Could've. Would've. Should've.

Joanna walked into the disaster of a bedroom with Isabelle at her side.

Isabelle growled.

"I know," Joanna said to the dog.

"She doesn't like me," Kaylee said.

"She'll warm up to you," Joanna reassured her. Then she giggled. "Isabelle still keeps Harry in her crosshairs."

"Perhaps Harry and I have something more in common."

"Let your guard down and she'll come to you. It worked for me and I never had any experience with pets. How about you?"

"We had a poodle named Daisy because my dad was allergic to fur, so Daisy was perfect because poodles are hypoallergenic. Daisy got old and died. We all cried for months. After Daisy died, none of us—my dad, mostly—couldn't bring ourselves to get another dog."

"That's tragic."

"It was."

"But now we can all share Isabelle. She's very loving and nonjudgmental. I can attest to that."

"Maybe she knows I don't belong here."

"I didn't belong at first, and it didn't seem to matter to her. In fact, she made it a point to accept me as I was."

"You mean as me."

"I have a feeling she already knew the score."

"Whatever."

"How about I straighten the dresser drawers while you tackle the closet?"

Kaylee accepted Joanna's offer. After all, Kaylee made out better because the closet would be the easiest to straighten up.

While Joanna sorted the dresser drawers, Kaylee tackled the closet. She hung Lou Ann's clothes back on their hangers and then knelt to straighten the shoes that had been tossed in all different directions.

Damn. They really messed this place up.

Kaylee matched the pairs of shoes and set them in neat parallel rows.

There! Done!

Something touched her leg.

Kaylee looked down to discover that it was Isabelle who was rubbing against her legs.

She leaned over and petted Isabelle.

"Hey, you."

She could swear the dog smiled back.

Kaylee stroked Isabelle's back. It was so silky.

"See?" Joanna cheered.

Isabelle remained next to Kaylee.

"Oh, you're such a traitor," Joanna teased the dog.

Isabelle trotted over to Joanna, bumped her nose against Joanna's leg, and then returned to Kaylee.

"Daisy and Isabelle would've been fast friends."

"They sound a lot alike."

But, unlike them, they were dogs.

The only reason Kaylee had her life destroyed was because she looked like Joanna. She hadn't admitted it out loud, but the thought lingered in her head like a hangover from hell.

"The closet's all done," Kaylee announced.

"And I've finished putting the dresser drawers back in order," Joanna said.

"Just in time with a half an hour to spare."

"Yeah, let's get out of here," Joanna said. "Hopefully Lou Ann won't notice we were in here—that we invaded her space."

"But I…we…found what I needed."

Kaylee scored not only her wallet with her driver's license, but also money. It was a successful start to her trip back to Greece.

She was about to close the closet door when she looked up. There were what appeared to be a stack of photo albums on the top shelf.

Kaylee reached up and took the three thick albums down.

"Oh, Lou Ann packed those when we stayed in your house in Miami. There are pictures of you as a baby in one of them. Lou Ann showed them to me. I was clueless about who was in the pictures, but then Lou Ann continued to talk about them. I just kept nodding my head and agreeing."

Kaylee sat on Lou Ann's bed and opened the first album.

Page after page were photos of Lou Ann and Kaylee's dad as kids growing up in Miami. She recognized Grandma and Grandpa's house down the street from her house.

Kaylee's eye's burned wet and hot.

"What's going on?" Joanna asked softly .

"There are photos of my grandma and grandpa. Grandma was very sick. She had Alzheimer's."

"Alz...what?"

"Alzheimer's is a progressive disease of the brain, where bit by bit a person can't remember people, family members, although sometimes they remember things in their past. They eventually die of it. Then my Grandpa, who couldn't live without her, shot himself. He was a state trooper. I guess that's why Lou Ann's a sheriff. I was just a baby when that happened. My dad never talked about it. My mom told me about the whole incident, and how my dad and Lou Ann argued about the house. It was eventually sold. Lou Ann wanted it that way and Dad didn't. She pressured him to sell it and then split from Miami to Clearwater."

"Wow! I had no idea."

"It was complicated. Still is, as far as I'm concerned."

"It hurt Lou Ann terribly. She was a wreck at the funeral. I heard her say that she should've made up with your dad long ago. She blamed herself."

Kaylee closed the first photo album and sniffled.

"Lou Ann loves you despite the time that got away."

"She loved...loves...you," Kaylee said.

"But she thought I was you. She was going to care for you. She did. Her love was for you. It didn't matter that it was me. And when I came clean, she was willing to search the world for you. But neither she nor Harry gave up on me, and they very well could've taken me back to where they found me."

Kaylee nodded. "I'm glad they didn't. You deserve a home."

"You don't?"

"I do."

She'd wished for her aunt to rescue her from Newell's and Margo's abuse, not to mention that smelly monster, Otto, but Lou Ann didn't get there in time. And now Demetrios was dead. Lou Ann shouldn't have come to Greece at all. Now Kaylee would struggle to forgive her, but honestly couldn't. Lou Ann wasn't the aunt she expected.

Kaylee would pretend to fit in until she could leave for Greece.

"Here, open this one," Joanna urged.

She'd had enough. She didn't want to look at any more painful memories.

Joanna tapped the top of the album.

"Open it! Open it!"

Kaylee relented.

She opened the next album to find her parents' wedding photo. She zeroed in on Lou Ann as maid of a honor.

"She looks so young," Kaylee said.

Kaylee flipped through the pages before Lou Ann returned home.

There were her mom and then her dad, and finally Lou Ann, cuddling her as a newborn.

"That's the one I saw while we were in Miami," Joanna said while leaning over to look at the photo.

But it was the next photo that seized Kaylee's heart.

Lou Ann was sitting in a child-size chair, and three-year-old Kaylee sat across from her at the tiny play table. It was tea time.

God, she remembered those times. Lou Ann would bring these big fat, vanilla creme cookies from a bakery. They would sit at the table and sip orange drink that was supposed to be tea and eat the best vanilla creme cookies she'd ever tasted. The cookie would softly crunch in her mouth and then release a burst of sweet vanilla on her tongue.

Kaylee licked her lips. She could still taste those cookies. Maybe there was a bakery in Clearwater that had the same vanilla creme cookies as those in Miami. Probably not.

Kaylee stared at the rose pattern on the tiny cups on the matching child plates. This was probably why she particularly loved that white sundress with tiny roses that Demetrios gifted her.

Roses. That's what connected her and Demetrios, and her and her parents, who had presented roses to her after a ballet recital. Roses. The path to love.

Kaylee closed the album. She loved Lou Ann of the past. But neither she nor Lou Ann were the same as they were during those tea times. But there were no tea times anymore. Maybe both she and Lou Ann wished for the simplicity of years gone by.

Kaylee replaced the photo albums on the shelf in Lou Ann's closet… where they belonged.

6

Lou Ann finally finished typing up the report in her laptop at her station desk.

By now surely Diedre Kramer had been fingerprinted, photo'd, and processed and was probably shaking in her cell while wearing an orange jumpsuit. Her clothes would've been taken away and stored. The gun, which it turned out wasn't loaded—evidence. Diedre was in serious trouble.

Lou Ann closed her laptop.

It was time to go home.

She was about to get out of her seat when her phone rang.

Shit! It was Glenda Martinez.

"Hello, Chief Deputy Sheriff Martinez," Lou Ann answered while her heart thumped in her chest.

Ordinarily, she had a good relationship with Glenda, who was in the process of approving Lou Ann's promotion to sergeant, pending Sheriff Robert Carson's final sign-off.

"I know it's late and you've had quite an adventurous first day back."

That was an understatement.

Here comes the "but".

"Can you come by my office at 0800 tomorrow?"

"Sure."

"Good. I'll see you then."

No "But," but it might have well been said. It felt exactly like a "but" with all the psychological responses associated with that three-letter word.

The call reverberated in Lou Ann's head.

She should've waited outside the bank.

But she didn't, and she knew deep down that, given the

circumstances, she wouldn't have changed her actions. You can't teach instinct. *But* she wasn't going to say that to Glenda. Dan Mathew's must've filed a formal reprimand. Nothing she could do about it tonight *but* lose sleep.

But...but...but, she groused to herself all the way out the door.

Kaylee watched Joanna fill Isabelle's food and water bowl. She used to do the same for Daisy. Maybe she'd get a dog in Greece. Her dog could help with the grief that couldn't leave her head. She was sure Peter and Vasiliki needed a dog too. Maybe they could pick out a pooch together.

After Isabelle finished her dinner, she walked over and sat next to Kaylee.

Kaylee scratched Isabelle behind her floppy ears.

Isabelle closed her eyes, relishing the massage.

"You've picked her favorite spot," Joanna said.

Kaylee grinned. "I guess so."

Yes, she'd definitely adopt a dog.

But as much as she and Isabelle were forming a bond, she recognized Isabelle belonged to Lou Ann and Joanna. If Demetrios were alive, he would have bought her any kind of dog she desired. But she'd look into adopting one. They must have a humane society in Ekali. She'd ask around.

"I'll heat up the macaroni and cheese while you heat up the green bean casserole," Joanna suggested.

Kaylee scrunched her face behind Joanna's back. She had to continue playing nice so she could eventually break free.

"Sure."

Kaylee opened the refrigerator and removed the glass-covered clump of congealed green.

She walked toward the oven and shoved the casserole dish into the oven next to the macaroni and cheese.

At least Harry understood her aversion to green beans of any sort. Even her mom quit scooping any of it on her plate.

She'd never gotten sick eating green beans, but she had an aversion to the vegetable. Strangely, she liked broccoli and even Brussels sprouts, which many others wouldn't venture to eat.

Here she was disparaging food that wasn't in the same category as what Margo had dumped on her paper plate. Most of it ended up in that grubby toilet where it belonged.

Chicken was the final entree that made it into the oven.

Kaylee sniffed the chicken. Even cold, it smelled heavenly.

Kaylee smiled.

Here's to you Margo.

Margo didn't deserve to eat prison food which was surely several steps above what she forced down hers and Joanna's throats.

The oven timer went off and just in time because Lou Ann was home.

Lou Ann drove the cruiser into the driveway and stopped next to her car. She cut the engine, closed her eyes, and took a deep breath.

Despite what happened today, not to mention what awaited her tomorrow, she wasn't going to unload her problems on Kaylee or Joanna. They had their own problems to deal with.

She used to unload her burdens to Harry, and he to her.

But she needed to handle this on her own.

Lou Ann exited her cruiser and locked it for the night.

Then she looked at her sedan. She might be driving that exclusively after tomorrow's appointment with Glenda Martinez. But she was more concerned about what edict would come from Sheriff Carson, with whom she had no history other than attending departmental social events. Even then she only politely engaged with him for a minute at the most. Yet he ultimately had the say-so on her career or lack of one. Maybe it would be a reprimand or a suspension, either of which would leave a black check mark on her record.

She headed to the front door. Her belt felt extra heavy tonight. She couldn't wait to get it off.

Joanna opened the front door before Lou Ann could reach for the doorknob.

"Wow! You must have had a hard day," Joanna said.

Kaylee stood behind Joanna looking solemn.

Did her shitty day show that much?

But then Isabelle rushed past Kaylee and Joanna and jumped to greet Lou Ann.

It was a relief to come home to a family despite her ongoing struggle to keep everyone together.

"Come on in and relax. Kaylee and I have dinner prepared—well, heated leftovers."

"You guys didn't have to wait for me."

"We wanted to."

"I'm just going to go to the bedroom to get this stuff off and change into something a lot more comfortable."

Except tonight there wasn't going to be anything that would make her more comfortable.

* * *

Lou Ann sat on her bed and stared at her image in the dresser mirror. Her tired eyes stared back at her. She unhooked her belt, and it thunked onto the bed. Although her belt weighed fifty pounds, it was like releasing a hundred.

She unbuttoned her uniform shirt and unbuckled the pants. She was finally free of her uniform.

But as much as she lamented her day, Diedre Kramer's day was a thousand times worse. The woman's life would never be the same.

But Lou Ann didn't know what was going to happen to her tomorrow, so she wouldn't jump down that rabbit hole.

She exchanged her uniform for shorts and a T-shirt and traded her heavy work shoes for flip-flops but kept her hair in a ponytail. She couldn't stand to have her hair cling to her neck because the Florida summer evening remained hot and humid.

Harry couldn't reveal his location, but he probably was somewhere cooler tonight.

Lou Ann went to her closet to hang up her uniform and secure her belt.

Hmmm. Something seemed a bit different, but she didn't know what in particular it was. Everything was in place. Just how she had left it. Yet something was off.

She rubbed her eyes. It was surely the fatigue finally settling in.

A cold beer and warm dinner were just what she needed, but not in that order.

Lou Ann walked into the kitchen grateful that she didn't need to prepare anything tonight. Joanna and Kaylee had completely taken care of that—and tonight she needed that kind of caring support.

"You look better," Kaylee said.

"Have a seat. We'll serve you tonight with your own dinner. Well, Harry's mac and cheese."

"Thanks. Don't mind if I do."

She sat at the kitchen table and allowed the girls to serve her.

Leftovers always tasted better the next day.

She'd bolted out of Java and More during lunch after only three bite-fulls before dispatch called.

Lou Ann stabbed her fork into the chicken on her plate.

Really. What was she supposed to do? Stand there and do nothing until she was "rescued"?

Bullshit!

"Is the chicken too tough?" Kaylee asked. "Because you've sort of assassinated it."

Lou Ann pulled the fork out of her chicken. "No, it's just right."

Joanna raised her eyebrows.

"Sorry. I've just had a frustrating day."

It was the kindest way to put it. But she didn't want to spend anymore time thinking about the shift from hell and ruin dinner. She'd leave replaying the day to the privacy of her own bed.

"I'm sorry about that," Joanna said.

"Thanks. I appreciate it."

The three of them began to eat with only the clatter of silverware filling the silence.

Lou Ann stood from the table, and out of habit, began to clear the plates.

"We'll get it," Joanna said.

Lou Ann sat. After she and Harry split, she'd gotten used to taking care of herself at home, and she'd always been independent on the job. Now that all was changing, and she needed to learn to accept both.

She watched Joanna and Kaylee load the dishwasher.

Although they worked cooperatively, she detected the undercurrent of tension between them. It must have been hard for Kaylee to be uprooted twice. And then there was the fact that Joanna was here first, and that she had masqueraded as Kaylee, reaping Lou Ann's and Harry's affection. Kaylee must still feel like the odd one out of this cobbled-together family.

She'd have to start giving Kaylee extra attention. Joanna would understand.

And if she was suspended or worse, terminated, she'd have a lot of extra time to spend with Kaylee and Joanna, a situation that she suspected none of the three of them really wanted.

Lou Ann swore she'd stop being overbearing. Both Joanna and Kaylee had on separate occasions accused her of trying too hard.

But that was always her quirk—to be in charge. That stubbornness failed with her brother, Lyle, as well as Harry, Joanna, and Kaylee, and now it would surely fail with her superiors.

Although she wasn't going to completely change enough anytime soon, but from today on she'd have to start trying.

"Hey, why don't we watch an after-dinner movie?" Lou Ann suggested.

"Sounds good," Joanna said.

"I could go for that," Kaylee echoed.

Her plan to become more flexible just started.

Lou Ann, Joanna, and Kaylee headed into the den—okay "family room." Isabelle trotted alongside them and as soon as they were all seated on the the couch, Isabelle jumped into Lou Ann's lap.

"Thank you, Isabelle," she whispered into the dog's ear.

Isabelle gave a "you're welcome" bark.

Isabelle lay warm in Lou Ann's embrace while she stroked the dog's silky back.

That part of her life never changed, and it never would.

Isabelle always sensed when someone needed her, and tonight it was Lou Ann.

"So what should we watch?" Lou Ann asked.

"Action adventure," Joanna called out.

"I vote for a romantic drama," Kaylee said.

Romantic drama already surrounded all their lives.

"Let's just see what the offerings are," Lou Ann said.

Joanna grabbed the remote.

"Oh, here's one for everyone. A couple in dire straits rob a bank. Action-adventure and romance."

"Ooh, yeah," Kaylee agreed.

Ohh, no.

Lou Ann gently dislodged Isabelle from her lap.

"I'm going to go get a beer. I'll be right back."

If she was going to make it through this movie, she desperately needed a beer.

Be flexible, she reminded herself.

"Bring me one too," Kaylee called.

"Me too," Joanna chimed in.

"No. And no. Two Cokes it is."

"We were just joking around," Kaylee said.

"Okay."

Time to check how many beers still left in the fridge.

Lou Ann opened the fridge and counted the beers. The six-pack that Harry bought was still there, untouched. She took out a beer, and when she turned around she found Kaylee and Joanna right behind her.

Lou Ann then removed two Cokes and handed one to each while Joanna reached into a cupboard and snagged a bag of chips.

"To go with your beer and our cokes for the movie," Joanna winked.

"Good idea," Lou Ann said.

Anything to keep her occupied during the *chosen* movie.

Lou Ann grabbed one of Isabelle's treats, and the three returned to the den.

Lou Ann set her beer on a coaster on the coffee table and pointed to two other coasters where Joanna and Kaylee placed their drinks. Joanna set the bowl of chips in the middle.

"Ready?" Joanna asked.

As ready as Lou Ann could be to spend the evening watching a bank robbery movie—art about to imitate life.

Joanna clicked the movie into action.

Lou Ann sipped her beer.

Five minutes later she was into the movie. It was more romance than felony. And the felony part was laughable.

"Wow! Aunt Lou Ann, is that really what happens when the police respond to a bank robbery?" Joanna asked.

"It's fiction!" Kaylee said before Lou Ann could answer.

"No. Kaylee's right. The situation wouldn't really play out like that. It's a movie."

And it had been a decent escape until Joanna's innocent inquiry.

Her day wasn't remotely similar. She only wished it was all a movie instead of real life.

Lou Ann took another swig of her beer and tossed Isabelle one of her doggy treats.

Isabelle devoured her treat and began to eye the chips.

"Okay. But just one."

Lou Ann flipped a chip to Isabelle, who caught it in midair and happily crunched it.

Back to the movie.

"I wish I had someone sweet and who cares about me like this couple," Joanna lamented.

Lou Ann glanced at Kaylee, waiting for her response to unrequited love, but Kaylee only looked down in silence.

Apparently Joanna also caught on to Kaylee's nonverbal response.

Joanna simply offered the bowl of chips to Kaylee, who took four, piling them into her palm.

The movie continued until it finally culminated with a satisfactory ending.

Lou Ann had finished her beer, and the girls, their sodas. The chips were gone, and Isabelle snored at Lou Ann's feet.

The movie wasn't that painful after all.

Joanna stretched and clicked off the TV.

Kaylee yawned. "I'm headed off to bed," she said.

"Me too," Joanna said.

"Good night you two. Since you guys cleaned up after dinner, I'll take care of this stuff."

"Thanks, Lou Ann…I mean Aunt Lou Ann," Kaylee corrected herself.

"You're welcome."

Like Lou Ann, Kaylee was trying her best. Stubbornness ran deep in the Jasinski line.

The girls took off to the bedroom they shared. She'd have to look into getting Kaylee a private space. Initially both she and Harry thought Kaylee and Joanna would benefit from sharing a space where they could heal together. But that's not what appeared to be happening. Greece and Demetrios had changed Kaylee forever. The only thing she and Joanna shared was an ugly past. And Joanna had never known physical love, only physical abuse.

In addition to her departmental meeting tomorrow, Kaylee and Joanna had their own upcoming meetings with psychology, gynecology, and neurology—every "ology" they needed to help glue their lives back together—if that was even possible. Lou Ann prayed it would be.

Lou Ann collected the remains of movie night and stored them in the kitchen before heading to her bedroom.

She would have to get up earlier to make her appointment at headquarters. She didn't want to imagine who would attend besides her and Glenda, but her brain decided differently.

She undressed, put on her nightclothes, and brushed and flossed her teeth, hoping the bedtime ritual would help her get settled for the night.

Lou Ann pulled back the covers and climbed into bed.

She was just about to set her cell phone alarm when an incoming text pinged.

Maybe the meeting was cancelled or moved? Or wouldn't take place at all, which could be either good or bad news.

Lou Ann took a deep breath and opened the text.

It was Harry.

You up?

Yep.

Harry's text stopped. Instead, Lou Ann's cell rang. It was Harry's ringtone.

"Hey, what's up?" he asked.

Where should she start?

"Lou Ann?"

"Yeah, I'm still here."

"Bad first shift back?"

"Bad doesn't begin to describe it."

Lou Ann paused and balled her fist.

"What happened?" he asked softly.

"I responded to a bank hostage crisis."

"Damn. I just got back from a marathon of an interrogation, and I haven't checked the news."

"Neither have I. I'm sure I'm on it."

"Thank God you're all right."

"No, I'm not all right."

"You know that's not what I meant."

"You're still on my call list if something happens to me."

"Good to know. You're still on mine too." Harry hesitated. "You want to tell me about it?"

"I was having lunch…or trying to…when the dispatch came. I rushed to the bank, assessed the situation, and went inside."

"Alone?"

"Yes."

"Shit."

"It was a distraught woman who I could tell didn't know how to use her gun. Plus her hands were shaking. She came with me willingly. Cried the whole time. Her, not me."

Harry chuckled at her joke.

"Anyway, turned out her husband ran off with all the money in the account, and most of the possessions in her home, and with a much younger woman."

"Ouch."

"Yeah."

Harry swore he didn't stray much. But they were in the process of working past that.

"So when SWAT got there, they and my stick-up-his-ass superior, Dan Mathews, were pissed. Don't blame them. But you know, you can't teach intuition."

"I agree. So, you're in deep shit?"

"Don't know. Have an early morning meeting."

"Be respectful. Arm yourself with the facts. You'll be all right. I'm done and I'm flying home tomorrow afternoon. I'll be there as soon as I can. In the meantime, try and get some sleep."

"Thanks, Harry."

"Don't mention it."

"Love you."

"Love you too."

Lou Ann ended the call, set her alarm for an hour earlier, and closed her eyes, praying for sleep.

7

Lou Ann's alarm shouted in her ears. With her eyes blurry, she reached for the cell and smacked off the alarm. No snoozing this morning. She must have dozed off in the past hour because she'd looked at the time every half hour since she got into bed. She probably hadn't gotten even a smidgeon of REM sleep.

Shit. That was exactly what she was going to look like today.

She flipped off the rumpled covers and headed for a shower. Eye drops and plenty of makeup would be essential this morning, along with courage and conviction. Conviction. Maybe she'd be convicted today.

Lou Ann trudged into the shower and stared at the shower-head. This wasn't how she imagined the return to her duties would end. *End. Finished. Don't let the door hit your ass on the way out.*

What would she tell Kaylee and Joanna? Harry? He'd be the first to know.

How ironic that he would be picking up her pieces after she'd ripped him to shreds.

Perhaps she did overreact. Harry might have been telling the truth all along that he didn't have sex with that woman from the bar, and that he truly was in the shower when his female colleague answered his cell because the two of them had no choice but to platonically share a Madrid hotel room.

Overreaction was no stranger to her. And look where that got her? In trouble, that's what.

She showered quickly. There was no time to relax. She had to just get in the cruiser, drive to headquarters, and walk in to that appointment, ready and armed with only the facts, as Harry put it.

He should know. He'd been in ankle-deep shit before and every time he managed to emerge unscathed.

But this was her first time. She was an "unscathed" virgin.

Lou Ann instructed her pounding heartbeat to knock it off while she brushed her teeth, dried her hair enough to slick it into her standard ponytail, and added just enough makeup to cover the bags under her eyes. She then looked into the mirror and grimaced. It would have to do. Insomnia was a bitch to hide.

She put on her uniform including her Kevlar and strapped on her belt, possibly the last for awhile…or longer.

She looked in the mirror again and said aloud, "Go."

Lou Ann pulled her cruiser into the Largo headquarters reserved parking. As of 0740, she was still considered reserved. She cut the engine and sat. She didn't want to be too early or too late or worse have to sit outside Glenda's office sweating while her dread escalated by the minute.

So she sat in her cruiser and steadied her bouncing knees.

Stop it! Stop it!

She took a cleansing breath, exited her vehicle, and headed in for her appointment..

A security officer met her.

"Gunbelt , please," he instructed.

Lou Ann removed her belt.

"We'll keep this for you," he said.

Was this temporary or permanent? She'd rather not know.

"Where are you headed, Deputy Sheriff Jasinski?"

"I have an appointment with Chief Deputy Sheriff Martinez at 0800."

"Fourth floor, room 420. Elevator's down the hall."

"Thank you," she kept her answer respectful even though she'd been to Glenda's office before. However, he was obligated to repeat the same information with everyone.

Lou Ann walked to the elevator bank and pressed the button, then stood waiting for the stainless steel doors to open.

She heard someone walk up behind her.

"Good morning, Deputy Sheriff Jasinski," Lieutenant Dan Mathews, her nemesis superior said with smack of sarcasm.

Lou Ann turned around and responded politely, "Good morning, Lieutenant Mathews."

The elevator dinged and the doors opened.

It killed her, but she waited for him to enter the elevator first and then followed.

Lou Ann pressed the fourth floor button and the doors closed.

Dan's office was on the third floor, but he didn't choose it.

They were going to the same place…Glenda's office.

The ride remained silent.

She knew the game of intimidation well and didn't speak to him either.

The doors parted on the fourth floor and Lou Ann let Dan exit first.

No way was she going to walk in front of him or next to him.

"Please have a seat, Deputy Sheriff Jasinski. Chief Deputy Sheriff Martinez will be with you shortly,"Glenda's receptionist said.

Dan Matthews walked right past Lou Ann and into Glenda's office.

What an arrogant SOB.

Lou Ann sat in a chair in Glenda's office waiting room.

The only sound came from the receptionist tapping on her computer keyboard.

Lou Ann glanced at her watch. It was 0815. They were probably already set up in there but purposely played games with her, waiting for her to become completely off point. But she was going to wait patiently.

She replayed what Harry suggested during their phone call last night in her head.

Stick to the facts.

Glenda's door opened and she beckoned to Lou Ann.

"You can come in now, Deputy Sheriff Jasinski."

Lou Ann stood, straightened her shoulders, and walked into Glenda's office.

She assessed the room without being obvious.

Sheriff Carson sat in a chair 90 degrees and to the left of the front of Glenda's mahogany desk and Dan Mathews sat in the same position on the right side. An empty chair faced Glenda's desk. That one was for Lou Ann.

Glenda resumed her position behind her desk while Lou Ann sat in the hot seat.

"We're here to discuss the incident at First National Bank on State Street yesterday. I believe Deputy Sheriff Jasinski that you were dispatched at…." Glenda glanced at her computer screen, "1232."

"That is correct," Lou Ann replied.

Why wouldn't it be? It wasn't up for debate. That's what the log indicated. She recalled how she bolted out of Java and More, but she didn't offer that bit of information.

Stick to the facts.

Glenda continued, "So you arrived on scene at…?"

"My cruiser clocked 1238."

It was all in Lou Ann's report, but they were going to put her through her paces.

"That took six minutes," Sheriff Carson said. "Impressive," he added.

"And where were you when you received the dispatch?" Dan added, his tone crisp.

"Deputy Sheriff Jasinski responded well, without delay," Sheriff Carson interjected. He looked at Lou Ann. "You can answer."

"I was at Java and More restaurant when I got the call that I responded to immediately as standard," Lou Ann responded in an even tone.

"So you weren't patrolling that area?" Dan shot back.

"I was at a restaurant having lunch, so no, I hadn't been dispatched to any scene prior to the one at 1232," Lou Ann answered.

"Slow morning, huh?" Dan picked at her.

"I did not receive any dispatches prior to 1232," Lou Ann repeated.

"Deputy Sheriff Jasinski has already answered that question, Lieutenant Mathews," Sheriff Carson reminded Dan. "May we please move on?" he added.

"When you arrived at First National Bank, what was your first response?" Glenda asked.

Dan was probably salivating at the inquiry.

"I parked my cruiser in front of the bank, then exited my vehicle, ready to respond."

"You mean ready to discharge your firearm," Dan goaded her.

"I was ready to respond," Lou Ann repeated.

She continued, "I approached the glass door with caution, but with outward confidence. I observed one woman who did not handle her firearm with any knowledge."

"How so?" Glenda asked.

"Her hands did not grip the firearm properly and her finger was not on the trigger. Her hands were shaking and she waved the fire arm around haphazardly. I opened the bank door and calmly conversed with her. I noted that the gun's safety was still engaged."

Sheriff Carson raised his eyebrows while Dan scoffed softly.

"Continue, please," Glenda prompted Lou Ann.

"The distraught woman lamented that her spouse had emptied the bank account and left her. I empathized with her situation. She willingly let me restrain her and I led her to my vehicle and placed her, cuffed, in the back seat. I forgot to add—and it's in my report—that I notified dispatch that the situation was under control and that no one was injured. I waited for SWAT to arrive and that is when Lieutenant

Mathews also arrived on scene. The jail van arrived and the woman was transported to the county jail. My report was completed prior to the end of my shift."

"I see that," Glenda confirmed.

"I commend you for being astute enough to ascertain that the gun's safety was engaged," Sheriff Carson said.

Dan didn't utter a peep. However Glenda nodded.

"I also understand that the confiscated gun was not loaded," Glenda said.

"Yes, but she…Deputy Sheriff Jasinski…didn't know the gun wasn't loaded. It could've been," Dan said while shaking his head.

"The safety was on," Lou Ann drove home the crucial point.

"Thank you for coming in," Glenda acknowledged.

Glenda blinked at her own comment.

Lou Ann's appointment was hardly voluntary.

Sheriff Carson and Glenda stood and then Lou Ann stood afterward out respect for their rank. Dan delayed standing, probably scowling inwardly that the inquiry didn't go the way he intended. He failed to gain traction to discredit her.

Lou Ann shook everyone's hand, even Dan's, who gave her a limp grip.

"We'll take everything into consideration regarding the facts obtained during this meeting, and we'll notify you, Deputy Sheriff Jasinski, of our final decision regarding this incident."

"Thank you," Lou Ann said.

Glenda ushered Lou Ann out her office and closed the door.

Lou Ann couldn't do anything more. They were in there discussing her and Dan would certainly continue to push to punish her.

Lou Ann nodded to the receptionist, who gave her a sympathetic look.

How many had passed by her after leaving her boss's office.

Maybe she misjudged Glenda's and Sheriff Carson's neutral or at best, positive responses.

She stood at the same elevator bank, but this time waited alone.

The elevator arrived and carried her back down to the lobby level where her gunbelt was returned to her…for now.

Lou Ann walked out of the headquarters and squinted to adjust to natural daylight. She'd just spent over an hour inside with fluorescent lights and the morning sun stabbed her eyes.

"Lou Ann!"

She narrowed her eyes to see Harry leaning against his car.

What a surprise! She ran over to him.

"Harry! I thought you weren't arriving until this afternoon."

"I took the red-eye."

He studied her.

"And…how did it go?"

"I stuck to the facts."

"Good."

"The Chief Deputy Sheriff and Sheriff asked me concrete questions, but my lieutenant was hellbent in tripping me up, on purpose. But I stayed steady, responded only to the stated questions and didn't elaborate. But they're up there now discussing me. At least I've got my belt, and I still have my cruiser, so I'll go about my duties until I hear different."

"You're not going to hear different if the big guy, who trumps your lieutenant, has your back, and don't forget that. As an aside, what do you want for dinner tonight?"

"Surprise me."

Harry grinned.

"I'm planning to."

8

Harry waved to Lou Ann while she drove off in her cruiser.

Everything would work out, he told himself, for Lou Ann, and for him and Lou Ann.

He wouldn't screw up again. She'd just started to trust him again. She even gave him a key to the house since she'd changed the locks after kicking him to the curb. No more jamming his foot in the door to sneak his way into the house they once shared. Here was his second chance to redeem himself. But just in case, he'd still keep his apartment.

Harry whistled while he drove to the house. Lou Ann used to wince when he whistled. He would no longer do it in her presence, but he was alone in his car, so he whistled all the way to Clearwater.

When he arrived at the house, he cut the engine and the whistling.

He then got out of the car, strode with a bit of a skip to the front door, and took out his house key.

First he called his name through the door so he wouldn't scare Joanna and Kaylee.

He stuck his key in the door to find it unlocked then opened the door to find neither Kaylee or Joanna.

"Hey! It's Harry. I'm hooome," he called louder.

Still nothing.

What the hell?

He walked through the house, and the last thing he wanted to do was call Lou Ann, especially after this morning.

Shit!

Come to think of it, Isabelle wasn't here either. She always took it upon herself to bark at him.

He walked further toward the kitchen.

And then he saw the three of them through the kitchen's sliding door romping in the backyard. They didn't hear him come in. The unlocked front door? He'd address that later.

Harry stood at the glass door, waiting to be seen.

Of course Isabelle saw him first and barked.

Love you too, Isabelle.

Kaylee and Joanna turned to see what Isabelle was barking at.

Harry waved to them.

They waved back and ran toward him.

Harry opened the glass door and stepped outside.

"I called, but no one answered," Harry said.

"Sorry. We were having fun playing tag with Isabelle. She's really amazingly good at it," Joanna said.

"Yeah, where did you think we went? We don't have any transportation," Kaylee added.

That much was true.

He decided to let her comment go. Kaylee was still pissed about being hauled out of Greece to suburban Clearwater. The rest of them were pretty happy here except for her. Perhaps if he were forced to move to some place he found strange and lonely, he'd probably pine for where he'd started putting down roots, too. That they were both a work in progress to fit into Lou Ann's world—they had that in common.

"How about pizza for lunch?" Harry offered.

"I could go for that," Joanna said.

"So could I," Kaylee finished for him.

"Great. I'll order a large with…."

"The works," Kaylee replied.

Joanna frowned. "But no anchovies."

"Ya didn't even have to even mention that," he teased.

Harry called the local pizzeria that was still in his phone. The last time he'd picked up a pizza was when he showed up at the house offering the pizza to get on Lou Ann's good side only to learn that her brother and sister-in-law had died in a car wreck and that she was the sole guardian of a niece who Lou Ann hadn't seen in years. Turned out it was actually Joanna. And here he was with pizza again. What could go wrong?

The pizza arrived in less than thirty minutes, so he tipped the driver and brought the big, steamy cardboard box to the kitchen table.

Joanna grabbed plates while Kaylee brought three glasses to the table.

Harry reached inside the fridge and took out a two-liter bottle of soda.

The irresistible scent of warm doughy pizza wafted to his nose.

He'd slept fitfully on the red-eye, and when he landed he drove straight to the Sheriff's office hoping to catch up with Lou Ann, and now he was so hungry he could eat the whole pizza in one sitting. But he'd hold off till the girls got theirs first.

Kaylee and Joanna each had two slices while he wolfed down four.

"Hungry, huh?" Kaylee commented.

Harry rubbed his belly. "I was starved, but that pizza sure hit the spot."

Together they'd devoured three quarters of the pizza, leaving plenty for Lou Ann after what must be a long and difficult day.

Pizza. Great for what ails you, except when someone dies.

Harry stretched and his eyelids began to flutter.

"If you guys don't mind, I'm going to take a nap. I'm full, and I'm beat."

"Sure. Go ahead," Kaylee said.

Harry yawned and headed to the bed Lou Ann and he once shared, and he prayed they would share again in the future.

But an afternoon nap was harmless.

He'd be up and out well before Lou Ann returned home.

Harry took a deep breath and lolled his head back onto the pillow on the side of the bed that used to be his.

Kaylee went into the bedroom she shared with Joanna and grabbed her wallet that contained her driver's license, in case she was stopped, and the twenty-dollar bill, and then returned with it.

"We can't be too careful. After all, I'm driving."

Kaylee followed Joanna out the front door and locked it.

Isabelle sent them sad doggy looks from the front window.

Joanna brought her finger to her lips.

"Shhh," she begged Isabelle to remain quiet. "Shit! She's going to bark and wake Harry."

Isabelle quietly backed away. "See?" Joanna said. "Isabelle and I have an understanding."

Kaylee arched her brows. "Perfect."

Kaylee clicked open Harry's car doors, and Joanna climbed into the passenger side while Kaylee slid behind the steering wheel.

Kaylee winced while she started the engine.

She and Joanna looked at each other and waited for Harry to rush out and catch them commandeering his car, but he didn't appear.

"We're just borrowing it," Kaylee reassured Joanna.

"Thirty minutes, and that's it. Maybe you don't want to stay here, but I do. You'll have Greece and I could end up back out on the streets."

Kaylee nudged Joanna. "Nah."

"How about we just go to the main drag and look around. We'll be back before you…or Harry know it."

"Okay."

"There you go!"

Kaylee maneuvered the car out of the driveway.

She hadn't driven in months, and the steering wheel felt foreign in her grasp.

But after two blocks and two turns, she was in control once again.

She passed two traffic lights and turned right.

Damn, there was a lot of traffic in Clearwater. It rivaled Miami where she passed her driver's license road test on the first try. So did her best friend, Shawna.

But Jimmy was really pissed when he failed that same day. They tried to reassure him it was okay, because others failed too, but he stomped away, and didn't talk to her for three days. Kaylee knew it was because he was embarrassed. He ended up passing on the second try, but they never spoke of that day. She imagined he just wanted to forget the whole thing since now he had a license too. Jimmy could be really difficult. But he was in her rearview mirror. Kaylee sniffled. Demetrios was too— permanently.

"Hey, are you okay?" Joanna asked. "Let's go back," she added.

"Okay. But look over there, Joanna. There's Coffee Cafe! I got my twenty on me. I'll treat you and me to iced coffees. That's gonna feel awesome on a hot day like this."

"I thought you were saving up to go back to Greece."

"Twenty dollars isn't going to be near enough. Come on. You know you want one."

"I…I've…only seen them, and I don't know how or what to order," Joanna admitted.

"Not to worry. I'll order for us both. Trust me, you'll like it."

Kaylee pulled into the drive through lane.

"What can I get you?" the woman at the window asked.

"Two large vanilla iced coffees, both with cream and sugar."

"You got it," the woman said.

Kaylee watched Joanna's eyes widen and her lips curve into an anticipatory smile. Joanna's past life, and even her much-improved present one, left her behind what everyone else took for granted. But Kaylee had it all, most of her life.

"That'll be $7.50."

Joanna's eyes got even bigger.

Kaylee gave the woman the twenty, and she gave Kaylee back her change.

The woman then handed Kaylee the two iced coffees, one at time, and Kaylee handed Joanna her coffee and put hers in the cup holder.

"I had no idea that coffees like these cost so much," Joanna said.

Kaylee laughed. "Well, they're not just coffees, but special ones."

Kaylee pulled back into traffic and then grabbed her iced coffee from the cupholder and took a long drink through the straw.

"Ah! I forgot how good these go down."

"Do they have coffees like these in Greece?"

"Better! But these will do for now."

Kaylee drove along the main drag and spotted a mall.

"Ooh, let's go in there! I haven't gone into a mall in ages."

"I've been in the one in Miami a few times."

"So have I!"

Kaylee stopped at a light and Joanna and she looked at each other. Neither had mentioned Miami and the horrors they each suffered at the hands of Newel.

"Do you still want to go?"

"Yes!" Joanna said with a firm nod.

Burying Newell was more than knowing he was six feet under.

Kaylee nodded. "Then we'll go and look around."

Kaylee entered the mall parking lot.

"What luck! There's a spot right by the main entrance."

Joanna clapped her hands.

Kaylee parked in the coveted space, and she and Joanna hopped out of Harry's car. Kaylee clicked the remote and the car beeped, signaling the doors were securely locked.

"This is so cool. I'm glad we came!"

Kaylee grinned. "Beats sitting inside or in the backyard. Isn't it good to get out?"

"Sure is!"

Kaylee knew Joanna would have a good time. They both badly needed the release.

They skipped to the mall entrance and Kaylee opened the door.

"After you, my friend!"

They bounded inside and straight to the department store's makeup counters.

Kaylee's heartbeat suddenly flickered to her neck recalling how her bedroom bathroom at Demetrios's mansion easily had five times more high-end makeup than they had here.

But then reality invaded and for the moment it didn't matter that

Kaylee only had a few dollars left after those coffees, which was totally worth it, because these make up samples were free.

Kaylee and Joanna bopped from counter to counter.

Kaylee dipped a disposable applicator into a lipstick pod and approached Joanna. "I think this color would look great on you."

Joanna backed away.

Damn you, Margo!

"It's all right. You can choose whatever you like."

That's all it took.

Joanna puckered her lips while Kaylee applied the neutral color.

"You look awesome. Take a look into the mirror."

Joanna peered into the counter's mirror and smiled.

"Great. Now pick one out for me," Kaylee said.

Joanna scanned the samples, chose a pale pink, and applied the lipstick to Kaylee's lips.

Kaylee smacked her lips and glanced into the mirror.

Demetrios would have liked this shade.

By the time they reached the end of the makeup counters, both sported foundation, eye shadow, blush, mascara, and lip color of their own choosing.

"I bet Margo looks like shit these days," Joanna said.

"Yeah, it's really hard to coordinate with prison orange!"

They both chuckled.

Armed with their new faces and sample bags that the cosmetic sales ladies had given them, Kaylee and Joanna maneuvered through the mall crowd. No doubt many ducked into the air conditioned mall to avoid the sweltering Florida summer day, including them.

Their next stop was the food court, where they took advantage of tooth-picked samples from every food spot.

Joanna glanced at the mall clock. By Harry's car clock, they'd been gone for two hours.

"We better head back."

"Okay," Kaylee agreed. "But we did have an awesome time, right?"

Joanna grinned and nodded. "The best!"

Harry stretched. He'd desperately needed that nap. He smacked his lips and sat up on the side of the bed.

How long had he been out? He reached for his phone.

Hmmm. Two hours. Time for him to get up. He checked for any text messages. Nothing work-related, or from Lou Ann. Hopefully she was too busy to text.

Perhaps the girls would like to go out somewhere since they were probably going stir-crazy from being cooped up in the house.

Harry stood, straightened the dent he left on the bed, and walked out of the bedroom.

"Kaylee! Joanna!" he called.

No answer. They must be out in the backyard.

Isabelle met him in the kitchen.

He waited for her to bark at him, but apparently she'd changed her mind for some reason.

Harry leaned over and petted her.

"So, maybe we're friends?" he asked her.

Isabelle looked up at him with her doggy brows raised.

Then she toddled off to her empty water bowl.

"So that's it?"

Harry picked up Isabelle's water bowl, filled it, and set it back down at her spot.

"We'll have to talk to the girls about this," he teased the dog.

She lapped up the water and then whined.

"Out?"

Isabelle barked.

"Okay, let's go outside and talk with the girls."

Isabelle hesitated.

"What's the matter?"

Then she backed up.

"Come on. We're doing well here. I'll go with you. I'll give you a biscuit if you do."

That's all it took.

Isabelle trotted alongside him to the glass doors.

He slid them open, and he and Isabelle stepped out into the backyard.

But Kaylee and Joanna weren't there.

Isabelle pee'd and then they both went back inside.

"Here's your biscuit as promised."

Harry handed a biscuit to Isabelle who happily chomped away at it.

The girls were probably watching TV in the den.

He went in there. They weren't there.

The bedroom.

He checked for them there. Nope.

Maybe they went out for a walk…without Isabelle.

He went to the living room credenza to get his keys.

He'd catch up with them. It was hot as hell outside and he'd offer them an air conditioned ride back. Then he'd take them out. The beach would be nice.

He reached into the bowl on the credenza to get his keys, but the bowl was empty.

What?

He could swear he put them there.

No. Was he so tired that he left the keys in the car? Joanna did open the door when he got home.

He'd check his car.

Harry stepped outside the front door.

Shit!

His car was gone.

He must have left the keys in the car and someone stole it!

But then he saw his car being pulled up into the driveway with Kaylee driving and Joanna in the passenger seat.

Red-hot anger spread across his face, and it flushed to his ears.

His chest seethed.

Harry gritted his teeth and shot his finger at them while waiting for his angry words to catch up.

Kaylee and Joanna got out of Harry's car. While Joanna fled past Harry with her head down, Kaylee stared straight at him while slurping what remained of her iced coffee.

He was a lamb compared to the demons she'd faced, even killing one, and was positive she was instrumental in Newell's demise. It was her shot that killed Newell, and everyone else shot at an already-dead piece of shit.

Even with Harry fire-hot pissed-off demeanor, he didn't frighten her.

"We only borrowed it. You were asleep."

He threw darts from eyes right at her.

Was that all he had?

"Okay. I should've left note."

"A note?" he spat back.

"Yeah."

"You stole my car."

"Borrowed," she pointed out again. "It's not stolen. It's sitting right there. If I wanted to steal it, then I wouldn't have returned it."

"Get in the house!"

Kaylee narrowed her eyes and shook her head. Now she was equally red hot.

"You're not my father!"

Harry took an angry step forward but then retreated.

She won.

Kaylee sashayed past Harry.

She felt his heat and she knew he felt hers.

Kaylee went straight to the bedroom where she found Joanna sitting with her shoulders hunched.

Kaylee shut the door and locked it.

Now she had control of the locks.

"I thought you said you had a good time. Fifteen minutes ago you were all happy."

"I just didn't know he'd wake up."

"So? He'll get over it."

"I like Harry. I've never had anyone to disappoint before."

"Harry's no saint. And neither is Lou Ann."

"And what are we?" Joanna asked.

"Damaged."

Harry sat on the sofa in the den and dropped his head in his palms.

It was easier on everybody when they thought Joanna was Kaylee.

He wished she still was.

Try as he might, he just couldn't connect with Kaylee. Neither could Lou Ann.

But Kaylee had no intention of letting her guard down.

They all needed to see the psychologist, because without help, Kaylee and the rest of them didn't stand a chance.

Harry bet that Kaylee was just waiting for him to call Lou Ann so they could gang up on her.

Yeah, that wasn't going to happen.

Isabelle toddled up to him.

"Did you know what they were up to?"

Isabelle laid down and rested her snout on his feet.

"You're excused."

At least he was making headway with Isabelle.

Then his cell pinged a message.

It was Lou Ann.

How's your day been?

He wasn't about to elaborate.

Okay. Just tired.

Me too. Home on time tonight.

Saved you pizza.

He left out a helping of heartache.

Thanks!

You're welcome.

How's Isabelle?

Believe it or not, she has her chin on my foot.

Lou Ann texted a thumbs-up emoji.

Kaylee and Joanna?

He definitely wasn't going to elaborate. That was an intense discussion for later. At least till after she had a slice of pizza.

In their room.

Behind a locked door, he imagined. He hadn't even tried to go there. It was best for them all to go to their own corners to cool off.

And he needed a long cool-off period. Kaylee? He shrugged.

He thought he and Kaylee were on the same playing field that day on the stoop after the green bean crisis. But just when he thought they bonded, today happened.

"Come on, Isabelle. Let's go into the kitchen. You get a biscuit and I get a beer."

Isabelle's ears perked.

"Sounds like a good deal, huh?"

Isabelle barked.

So the day wasn't a total loss.

Harry never thought he'd see that day when he wasn't in Isabelle's crosshairs.

Now if he just wasn't in Kaylee's either.

Joanna sat on the bed next to her cosmetic sample bag from the fatal…or might as well be fatal… afternoon joyride.

But she'd gone along with it.

She'd done worse, but she was trying to change, and Lou Ann and Harry had helped her plenty. But that might not be the case anymore.

It didn't matter for Kaylee because she'd fly out of here the first chance she got. And after witnessing Kaylee in Greece and how her heart was ripped in two when Newell shot Demetrios in the back like the coward he was, Greece should be her home.

Newell deserved being riddled with gunfire, but a slow, painful death would have been far more satisfying. And although Kaylee made Otto suffer with his face all cut up and a fork poked hard in his eye, Joanna beat Margo to near death. Too bad that like Kaylee, she didn't finish the job.

Neither Kaylee nor she were arrested for their deeds, but Harry could've—and probably would've—reported his car stolen had they not pulled into the driveway just in time. Then she and Kaylee could've very well seen the inside of a jail, something Joanna had luckily skirted many times.

Kaylee tossed her sample bag onto the dresser.

"He'll get over it," Kaylee said.

"It's not a matter of Harry getting over it, it's that he's not going to trust us, and he's going to hover over us like a hawk from now on. And you better keep this in mind if you want to get out of here to Greece."

"Don't worry about me. I escaped Newell…temporarily. Lou Ann and Harry wouldn't even bump my pulse."

That was true.

Joanna had considered going with Kaylee to Greece, but after today, and frankly, because of Kaylee's persistently shitty behavior, she changed her mind. She needed to stay in Clearwater and build a stable life, one she'd never experienced—that is if she hadn't fallen on the dark side of Harry and Lou Ann, because surely Harry would tell Lou Ann about what they did today.

The bottom of Joanna's feet began to get as sweaty as her palms, which she wiped on the sides of her shorts.

Kaylee zeroed in on Joanna's nervousness.

"Take it from me. The last thing you want to do is look nervous…or worse, scared."

Newell had killed Kaylee's soul and robbed her of happiness. How sad. Although Newell, Otto, and scores of men had violated her, at one point she became so ill that she had become practically and fortunately unconscious and unable to feel anything more that was done to her. Even Newell, who was a doctor, thought she was dead. And she must have teetered horribly close to death.

But Kaylee fought Newell to the end.

Even though Kaylee and she looked scarily alike, they couldn't be more different.

9

After leaving headquarters and Harry, Lou Ann's shift so far had been uneventful. No bank crisis. No domestic violence. Not that she remotely wished for either, because all her adrenaline was spent in the meeting. But it could ramp up at any minute, because that was the "job"—to be ready for anything anytime.

And she needed anything short of a disaster to help keep her mind off of whatever her fate would be.

The driver of a red Porsche sped right past her at 35 miles per hour over the speed limit.

Didn't he see her here? Or maybe he did and welcomed the chase.

But there would be no high-speed pursuit. The last thing she wanted to do was buck the rules, especially after the meeting this morning.

Lou Ann sped up enough to spot him swerving to the right on the main drag. She drove a block farther hoping to catch sight of him.

And she did.

The driver of the Porsche slowed, taunting her.

Lou Ann engaged the cruiser's strobe lights.

The driver pulled off the road.

Lou Ann's heartbeat ramped up. It could be a trap.

She ran the car's license plate, banking that the car was stolen, or that the driver had a record, or both.

The plate popped up and Lou Ann widened her eyes.

The car was registered to Jake Regis, her ex before Harry became her ex, who no longer was her ex, sort of.

The complications of her life, just took a more-than weird turn.

Lou Ann exited her vehicle and approached Jake's luxury car. Figured he'd be driving that car, vain as he always was and still appeared to be.

Jake rolled down his window and shot her a toothy white smile.

"Hey, Lou Ann. I thought that was you!"

She didn't smile back. Instead she remained straight-faced with her eyes hidden beneath her shades.

"Do you know how fast you were going, sir?"

Jake chuckled. "Sir?"

Lou Ann pressed her lips together.

Jake apologetically shook his head. "I'm sorry, Deputy Jasinski. No, I do not know how fast I was going."

He damn well did.

"You were doing 65 in a 40-miles-per-hour zone."

"I was? I mean I guess I was. You would know."

"Are you in some kind of a hurry?"

"Uh...no."

"License and registration, please."

"I hate those words."

"I wouldn't have to say them if you hadn't been speeding."

"You're right, as always."

Lou Ann sighed inwardly.

Jake reached into his glovebox, retrieved the requested documents, and handed them to Lou Ann. Everything was in order.

"I'll be right back."

Lou Ann took Jake's documents back to the cruiser while Jake waited in his cherry red car.

She entered the information. Oddly, he had no speeding tickets...or hadn't ever been caught speeding.

Lou Ann returned to Jake and returned his documents along with a speeding fine.

The fine would be only pennies to him, a perk of being the head of his own law firm.

"You can contest this, but I wouldn't recommend it since I have you clocked at 25 miles over the limit." Lou Ann finally gave him a grin.

"Have a nice and *safe* day, sir."

"I will. It was nice to see you again, and to be under your radar," he added.

He shot her another grin and then slowly pulled away.

Jake had that planned. He knew that was her sector.

But why? They broke up long ago. He'd moved on and so did she, with Harry. Maybe word was that she wasn't with Harry anymore, but she was again. And hopefully for good this time. What she had with Jake, even during the good times, paled in comparison to what she had with Harry, even in the bad times. Even when she hated Harry, he was still in her head. Jake only left an empty spot she never noticed. That empty spot just resurfaced.

Lou Ann just returned to her cruiser when dispatch notified her to return immediately to headquarters. The decision had been made. Her steady feelings that the meeting ended as well as could be expected were apparently wrong.

Lou Ann swallowed past the lump in her throat and notified dispatch that she was on her way.

Shit! Her career was done. What else was she suited for?

She came up with nothing during the fateful drive back to headquarters yet again today. At least she got a speeding fine to show for it.

Lou Ann pulled her cruiser back into the department parking garage. Harry would not be waiting for her again, and she couldn't begin to rehearse what she was going to tell him and Kaylee and Joanna when she returned early from her final shift.

She cut the cruiser's engine and drew a deep breath before getting out.

Dead deputy walking.

Lou Ann entered the lobby and surrendered her gunbelt before going to the elevator bank. Fourth floor again.

She walked out of the elevator and walked with her chin up to Glenda's office.

The receptionist sent her right through. At least she didn't have to wait. She, and apparently her superiors, wanted to get this over with.

Lou Ann entered Glenda's office to find Glenda and Sheriff Carson waiting for her. At least her nemesis, Lieutenant Dan Mathews, was absent. They'd spared her that indignity.

Lou Ann shook their hands and stood like a defendant awaiting the judge's decision.

"Unfortunately, we can no longer have you in this department as Deputy Sheriff," Sheriff Carson stoically announced.

Her knees quivered beneath her uniform.

That was that. It was done.

Then Sheriff Carson extended his hand to her.

She had no choice but to shake it.

"You are no longer Deputy Sheriff Lou Ann Jasinski because you will now be Sergeant Lou Ann Jasinski."

The room began to spin. Lou Ann blinked to steady herself. *Is this a dream?* Did she hear that?

"Sergeant Jasinski?" Glenda called.

"Um…yes. Present."

"Congratulations."

No way was she going to ask why this was happening.

"Finish your shift and tomorrow, report back here for your reassignment," Glenda said.

"Thank you, ma'am."

Glenda grinned. "Now, get going."

"I will."

Lou Ann left Glenda's office and zombie-walked to the elevator bank.

She returned to the lobby and had her gunbelt returned to her.

"Have a nice day," the security officer said.

"I intend to. You, too," she said.

Lou Ann walked out into the sunshine and walked with a lilt back to the garage, where she got back into her vehicle.

As soon as the door clicked shut, Lou Ann shot up her hands.

"Who hoooo!"

Harry paced from the kitchen to the den in circles. He needed to blow off steam before he engaged Kaylee and Joanna, who surely followed Kaylee into the arena of lies and deceit. They'd taken his car without permission. Kaylee knew he'd never give that permission, and she would be right.

It was hard to keep them corralled at home. It was natural for them to go out and enjoy freedom that they thought they would never have again. He understood better than they thought he did.

Harry stopped pacing and Isabelle, who'd followed him along at his heels, came to a halt too.

Kaylee and Joanna didn't want to have him and Lou Ann shadowing them forever.

Harry massaged his face.

He didn't want to reward their behavior, but perhaps he and Lou Ann could swing a car for them. Kaylee had a driver's license, but Joanna didn't. He'd teach Joanna how to drive so she could get a driver's license.

If he and Lou Ann continued to keep them hostage, more of the same would happen again. But if they got them a car then maybe Kaylee would stop fighting them.

Harry looked down at Isabelle.

"Well, here goes."

Isabelle wagged her tail.

"I see you agree, but I must say I think you're a bit biased."

Isabelle barked.

"All right, we'll do it your way."

Isabelle toddled alongside him as he made his way to Kaylee and Joanna's shared bedroom.

He made a fist to knock but thought better of it and relaxed his hand before he rapped on the door.

Neither Kaylee nor Joanna answered. But he heard them scurrying around behind the door.

He looked down at Isabelle who furrowed her doggy eyebrows.

Harry shrugged and rapped on the door again.

The door knob rotated and the bedroom door opened a crack.

"Can you guys meet me in the den?"

They needed a level playing field.

"We'll be there in a minute," Kaylee said.

"Okay."

Harry backed away. The invitation was extended. Now all he had to do was keep his cool and not rehash the car incident with anger. The heat between them had dissipated to lukewarm. It was the best he could offer at the moment.

He and Isabelle returned to the den, sat on the couch, and waited for the treaty negotiations to begin.

Kaylee and Joanna quietly appeared at the doorway and hesitated.

Harry gestured for them to enter, and they approached slowly.

Joanna sat on the other end of the sofa from Harry, while Kaylee sat cross-legged on the floor.

At least they showed up.

"I understand that it has been difficult for the two of you to be cooped up here at the house and that it's natural for you to want to get back out into the world."

Kaylee studied him intently, while Joanna leaned forward. He had their attention.

"However, commandeering my car was the wrong way to go about it. Do you get where I'm coming from?"

Kaylee nodded while Joanna said, "Yes."

Progress was being made, and so far no one had stomped out of the room, including him.

"I've been thinking about this and…no promises…but I'll speak with Lou Ann if—and that's a big if—we can manage to get a car for you two. We can't do two vehicles."

"That would be acceptable," Kaylee said.

"It's fine, but I can't drive. No one ever taught me."

"I'll handle that. We'll work on that so you can get a license."

"Thank you, Harry."

"Don't thank me too quickly because we still need to discuss all this."

"I can't wait for Aunt Lou Ann to come home so we can talk about it!"

Kaylee rolled her eyes. "I don't think she's going to go for it. She's all about control."

"That's not completely true."

Lou Ann could be rigid sometimes. It was hard for her to shift from the rigors of the job to the pure release of home. He could relate to that too. They shared that trait.

Harry continued, "She's adjusting, just like you. But tonight is not the night to mention any of this. She's having a very hard day. Tonight I'm not even going to mention you taking my car."

"What's going on?" Joanna asked.

"I'm not sure. But treat her gently when she gets home."

"That's fair," Kaylee said.

"I'm glad you see it that way."

"Why don't you two feed Isabelle and then take her for a walk…on foot."

"That's what walking implies," Kaylee replied.

"Just checking," Harry said.

"By the way, your car needs a tune-up," Kaylee added on her way out of the room.

"I know that," he called back at her.

Damn. She was right.

Harry remained on the couch. He heard Isabelle crunching on her food and then lapping up her water. The leash went on and Kaylee, Joanna, and Isabelle went out the front door.

He purposely didn't check where they were headed. As long as his car engine didn't start, he was okay.

It was better that they'd aired everything before Lou Ann got home.

Harry looked at his phone and was about to text her, but didn't. She needed space and a quiet night at home.

He'd see to it that she wouldn't have one more crisis to handle. One big one was more than enough.

10

Lou Ann parked her cruiser on the side the house, where Harry couldn't see it. She didn't call or text Harry about her promotion on purpose, planning to surprise him.

She cut the engine and crept to the front door. She made a wrinkled face.

Then she opened the door to find Harry on the other side.

"I didn't hear the cruiser."

He peeked past her to find it, and then harder.

She worked to suppress a smile, almost blowing her acting.

He took one look at her fake-scrunched face and opened his arms.

Lou Ann bowed her head.

"I'm no longer a deputy sheriff. They did let me finish my shift."

"Oh, babe. I'm so sorry."

He wrapped his arms around her.

"Is there anything I could do for you?"

Lou Ann pulled away from him and grinned.

"You can take me out to dinner, because I'm a sergeant now!"

Harry pointed his finger at her.

"You…deserve it. Congratulations!"

Now came the happy hug.

Kaylee and Joanna came in the front door with Isabelle on her leash.

Kaylee and Joanna looked at each other.

"We didn't mean to interrupt anything here," Joanna said.

"Yeah, we'll head in to our bedroom. Come, on Isabelle," Kaylee said.

"Well, you might as well go there to get ready, because we're all going out to eat to celebrate."

Joanna jumped up and down. "We're getting the car!"

"What car?" Lou Ann asked.

Harry shook his head. "Uh, I'm thinking of getting another car."

"I thought you couldn't part with yours."

"Just considering it."

"Okay. I'm going to get out of this uniform."

Lou Ann practically skipped down the hallway to the bedroom.

Sergeant Jasinski! Sergeant Jasinski! She hummed to herself.

Once inside, she closed the door and then whipped off her gunbelt. She yanked off her uniform and then danced around in her bra and panties, then paused in front of the dresser mirror and saluted to her reflection.

High on giddiness, she didn't hear the door open.

"May I join in the festivities?" Harry asked.

Lou Ann startled to a halt.

Shit! He saw that.

"How long have you been standing there?" she sheepishly asked.

"Long enough to see you over-the-moon happy!"

Lou Ann jumped into his arms and he caught her. She wrapped her legs around his waist and hugged his neck.

"Here's to the new you!" he said.

"I still can't believe it. They called me back later this afternoon, and I thought I was done for. I still can't get over it!"

Harry spun around with Lou Ann attached to his hips.

"I hope it isn't inappropriate to treat a sergeant this way," he teased.

"Most inappropriate, but please don't stop!"

Harry stopped twirling and tossed Lou Ann on the bed.

"This is about to get more inappropriate," he growled.

"Mmm. Interrogate me, Special Agent Boxer!"

Harry whipped off his shirt.

"Where were you at 0800 today?"

Harry's exposed chest caused her mind to stutter.

"I was being questioned," she finally answered. "But at 1400 I prevailed."

"Hmmm. So you are free now?"

Her heart jackhammered in her chest. Here she was, beneath the man she once so wanted to hate but now so wanted to love. *May her heart survive this time.*

"I'm free at the moment."

"Fabulous. So am I."

"Harry," she whispered.

"One second."

He rolled off her and lowered his shorts.

"Let freedom ring, baby!"

Their skins began to melt into one when a knock came at the door.

"We're ready to go," Kaylee called.

Then she and Joanna giggled.

Lou Ann sighed. "I did say we're going to go out."

"Uh-uh. You're not going to get out of this interrogation. To be continued. We'll reconvene here at 2130."

"I'll be here."

Lou Ann quickly put on a sundress, and Harry redressed and shifted his over eager, and way too happy response.

"Ready when you are," Lou Ann teased.

"After you…my dear suspect."

Humor was always his best foreplay.

They'd arrived at Taste of Italy, his and Lou Ann's favorite restaurant from the past, and now the present and hopefully the future.

They were seated at a table by the window, which happened to be Harry and Lou Ann's favorite spot.

"When I called for a reservation, I didn't plan on this booth," he cautioned.

Lou Ann smiled. "My good fortune continues."

They sat at that booth as lovers and as fighters. It had their messy footprints all over it.

He and Lou Ann had accepted it as an important part of their past and their recommitment to their future.

They'd been back since but never at this booth.

"I'm sorry," he started to get up.

He automatically made the reservation out of habit, and without thinking.

It was supposed to be her congratulatory dinner.

He messed up.

Lou Ann extended her hand across the table to Harry and he rested his upon hers.

"It's okay, " she said.

"What's okay?" Joanna, who sat next to Harry, piped up .

"Um, must be the night for restaurants, because all the others were booked solid," Harry lied.

His and Lou Ann's past wasn't open for discussion. It was private between them even, though Joanna knew only a small part of their rocky past. Kaylee didn't know much about it, and as usual, didn't seem to care.

"It looks and smells like an awesome place," Joanna grinned.

"I prefer Greek food. But I suppose restaurants here couldn't begin to compare to real Greek…in Greece," Kaylee snootily proclaimed.

Lou Ann nodded. "There's nothing like the original."

Brava!

Kaylee arched her brows in surprise but offered no words in return.

A waiter approached and handed out the menus.

"May I offer you drinks? Appetizers?"

"A glass of red for me and the lady," Harry said.

Kaylee raised her hand. "Me too."

The waiter paused.

"No, not you too. Cokes for the young ladies. And some bread will be fine."

"I'll return with your drink and the bread, and I'll take your entree orders when you are ready."

"I drank wine in Greece."

"Well, this is the United States, and you are legally underage."

"I was a Lady in Greece."

"And you're a young lady here," Lou Ann said.

The waiter brought the two glasses of wine and the two Cokes and set the bread and pats of butter in the center of the table.

"Thank you," Lou Ann said.

"Have you decided on the entrees?"

"I'll have the lasagna, please," Lou Ann said.

"Spaghetti and meatballs for me," Harry ordered.

"Kaylee? Joanna?" he inquired.

"I'll have the lasagna too," Kaylee said.

"Sounds good, but I'll also have the spaghetti and meatballs," Joanna said.

"Very well," the waiter said, and then collected the menus.

Harry raised his glass.

"To Sergeant Lou Ann Jasinski!"

"Salut!" Kaylee said.

"Yeah, salut!" Joanna echoed.

"Thank you, you all!"

Lou Ann and Harry sipped their wine while Kaylee and Joanna their sodas.

Kaylee put down her drink and hugged Lou Ann, who appeared as stunned as Harry felt.

"Congratulations," Kaylee said.

"Thank you, Kaylee."

"You're welcome."

"I guess we'll have to start calling you Aunt Sergeant Lou Ann," Joanna teased.

"Well, fall in and eat. And that's an order," Lou Ann winked.

Even Kaylee grinned at that.

Harry couldn't figure out Kaylee. Such a willful girl. Hot and cold. Light and dark. Kaylee was truly a tortured soul who just couldn't find her way to fit in, unlike Joanna, who craved to fit in and so far successfully.

When the food arrived, they dug into a rare happiness for everyone. Even Kaylee became surprisingly animated.

After the huge Italian meal, they pushed back in their chairs, satiated physically and psychologically. No smirks or rolling eyes.

Harry exhaled. A night that could have been tense and ruining it for Lou Ann turned out to be darn near perfect.

Now it cleared the private path for him and Lou Ann.

11

Harry pulled into the driveway and Lou Ann, Kaylee, and Joanna got out of his car. Lou Ann waited for him get out and lock the car, and then they followed Kaylee and Joanna to the front door.

Isabelle stared out the front window and barked a greeting.

"Looks like someone is happy we're home," Lou Ann said.

Harry wrapped his arm around Lou Ann's waist.

"She's not the only one happy we're home."

Lou Ann reached for her keys and unlocked the door.

Isabelle circled everyone, including Harry.

Lou Ann raised her brows.

"Wow! Apparently something remarkable happened while I was out."

Harry shot a glance at Kaylee and Joanna.

"Yep, a lot did happen."

Kaylee yawned. "I'm whipped."

"So am I," Joanna echoed.

Kaylee winked at Harry. "It's been a long day. We're going to turn in."

Harry stretched. "Yeah, I think we should all call it a night."

After Kaylee and Joanna left for their bedroom, Harry nudged Lou Ann.

"We have unfinished business," he whispered in her ear.

"Yes, we do."

Harry led Lou Ann into the bedroom and quietly closed the door.

"Where were we?" he asked.

Lou Ann pulled off her sundress and lay across the bed.

"Right here." Lou Ann grinned. "Aren't you going to continue to interrogate me?"

"I've no further questions."

"Now what?"

"This."

Harry crawled toward Lou Ann.

She could back out at any moment, but the sweat on the back of her neck and the rising heat clear to her belly convinced her to stay.

She slid off all that still covered her body, and Harry did the same blindly, because his eyes were riveted on her.

"Harry," she whispered.

"I know." He reached into his shorts pocket—his shorts already in a heap on the bed—and pulled out a condom. "Don't take this the wrong way. It was only meant for the right moment…with you."

"It's okay to quit apologizing."

Harry bowed his head.

"Thank you."

Lou Ann patted the mattress. "You're welcome. Now put that on and get over here."

Not that she didn't trust where he'd been, because she honestly this time knew he hadn't strayed or even considered it, but she was responsible in different ways for two difficult teens, and the last thing she needed was a baby in the mix. Luckily, he agreed. Plus, she'd already taken more than a leave of absence to search for Kaylee. That, and she'd just been miraculously promoted to sergeant. And with Harry's unpredictable assignments, she had more than her hands full.

Lou Ann drew a deep breath and hushed her mind, letting her body speak for her.

It was as if his lips never left hers, the memory of them so sweetly refreshed.

She'd refused to remember how good they were together. Now the release of all that anger and disappointment only made what was between them even hotter.

His fingers, hands, and mouth returned without a stutter, knowing the map to every one of her crevices and nooks.

She tilted her head back, offering her neck, and he took full advantage of it.

They rocked and filled each other until the room spun around them.

What had been unsaid and hanging over them was no longer.

Harry shivered and Lou Ann drew him closer, hoping to hide her own quaking.

She ran her fingers through his mussed hair and released him.

Harry rolled off her and lay on his side, facing her.

"Stay," she said.

He hesitated.

"I have to feed my fish."

"You got fish?"

"Yeah. Perfect pets for a small place. I was lonely."

"And now?"

Harry grinned.

"Not so much."

Harry stretched. He automatically woke predawn as if his body warned that it was time to leave. He scooted toward Lou Ann and kissed her forehead. Should he wake her? If he didn't, he risked ruining all that he had prayed for—a second chance with the only woman he truly loved and nearly betrayed…thankfully not physically, although she with good reason accused him of it—but unfortunately emotionally. He'd wrecked her, himself, and the two of them. He couldn't do it again.

He gently shook her.

"Hey, I have to go for now. I need to tell you that."

"Thank you for not just leaving."

"I'll see you later, and if I'm called out, I'll let you know. I love you, and we'll take it from here."

"Here is a great place to start."

Harry dressed and returned to settle his lips on hers.

"Think they know?"

Lou Ann laughed.

"Yeah."

"I don't want to keep sneaking around."

"I don't want you to either." She winked. "We'll work something out."

"My thoughts exactly. Have a great first day as sergeant, and then tell me all about it."

"I promise."

Harry blew Lou Ann a kiss and walked out the door to find Isabelle siting by it.

"Did I take your spot?"

Isabelle growled.

Harry opened the door, and Isabelle trotted past him.

And we were doing so well.

12

Lou Ann wolfed down a bagel. Last night with Harry left her pleasantly but precariously late for her first day at headquarters as a sergeant. Today she'd find out her assignment.

Kaylee and Joanna were still fast asleep.

Lou Ann left them a note to have a great day, and to help themselves to breakfast and lunch, and that she should be home by seven or earlier.

And that they could call or text if they needed anything.

She donned her deputy sheriff's uniform for the last time.

Before leaving, she bent over and hugged Isabelle.

"I'm sorry you felt left out last night. It won't happen again, but you and I may need to share the bed with Harry…every once in a while."

Isabelle twisted her mouth.

"It will be okay. I promise. You're still my number one, but we have to make room for not only Harry, but Kaylee and Joanna. They need your company and love too. But you knew that already, didn't you?"

Isabelle woofed affirmatively.

"Good girl." She narrowed her gaze at Isabelle. "How do feel about fish…the kind that swim?"

Isabelle arched her brows and then pit-pattered away.

"I'm guessing you'll think about it," Lou Ann called. "Bye, baby."

Lou Ann locked the front door and then got in her cruiser for probably the last time.

A change happened last night and another would happen today.

She smiled wide, thinking about the one last night. But for the time being, it was better for both of them not to rush, and have him keep his apartment and his fish for now.

Lou Ann pulled into the parking garage at headquarters, but instead of her knees shaking and her heart pounding anticipating doom, they now did from excitement.

She exited her vehicle, puffed her chest out, and pinned back her shoulders. Not even Lieutenant Dan Mathews could ruin her day.

Lou Ann let out a muted laugh. He was probably aware of Sheriff Carson's and Glenda's final decision, having avoided her at the final meeting.

But they'd have to work together at times, she imagined, because he was still her superior.

She proceeded to the lobby where the security officer smiled at her.

"Good morning, Sergeant Jasinski. Deputy Chief Glenda Martinez is expecting you."

"Thank you."

He didn't take her gunbelt this time.

Lou Ann went to the same elevator bank as before, pressed the up button, and waited. This time she rode up to the fourth floor, happily alone. No Lieutenant Dan to curb her enthusiasm.

It was pleasant ride to the fourth floor and Lou Ann walked straight to Glenda's office. She paused and took a deep breath before entering the chief's office waiting area.

The same receptionist greeted her.

"Good morning, Sergeant Jasinski. Go right in."

"Good morning, and thanks."

Lou Ann ventured inside Glenda's office.

Glenda stood behind her desk. "Ah, there you are. Right on time."

Lou Ann nodded and saluted.

"Please, sit."

Lou Ann sat after Glenda made herself comfortable behind her desk.

"So how does it feel?" Glenda asked.

"Good. Happy. Overwhelming," she admitted.

"I remember the feeling. Still do feel that way now and then," Glenda said.

"Today is a paperwork day, and then you'll meet with Lieutenant Dan Mathews. Then you two will join me for lunch."

Glenda met Lou Ann's gaze at the mention of Mathews.

"I look forward to having a working relationship with Lieutenant Mathews, and paramount with you, chief and Sheriff Carson. "

Glenda smiled. "Good. You'll now be included in many departmental meetings."

Lou Ann nodded. But inside her heart did flip-flops. She'd long dreamed of this chance to be accepted and heard. To truly make a difference.

Glenda led Lou Ann to a conference room and pointed to a chair where a thick envelope awaited her on the table alongside of it a pen.

"This will take you about two hours to complete and sign. Lieutenant Mathews will meet you here at 10:00."

Glenda left the room.

Lou Ann opened the envelope. So much for making a difference, at least today.

She went through page after page of policies and procedures governing Sergeant Sheriffs, and signing and attesting at the end of each section until her hand cramped.

And just in time, because her nemesis and superior, Dan Mathews, entered the conference room.

"Are you done?" he asked.

"Yes, sir."

"Took you long enough."

"I read through all the sections carefully," she answered.

Lou Ann straightened the papers into a thick pile with the edges completely flush, pushed them back into the envelope, stood, and handed the envelope to Dan Mathews.

He grunted and accepted it.

This was going to be a long, hard relationship.

"Come with me. You'll need a new tag, photo, and new uniforms."

"The cruiser?" she asked.

"Remains assigned to you."

She followed Dan out of the conference room and acquired everything he'd described.

Lou Ann ran her fingers over the starched white shirts with the sergeant stripes on the upper sleeves, and two pair of new beige trousers to complete her new official look. The photo and ID swipe turned out better than her deputy one.

"Women's locker room is over there. You can change into your appropriate uniform and turn in the old one you have on today, and bring any you still have in your possession to headquarters tomorrow."

"Yes, sir."

Once in the locker room, Lou Ann shed her deputy uniform and replaced it withe the sergeant one.

She looked in the mirror and grinned. She couldn't wait to show Harry and the girls, and Isabelle of course.

She quickly adjusted her ponytail, and with her chin held high, walked out of the locker room to where Dan stood waiting for her.

He made no further comment, but simply walked away.

Lou Ann silently and dutifully followed him.

They stopped in front of Glenda's office.

The bagel she gobbled down earlier this morning had long since been digested and her stomach chose this moment to growl a complaint.

Dan whipped around and glared at her, but once again said nothing.

He didn't have to. He was directly in charge of her, and that must have made him larger than his five foot eight stance which she was sure gave him his Napoleonic swagger.

But she intended to give him his due, no matter what. Sheriff Carson already had his eye on Dan, and not in a good way. However Dan was efficient, and that kept him squarely in his position.

"Ready for lunch?" Glenda asked.

Dan stoically glanced at Lou Ann.

"Apparently so," he said.

"Good, because I'm starved. Consequences of a breakfast on the run."

Man, could she relate. She pictured Dan getting up at the crack of dawn to have a hearty breakfast.

"The uniform suits you," Glenda said.

Once again, no comment from Lieutenant Dan.

Never mind, because she and Glenda were on the same page, and that counted more than Dan's shitty silence.

Lou Ann's phone vibrated an incoming message.

She quickly glanced at it, since she was behind Glenda and Dan.

Shit! Kaylee and Joanna's gynecologist appointment was this afternoon.

How could she have forgotten about that?

Dan turned around.

"Is there a problem, Sergeant Jasinski?"

"No, sir," she lied.

Her heart thumped in her chest.

What now?

She had no choice but to excuse herself.

Then another text came. This one was from Harry inquiring how she was doing.

She was screwed.

"I'll join both of you in one second. Family matter."

Dan rolled his eyes.

"No problem. I'm sure you'll join us shortly."

Shortly wasn't what was about to happen.

Lou Ann called Harry.

"Hey, what's up?"

"I'm in deep shit. I'm a terrible mother…aunt. I forgot that Kaylee and Joanna have a gynecology appointment at 2 pm."

"Okay, easy. No problem. I'll take them there. I haven't been called out. It's all good. Don't leave. I got it."

"200 State Street, suite 404."

"We'll be there."

"Dr. Zimmer sent the referral, and all the paperwork should be there. Insurance card is in the top dresser drawer."

"Do what you need to do. I'll take care of everything and I'll text you later."

"Harry…Thank you," she said over the lump swelling in the back of her throat.

Lou Ann hung up. Harry had once again come to her aid. This time the only funeral she'll have to attend might be for her career.

Lou Ann hurried inside the headquarters officers' dining room just in time to join Glenda and Dan.

"Everything all right? Glenda asked.

Dan tightly grinned, ready to pounce on the opportunity to expound on why she should not have been promoted to sergeant, given her multiple distractions.

Lou Ann looked straight at Dan, and then at Glenda.

"Everything is fine."

She got a tray and proceeded along the dining room's lunchtime offerings.

"Everything looks absolutely delicious."

<h1 style="text-align:center">13</h1>

Harry sprinkled fish food into the tank.

"Sorry, guys but I gotta go."

The fish wiggled to the top of the tank and began to devour the food.

"I'll see myself out," he said to them.

He pulled out of his parking garage while passing by the empty second space assigned to him. Perhaps in time his space would be empty too along with his apartment once his lease expired.

Harry continued to Lou Ann's, and formerly his house, where he'd continue to exercise a mix of caution and hope.

Fortunately, he hadn't been called away. All he had was a Zoom meeting later this evening, and he had the whole day free to help with Kaylee and Joanna as he'd promised to do.

Trust was beginning to blossom between him and Lou Ann, and he'd text her later to reassure her that they all made out fine so she could focus on the important day.

He parked in the driveway and got out of his car.

How hard could this be?

He knocked on the door.

Lou Ann had given him a key, but he wasn't at that point yet to use it.

Kaylee opened the door.

"Why didn't you just come in?"

"Uh…you might not have been decent."

"Decency has been gone for a while."

That was true.

"Hey, Harry!" Joanna greeted him behind Kaylee. "What a surprise!"

Harry entered the living room and paused.

"I'm here to drive you to the lady-parts doctor."

Kaylee laughed. "Harry, it's called a gynecologist."

"Ummm…yeah…so …uh…get ready. I'll wait for you two in the den."

Kaylee walked away with ease, while he noted Joanna's cheerfulness draining away while she trudged behind Kaylee.

He ventured into the kitchen to get a drink of water.

A muffled discussion was happening behind their closed bedroom door, and then Kaylee and Joanna came out.

"All set, "Kaylee said.

"I was just getting a drink of water."

"Yeah, okay. Come on, Joanna."

Harry chugged his glass of water and followed the girls out the door, using his key to lock it.

Kaylee and Joanna climbed into the back seat.

Suddenly he felt like a chauffeur, but his job was to drive then to the gyno-whatchmacallit.

Kaylee and Joanna remained quiet during the ride.

He made a right at the doctor's office parking lot, and pulled into the last available space.

"Busy place," he said, breaking the silence.

Kaylee and Joanna climbed out of the back seat and proceeded to the office.

They turned around when they noticed he was following them.

"We can take it from here, Harry," Kaylee announced.

"I need to go inside and fill out some insurance forms."

"Whatever," Kaylee responded.

Kaylee opened the office door and she and Joanna and then Harry entered.

Women of all ages and shapes, including some very pregnant ones, looked straight at him, dressing him down as to why he dared enter their domain, and even accompanying two young girls.

He nodded a polite hello to them and they scrunched their faces before returning to their office magazines, while still obviously periodically staring at him.

Kaylee and Joanna sat while Harry approached the woman behind a glass partition. The glass boundary doors rattled open.

"May I help you, sir," the receptionist asked loudly.

Could she possibly have brought more attention to him?

"I believe Kaylee Jasinski and Joanna Stemple have appointments this afternoon."

"And you are?"

"Harry Boxer, a friend of Lou Ann Jasinski, their guardian. I think she called earlier. She's detained and couldn't be here…so…I'm here in her place."

The receptionist typed across her keyboard. "Yes, I see that."

Good, you miserable…

The stoic receptionist held out her hand. "Insurance card, please."

Harry pulled his wallet out of his back pocket, flipped out the insurance card, and surrendered it to the woman.

"One minute, please."

The woman scanned the card and handed it back to him. She then gave him a loaded clipboard and a pen. "Sign these payor forms and have the girls fill out the rest."

The receptionist yanked the glass partition shut.

Harry walked over to Kaylee and Joanna and sat next to Joanna.

He read over his part of the forms, signed them, and then handed the clipboard to Joanna.

"You're supposed to fill these out and then give the rest to Kaylee," he whispered.

Kaylee rolled her eyes.

"Okay, Uncle Harry," she said loud enough for the waiting women to narrow their eyes directly at him.

Harry sighed and forced a smile at the surly women.

They looked away and returned to flipping their magazine pages.

Joanna shook her head while checking a series of boxes and then quickly scribbled a response and shoved the clipboard to Kaylee as if the questionnaire had sapped her strength.

Kaylee penned her response, barely batting an eye.

She leaned over Joanna and passed the clipboard to Harry.

"Done," she said.

Harry stood and just as he expected, the magazine pages went silent.

He walked over to the receptionist and gently tapped on the glass.

The partition slid open and Harry handed over the clipboard.

"Have a seat, Mr. Boxer. The nurse will call the girls."

"Okay. Thank you."

The receptionist nodded and then resumed her hiding spot beyond the glass.

By the look of the packed waiting room, no wonder the receptionist needed a shield to hide behind. Hmmm. He would too.

Harry returned to his seat next to Joanna.

The room emptied of most of the pregnant women and an older woman was called back before the nurse returned to call for Kaylee, who stood and walked with the nurse until both disappeared behind a door.

Joanna's knees were bouncing at a mad rate.

Harry reached over and rested his hand on one of her knees to steady her.

The remaining women speared him with disapproving looks.

He tossed back a protective look, and that's what it took for them to sigh in retreat.

One down and one to go.

Kaylee dressed in the patient gown and sat on the edge of the exam table.

A woman and a nurse entered the room.

"Hi, Kaylee. I'm Dr. Turner How are you?"

"Okay," Kaylee answered.

The doctor sat and reviewed Kaylee's responses.

"I understand you've been through a lot."

"Okay," Kaylee repeated. "I'm not here to make you uncomfortable, so let's get on with it."

Dr. Turner smiled. "Ditto for me. I don't want to make you uncomfortable either."

"I see that your period was months ago."

"I'm not pregnant," Kaylee said. "That would be an impossibility. The only man I've been with is dead. You see my history. They never touched me…physically. Except for the woman who shaved me."

The nurse's eyes widened.

"It's all right if you can't take it," Kaylee said to the nurse.

Dr. Turner didn't flinch.

The doctor got her while the nurse was clearly uncomfortable.

"I've issues I'm dealing with so could we move on?"

Kaylee shifted.

"I've never been to a gynecologist before so you'll have to tell me what to do."

"I absolutely will. Today I'm going to remove an IUD that was placed inside you without your consent."

"They knocked me out and lied to me. I just found out about it. Just yank it out."

"I will. I'll have to put an instrument called a speculum inside you in order to remove the IUD, and I'll test for any sexually transmitted infections."

"Fine, but Demetrios didn't give me anything."

"Testing is standard," Dr. Turner reassured Kaylee.

"Lie back and put your heels in these things called stirrups. I'll keep you covered up, and I'll let you know everything I'm doing. No surprises."

Kaylee did as she was instructed.

She pushed her heels hard in the stirrups to keep her legs from shaking, recalling how Margo humiliated her while shaving her, and how she lay naked and splayed out shivering while Newell meted out her punishment. How he'd used that instrument to rip out the twig stump embedded in her heel. It still ached, but she forced herself to walk normally. She would not allow Newell to win, even from his grave.

Dr. Turner paused.

"Go on. Please take that thing out of my body."

"You may feel pressure."

Kaylee took a deep breath.

It felt nothing like Newell, or like Demetrios.

"The IUD is out. And I'm finished with the swabs."

Thank God.

Dr. Turner gently removed the foreign instrument.

"You can sit up now," she said.

Kaylee removed her heels from the stirrups and sat up.

"Is there anything you want to talk about today?"

"No."

"Do you need any birth control? I have to ask."

"No."

"All right. You can dress now and come out whenever you're ready."

"Okay."

"Is there anything I can do for you today?" Dr. Turner asked.

"No. I mean no thank you."

"You're welcome. The nurse will let you know how you can access a computer portal for your records and results. If anything comes back positive, I'll let you know. Everything between us is confidential."

"I appreciate that."

"You can call and ask for me anytime, and I'll answer as quickly as I can."

"Okay."

"Okay," Dr. Turner responded with a smile.

She'd have to thank Lou Ann for choosing Dr. Turner.

Kaylee returned to the waiting room just in time for Joanna to be called back.

"It's not so bad," Kaylee told her.

Joanna hesitated, glued to her seat.

She couldn't go through with this.

"Harry, I want to go home."

"It's going to be all right. No one's going to hurt you. I promise. I'm here. I can't force you, but I think you should stay."

A woman looked on sympathetically.

"He's right. It's not so bad."

As well-intended as the woman was, she had no idea what "bad" even meant. No one knew, not even Kaylee, about the horrors she had to endure. Pure evil. She had no Demetrios in her life. Only sweaty, foul men, including Newell, who left her for dead.

"Do you want me to go with you?" Kaylee asked.

Joanna shook her head and eyed the exit door.

She could still make a run for it.

The nurse waited for her patiently.

"Go on," the woman said.

Joanna stood, and her knees buckled so she fell back into the chair.

"We'll go," Harry said.

"Just a minute," Kaylee said.

She knelt in front of Joanna.

"I'm not going to lie to you. It felt strange at first. I even considered making a run for it. But I didn't, and I know you won't either. You survived. The scars will be there forever, but you have to trust that no one is going to hurt you here. Dr. Turner is all right. She won't do anything you don't want."

Harry waited a moment, then said, "It's your choice. You're in control."

Joanna stood.

She took the nurse's hand and went behind the mysterious door.

"You can come in here," the nurse said.

Joanna entered the exam room and stood there.

A woman that thank God didn't resemble Margo entered the room.

"Hi, Joanna. I'm Dr. Turner."

"Hi," Joanna said in barely above a whisper.

Dr. Turner patted the exam table. "Sit. It's okay. We'll talk."

Joanna slowly slid up on the table. The exam paper crinkled beneath her. Her palms were slick with sweat, and her heart pounded in her ears.

"It's okay. We don't have to do anything but get acquainted."

Dr. Turner reminded her of the kindness of Dr. Stephanie Zimmer and Nurse Lynn Davis at the Naples hospital where she'd been taken to after Newell and Otto dumped her at that crash site taking her for dead. She eventually trusted the doctor and nurse who saved her and took care of her.

"Mmm. It's okay. I'll do whatever you tell me to do. The people who took care of me at Good Samaritan in Naples would want me to take care of myself. I promised Dr. Zimmer that I would follow up with a gynecologist, so here I am."

"All I need to do is to test to see if the antibiotics took care of your infection."

"The gynecologist at the hospital took out the IUD that my captor put in, and I swear that I finished all the antibiotics."

"That's wonderful, and responsible of you. I reviewed the referral records that Dr. Zimmer sent. I just need to do an internal test, if that's okay with you?"

Joanna nodded.

"I'll need youth remove everything from the waist down, and you can put this sheet across your lap. The nurse and I will be back in a bit."

"All right."

Joanna eased off her clothes while eyeing the door. She covered herself with the sheet and waited.

A soft knock came at the door.

"It's Dr. Turner and the nurse."

"You can come in."

She just needed to get this over with.

"I know what a speculum is. Can you be quick about it? Ooh. That came out wrong. I didn't mean to be rude."

"It's okay. I didn't take it that way."

Kaylee was right. The doctor was gentle, and quick, as she had requested.

"All done," Dr. Turner said. "You can get dressed now."

After Dr. Turner and the nurse left, Joanna dressed lightning fast and exited the exam room just as fast.

Joanna bounded into the waiting room.

"We can go now, Harry."

Harry approached the receptionist.

"The insurance will cover the visit. Joanna?" she called.

Joanna's heartbeat leapt.

"What?"

"It's all right, sweetheart. These are the instructions for how to access the computer portal for your records and results."

Joanna grabbed the paper.

"Thank you," Joanna said.

"Okay, let's go, guys. I could go for a burger," Harry said.

"Me too," Joanna said.

"Yeah, that would be good," Kaylee agreed.

Joanna and Kaylee left the gynecologist's office, but it was Harry who ran out.

Joanna and Kaylee laughed.

Joanna pointed at Harry. "And I thought I would beat him to the car!"

14

Lou Ann sat next to Glenda and across from Dan at one of the officers' dining tables. Dan continued to glare at her.

Glenda loaded her fork and took a bite of the meat loaf. Lou Ann chose the same menu item, while Dan chose a loaded cheeseburger and fries.

He lifted the thick cheeseburger and manhandled it to his mouth, taking a hunk into his wide open mouth as an overt display of his manhood and superiority in rank over her. Yes, he ranked over her, but the manhood? Not so much.

Lou Ann scooped her fork into her mashed potatoes, brought it to her mouth, closed her mouth around it, and removed the fork completely clean and shiny, all while not taking her eyes off his stabbing glare.

It was a food war between them.

Glenda was too busy with her own meal and probably more important chief matters while Lou Ann and Dan engaged in petty ones.

Lou Ann decided to not play his game and chose to enjoy her lunch no matter what he decided to do. And she would enjoy her promotion too, despite Dan's intent to throw every obstacle he could at her.

It was clearly not about the bank incident. The guy genuinely disliked her, or was threatened by Glenda's and Sheriff Carson's support of her, or both. She bet on both because one day she'd become his boss.

Lou Ann took a big bite of her meat loaf and happily chewed it while staring back at Dan.

Then her cell pinged an incoming message.

Dan grinned.

"Excuse me. I have to answer this."

Lou Ann removed the napkin from her lap, set it down next to her plate to indicate she wasn't done with her meal, and stood.

"Go right ahead," Glenda said.

"I'll be right back."

Lou Ann entered the women's bathroom and read Harry's text.

Just letting you know everything turned out fine.

Thank you so much.

Not a problem. See you later.

Later, followed by a smiley face emoji.

Lou Ann washed her hands in case anyone walked in and thought she truly used the facilities, and then returned to the table.

"Crisis averted," she joked with Glenda.

"Crisis? Your day hasn't even started," Dan retorted.

"And I can't wait to get going."

Harry returned home with Kaylee and Joanna after a hectic afternoon of gynecology and a late lunch. Kaylee and Joanna hustled toward the front door while Harry sagged out of the car. They were the ones who underwent what he imagined were uncomfortable exams, but he was the only one who was apparently spent. He didn't even like going to his own mandatory doctor exams.

Kaylee and Joanna giggled at him.

"Ooh, does someone need a nap?" Kaylee teased.

He arched his brows. "I'll need several."

He unlocked the door and Isabelle jumped on Joanna and then Kaylee.

"We said we'd be right back," Johanna crooned to Isabelle.

Kaylee shook a bag attracting Isabelle's immediate attention.

"Doggy bag," Kaylee called.

Isabelle rushed behind Kaylee and to the kitchen.

That's a real doggy bag.

"Don't mind me because I'm home. And I paid for that doggy bag," Harry called.

But neither Kaylee, Joanna, or Isabelle responded.

Even his fish ignored him after he sprinkled fish food in the tank.

Lou Ann would be thrilled to find everyone's day had ended satisfactorily, dog and fishes included.

After Isabelle gobbled the leftovers, Kaylee and Joanna led her to the backyard.

Harry got the beer he'd been craving out of the fridge, shuffled to the den, and collapsed on the couch, glad the day was almost over. He'd just leaned back when the doorbell rang.

Harry set the beer on the coffee table.

"Hey, don't worry. I'll get it," he reassured whoever was in the silent kitchen.

He wondered who it could be. Maybe a neighbor complaining about the barking and the squeals. He'd promise he'd have it toned down even though it was only late afternoon. But an annoyance was an annoyance. He'd handle it diplomatically, so Lou Ann wouldn't get in trouble in the neighborhood, even though she was not the most sociable kind of neighbor.

Harry opened the door to find the mailman holding two letters with a green card attached to each.

Aw, shit! Certified letters. Lou Ann was about to be served.

"Do Kaylee Jasinski and Joanna Stemple reside here?"

Double shit! What could this be?

"Yes, but their aunt who's their guardian is at work. I'm here with them."

"Can you please sign for these two letters?"

"Sure."

Harry signed for the letters.

"Here's the other mail. Have a good day."

He read the letterheads which revealed these documents had come from the United States District Court, Southern District of Florida, Miami, Florida.

He opened the letters.

Just as he'd expected and dreaded.

Kaylee and Joanna were just subpoenaed to testify in three weeks as witnesses in Margo's trial.

Harry stashed the letters in the top drawer of the living room credenza.

Kaylee and Joanna opened the kitchen glass sliding doors and dodged inside, red-faced from romping in the backyard with Isabelle, who waddled inside with her pink tongue hanging out sideways.

Isabelle went straight for her water bowl and nearly emptied it.

"I sure could go for a cold one," Kaylee said.

"No beer," Harry responded.

"God, Harry. Who said anything about beer?"

Kaylee reached into the fridge and took out a pitcher of lemonade while Joanna got two glasses. Kaylee filled the glasses and then put the pitcher back in the fridge.

She shook her head. "When are you going to totally know me?"

"When you let me."

"Okay, that's fair."

She and Joanna grabbed their glasses.

Harry had left his beer on the table when the mailman delivered more than junk mail.

"Come on, Harry. Let's cool off and watch a movie on Netflix," Kaylee said

Kaylee sure knew how to push his buttons.

He knew about buttons. He was an expert in poking them. Lou Ann could testify to that.

May Kaylee know the right buttons to push to send Margo away for a long time.

More sheriff's staff left the dining room, leaving Glenda, Dan, and Lou Ann as sole occupants.

"Perfect. Privacy finally," Glenda said.

Dan fingered the straw in his emptied drink. "I've provided a list of meetings you are required to attend with the dates, times, and conference room numbers."

"We're glad to have you aboard," Glenda said.

Dan grinned with teeth clenched. "Yes, we are."

Lou Ann waited for the assignment Dan had prepared especially for her.

"Your first duty, besides attending every meeting, is to train a new graduate from the academy."

She'd expected to have to maneuver through a maze of paperwork. Busy work. But this was way better. She'd train whoever was assigned to her the right way.

Dan slid over a file to Lou Ann.

"Review this file tonight and meet me in my office—that's suite 303 on the third floor,"—as if she didn't know where his "cave" was—"where you'll meet your trainee. Also, I've compiled the forms you'll need to fully complete every shift with the trainee, and then you'll report to me by the day's end, where I'll review your reports and sign them off. Clear?"

"Clear, Lieutenant Mathews."

"You're excused for the remainder of the day. See you at 0800 sharp tomorrow morning."

"See you tomorrow too. And I'm confident that you'll equip your charge with the appropriate skills." Glenda said.

Lou Ann nodded to Glenda. "You can count on me."

"We intend to," Dan added.

Lou Ann walked to her parked cruiser, carrying the file of her future trainee. She unlocked the cruiser, and leaned over and set the file on her passenger seat before getting behind the wheel. She pulled out into the late afternoon.

Her day had prematurely ended after only two hours, but she could use the extra hours at home before tackling the file.

Lou Ann pulled into the driveway next to Harry's car, while her personal car was parked on the other side.

Her driveway was beginning to look like a parking lot, which was just fine with her.

She grabbed the file and got out of the cruiser.

The living room curtains parted, and Harry waved at her with a confused expression.

Lou Ann opened the door. "Surprise!"

"Is everything okay? Did I text at the wrong time?"

"No. After a day of paperwork, new ID, and new uniforms, my prick of a superior cut me loose early."

"Let me thank that prick."

Lou Ann chuckled. "Don't thank him too soon."

Lou Ann dropped the file on the credenza.

"How was the gynecology visit?"

"At the end I was the one running out."

Lou Ann kissed Harry.

"You deserve more."

"So do you."

Kaylee, Joanna, and Isabelle bounded into the room.

Isabelle jumped onto Lou Ann's legs.

Lou Ann hugged her. "I missed you too."

"I thought I heard your vehicle pull up," Joanna said cheerfully.

"Are you in trouble?" Kaylee asked.

"Nope. I just have work to do tonight."

"It's nice to have you home," Kaylee said.

Did I hear that right?

"Thanks."

"Harry actually did okay today. And so did Joanna, after we talked her down."

Joanna blushed and frowned. "Thanks a lot, Kaylee."

"I'm sorry I couldn't be there," Lou Ann said.

"That's okay," Joanna said. "At least it's over with."

Lou Ann decided to talk with Joanna and Kaylee in private later.

"Hey, we're watching a Netflix movie in the den. Come on, we can start at the beginning for you."

"Okay."

"Get comfortable and take a break. Pizza or Chinese for dinner?" Harry asked.

"Chinese," Kaylee and Joanna chorused.

"Fine with me," Lou Ann said.

At least she could enjoy her dinner companions, although she wouldn't mind if Glenda was included.

"Pause the movie for me while I get out of this uniform."

"We'll wait for you," Joanna said.

Lou Ann went into the bedroom and peeled off her old uniform for the last time. Tomorrow she'd put on her sergeant's regalia. She put on her shorts and a tee, ready to spend time with her family.

She practically skipped into the den and plopped on the couch next to Harry.

Kaylee rewound the movie. "I like this one so I don't mind watching it again from the beginning."

Harry got up. "I've seen this part. Beer?" he asked Lou Ann.

"Yeah. I really could use one."

"Done. I'll be right back."

Harry returned with a cold beer and handed it to Lou Ann.

"Thanks."

Harry grabbed his cell.

"Four happy family dinners," he ordered. "Is that okay with everyone?"

"Sounds great," Kaylee said.

"Yeah," Joanna agreed.

"That'd be my vote, too," Lou Ann added.

Happy family. She should actually thank Dan, but only tonight.

The door bell rang. This time it wasn't the mailman.

Harry paid and tipped the delivery guy, brought the big bag of food into the den, and set it on the coffee table.

"Dinner and a movie."

Kaylee and Joanna dug into the bag and pulled out the red and white cartons.

"I'll get the plates." Harry said. "Forks or chopsticks?"

"Chopsticks," Kaylee said.

"Joanna?"

"I'll try chopsticks. But I'll need tons of napkins."

Lou Ann smiled. "Me too."

She winked at Harry.

Harry knew she was proficient with chopsticks, and only said that to make Joanna feel better.

Harry returned with the plates, and they all sat on the floor around the coffee table.

And they sat as a happy family while eating and watching a movie together, including Isabelle, who didn't require chopsticks.

They'd cleaned their plates.

"Thanks, Harry," Kaylee said. And then looked at Lou Ann. "And you too, Aunt Lou Ann."

"You're welcome, Kaylee."

"I did pretty good with the chopsticks, didn't I?" Joanna asked.

"You're a fast learner," Lou Ann said.

"Can we have Chinese again?" Joanna pleaded.

"Absolutely."

Harry collected the plates and the emptied Chinese cartons.

"Looks like we were all hungry," Harry said.

"I'm stuffed," Joanna groaned.

"That's amazing because you dropped most of your food," Kaylee said, elbowing Joanna's ribs.

"Did not."

"I'm just joking."

The movie ended.

"That's enough for me. I'm going to flop on the bed and digest," Kaylee said.

"I'll join you," Joanna said.

Harry waited for Kaylee and Joanna to head into their bedroom.

"I'll talk with them tonight about their gynecology appointments, woman-to-woman. Nothing personal," Lou Ann said to Harry.

"Umm. Before you do that, and now that they're in their room, I need to show you something."

Harry went to the living room credenza, opened the top drawer, and took out the letters.

"These arrived certified earlier today."

"Subpoenas?" Lou Ann asked. "Margo?"

"Yeah. They don't know about it yet. I wanted to discuss it with you first. The trial starts August 31st."

He watched Lou Ann's cheerful expression fade and waited for her response.

Lou Ann rested her forehead in her palm and exhaled.

Harry reached for her other hand.

"The last thing I wanted to do was to give you these tonight, but it's too important to delay."

"It's not going to go away. I'd be upset if you hid this from me, even temporarily."

"I know. And Kaylee and Joanna need to know, even though technically because of the severe abuse, they won't be compelled to testify…."

"But I agree they should be offered the chance to do it," Lou Ann said, not only completing his sentence, but also his thoughts.

"There's a lot that happened today, to everyone, especially to Kaylee and Joanna. I think it would be best to tackle those letters tomorrow. And that will give us and them plenty of time to respond to the subpoena."

Harry nodded,"You're right. I'm sorry this is happening, again—that they'll have to relive this nightmare all over again, and in a courtroom full of people."

Harry kissed Lou Ann.

"I'm going to go now. You'll need to prepare for your new role tomorrow, and I have a Zoom meeting tonight."

"Harry…"

"You don't have to ask. Barring events out of my control. I'll be with you tomorrow night. And if I can't be, then I'll arrange to there via Zoom or FaceTime. Or whatever it takes."

Lou Ann walked Harry to the front door where they paused.

"Good night, Harry."

"Good night, Lou Ann."

Harry walked to his car, knowing Lou Ann was still standing there watching him because she didn't close the front door, but more important, he finally had her heart.

15

Lou Ann watched Harry drive away. It wasn't that long ago that she couldn't wait for him to leave in her in peace—to find pleasure in closing the door in his face and shutting him out of her life. Now the aloneness she once craved had become the loneliness she battled.

Were they ready to risk permanence and to allow the old wounds to resurface or maybe new ones to creep in?

No relationship was perfect, and their history more than proved that. But nothing worth having came without some risk.

And that also applied to caring for Kaylee and Joanna.

Lou Ann approached their bedroom door and gave it a gentle knock.

Kaylee opened it.

"Can I come in?" Lou Ann asked.

"Sure."

Kaylee opened the door wider.

Joanna was sitting on the edge of her queen-sized bed next to Kaylee's equally, large bed.

Even though the bedroom was more than cramped now, at least Joanna and Kaylee each had their own bed—their own mini-space.

Kaylee bounced to a sitting position on her bed.

Lou Ann maneuvered between the narrowly-spaced beds.

Joanna inched over and patted her mattress, gesturing for Lou Ann to sit, while Kaylee stretched across her bed.

"What's up?" Kaylee asked.

"I want to hear about how your visits with Dr. Turner went."

"It was okay," Kaylee said, not offering any more details.

"I was freaked out, at first, and almost ran right outside the door and back to the car," Joanna said.

Kaylee interrupted, "But I convinced her to stay."

"You, and Harry," Joanna countered.

"Yeah, that's what happened." Kaylee giggled. "You should have seen Harry. He was mortified!"

"He was uncomfortable, but I'm glad he was there," Joanna said.

"Yeah. He survived and so did we," Kaylee added.

"I'm glad, and relieved. I'm so sorry I couldn't be there with you too."

"I know you couldn't, given your new position, but you did okay picking out a good doctor," Kaylee said.

"She was really nice and gentle," Joanna added.

"Dr. Turner is the best," Lou Ann said.

"Yes, especially for first-timers."

Lou Ann's stomach clenched. She'd missed an important milestone in every young woman's life. Instead, she'd spent her day with Dan.

Lou Ann patted the bed.

"I'll leave you guys to do whatever you want. I'll be in my room doing my homework for tomorrow. But if you need anything, just knock."

"I don't miss homework," Kaylee said.

"I don't remember, because I never got past middle school. That is when I went," Joanna admitted.

"Kaylee?" Lou Ann probed.

"College isn't for me anymore."

Lou Ann was sure Kaylee had acceptance letters waiting for her. She had been so preoccupied with getting Kaylee and Joanna settled, and then settled in her own career, that she hadn't even thought about those college letters. How shitty.

Then Lou Ann reassured herself, because she had the mail from Miami forwarded to Clearwater. Those letters should be arriving any day now. The subpoena ones had no delay being delivered.

Lou Ann got up and placed her hand on Kaylee's shoulder.

"Don't count anything out," she said.

And that included more than college acceptances letters. Two particular letters waited for both Kaylee and Joanna.

But that discussion could wait till tomorrow.

Lou Ann sat cross-legged on her bed and shook the papers out of the thick envelope Dan gave her without revealing the candidate. But that kind of idiotic secrecy was just like Dan.

A photo of the candidate first caught her attention.

Her trainee was a male named Tim Farmer.

Gender wasn't important. His hard-working and attentive attitude was.

Lou Ann put the photo together with his file and began to read Tim Farmer's file.

Tim was 24 years old and had graduated in the bottom quarter of the Sheriff's Academy.

That was either a pro or a con.

She chose to look at it as a pro.

Either way, Tim was a wet-behind-the-ears recent graduate.

Lou Ann laughed. Dan assigned her a guy who might've struggled through the academy.

She'd train the guy without so much as a frown or a complaint, if only to stick it to Dan.

But that wasn't fair to Tim.

Lou Ann continued to review his file.

Tim graduated with honors from Clearwater High School, where he not only played football, but also was involved in ROTC—an unusual combination. He then obtained a degree in criminology, graduating in the top ten of his class.

Then why didn't he do well in the academy?

She graduated at the top of her academy class, but politics played into Dan's rise over hers. Now the playing field for her was rapidly leveling, and she'd make sure Tim was treated the same way.

Although he didn't need to include the personal details of his life, he apparently had no qualms doing it.

Tim was married and was a dog enthusiastic.

Bonus points.

Dan, on the other hand, had only a ferret to keep him company at home.

Poor little ferret!

Lou Ann tucked Tim's file back in the envelope.

She knew enough about him to get them started tomorrow.

Kaylee rolled to her belly and faced Joanna.

"Are you all right?" she asked.

"I'm okay. Why?"

"You were more freaked out than you admitted to Lou Ann."

"I think I was honest with her. But I think you underplayed it."

"Whatever. I just don't want to get into it because it's over."

"Dr. Zimmer had a gynecologist at the hospital remove the IUD Newell shoved inside me. Because of all the scum Otto led into my locked room, including him, I got badly infected. I had to be on antibiotics."

"I had no idea he put one in me. But he then he lied that he put me under to fix my ankle. Except he didn't do anything to my ankle, because when I unwrapped the half-assed bandage, I discovered no stitches. Margo lied and told me because Newell was such a fantastic surgeon, I couldn't see his "internal" stitches. I bled afterwards and thought I had my period." Kaylee pounded her fist into the mattress. "I was so stupid. I was lucky, though, that neither Newell or Otto raped me. I know you *were* raped. I'm sorry."

Joanna scooted off her bed and climbed into Kaylee's bed.

"Yes, that happened to me.And I'll never be same. I wanted to bolt out of the GYN office, because I was so ashamed of having an exam reveal the horror of what I endured was on display. Turns out it wasn't what Dr. Turner, her nurse, or the whole office thought—it was what I thought of myself. That I was dirty and diseased forever."

Tears spilled down Joanna's cheeks.

Kaylee hugged her. "I'm sorry what I saw. I can't help being so mean sometimes…well, actually a lot of the time."

"That's because you're a fighter, and I gave up. I wanted to die. You didn't."

"You and I became captive victims in different ways, but victims of the same demons. After I stabbed Otto and whacked Margo on the head, I thought I was going to make it. But I didn't, and I was humiliated and punished while tied to that damn bed. But Demetrios turned out to be my salvation. Sure, he paid for my company, but once he saw who I am, which he thought was you, he couldn't do it and called the deal off, returning the money to Newell. And for that Newell shot him—murdered him. Demetrios would be alive if it wasn't for me."

Kaylee's tears mixed with Joanna's.

"That's not true. He fell in love with you. I'm so sorry about all the terrible things that happened that day."

Kaylee twisted her ruby ring. She hadn't taken it off since he bought that it and put it on her hand during their outing to Athens, when she revealed who she really was. He was surprised, but it didn't matter to him. Her one true love was gone. At least she had the ring to remember him by. And soon she'd live where he had lived, and where he had intended for her to live forever. Lou Ann wouldn't understand. That was why she wasn't even going to hint of her departure. She needed to wait for the right time, and somehow acquire the funds to escape back to Greece and then to became a bona fide citizen of Greece.

Kaylee extended her hand to Joanna who took it.

They lay in Kaylee's bed together, no further words necessary between them.

16

Lou Ann grabbed her cell off the nightstand. Her alarm wasn't set to ring for another thirty minutes. She shut it off. Thirty minutes wasn't going to make a big difference and she was already awake.

She stretched and smacked her dry lips. Now she could take a leisurely shower with plenty of time to spare. She could actually eat a decent breakfast. Maybe her morning was too good to be true. She'd soon find out.

Lou Ann enjoyed a long shower compared to her quick in-and-out so she could squeak out the door just in time.

She sighed while letting the water massage her neck and back, two major stress points while maneuvering in her cruiser, especially when urgently called to respond to a 911.

But hopefully today would be a relatively moderate day so that she could get give Tim enough first-time experience without overwhelming him. But soon all-out craziness would hit, pushing him to be extra-ready to respond.

Although she couldn't guarantee a zero to sixty shift, she hoped Tim would have the right amount of first-time experience to build on, like it had been for her. She'll never forget or be grateful for Sergeant Alanna Morris's patience and excellent training. Alanna moved away due to her husband's job relocation, but the Pinellas County's Sheriff's Department's loss was Duvall County's gain.

Lou Ann would make sure to text Alanna later to let her know how being a training officer herself was going.

Lou Ann toweled off, dried her hair, and pulled it back into her standard ponytail. But instead of her longstanding beige deputy's uniform, she dressed in her starched white shirt with the Kevlar beneath it, and with her sergeant bars affixed to the sleeve. Then she donned creased beige pants to complete her new role.

She took a deep breath while checking her final uniformed look in the mirror, and she liked it.

Lou Ann walked out of her bedroom and stopped in front of Kaylee and Joanna's room.

She listened at the door. All was quiet.

She winced while cracking open the door, only to find Kaylee and Joanna sleeping peacefully together in Kaylee's bed.

Wow.

She slowly closed the door.

Something did happen after Harry left, and while she was ensconced in her room, raking through Tim's file.

Apparently all Kaylee and Joanna needed was to be left alone to find for themselves.

They would definitely need to lean on each other during their testimony in Margo's upcoming trial.

Lou Ann pressed the third floor button at headquarters on her way to where Dan "lived."

After exiting the elevator, she headed with a crisp stride toward Dan's office and knocked on his door with three rapid hits.

Hard footsteps grew closer and then Dan opened his door because he didn't have a receptionist. Every receptionist could breathe a sigh of relief.

"Good morning, Sergeant Jasinski."

Lou Ann did a quick nod. "Good morning, Lieutenant Mathews."

"Come in and meet your trainee."

Tim Farmer had a fresh young face, younger-looking than his photo. His red haircut was cut military style, but it was his freckles that made him look like a farmer.

Tim stood up straight, extended his hand, and firmly shook Lou Ann's hand. She didn't expect anything different.

He had a genuine smile and Lou Ann liked him immediately. But she wasn't going to show that to Dan, so she kept a straight face and returned Tim's handshake with extra firmness.

Tim Farmer's quizzical look was followed by a changed, stoic expression, and Dan's smug grin showed that her attitude worked. She'd explain everything to Tim once he and she were in the privacy of her cruiser.

"Before you head out, Sergeant Jasinski, I need you to fill out these forms and return them to me by 4:30 pm every day this week and possibly longer."

Lou Ann accepted yet another thick envelope from Dan.

"Yes, sir."

Dan waved to Lou Ann and Tim with the flip of his hand.

"Go."

Lou Ann and Tim went to the elevator bank and Lou Ann pressed the lobby level.

Tim remained silent during the elevator ride.

Lou Ann broke the awkward silence.

"My cruiser is parked in the department garage."

Tim simply nodded.

Perhaps she'd overdone it.

Tim followed Lou Ann to her cruiser.

She unlocked the driver and passenger doors, and Tim waited for Lou Ann to climb in first, then took his position, a mounted laptop and an AR-15 in between them.

This was going to be a long shift.

Once Tim was inside and buckled in, Lou Ann pulled out of the dim garage and to the sunny morning.

Both Lou Ann and Tim put on their shades, for not only sun protection, but also to keep their eyes camouflaged.

"I know it's tight in here with all the equipment, but we'll make it work. Eventually, once you're checked off, you'll get your own cruiser assigned to you and you'll ride solo. My objective is to make sure you are as attentive and safe, as any of us can be. This, as you know, is a risky and unpredictable job. A call can go sideways rapidly. That being said, you have to love what you do. There are rewards and you do make a difference."

"I agree."

Lou Ann decided that the best way to begin to bond with Tim was to first review the mechanics of the cruiser.

"You might be acquainted with departments vehicles from the academy, but nevertheless, let's review it." She pointed to the laptop. "You'll have a laptop at your fingertips, where you can run data on plates and access data bases for not only specific and important information, but also to protect you. Obviously you'll need to call for backup when encountering a dangerous individual or individuals. You never know who might pop out of a car or even a trunk to ambush you. Clear?"

"Clear."

Lou Ann wondered whether Tim had been made aware of her initial solo response to the bank crisis.

There may be times when you'll have to make a critical decision. I can't, and truthfully no one can, teach instinct. But when in doubt, it isn't a sign of weakness to call for assistance. You want to be able to go home at the end of the day."

That was meant as a segue to whom Tim Farmer was to return to home to at the end of his shift. But by his silence, he apparently wasn't ready to trust her with personal details.

Lou Ann continued with the workings of a department cruiser.

She pointed to the vertically-racked AR-15 between them.

"You'll continue to periodically attend and pass target tests. And although the rifle is secure, that doesn't mean that criminals can't get to it or strip you of it. Again, your absolute attention at all times on who or what are around you and your cruiser is paramount. There is, unfortunately, hate and violence just waiting for you."

"My wife's worst fear."

Ah, there it was.

"I'm responsible for two teenage girls, and in the back of my mind, I worry about what would happen to them if I'm not around," she shared.

"And your husband or significant other? How does he or she feel about your job?"

"Harry is my significant other, again. It's complicated. But he's an FBI special agent, so he's well acquainted with risk."

"Wow."

A chill snaked up her spine. What would happen to Kaylee and Joanna if both she and Harry never came home.

She threw the morbid thought out of sight and ino the back of her brain.

"My wife is a special needs teacher. But neither of us were ready for our baby girl, who decided to make a way-too-early debut."

"I'm sorry."

"It's over now. My wife, Ashley, developed severe pre-eclampsia—severe high blood pressure—at 28 weeks of pregnancy, forcing the early delivery of Susanna, our daughter. Both were in the hospital for a long time, Susanna longer. I almost lost them, all during my time at the academy."

That's why he graduated near the bottom. He risked his career for his family.

"Sorry for the litany."

"No, don't be."

Now was her chance to set their initial meeting straight.

"You might have decided I'm a ball buster. I had to act that way."

"You don't have to explain. I get it now. And I'm glad my balls are still intact."

Lou Ann and Tim broke out laughing.

"All right, let's get back to business," Lou Ann said.

"And we better have something to show for it."

Lou Ann winked. "I knew I liked you right from the start."

"Okay,"she continued. "There's a panel with a lot of buttons just to my right. You're right-handed, right?"

"Correct."

"Great. Once I rode with a predominantly lefty who luckily was ambidextrous."

Alanna was a lefty.

"This one engages the siren and lights, and this one engages the video screen and the video lens is mounted here on the windshield, and you need to turn on your body cam the second you step out of this vehicle, even though the video is on. The body cam is key."

"Got it."

"Here, in under the arm rest, is the thermal printer that you'll be well acquainted with. And your radar for clocking speedsters is here. You'll have to make a judgement call regarding the flow of traffic versus outright dangerous speeding, and then somewhere in between. Everyone responds differently to being stopped. You may be called names, or be greeted with lewd finger gestures. Keep calm and attempt to deescalate an angry or upset driver. Remember, you're not the bad guy."

Except for her ex, Jake, who gleefully sped past her and probably right now holding the printed ticket to his heart. She couldn't believe she dated that man.

"Let's ride around in my sector. You'll eventually be assigned your own patrol area."

Dispatch notified Lou Ann of a call about an intruder at 598 Hibiscus Avenue.

"Hit the lights and siren. We gotta go."

Lou Ann knew the upscale area well.

Lou Ann's adrenaline pumped, but she hid the response and asked Tim, "Remember everything I told you?"

"Attend to surroundings. Be prepared for anything to go sideways. Video on. Body cam to be engaged. Cruiser cam on. Taser left. Gun right."

"Correct."

The cruiser lights strobed red and blue, and the siren blared while Lou

Ann hurried through traffic to the scene.

Once they were in the suburb and on the correct avenue, Lou Ann cut the siren but not the strobes.

She pulled up to the house where the 911 originated.

"Ready?"

"Yes," Tim replied.

They exited the cruiser to find a woman running toward them waving her hands.

"Help!" she yelled.

"Is the person in the house?" Lou Ann asked.

"No, he's in the backyard."

"Is anyone in the house or the backyard?"

"Not in the house. The kids are at summer camp. But my God! Bailey is in the backyard with him."

"Bailey?"

"My dog. You have to save my dog from him."

"Him? Do you know him?"

"No, I don't and I don't want to."

"Can you go to your neighbor's house?"

"Not without my Bailey!"

"Okay, we're going to the back, but I need you to be safe. Go next door. We'll handle it."

The woman paced in the front yard and didn't heed Lou Ann's order.

"Ready?" Lou Ann asked Tim.

"Ready."

Lou Ann and Tim proceeded to the backyard.

But she didn't see "him", but that didn't mean he wouldn't pop up any minute.

And there was the perp—an alligator swimming in the pool, while Bailey, the white miniature poodle, barked and growled.

Lou Ann scooped up Bailey and walked out of the backyard with Tim at her side.

She approached the distraught woman and handed Bailey to her, who was still barking.

"Oh, thank you. Thank God Bailey is safe."

"Go back in the house with Bailey, and do not go in the backyard."

"We won't."

"Ma'am, we don't remove gators or any wildlife or animals. We're willing to stay here until Wildlife arrives," Tim said.

"I'm sorry. I panicked and called 911."

"It's okay. We're going to take care of the situation," he reassured the woman.

The woman and Bailey returned into the house.

"Should I cuff him and read him his rights?" Tim joked.

"Can you imagine the look on Lieutenant Dan's face when I report that we responded to a home invasion on your first shift?"

"Will I get credit for this?"

"Absolutely. You did everything by the book, because it might not have been a gator. Remember. Sideways!"

17

Joanna stretched and smacked Kaylee's back.

"Hey!" Kaylee protested.

"I'm sorry."

Kaylee rolled over. "It's okay," she sleepily muttered.

The two had a bonded moment last night, which thankfully extended into the morning.

Joanna glanced at the clock.

"It's ten o'clock!"

"Yeah, and we both needed the sleep."

"Thanks for letting me stay with you."

"No problem. My best friend, Shawna, and I always ended up in the same bed when I slept over, or if she did."

"I never had a best friend, so I didn't know any different. I just got a glimpse of those like you and Shawna. My mother and I moved a lot, or rather more like we were evicted a lot."

"Shawna and I are no more."

"Why?"

"You know why."

"We're untouchable."

"That's right. Nothing will be the same for neither of us."

"Well, at least we untouchables have each other."

Kaylee was not only Joanna's best fiend, but also like a sister. She'd always dreamed of having a sister. Someone she could confide in. Someone who would love her unconditionally. Who would champion her as Joanna would champion her. Did Kaylee see her in the same way? She prayed so. And after last night, maybe it could really be that way.

"Lou Ann's gone and Harry isn't here. We have the whole house to ourselves," Joanna said.

"I'm liking the way you think."

Happy warmth spread throughout Joanna's body.

Whoopee! Kayla finally accepted her!

She wasn't orbiting by herself anymore.

Joanna vaulted out of Kaylee's bed.

"Let's go make breakfast!"

"Okay. I'll be there in a minute."

"I'll meet you in the kitchen," Joanna caroled.

She skipped out of their shared bedroom.

They were two of a kind, and damn, it felt good!

Kaylee and Joanna needed each other last night. It was a midnight confession. But in the light of day it wasn't the same. Although the last thing she wanted to do was to hurt Joanna, or herself. Weirdly, she had become like Joanna, self-sufficient and untrusting.

Yeah, they were simpatico. But for someone who'd spent most of her time on the streets, Joanna seemed very childlike at times.

But Kaylee grew up with a mom and dad. Joanna had no experience with any kind of quality interpersonal relationships, and Kaylee wasn't convinced she was the one to teach Joanna about them.

However, Lou Ann and Harry were doing a good job so far.

But Kaylee's commitment to Joanna was a bit iffy. Besides, it might not be in Joanna's or her best interest to build on a commitment because soon she'd be off to live in Greece.

But that wasn't today.

Kaylee push out of bed, headed into the kitchen, and found Joanna frowning at an empty frying pan.

Joanna's frown turned into a pout.

"I don't have any idea how to make pancakes," she sniffled, blinking back tears.

"I'll show you how to do it."

She used to help her dad make pancakes, his specialty. But now she had to fly solo.

"You get a mixing bowl out of that cupboard, and I'll get the ingredients," Kaylee instructed.

They met at the kitchen counter to pursue a common goal, to make edible pancakes.

Kaylee dumped the ingredients into the bowl while Joanna whisked them together.

"That looks about right," Kaylee said. "I'll heat the pan, and then you'll take a ladleful and pour it in."

"Okay."

"Ready," Kaylee told Joanna.

Joanna poured the mix into the pan.

"Perfect," Kaylee encouraged her.

"Now what?"

"You wait until the top begins to bubble, and then you flip it over with this."

"Now," Kaylee said.

"Ummm."

Kaylee grabbed the spatula and flipped a pancake.

"See? Not so hard. You do the next one."

One by one Kaylee and Joanna created a short stack for each of them.

"Sorry a few of them are lopsided," Joanna apologized.

Kaylee nudged Joanna. "Lopsided pancakes are the best kind."

"They don't look like the ones Brad made."

"Brad?"

"Yeah, Brad Jarett, the sheriff who visited me in the hospital and then got in contact with Lou Ann because he recognized the last name, Jasinski, since he went to sheriff school with her."

"You mean academy."

"Yeah. Then I spent the night at his house with Lou Ann and Harry before we went to your house in Miami and then the funeral."

"Stop! Stop!"

Kaylee wanted to plug her ears about Miami and her parents' funeral, but it was too late because Joanna had already prattled on.

"What, again, does this have to do with pancakes?"

"At breakfast, Brad made these perfectly round pancakes and he decorated mine with a whipped cream smiley face. Brad's the best, next to Harry, of course. You remember? He was in Greece to help rescue you. He put a lot of bullets in Newell."

Kaylee jabbed her finger at Joanna. "I didn't need to be rescued, and it was my shot that killed Newell."

"I'm sorry. I didn't mean it that way. And don't ever say you shot and killed Newell because you can get into serious trouble. They all shot Newell not only to make sure he was dead, but also to cover for you."

"I'll take responsibility," Kaylee demanded

"No, please don't. Trust me. Let it go. I don't want anything bad to happen to you. I don't want you to go to jail."

Joanna hugged Kaylee.

"It's all right. I'll let it go," Kaylee said, only to reassure Joanna, because she knew she was the one who put Newell in his grave.

Kaylee changed the subject. "Let's sit and eat."

"Sounds good to me."

They sat at the kitchen table while still in their PJs and dug into the pancakes.

"Mmm. These are actually pretty good."

"They are. You did a good job."

Joanna smiled between bites.

"No, we did a good job!"

18

Lou Ann pulled the cruiser into the headquarters parking garage. She cut the engine and looked at Tim, her trainee until Dan Matthews told her he wasn't.

She took out the envelope that contained Tim's daily review.

"Don't look," she teased.

Tim looked away.

Lou Ann checked off all excellent check marks for the day—including their response to the 911 home invasion call—and in a small addendum at the bottom of the page, she noted that the home invader was a dangerous alligator and that Tim, was correct in his response to secure the safety of the woman and her pet while Wildlife was notified. She'd done that, but Tim, who was in agreement, and she'd see to it he got credit for everything in relating to his trainee experience.

"All done. Let's go meet with Lieutenant Mathews."

Lou Ann and Tim exited the vehicle and walked to headquarters.

Once inside, they passed through security and took the elevator to Dan's third floor office, just in time for Dan's 4:30 pm deadline.

"Wait out here while I hand over your review for the day."

"Got it."

Lou Ann knocked on Dan's door, and he answered right on time.

"Come in, Sergeant Jasinski."

Lou Ann stepped into *his den* and gave him the envelope containing Tim's review.

"So how did he perform?"

"Excellent, sir. He is well versed in the vehicle's controls, and he was nothing but professional."

Dan opened the envelope and browsed through Lou Ann's review of Tim's first day.

"Mmm. 911 call about a home invasion. Back up called?" he prompted her.

"As noted in my addendum, it wasn't necessary as the invader was an alligator, which we both evaluated and confirmed after ascertaining the home owner's and her pet's safety. Wildlife was called and responded to the incident. Everything was done according to procedure, and Tim responded with caution but not alarm."

"Hmmm. All right. You're dismissed. Oh, wait. Now that you're a sergeant, your office will be next to mine."

"Office?"

"Yes. What did you think was going to happen?"

Lou Ann stood silent.

Ass.

"What about my cruiser and my sector? And the rest of my shift?"

"My, you're so full of questions."

She refused to take his bait.

"I told you, you'll retain your cruiser in the event that you have to go out in the field. Tim will assume your sector, and cover the remaining part of your shift. So, if you don't have any further questions, go home. Be here at 0800 again. And send in Deputy Farmer."

"Yes, sir."

Lou Ann turned away and winced. An office next to Dan's would be like falling into hell. She liked being out and independent. Now she'd be trapped under Dan's hawkish eyes. She was thrilled to be promoted to sergeant—the prestige and the pay—but she hadn't counted on landing right in front of Dan's shitty radar. But she'd have to get used to it. Avoiding him wasn't going to be possible.

She stepped out of Dan's office and shut the door.

Tim was waiting down the hall.

Lou Ann approached him and said, "I softened him up as much as possible. He read my review. You're good to go in there. Just…"

"Yep, I know."

"See you tomorrow. Same place. Same time."

"Looking forward to it. Thanks for everything today, Lou Ann…I mean Sergeant Jasinski."

Lou Ann chuckled. "You're welcome, *Deputy Sheriff Farmer.*"

She laughed to herself all the way to her cruiser.

Tim was going to be just fine.

But she suspected she wasn't going to be.

Kaylee looked into the sink full of dirty dishes, bowls, and forks left over from this morning's pancake breakfast.

"We'd better clean this up before Lou Ann gets home."

The last thing Kaylee wanted was to be blamed again for anything she did or didn't do. She didn't have the energy to defend herself. But soon she wouldn't be around to hear it ever again.

Joanna leaned over the sink.

"Ooh, I didn't realize we made such a mess. I guess we forgot all about it," Joanna said. "This stuff really got plastered on. I don't think the dishwasher will take care of it."

"Yeah it will. We just need to hot rinse these off before loading them in the dishwasher."

Kaylee rinsed while Joanna loaded the dishwasher.

"Done!" they high-fived when they finished.

"What do you think we should have for breakfast tomorrow?" Joanna teased.

"Cereal," Kaylee answered.

They bumped fists.

Joanna was really okay. Kaylee regretted giving her a hard time.

"This is really sad. We've been in these pajamas all day. Let's get changed into real clothes and take Isabelle for a long walk," Kaylee said.

"Yeah, we are pretty pitiful."

"The pajamas, yes. Us, no."

It was the first time since she escaped from her cell, and from Newell, that she hadn't thought of herself as pitiful. Demetrios began to change that, but the hope she had for a sliver of time had once again vanished.

"Hey, are you okay?" Joanna called. "You were staring off into space."

"I'm all right. Let's get changed."

Greece began to slip further and further away. But she owed it to Demetrios to manage the mansion. That was his dying promise and request.

All that I have is yours.

Joanna slipped the harness over Isabelle's head, secured it around her belly, attached the leash, and then gave her a pat. "Are you ready to go, girl?"

Isabelle wagged her tail.

"And are you ready to go?" she called to Kaylee.

Kaylee trotted into the living room.

"Ready."

While Joanna held Isabelle's leash, Kaylee opened the front door, then the three emerged into the late afternoon sunshine.

Kaylee locked the door.

Last time she and Kaylee ventured out, Kaylee convinced her to take a joy ride in Harry's car. Harry wasn't here, nor Lou Ann. But Lou Ann's personal car was parked in the driveway, and both she and Kaylee knew where the keys were located.

Kaylee walked past it without so much as a glance.

Joanna exhaled. Kaylee was finally adjusting, and even pleasant.

It wasn't like Kaylee to surrender, but perhaps she was slowly accepting that this is where she belonged instead of Greece.

Isabelle took the lead and led Joanna and Kaylee around the dog's favorite neighborhood blocks.

"At least Isabelle knows exactly what she wants. She knows her path," Kaylee said.

"Do you?" Joanna ventured to ask Kaylee.

Kaylee shrugged.

Joanna left it at that.

Joanna and Kaylee both went silent.

Isabelle's clicking toenails were the only sounds.

"Kaylee?"

"Yeah"

"I want to tell you something but please don't laugh at me."

"Okay. I won't. What is it?"

Joanna cleared her throat.

Should she admit it? Or make something up on the fly?

Kaylee waited.

Here goes.

"When I left the hospital in Naples, Lou Ann brought me to her friend's house, Sheriff Jarett—Brad. You met him."

"Yeah, you told me he was a pancake master."

Joanna laughed. It was true.

"I spent the night in one of Brad's daughters rooms. The girl had all these Barbies. I never had one. I only saw them in stores or on TV." Joanna hesitated. "I picked up one of them. Her hair was so soft and long —blonde, like you and me. I didn't want Lou Ann, or Harry, or Brad to see me playing with a doll, so I hid her under my pillow. I want one of my own. I know it's silly. You're the only one I've told. You can laugh now."

Kaylee turned to look at Joanna.

Isabelle clip-clopped on.

"So, you want a blonde one?"

"Yes."

"All right. I'll ask Lou Ann if we can go shopping."

Joanna's palms sweated in the heat of the afternoon.

"Please. I don't want her to know. Or Harry. I'd be so embarrassed."

"I'll take you. We'll make up some excuse."

"Are you shocked?"

"No. It's okay. I always liked my Barbie Dolls."

"Thank you."

"Don't mention it."

What was the big deal about Joanna wanting a Barbie?

But Joanna saw it as a big deal.

Getting a Barbie doll was a simple fix.

Returning to Greece was not.

She'd keep Joanna's desire for a doll a secret, and in return, she'd have Joanna keep her secret.

That's how secrets worked.

She and Shawna, her best friend in Miami, always shared secrets. How many times had they slept over each other's houses giggling about their secrets? Neither she nor Shawna ever betrayed each other. They trusted each other implicitly. But Miami and Shawna were in her past.

Joanna wasn't Shawna, but somewhat close enough. But damn! She was so needy. Although Kaylee understood her neediness. Joanna never had a "Shawna" in her life.

"Hey, Isabelle! Slow down!" Joanna called, ripping Kaylee out of her memory of Shawna and the home she left behind, including all her Barbie dolls.

Kaylee nudged Joanna.

"If Isabelle wants to run, let's run with her."

Kaylee and Joanna laughed while Isabelle pulled them along together.

Hmmm! Isabelle did that on purpose! Smart dog!

19

Lou Ann pulled her cruiser into the driveway but kept the engine running and the AC on full blast. Florida, whether in the morning, afternoon, or evening, was wicked hot in the summer.

Between handing Tim's daily review to Dan and then not hitting one red light, she was home earlier than expected.

She took out her personal cell and speed-dialed Harry.

He answered after the first ring.

"Wow! That was quick," she said.

"I could say the same for you. Home early or terminated early?"

"Home early, and no I haven't been terminated or demoted…yet."

Harry chuckled. "Same Lou Ann."

She chuckled back. "Want to trade me in?"

"No. Never. I love the way you are. Always have, by the way."

"Hmmm."

Harry still made her hum.

"I'm allowed early dismissal because my trainee was solid. Actually, he was more than solid. He's going to be one hell of a deputy, and hopefully maintain a respectable distance from Dan. Me? Not so lucky."

"He? Huh?"

"Yeah, wet behind the ears baby, meaning not for me. You? Ironically, just right."

"Aw, shucks."

"Coming over tonight? Subpoena letter, right?"

"Of course. I was hoping you might need me for more."

"Didn't I mention that?" she teased.

"Umm. Nope."

"Well, bring clean underwear."

"You're in luck because I just happen to have some."

"You mean you just bought some."

"Nope. Did that in Naples, remember?"

"Okay. Now I do."

"I'm a big boy now, and I can do my own laundry."

"Fantastic. I have a pile here you can work on."

"Will do. Can't guarantee girly things will come out right though."

Lou Ann laughed. "You can be my trainee."

"Promise?"

"Promise. I'll be over around six, and I'll bring spicy Thai."

"Spicy, huh?"

"Yes, very hot."

"Okay, see you at six."

Lou Ann stepped out of the vehicle in time to see Kaylee and Joanna trotting up the driveway behind Isabelle, who was wagging her tail and panting with her pink tongue lolling sideways out of her mouth.

"You're home early," Kaylee called.

Isabelle pulled Kaylee and Joanna straight to Lou Ann.

Lou Ann squatted and hugged Isabelle, reveling in doggy kisses.

"Oh, so happy to see you too."

Then she looked up at Kaylee and Joanna.

"We're also happy to see you home," Joanna said.

Wait for it.

"Absolutely," Kaylee said. "Let's all go inside. Isabelle and the rest of us definitely need cold water to cool off." Kaylee pointed to Isabelle. "This girl can run. We're pooped."

"Even with those short little legs and sausage body, I think she dreams of being a canine officer," Lou Ann said.

Kaylee stroked Isabelle's back. "Dare to dream, little one."

Lou Ann couldn't and wouldn't stifle Kaylee's dreams. Kaylee needed those dreams for now. She'd let her lose them in her own time.

Dreams—realistic or not—everyone needed them.

Hers, to have a family, was coming true. Not only did she have Isabelle and Harry, but also Joanna and Kaylee, and she desperately wanted Kaylee to know that.

Lou Ann fished in her pocket for the house key, but Kaylee whipped hers out faster.

"I got it," she said.

At least she was responsible enough to lock up the house when she and Joanna left with Isabelle.

"Thanks," Lou Ann said.

"No problem,' Kaylee answered.

They ducked into the house and away from the heat.

Isabelle went straight to her water bowl.

"Just a second, Isabelle," Kaylee said.

She reached into the fridge and pulled out several bottles of water and then poured some in Isabelle's bowl, who eagerly lapped it up.

"Have a seat, Lou Ann," Kaylee said.

Where did the real Kaylee go?

The new and improved one had arrived!

It didn't matter that she didn't call her Aunt Lou Ann. Her Aunt Lou Ann had left years ago. And that was on her and her brother Lyle, Kaylee's dead father.

Lou Ann had left Miami for Clearwater, not just for a new position with the Sheriff's Department, but admittedly to avoid a family confrontation. Ironically, she now recognized that one can never run away from family drama. It was a natural part of a real family. She learned that too late.

The three sat at the kitchen table, sipping on iced cold water.

It was the best part of Lou Ann's day.

All too soon it might become the worst part.

"Harry's coming over tonight and he's brining Thai food for dinner."

A warm-up for unsettling news.

"What's Thai food? I've never had that," Joanna said.

"You'll like it. It's spicy, but so good," Kaylee replied.

"Okay, I'll give it try. Anything would be better than Margo's slop."

"While we're eating fabulous Thai, Margo is finally swallowing prison slop."

'Too bad I didn't knock all her teeth out. Then she'd have to gum her food," Joanna said.

Kaylee and Joanna raised their bottles of cold water and bumped them.

"To justice," Kaylee said.

"To justice," Joanna repeated.

If they only knew.

Lou Ann heard Harry's car putter into the driveway.

The evening was now in motion.

She stepped out the front door and waved to him.

He waved back and cut the engine.

"Hey," she called.

"Hey, yourself!"

Lou Ann trotted to his car.

"Can I help you with the dinner bags?"

"Sure."

He handed her two food-filled paper bags and grabbed the other two from the front passenger seat, got out of his car, and shut the door.

"Wow! You really went all out."

Harry had picked up the order at the Thai restaurant where they used to grab take out dinner.

Lou Ann chuckled.

They'd sit in bed eating Thai. It was one of her best memories of her and Harry. But tonight it would be another kind of memory.

Harry hesitated.

"Um. It was second nature to get the Thai."

"It's okay. It will always be our place and maybe now Kaylee's and Joanna's too. It will soften the blow. I know it will."

"All right. Let's do it."

Lou Ann and Harry went inside together.

"Dinner's here," Lou Ann called.

"I'll get the plates," Harry said.

Kaylee bounded into the kitchen.

"That smells terrific. It's been forever since I've had Thai!"

Lou Ann nodded. "This is the best Thai place in Clearwater and beyond."

"I can attest to that," Harry added.

Joanna walked into the kitchen and sniffed.

She looked at the assortment of rice and noodles and sauces and vegetables with furrowed brows.

Kaylee patted a chair "Come sit next to me. You'll like it," Kaylee said.

Joanna sat and stared at the buffet style Thai food gracing the table.

Kaylee loaded her plate with a glop of everything, and Lou Ann and Harry filled their plates.

Lou Ann looked up at Joanna and then at Joanna's empty plate.

"There's plenty of rice. Start with that," Lou Ann said. She pointed to a mild dish. "Then you can add this. If you don't like it that's okay. I can fix you something else."

Joanna shook her head at Lou Ann's offer.

"I ordered this one especially for you," Harry said to Joanna. "It's not too spicy."

"Try it," Kaylee begged.

Joanna scooped tiny portions onto her plate.

Lou Ann smiled at Kaylee. Kaylee's perpetual sourpuss was thankfully fading. Lou Ann and Harry had agreed to be patient with

Kaylee. Joanna, who shared the atrocities of Newell's gang, had the most positive impact on Kaylee. Tonight and on into Margo's upcoming trial would probably reopen all their wounds.

The best Thai food in the world wouldn't be enough. But the best Thai shared among family had the best chance to help salve those wounds.

Chopsticks clicked.

And then it happened. Joanna loaded not one offering of Thai, but two!

She chewed and swallowed the unfamiliar food.

Joanna set down her chopsticks.

"Mmm. It really is good!."

"I told you so," Kaylee said.

"I think I'll try this, too."

Joanna laughed at herself after dropping the food off the chopsticks before she could get the bite to her mouth.

Everyone laughed along with her.

Joanna was getting stronger and stronger. Kaylee was always that way. Chopsticks aside, they would soon need each other even more.

"You guys take it easy, since both of you had a hard day. We'll take care of the rest," Kaylee said.

Kaylee and Joanna collected the dinner plates and loaded them into the dishwasher.

Lou Ann and Harry stared at each other.

Then Harry reached his hand across the table to Lou Ann, and she offered hers.

They sat across from one another with their hands joined while Kaylee and Joanna were distracted.

"It'll be okay," Harry mouthed to Lou Ann, who nodded.

They would discuss the letters and explain the options available to them to Kaylee and Joanna.

Options—something that neither had while in captivity and even going forward. Lou Ann and Harry would leave it up to the girls to choose the path right for them, and support whatever each of them decided.

"Let's go to the den," Lou Ann said.

"All right," Joanna said. "Are we going watch a movie, or play a game?"

Lou Ann shook her head "No, um, Harry and I need to talk to you two. We need to have a family meeting."

"This is about the car, isn't it?" Kaylee blurted.

Lou Ann gave her puzzled frown. "Car?"

"No it's not about the car. We'll talk about that latter."

Harry looked at Lou Ann, noticing her obvious confusion.

"For another day," he said.

Kaylee's eyes grew big, and Joann's bigger.

"What's going on?" Kaylee asked. "Are you two splitting up again?"

Joanna went pale. Her brows furrowed as she looked between Lou Ann and Harry.

"No," Lou Ann and Harry said at the same time.

"Something's obviously wrong, and I want to know what it is, now! Not in the den, but right here, right now!" Kaylee demanded.

Kaylee pulled out a kitchen chair and plopped into it.

"Sit down, Joanna," Kaylee said.

Joanna hesitated, but then pulled out a chair and sat next to Kaylee..

"Shoot," Kaylee said, straight-faced.

Lou Ann looked at Harry.

"I'll get the letters," Harry said.

"Letters? What letters?" Kaylee asked, her voice high and urgent.

Joanna sat quietly while circling her thumbs on the table.

Harry returned with the two legal letters and sat next to Lou Ann so they both faced Kaylee and Joanna.

'What are those letters?" Kaylee demanded.

"They arrived yesterday," Lou Ann began.

"Oh, yesterday? And you've just decided to tell us now?"

"Kaylee, Harry and I needed to discuss these first so we'd be able to explain your best choices to you."

Oh, my gawd! Will you just spit it out?!" Kaylee yelled.

Joanna kept shaking her head.

Harry read the subpoena letters.

"I knew this day was coming," Kaylee said.

Joanna pushed back her chair, stood, and bolted out of the kitchen.

Lou Ann should have done it yesterday, but she thought that coupled with their recent visit to the gynecologist, it would be too much. But she was convinced that the response would've been the same. And it was.

But she and Harry were united and would be there as a shield against the eventual fallout. Still, Kaylee saw it as a betrayal and Joanna as a resurrected nightmare.

Kaylee then stood and glanced at Lou Ann and Harry.

"I'll go after her," she said.

Harry wrapped his arm around Lou Ann's shoulder. "At least they ate first…we ate…as a family."

Harry had a point.

But as Kaylee said, it was an eventuality that she and Joanna had to face. Except this time they weren't alone and helpless.

Joanna sat on the edge of her bed, shaking uncontrollably.

The bedroom door squeaked open.

"Can I come in?" Kaylee asked.

"It's your room," Joanna said, her voice quaking.

"It is, but if you want to be alone…"

Joanna sniffled. "Don't leave."

Kaylee entered and closed the bedroom door.

"They didn't tell me to come."

"I figured as much."

Kaylee sat next to Joanna on Joanna's bed.

"Maybe we'll sleep in your bed tonight."

Joanna shrugged.

"Or not."

Kaylee waited.

"I can't go to the trial."

"Okay."

Joanna took a long sniff.

"They'll arrest me."

"What?"

"Margo will tell them how I beat her."

"First off, that happened in Greece, and no one filed any charges there."

"That's because Harry and Brad covered for me."

"Partly. But you and I know Margo. She will never admit that you kicked the shit out of her. She's vain. I hit her over the head with a tray and I stuck a fork in Otto's eye. And that was in Miami, the United States of America. Am I worried? Hell no. For the reasons I just said, and you shouldn't be worried either. I'm going to go to the trial and tell everyone what she did to us. How she humiliated us. How she groomed us. How she allowed—or was complicit in—Newell and Otto's torture. You had it worse. She stood by while Otto and his scummy gang took turns raping you. They were even convinced you died. But you survived. I don't know how many others didn't survive or were left with nightmares like us."

Joanna went silent.

Kaylee was right. It had to be done. Newell and Otto had a fitting ending. Now it was Margo's turn.

"I'll go."

Kaylee hugged Joanna.

"I'll be right there with you, and so will Lou Ann and Harry. You and I will finally finish that chapter of our life. It will never fully be erased from our memories, but we have the control now. Shall we use it?"

"Yes."

Kaylee stood and held out her hand to Joanna.

"Let's go and hear them out."

Joanna took Kaylee's hand.

Theirs was a bond only they could share.

Kaylee led Joanna by the hand out of the sanctuary of their bedroom and into the hallway, where she released her hand.

Joanna needed to do this part on her own. Kaylee wanted to do it for revenge, and she couldn't wait to see Margo's face again.

Kaylee whispered in Joanna's ear, "I have your back."

"I know," Joanna replied and then took the lead into the den where Lou Ann and Harry sat on the sofa waiting for them.

Joanna and Kaylee sat in chairs on either side of the sofa so the family formed a semi-circle.

"We're ready to talk about our next steps," Kaylee said.

Joanna nodded.

"Okay, here's the deal," Harry began. "First of all, although these are subpoena letters, because of the circumstances...physical and psychological abuse involved in sex trafficking...you aren't compelled to testify...meaning no one will pursue you if you do not appear."

"We can respond in that manner if you choose not to appear," Lou Ann said.

"It's completely up to you," Harry added. "We'll support you either way. You can take a few days to think about it."

"We already decided. We'll testify," Kaylee said.

Lou Ann and Harry looked at Joanna.

"Are you sure, Joanna?" Harry asked.

"Yes."

"Do you know when Margo's trial begins?" Kaylee asked.

"In three weeks, on August 16th."

"Tell whoever that Joanna and I will be there."

Three weeks would give Kaylee ample time to practice her responses in court and to coach Joanna, while she did the same.

They were going to nail that bitch, and it was going to be sweet!

"So that's that," Kaylee said. "Let's get on with the rest of the

evening."
Kaylee stood.
"I'll be right back."
She returned with a board game and set it on the den's coffee table.
"Let's play, The Game of Life, shall we?"

20

Lou Ann arrived on time at headquarters to pick up Tim for his second day of training.

She paused for a moment in her vehicle.

Margo's trial was scheduled to begin in three weeks. She had to be there. But she'd have to request another time off day to Dan, who would either deny her request with glee or revel in going straight to Glenda, recommending her demotion. She'd already taken a leave of absence for Greece. Additional requests would not be approved.

Then she took out her cell calendar. Yes! She could put in for a personal day. Kaylee and Joanna's testimony would take a day. They'd travel to Miami and back with Harry driving while she slept in the car, and she'd be back on the job the next day. Lou Ann nodded to herself. Problem solved.

Lou Ann stepped out of her cruiser and straightened her shoulders, determined to deal with Dan and to have a productive shift with Tim. Everything was going to fall into place.

She strode into the lobby with a renewed purpose.

"Good morning, Sergeant Jasinski," the security officer said.

"Good morning."

She passed through security and up to the third floor, where she passed by her empty assigned office and on to the next one, Dan's. After she completed Tim's training, she'd take the time to furnish her office. For now she at least had the key to her office—her future.

Lou Ann rapped on Dan's door.

"Enter," he called.

She opened the door to find Dan sitting stoic behind his desk while Tim stood straight in uniform and ready.

Dan shoved an envelope across his desk.

"Fill this out and as usual return it to me by four thirty. And by the way, here's your court date."

Lou Ann's thoughts spun around in her head. How did he know about Miami? How did he know about anything? Was he spying on her? No, that wasn't possible. She was just being paranoid.

She tilted her head.

"What court date?" she asked.

"Some idiot who you gave a speeding ticket is fighting it."

"Fighting it? There's nothing to fight."

"As stupid as it is, he has the right to be an idiot. Bottom line, you've gotta waste your time and mine."

Lou Ann examined the paper. Shit! She was due in court in three weeks. Then she read the name—Jake Regis, her ex.

"Unbelievable," she muttered.

Jake had screwed her once again. She thought she'd gotten rid of him for good. Apparently not.

What if it was the same date as the day Kaylee and Joanna were set to testify in Margo's trial?

Lou Ann couldn't get out of this unexpected hearing. Damn him!

"Don't just stand there," Dan waved his hand. "Go! I've got my own shit to do."

Tim stood silent.

Lou Ann beckoned to him. "Let's go," *and leave Dan with his shit.*

It definitely wasn't the right time to request a personal day. Plus, to complicate matters, she'd have to confirm the date Kaylee and Joanna and Harry and she were to be in Miami.

Lou Ann sped down the hallway and to the elevator bank, where Tim caught up with her.

"Trouble?" he asked.

She stared at the closed elevator doors.

"Might be."

"I can't believe that guy is going to contest a speeding ticket."

"I can. I know him."

"He's gotten tickets before? A record?"

"Yeah, he has a record—with me." Lou Ann turned and looked at Tim. "But that's between you and me."

"Absolutely."

"I used to date the vain guy…briefly. I cut it off. He knows where I patrol, and I swear he did it on purpose."

"What are you going to do?"

"I have to appear in court as the ticketing deputy. I don't have a choice. I just…"

The elevator doors opened to reveal three people in the elevator.

She and Tim got in and off at the lobby level, both letting the three people out first.

Tim kept up with Lou Ann while she moved at a rapid clip to the parked cruiser. Anxious steam whipped from her nostrils.

She unlocked the vehicle and got in. Tim swooped into the passenger seat remaining silent.

"We'll be off in minute," she said.

She took out her personal cell and texted Harry, praying he'd be available.

When is the court date?

Lou Ann waited. Her heartbeat chugged.

He was probably unavailable. It's not like he no longer worked. Lou Ann shook her head. She'd become dependent on Harry. She'd have to search for the beginning of Margo's trial date on her own when she got home. Nothing she could do about it now.

"Let's ride," she said

She started the engine and pulled out to begin Tim's second day of training.

She'd just turned the corner out of headquarters when dispatch notified her of a heated argument at a popular breakfast place.

"They're starting early today," she said.

Tim engaged the cruiser's lights.

"Morning traffic. You never know what to expect of an argument when someone calls for help."

"You aced it," Lou Ann said.

They arrived at the restaurant to find two women slugging it out while men gathered to watch the melee.

"I bet you thought were responding to men."

"That was my assumption."

"Mine too. Shall we?"

"Let's do it."

Lou Ann and Tim excited the vehicle. Women's' fists flying were the only weapons she saw.

Lou Ann stepped forward.

"All right. Break it up. I need all of you, except these two ladies—and I use the term 'ladies' loosely—to go back into the restaurant."

The crowd of mostly grown men left.

The women scowled at each other, but dropped their fisted hands to their sides.

"What's the problem here?" Tim asked.

The women glanced at Tim and then their eyes went straight to Lou Ann.

"The deputy asked you a question," she said, allowing Tim to handle the dispute.

The women returned their attention to Tim.

"We were all going boating after breakfast. They agreed to pick up the bill because me and my husband do it all the time. But they tried to stiff us again, and when I said so, she got mad and poured syrup on my new dress. She did it on purpose!"

"It was an accident. When I got up from the table, my plate of pancake syrup slipped off the table and accidentally dripped on her dress. And we weren't going to stiff you. Not that it matters since you make a shitload of money. And no, we don't want to get on your boat anymore."

"Uh, well that's good because you're not welcome anymore."

"Well, you're not welcome anymore at my daughter's wedding."

"Your daughter is marrying my son—which by the way—we're also paying for!"

This was one messed up family.

Lou Ann raised her hand. "Whoa."

The husband of the woman with the boat came out of the restaurant.

"The bill's paid," he said.

"Of course it is," she sneered.

The other woman's husband arrived.

"Let's go dear," he said.

He looked at Lou Ann and Tim.

"I'm sorry for the scene, deputies."

"Since no one is physically hurt and the bill is settled, I need you all to separate and peacefully go about your separate business. We'll stand here and make sure that happens. You're not to return to this restaurant again. Ever. We don't want to get called for any other fighting because if we do, we'll have to take all of you in. Is that understood?"

"Yes, ma'am," the boating husband said.

"Won't happen again," the other husband said.

"Ladies?" Lou Ann asked.

"All right," one said.

"Fine by me," the other said.

Lou Ann and Tim watched the couples leave the premises in separate vehicles.

After Lou Ann and Tim spoke with the manager at the restaurant, who was in agreement with Lou Ann's punishment, she and Tim returned to the vehicle.

Lou Ann's cell pinged.

Trial starts Aug 15, testimony Aug 16. Sorry for delay. Was in meeting.

Thanks. Sorry to bug you.

No bug. Back in meeting in ten. See you tonight.

K.

Lou Ann took out her court appearance, read through it carefully, and sighed at the April 12th date.

"Families," Tim commented.

Lou Ann nodded as she put away the document.

"Ties that bind can really chafe."

After the ladies' fight scene at the restaurant, they responded to a department store's detained shoplifter, infamously known as "Queen Marie," who preferred to be called a professional booster. Queen Marie sat handcuffed in the back of the cruiser while Tim responded to the call about Rocko, the mischievous terrier, who didn't dig a hole deep enough under a fence to fit his body through, consequently got his head stuck in the fence between his owner's and neighbor's. Apparently, like Queen Marie, Rocko was a repeat offender.

Tim extracted the whimpering dog's trapped head.

Rocko was sentenced to leash probation while the hole in the fence was fixed.

Halfway through the day, Lou Ann allowed Tim to take control of the vehicle while she supervised from the passenger seat.

As usual, Tim more than met her expectations, and after they dropped Queen Marie at the county jail, she and he returned to headquarters.

"Stellar second day on the job," she said to Tim while he parked her cruiser.

"You're a stellar training officer," he replied.

"Accolades will get you everywhere."

"So will truth."

"Thanks for the compliment, but always keep truth in mind no matter the temptation."

"Will do, Sergeant Jasinski."

They arrived at Dan's office, and she let Tim knock on his door.

"Enter," she mouthed.

Tim grinned.

"Enter," Dan bellowed behind his closed door.

Lou Ann shot Tim a thumbs-up and he entered Dan's lair first.

Lou Ann followed.

Dan set his folded his hands on the desk.

"Well…"

Lou Ann slid Tim's review across Dan's desk.

"Hmmm. I see Queen Marie has made a return to her royal cell."

Lou Ann smiled at Dan's rare attempt at humor.

He perused the other reports.

"That's new. A women's fight club."

"Not really. No one got hurt. No one landed any punches. The couples involved left separately without further incident, and are barred from patronizing that establishment."

"And a dog with his head stuck?"

He stared at Tim.

"Nice dog with poor planning skills," Tim joked.

Dan snickered.

Apparently she and Tim had entertained Dan—one for the books.

Lou Ann decided to take advantage of Dan's jovial mood.

"Dismissed," Dan said.

"Same time, same place?" Tim asked.

"Why wouldn't it be?" Dan answered.

"See you at 0800, Sergeant Jasinski."

"Absolutely, Deputy Farmer."

Tim departed with a spring in his step.

Dan looked up from his desk.

"Do you need something, Sergeant Jasinski?"

"Yes," she replied.

"Go on."

"I'm requesting a personal day on August 16th."

"For?"

"Personal reason."

"Obviously. You already have a half a day on the 12th to appear in court on that contested ticket."

"And I will be there on official duty."

Dan rolled his thumbs while staring at her.

Back to his old, acerbic self.

"All right approved. Go. And do something with that office of yours that I went to great lengths to get for you."

Actually, it was Glenda who'd secured her an office and apologized because that it was next to Dan's.

"And I appreciate that and the approval. And I will move in once Tim is ready to fly on his own, which I have the utmost confidence he will do soon."

"Duly noted. You're free to go."

"Thank you, sir."

"Yeah, yeah."

Lou Ann turned and strode out of Dan's office, and once she closed his door, she sashayed to the elevator and hummed all the way to her cruiser.

An unusual and humorous day—she'd take it.

After securing her day off for Kaylee's and Joanna's testimony in Miami, Lou Ann still needed to tell Harry about her court date with Jake. When Harry wasn't in her life, it didn't matter. Now she was compelled to let him know about her ex before he learned about it some other way. They were rebuilding their relationship on trust, so she would be transparent. Who knew? The knucklehead might start calling her, and she'd have to backtrack and explain him to Harry.

Miscommunication and cover-ups were what brought them down. She couldn't go through that again, and she was positive Harry didn't want to either.

They'd pledged to do better, and so far their relationship was once again blooming.

Lou Ann walked into the house and Isabelle swarmed her. It was always their routine. Isabelle was always glad that Lou Ann arrived home safe.

"Yes, I'm home baby. I'm home."

Isabelle swished her tail so hard that her long body rocked.

Kaylee and Joanna trotted toward her.

"Hey! You're home!" Joanna cheered.

Kaylee grinned. "Home early for good behavior again?"

Lou Ann smiled and nodded. "Yes."

"Harry called," Joanna said. "He'll be over shortly."

"Joanna and I made a big bowl of salad for dinner. It's too hot for anything else."

"Thanks, guys. It's great to come home and not worry about dinner. Salad sounds great. That you guys put it together makes it even greater."

Even Kaylee smiled wide.

"Isabelle's already fed and walked," Joanna said.

"Wow! I don't know what do with myself."

"You can change out of that uniform. I'm sweating just looking at it," Kaylee said.

"It's at least as hot as it looks, maybe hotter."

"Hey! Harry just pulled up!" Joanna said.

"Let him in and tell him I'm in the bedroom."

"Woo hoo!" Kaylee teased.

"It's not like that… hopefully would be later. I need to talk to him."

"Ooh. Has he been bad?" Joanna jumped in.

Lou Ann propped her fists onto her hips. "What is it with you guys?"

The girls giggled.

Lou Ann grinned. "Just send him back."

"Okayyy," Kaylee and Joanna sing-songed in unison.

Lou Ann passed by them while shaking her head.

At least no one slung any fists in this family.

Lou Ann peeled off her uniform.

Ah, relief.

A knock came at the bedroom.

"Are you decent in there?" Harry joked.

"Nope," she replied, but then laughed.

"I'm coming in!"

Harry slipped inside the bedroom, shut the door, and whistled. He waggled his brows.

"You gonna wear that for dinner?"

"Under my shirt and shorts."

"Dang."

Lou Ann finished dressing.

"The girls sent me up here."

"That's because I asked them to."

Harry sat on the bed. "What's up?"

"Dan approved my request for August 16th."

"I'm sure you're relieved. I know I am, and I'm sure Kaylee and Joanna will be too."

"But I have to be back to Clearwater for a mandatory August 17th meeting."

"No problem. Testimony should take a day. I'll drive to Miami and back home so you can rest. We'll make it work."

"That's what I was going to suggest."

"I've cleared my calendar too, so problem solved."

"Um, I've another court date I need to tell you about."

Harry tilted his head. "Another court date?"

"Yeah. I gave this guy a speeding ticket, and he's contesting it."

"You're kidding."

"Nope." Lou Ann paused.

Transparency, she reminded herself. Miscommunication was the death knell of their relationship before, and she wasn't going to allow that to happen again.

"I used to date the guy I gave the speeding ticket to...before I met you," she added.

Harry arched his brows.

"His name is Jake Regis. I had no idea who he was when he streaked past me. It was only when I pulled him over that I recognized him. He's contesting the ticket just to get to me because I broke up with him."

"I don't get why he's surfaced after so long,"

"Jake is vain, and that's why I couldn't stand being with him any longer. He persisted in calling me after we broke up."

"How did he know we'd broken up?"

Lou Ann looked at Harry. It had to come back out.

"Jake dated the woman from the bar."

Harry hung his head.

"I still regret that night. We had a fight—one too many—and I got hammered. I ended up at her house as you already know. I'm so sorry she hounded you. She was a sick person. She staged it all. Nothing happened except the end of our relationship."

"And that's why I'm telling you about Jake, because I suspect he's going to try to insert himself in my...our...life."

Harry stood. "I'm going to be in that courtroom."

"Not necessary. Because if he persists, I'll slam him for stalking. I'll make that abundantly clear. I just want you to know in case that happens."

"All right, I won't go. I'll let you handle it. But the minute he starts calling or coming around or following you, then all bets are off."

Harry the hero!

Lou Ann wrapped her arms around his neck and kissed him long and hard. He deserved it.

"Thank you, and I love you, "she whispered.

"Love you back, and I always have."

"I know."

Joanna and Kaylee leaned their ears toward Lou Ann 's bedroom door, and frequently Harry's too.

Joanna wished that Harry would soon share it with Lou Ann every night. Joanna was positive that Kaylee felt the same. Kaylee, too, had taken a shine to Harry even if she did drive off in his car while he napped.

"Lou Ann's going to court," Kaylee whispered.

Joanna's heart hammered fast in her chest and her palms got sweaty.

"Do you think she's in trouble?" Joanna asked.

"No. She has to testify," Kaylee answered.

"Like us. No. Yes."

"Which is it?"

"She's not on trial like we're not going to be on on trial. But this is ticket shit. It's a minor inconvenience for her. But we're not minor inconveniences. This is a city problem. Ours is a state one with international implications. This is a little court. Ours will be a courtroom with lots of people, a jury, and a judge. A judge decides tickets. A jury will decide Margo's fate. Got it?"

Joanna stuck out her bottom lip.

"I'm not stupid. I'm scared."

"I'm scared too. But, like Lou Ann, we got to go, right?"

Joanna nodded.

She couldn't back out and leave Kaylee alone. Plus, nothing would please Margo more than to see Kaylee but not her, knowing that Margo had once more controlled her—frightened her.

Footsteps approached the bedroom door.

Kaylee yanked Joanna's hand and pulled her into their bedroom.

They bounced to a sitting position on the edge of Joanna's bed, feigning innocence.

Lou Ann and Harry stopped at the open doorway.

Did they hear them scurry away?

"How about going to the diner for dinner tonight?" Harry asked.

They'd made it to the bedroom just in time.

Harry grinned at Joanna. "Mondo fries are on me," he joked.

Joanna and Lou Ann laughed.

"Mmm What's so funny?" Kaylee asked.

"Inside joke. There is no such thing as mondo fries. Harry just teased me about them the first time we went to that diner. You'll like it there."

It was just like when Kaylee reassured Joanna about Thai food.

Kaylee was an adventurer.

She? She'd stick to fantasy mondo fries…for now.

21

Last night's diner dinner was for the four of them, but this morning, Harry's omelet with a side of strawberries was just for the two of them, while Joanna and Kaylee snoozed.

She sat in courtroom A and then turned in her seat to see Jake strolling up the aisle wearing a designer suit and tie with brown leather loafers.

His finances apparently continued to overflow as bountifully as his ego.

He probably drove to court in the same cherry red Porsche that sped right past her.

Jake used to have three cars: two flashy muscle cars, including said Porsche, and for more sedate action, a Beemer.

He was a gold-card carrying attorney who spent more time looking in the rear view mirror to check himself out and see who was checking him out than looking at her. Although he did gift her a diamond necklace and matching diamond earrings that she only wore in his presence since the jewelry didn't t fit with her deputy lifestyle.

They'd met at an outdoor Clearwater bistro when he approached her and her, bestie and her best training officer, Allison, along with his pal, who was remarkably understated, and who Allison ultimately married, and was still happily married to.

They doubled dated a few times when Jake was the ultimate gentlemen, but when she and Jake went solo, he transformed into a complete egomaniac. He owned luxury cars and a top-flight condominium overlooking the water where, of course, his big-ass boat was moored. But he was a bigger ass in public. And he bragged that he was big otherwise, which wouldn't have mattered to her, but the "wonder dick" was nowhere near what it was cracked to be and neither were his sloppy kisses. Money can't buy everything, including humility, a warm heart, and a gentle embrace. Turns out, Jake was the poorest man she'd ever met.

Jake flashed Lou Ann his white, toothy grin and sat opposite her.

Judge Graham sat behind his desk and nodded to Lou Ann. She'd appeared before him in more complex cases that really mattered. The judge turned his attention to Jake.

"Mr. Regis, where is your attorney?"

Everyone in the Pinellas County courtroom knew Jake Regis.

Jake stood. "I'm representing myself, sir."

Judge Graham sighed. "Have it your way. Let's get on with it."

The judge looked down at his docket.

"On what grounds are you contesting this speeding ticket? Deputy Sheriff Jasinski clocked you exceeding twenty-five miles per hour over the well-signed speed limit."

"There were other vehicles exceeding the limit."

"Come on, Mr. Regis. You know better than that. None were twenty-five miles over the limit. There's a grace for just over the limit, and that doesn't include you."

"That may be so, but Deputy Lou Ann Jasinski and I have a past relationship, and I'm attributing that to her prejudicial response."

Huh! Ass! Such a liar!

"Judge Graham, I didn't know who Mr. Regis was until I stopped him for speeding. I do know Mr. Regis. However our relationship is from the distant past."

"Bottom line, Mr. Regis," the judge said. "The ticket stands. Now get out of my court room, for now."

"Next case, please!," the judge announced.

At least Jake only wasted fifteen minutes of her time today, added to an unfortunate month out of her life.

Lou Ann stood and began to leave the court room.

"Lou Ann," Jake called. "Wait up."

Shit!

Lou Ann sped out of the courtroom.

But Jake still caught up with her outside.

"Hey, I just wanted to see you again."

"This is not how you do it, nor will it ever work in the future."

"I get it. You look good."

"You look and act the same. So seriously, buzz off."

"I'll make like a bee. Bye Lou Ann."

Lou Ann hurried to her cruiser, but Jake didn't follow her.

She climbed into her cruiser and shut the door.

Although Jake was nowhere to be seen, he was right there in her head. *Damn him! How did I even last a month?*

Lou Ann kept flinging Jake out of her head. He not only humiliated himself, but also embarrassed her.

Like Judge Graham said, what a waste of time!

By the time she pulled into the headquarters lot, the space Jake took up in her busy brain had shrunk to a minor annoyance in her head, because now she had to deal with a real nemesis, Lieutenant Dan.

She'd quickly fetch Tim and be back on shift and blessedly away from yet another prick.

Then her personal cell rang. It was Harry's ring tone.

"Hey, how did it go?"

"Arrr. Thanks for reminding me."

"That didn't take long."

"It was too long for me and the judge."

"So he had his five minutes."

Enough of Jake.

"What are you up to today?"

"After I make breakfast for the girls, I'm heading to the field office. Hopefully I'll get assigned a local case. If not, I'll give you as much notice as I can."

"It's okay. Do what you need to do, because you can't tell me anyway. We're all right either way."

"I want it to be all right this time around."

"Mistakes are the best teachers."

"And I promise to be an attentive student."

"A plus for the call!"

"I will humbly accept that since I never got A's in school! Talk to you later!"

"Okay, babe."

Lou Ann hung up and grinned.

She and Harry, they were worth fighting for.

Now off to Dan's office. At least Harry put her in a good mood.

Lou Ann took the elevator to the third floor, ready to joust with Dan. Anybody was better than Jake. Even Dan.

Lou Ann rapped rhythmically on Dan's office door and then scooted inside before he could say "enter."

Dan looked up at her from his desk. He seemed smaller to her than usual. Or maybe she was standing taller. Or both.

Whatever. She was here for Tim's training shift.

"Today is Deputy Farmer's last day."

He quit already?

"You've done an excellent job with him so tomorrow he'll start his shift alone with his own assigned cruiser."

Lou Ann nodded. "That's great and thank you, sir."

Dan stood and slapped Tim on the back. "Thanks to you this guy is really going somewhere. I smell a promotion for him in the near future."

"Wonderful."

Only took her seven years to make sergeant. Nothing against Tim. He was catching on fast. But he needed rookie time. Jake and Dan—two pricks drawn on the same page.

"Let's roll, shall we?" Lou Ann said to Tim.

"Go get em!" Dan added."

"Final review due at four-thirty," Dan tossed at Lou Ann.

"As usual."

"I'll see you, Jasinski, at 0800 tomorrow in your office."

"Yes, sir."

He waved her on. "Dismissed."

Yeah, she was definitely being dismissed.

Kaylee peered out the living room window. Lou Ann was getting home later than usual.

Kaylee opened the door for her, and Lou Ann trudged inside.

"Court didn't go well?"

"No. I mean yes, because it was over before it began. It was a sham case."

"So your ex-boyfriend was a real dweeb?"

Lou Ann tilted her head. "How did you know I used to date him?"

"Ummm."

"You were eavesdropping on Harry and me last night."

"Yeah, okay. We were."

"Sorry," Joanna said. "We won't do it again."

"Uh-huh. I'm really beat."

"Anything we can do for you?" Kaylee asked.

"Thanks, but I'm just going to lie down for a while."

"Is everything okay with you and Harry?"

"Yeah. Harry had a meeting today, and he's probably on an assignment he can't divulge to us."

"Okay. I know that this might be the wrong time to ask, but can I borrow your car to go with Joanna to Target? It's about two miles away."

"I know where the store is," Lou Ann said.

"Okay. Keys are in a bowl on the credenza. Just don't hit the cruiser on your way out—or any other vehicle."

Kaylee and Joanna widened their eyes at each other.

That was way too easy.

But Kaylee would get the keys and take off before Lou Ann changed her mind.

"Thanks, Aunt Lou Ann."

"You're welcome, and don't disappointment me."

"We won't. We'll be back soon."

Kaylee skipped to the living room.

"Let's go, Joanna. I have a surprise for you."

Joanna frowned.

"Not like last time. This time we have permission. And it won't take long, because I know what you need."

"I don't need anything."

"I promise you'll need this!"

Joanna shrugged.

"Come on. Time's a-wastin'!"

Joanna climbed into the passenger seat and buckled her seatbelt.

What is Kaylee up to?

Kaylee maneuvered around Lou Ann's parked cruiser and pulled out of the driveway.

"I liked Target in Miami. I only walked through it. I've never stolen from them."

"I also liked going to the one near my house in Kendall," Kaylee said.

And then she grew silent.

Until now Kaylee had always talked about Greece, but never Miami, until now. Miami was a great city. It was for Kaylee, anyway…or used to be. Joanna smiled, recalling that she too had a few good times there. But Newell robbed them of 99 percent of Miami sunshine. However one percent survived, and Kaylee just hit on the one percent that did.

Joanna peered out the window.

"Not a cloud in the sky," she said.

Kaylee leaned over the steering wheel and glanced up.

"You're right," she said.

Joanna leaned back in her seat.

Two percent and counting!

Kaylee pulled into the closest available parking spot.

"Looks busy tonight," Joanna said.

Kaylee grinned. "Not too busy for us."

It didn't matter to Joanna that she had no money. It was a treat just to be here and walk through all the summer displays.

Summer was always her favorite season because it was never too cold to sleep outside.

Now she had a safe place to lay her head no matter the season.

Kaylee winked. "Let's go."

Joanna hesitated.

Kaylee tapped Joanna's hand.

"Trust me, nothing illegal."

Joanna and Kaylee got out of the car and Kaylee locked it.

"Safety first, right?" Kaylee said.

Joanna nodded. "Safety."

Passing the throng of parked cars, they run-walked to the store's entrance.

"I'm so happy Lou Ann let us use her car," Joanna grinned.

Trust was a wonderful thing to earn.

"I was surprised too. She must have had a really hard day," Kaylee said. "We should get something for her too."

"Too?"

Kaylee grabbed Joanna's hand. "Follow me, my friend."

Clearly, Kaylee was on a mission.

She led Joanna to the toy department.

Perhaps it was a shortcut to another part of the store.

But Kaylee pulled Joanna to a halt.

"Here we are," Kaylee announced.

She and Joanna stood in front of rows and rows of Barbie dolls of all kinds and their mega-accessories.

Joanna's breath hitched.

"What is it?"

"Go ahead and pick one out," Kaylee said.

"I don't understand."

"What's not to understand? You never had a Barbie doll, and I know you want one. I'll buy you any one you want. My treat."

Joanna's face burned.

"I can't. I'm so embarrassed."

"There's nothing to be embarrassed about. For all anybody knows, you're getting this as a gift. It's self checkout too."

She should've kept her wish for a Barbie doll secret after spending the night in Sheriff Brad's little girl's room, a true Barbie paradise. But staring at all those wonders of Barbie dolls, she couldn't help but wish she had one of her own. She'd hoped to save enough money one day to get one, and here was Kaylee offering to buy one for her.

"Do you think I'm a freak?" Joanna asked.

"No. And I didn't come here to humiliate you. Barbies are awesome, and I want you to experience that," Kaylee squeezed Joanna's hand. "Go ahead."

"There are so many!"

"Yeah, that's Barbie planet. Take your time."

Joanna perused the rows of Barbies.

"Oh! I want this one! Nurse Barbie in scrubs. She reminds me of Nurse Lynn, who took care of me in the hospital in Naples. She brought me the best turkey sandwich that first night in intensive care. After everything that happened to me, and I was still so scared that Newell would find me after he thought I was dead, she was there helping me trust for the first time." Joanna turned to Kaylee. "I want to be a nurse someday."

"Then definitely get Nurse Barbie!"

Joanna took Nurse Barbie off the shelf and hugged Kaylee.

"Thank you. This is truly the best surprise! And thank you for not making fun of me."

"You're welcome, and you're welcome."

"Don't tell Lou Ann."

"I won't if you don't want me to."

"I just need for it to be a secret between us for now."

"Okay."

"What should we get for Lou Ann—I mean you, since I don't have any money...yet."

"Eh. You don't have to owe me anything. The Barbie doll is a gift. Besides I've got plenty of money to spend thanks to the double life insurance money from my parents."

Joanna double hugged Kaylee.

Kaylee wiped away tears at the corners of her eyes.

"Let's get going," she said.

Once Joanna testified against Margo, then she'd get a job and make money the honest way instead of selling other people's garden flowers on the busiest Miami streets. No more of that...ever.

Joanna and Kaylee began to walk down aisle after aisle hoping something would "scream" Lou Ann.

Lou Ann's overloaded keys clanked in Kaylee's purse.

Joanna snapped her fingers. "I got it! She could use a nice keychain."

"That is an excellent idea."

They hurried to jewelry section.

Kaylee and Joanna picked out the same keychain—one that had the gold scripted, LOVE hanging from it.

They nodded to each other.

"It definitely screams Lou Ann," Joanna said.

"Done! Let's check out and go home."

Home!

Lou Ann stretched and sat up in bed. She'd needed that power nap. Her eyes widened at the time on her cell. She was only going to close her eyes for fifteen minutes max., but an hour and a half had passed.

Crap! Where were Kaylee and Joanna and her car?

She began to text Kaylee, who was responsible for the car.

She was about to send the text when she heard her vehicle's engine in the driveway.

Just in time.

Lou Ann deleted the text and started to go to the front door but stopped. She needed to step back before exploding the trust that was starting to build among the three of them.

Instead, Lou Ann went to the kitchen and sat pretending she'd been there all along.

Kaylee and Joanna came in the front door.

"Did you have a good nap?" Kaylee asked.

"Yes, and I'm now refreshed," she fibbed.

Lou Ann looked at the Target bag.

"What did you get?" she asked.

Kaylee shrugged. "This and that."

Lou Ann focused on Kaylee.

"This and that were on sale?"

"Yes. 'This' was 25% off and 'that' was buy one and get one free," Kaylee joked.

Joanna giggled.

"Ha-ha," Lou Ann replied.

"We'll be in our room," Kaylee said.

Lou Ann stood. "Dinner will be ready in half an hour."

"Did you start anything yet?" Kaylee asked.

"No. I was going to heat up something."

The Thai food was all gone, and Harry must be surely on an assignment since he hadn't called. It would be just the three of them tonight.

"How about UBER Eats Mexican. I could go for tacos."

"Okay."

It was less work for her and the heat from the oven would be stifling this evening. The temperatures hadn't dipped below 83 degrees.

"Great. I'll order," Kaylee said.

Then Kaylee and Joanna scurried to their room.

There apparently was a lot of mystery between "this" and "that."

Lou Ann retrieved a Diet Coke out of the fridge and sat back down.

What were they up to this long?

The doorbell rang and the door cam showed a young guy holding a paper bag.

Kaylee rushed out and handed Lou Ann a wad of bills.

"My treat and tip included."

The guy handed the paper bag to Kaylee and smiled wide.

"Here you go and thanks for the tip."

"No problem," Kaylee told him and then closed the door.

"He was nice," Lou Ann said.

Kaylee turned and walked away with the bag full of food.

It was too soon, but Lou Ann was sure Kaylee would eventually find someone her age now that her ex-boyfriend was out of her life.

But Demetrios, to whom Kaylee had pledged her love, was permanently gone from from her life.

But Lou Ann refrained from going there. It would only reopen Kaylee's still-fresh wounds.

And the parade of filthy men who'd stolen Joanna's ability to have a normal healthy relationship.

Joanna would understandably, be psychologically skittish for quite some time.

Lou Ann missed the gynecology appointment, but she wasn't going to miss the therapy appointments coming up, especially since Kaylee and Joanna were due to testify at Margo's trial which was three short weeks away.

Kaylee, Joanna, and Lou Ann sat at the kitchen table and loaded their plates with tacos.

Taco sauce ran down Joanna's chin, and she wiped her mouth and chin with a napkin.

"And there aren't any chopsticks involved," she joked.

They all chuckled.

Lou Ann finished seconds and leaned back in her chair.

"That was good," she said.

"Should we?" Kaylee asked Joanna.

"I think now would be a good time," Joanna replied.

"I'm confused." Lou Ann said.

"Go in the den," Kaylee ordered Lou Ann. "Please,'"she added.

"All right."

Kaylee and Joanna once again disappeared.

"Come on, Isabelle. We've been ordered to the den."

She could swear Isabelle grinned.

Lou Ann narrowed her eyes at the dog.

"What do you know that that I don't?"

Isabelle trotted away, her tail wagging.

Lou Ann burrowed into the end of the couch and waited for Kaylee and Joanna to return.

She scrolled through her text messages. Nothing from Harry. But she could handle his absence better this time around and it helped that besides having Isabelle at her side, she now had Kaylee and Joanna.

Kaylee and Joanna returned to the den, both with huge smiles.

Kaylee handed Lou Ann a flower-printed gift bag.

"There's a card inside," Joanna cheered.

Lou Ann's heart warmed.

Kaylee and Joanna bought her a gift!

It didn't matter what was inside the bag, because they thought of her and that was more than enough.

"Oh my!"

Joanna clapped. "Open it!"

"Okay."

She opened the card first and read, "To our Aunt Lou Ann, who took us in despite a change in her once-peaceful life. We thank you, and don't tell you often enough how much we love you. So here's something to help you to know and remember that."

Lou Ann peeked in the gift bag and peeled away pink tissue paper. Then she lifted out the gold keychain with the scripted "LOVE." Tears spilled down her cheek. She sniffled.

"This is the best gift I've ever received."

Isabelle barked.

"We noticed your keys were mounted on a plain ring. This one is classier and it fits how we feel about you, even though we've been such a pain in the ass to you. Me, especially," Kaylee said.

"You're my family on the good days and the more challenging ones, " Lou Ann said, her voice throaty.

She got up and hugged Kaylee and Joanna. "And thank you for being patient with me."

Never did Lou Ann ever imagine having an instant family. Miscarrying her and Harry's baby ripped her heart in two. But Kaylee and Joanna weren't babies. Although the two girls came with complicated and horrific baggage, they were meant for her and Harry, and from the way Harry's eyes lit up on those days and nights he spent with them, she was positive he felt the same.

"That's okay. We've all had our moments, and I'm sure they'll be many more," Kaylee said.

"I hope so," Lou Ann blubbered.

Then Lou Ann's cell pinged an incoming message.

Her smile pushed into her cheeks.

It was Harry.

"Sorry, long day. How are things?"

"Things are great. The three of us had an awesome night."

"Without me? "

"Just girls' night."

"Don't fit in there!"

"You'll always fit in."

"Miss you and be back in two days, so two more girl days."

"Miss you more and the girls do too."

Lou Ann fingered the "LOVE" keychain.

"Love you."'

"Love you too."

Lou Ann ended the call.

She removed her keys from the plain silver ring and she and Kaylee and Joanna slid them onto the new keychain.

"Isn't that better?" Kaylee asked.

Lou Ann dangled her LOVE filled keychain.

"Yes. It's absolutely perfect!"

22

Lou Ann palmed the Love keychain in the psychologist's waiting room while she waited along with Harry for Kaylee and Joanna to be called back for their respective appointments. Dan assigned her to the night shift. He did it on purpose to test her mettle, even though she was now a sergeant, and to force her complete loyalty to him, since she hadn't worked night patrol in almost a year.

Actually, he did her a favor because it freed her to be at Kaylee's and Joanna's psychology appointments without having to ask him for the day off. And secretly she looked forward to a temporary twelve-hour change. But she'd do it just this once. She needed to be at home every night for Kaylee and Joanna, and Harry too, and now that Tim was on his own, she'd decorate her new office to emphasize her role as sergeant, and that meant days only.

Lou Ann glanced at Joanna, who bounced her knees while she sat in a chair anticipating her turn, and then she zeroed in on Kaylee, who covered her face with a home decorating magazine that Lou Ann was sure Kaylee wasn't really reading.

Then she looked at Harry's red-streaked eyes. He'd stayed up all night preparing files so he could be here this morning.

Harry blinked and suppressed a yawn.

Lou Ann reached over and stroked the back of his hand.

"Thank you, and I love you," she whispered in his ear.

Harry grinned and gave her a "me, too," nod.

A slender woman with her auburn hair slicked back into a perfect ponytail and wearing equally perfect makeup walked into the waiting room. The woman looked to be in her thirties, same as Lou Ann, but that's where the similarity stopped. The woman wore, and Lou Ann meant "wore," a green pencil skirt that stopped just above the knee, and a yellow chiffon blouse, and wait for it…matching, yellow two-inch pumps.

Even Harry widened his bloodshot eyes at those yellow pumps.

Rorschach, anyone?

"Hello, I'm Dr. Deborah Stein," she announced.

Kaylee peered over the magazine and stared wide-eyed at the doctor, but Joanna's knees bounced double time.

Joanna's doctor, Dr. Zimmer, the put-together yet minimalist Naples hospital neurologist, had recommended Dr. Stein highly and mentioned that the two were medical student roomies. At least they both ended up working on the human brain.

Hopefully Joanna would go first before she jackhammered a hole in the floor. It was criminal to have her wait any longer.

But Dr. Stein looked straight at Lou Ann.

"Lou Ann Jasinski?" the doctor asked.

"Yes. That's me."

"Come with me, please."

What?

Lou Ann's brain did a double take, Harry blinked, Kaylee set the magazine on the table, and Joanna's knees took a break.

Lou Ann dropped the LOVE keychain in her purse and stood.

"Ummm. Okay."

Kaylee frowned. "What the hell just happened?"

"I want to know that too," Joanna said.

"You got me," Harry said.

What was going on behind that door? Neither he nor Lou Ann signed up for this. Both of them were just here to support Kaylee and Joanna.

Harry stared at the closed door, waiting for Lou Ann to pop back out.

Perhaps it was an insurance check? That made sense. Whatever the cost, he and Lou Ann would pay for Kaylee and Joanna's therapy.

He glanced at his watch. Fifteen minutes had passed, which was plenty of time to square away any payment due.

Harry stood.

"I'll be right back," he told Kaylee and Joanna. "I'm going to see what's going on so you can get on with your appointments."

He walked to the door and was about to knock on it when it opened. But neither Lou Ann or Dr. Stein appeared. Instead a guy wearing navy trousers, a blue pinstriped shirt with the top button undone stood there.

"Mr. Boxer?" he asked.

You're shitting me!

"Yeah."

"Great. I'm Mike Connor, Dr. Stein's associate. Please follow me."

"My girlfriend is still in there, and we're both here for the girls, who do have appointments. Neither I nor Lou Ann Jasinski have appointments."

"Yes, they do, and Dr. Stein will be with them shortly. I just want to speak with you briefly."

Harry looked at Kaylee and Joanna.

Kaylee rolled her eyes. "Go ahead. Joanna and I will go to lunch."

"Nuh-uh."

"I'm kidding. We're not going anywhere. I already hijacked your car once, so we're stuck here."

Harry followed Mike.

"What's going on?" he asked.

"Dr. Stein and I just want to assess how things are going with the family dynamics. It's really to help us with Kaylee and Joanna."

"To be blunt, Lou Ann and I are prepared to only pay for Kaylee's and Joanna's session or sessions as needed."

"There's no charge, Mr. Boxer. As I mentioned, this is only meant to help plan Kaylee and Joanna's therapy. That includes the whole family."

"All right."

He was doing it for Kaylee and Joanna, and he was positive that Lou Ann was too.

But they should've been told ahead of time instead of ambushing them. Then they would've come prepared.

Mike led Harry to a room and closed the door.

"Please have a seat Mr. Boxer."

"You can call me Harry."

"Okay, Harry."

Harry sat in oversized brown leather chair that faced Mike's dark mahogany desk.

Mike sat behind his desk and leaned forward toward Harry, who pushed farther back in his chair.

"How often would you say that you see Kaylee and Joanna?"

"As much as I can. My job assignments can be unpredictable."

"And what is it that you do?"

"I'm an FBI Special Agent."

Mike arched his brows.

"Wow. I apologize for calling you mister."

"It's fine. I'm not here in a work capacity, so Harry is perfect." Harry paused and continued to answer, "It's been between three to five times a week, mostly to have dinner together with the girls and Lou Ann, followed either by a movie streaming or a board game."

"Sounds like a good time."

"It is. For instance we found out that Kaylee detests green beans but loves Thai, and Joanna likes hamburgers and fries at the local diner, and she's taken to Thai, which she never had before and has even got pretty decent with chopsticks. And, at Kaylee's request, we played the game of Life the other night."

"Interesting choice of a game," Mike commented.

"Yes."

Mike tilted his head.

Harry sighed inwardly. He'd have to offer Mike more details, and it would help Kaylee.

"I think Kaylee chose that particular game because that night we all talked about the girls testifying in an upcoming trial—in three weeks—involving one of the Miami traffickers who mostly functioned as a groomer, but her involvement was actually deeper."

Mike nodded. "Yes we have the disturbing background for both Kaylee and Joanna."

A few seconds of silence passed.

"Getting back to the girls, I get the impression that Kaylee is having more trouble adjusting."

"Although they are strikingly and weirdly nearly identical, which contributed to how they became involved with the same traffickers, Kaylee and Joanna share the same trauma, but how they've responded is completely different. Kaylee is very outspoken and at times defiant, but inwardly I believe she feels abandoned. Joanna had a horrific past with multiple assailants, and she's more…uh…timid…or perhaps extremely cautious. She mostly defers to Kaylee, which gets her in more trouble, but she keeps doing it anyway."

"How so?"

"Kaylee commandeered my vehicle without permission and convinced Joanna that everything would turn out all right. They apparently went to browse the local mall, only to return to my anger….disappointment. Hasn't happened again. Recently, Kaylee did ask to use Lou Ann's car and she cautiously agree, and they returned her car on time. I think it was a step forward. Plus, they even bought her a gift, a keychain with the word 'love' in script, attached that she's over the moon about, and that she sorely needed."

"I see that mutual trust among all of you is an evolving process."

"Absolutely."

He wasn't about to mention the ongoing, blooming trust between him and Lou Ann.

"Thank you, Harry. You've been very helpful."

"Don't mention it."

Lou Ann sat facing Dr. Stein.

"I'm glad that we have this time together," Dr. Stein said.

"How can I help you?" Lou Ann asked.

Clearly this wasn't about an insurance issue.

"I want your feedback about how Kaylee and Joanna are adjusting."

"Hmmm. They each came with their own unique response to a horrific past. It's complicated but we…Harry and I…we found that it wasn't Kaylee who we brought back from a Naples hospital, but actually Joanna. We'd already bonded with Joanna, and the bond remains even after she finally confirmed her real identity.

"When we did find Kaylee while she was in Greece, she was reluctant to come with me, because unfortunately we'd been estranged since she was a toddler due to a disagreement between Kaylee's dad…my brother, and me, but through no fault of Kaylee. So we're working on a strained relationship on top of the abuse by her traffickers.

"She ultimately was trafficked to Greece to a billionaire, Demetrios Sakalis, who apparently fell in love with her at first sight and refused to buy her like a slave. They were only able to have a brief love affair before he was killed by one of her traffickers, who was then taken out by Harry, and his FBI colleague.

"My sense is that Kaylee has not yet processed the violence surrounding his death, and she pines for him. I think she's still angry with me on both accounts, but more recently, there have been times when she and I, and she and Joanna, have been bonding. Joanna is more sedate, and I think deep down she believes she doesn't belong to us like Kaylee. But we make sure to remind her by actions and words that we couldn't love her more."

Dr. Stein looked directly into Lou Ann's eyes. Something deep was about to come.

"Do you find that you favor Joanna?"

And there it was.

"I love them both. Kaylee is challenging and "devilish" at times and Joanna is…easier…grateful. Plus, Harry and I have known Joanna longer —since she was masquerading as Kaylee and then herself."

"Do you feel guilty about that?"

"About what?"

"About favoritism."

"I feel guilty that because of a stupid estrangement from my brother, I hadn't seen Kaylee all these years. She never understood, because she was just a baby when it happened. Then she survived the car accident that killed her parents. She's only seventeen, and has suffered tremendous losses that others will never experience. I do love her deeply, and every day I strive to show her that, even when she pushes all my buttons. I'm sorry I've been going on and on."

Whose therapy session is this?

"Having an instant family including teenagers is hard enough. Teenagers with highly emotional pasts are especially taxing. I know you and Harry—your boyfriend, right?"

It was so strange to call Harry her "boyfriend." He wasn't her husband and lover wasn't the right word.

"Yes, Harry is my partner."

Dr. Stein continued, "I was just saying that you and Harry are providing both Kaylee and Joanna with stability and support. Kudos to you both."

"Thank you. That means a lot to both of us."

Lou Ann reached into her purse and took out her LOVE keychain.

"A gift from Kaylee and Joanna."

"That's lovely."

"It absolutely is."

Joanna bounced her eyes from Lou Ann to Harry, who came back into the waiting room together. Her heart thudded with alarm, because either she or Kaylee would be next.

Dr. Stein entered the arena of Joanna's anxiety.

Please don't call me. Please don't call me.

"Joanna," Dr. Stein announced.

Her pleas failed.

Thump-thump. Thump-thump.

She saw Lou Ann's arm extend to her in slow motion.

But she needed to do this alone.

Joanna pressed her feet into the carpet and forced her body to a stand.

"Come this way," Dr. Stein said with a soft-spoken voice.

Thump-thump. Thump-thump.

Joanna put one foot forward and then another and then another, as if she was walking on the moon.

She followed Dr. Stein, praying she wouldn't fall over and knock the doctor off her feet.

But Joanna made it past that door and was still standing.

She entered Dr. Stein's office and sat, as directed, into the cushy tan leather chair. She stared at the calming pale yellow walls.

The rolling wheels of Dr. Stein's chair echoed in Joanna's head. Her head—the one Dr. Stein was about to enter.

She'd never been to a psychiatrist. That wasn't completely true, because she did see a psychiatrist while she was in the hospital at the behest of her neurologist. But Nurse Lynn was there to help her through that. And Lou Ann would be there likewise at the end—hopefully the end.

Dr. Stein leaned back in her chair allowing personal distance between the two of them.

Joanna sighed with relief.

Did she really do that out loud? Would Dr. Stein think she was bored or disrespectful?

But no disapproval followed. Only a pleasant smile.

"It's kind of nerve-wracking being here, isn't it?" Dr. Stein said with a nod.

Joanna returned a quick nod.

She pressed her hands on her knees to keep them from quaking.

"I understand you've lived a bit of everywhere. How are you settling in with Lou Ann at her home? A permanent place, huh?"

"It happened unexpectedly, because I lied about who I was, but you apparently know about my background."

"Mostly, yes. Go on."

"I arrived after Kaylee's parents' funeral in Miami, where I'd been terrified that someone would recognize that I wasn't Kaylee, but that didn't happen. I managed to get a home and a family. I had food to eat that wasn't from a dumpster or stolen. Lou Ann gave me a bedroom. I fell in love with her dog, Isabelle. I've never had a pet. I lived the lie, because I was frightened that Newell would come for me. I even worried about that in the hospital. I was relieved to leave Miami, where all my nightmares live. Lou Ann and Harry are my family now, even after they found out who I really am. And they treat me like family. I wish and pray that it will be forever."

"I'm happy for you."

"I understand you share the bedroom with Kaylee. How's that going?"

"Ummm. Okay. It's gotten better. Kaylee was brought back from Greece, where I was supposed to be sold to a wealthy Greek man.

"Turned out he ended up with Kaylee, and it also turned out well for her. She lost her family and gained a kind man who I think in the end was ashamed he'd worked out an agreement with Newell. I understood her difficulty in coming to live with an aunt she didn't know. We obviously came from very different backgrounds. Funny that the only things we have in common was we are lookalikes who both suffered at the hands of Newell and his gang. Which only Margo survived."

The mention of Margo was like hitting the wrong key on a piano—made one wince.

Joanna's hidden thoughts began to spill out uncontrollably, and surprisingly, easily.

Was this supposed to happen? Are psychiatrists like psychics?

Joanna took a deep breath. More was to come before she left this room.

"How do you find Harry?"

"I like him. He's funny and kind. I liked him better than Lou Ann at first, but now equally."

"Why?"

"Harry didn't try as hard as Lou Ann. He let things happen more spontaneously. He let me be me, or who he thought I was. Lou Ann tried too hard. I think she, umm, felt guilty about her distance from Kaylee. And she thought I was Kaylee. She bought all sorts of things like new clothes and her—I don't know—her actions were a bit stiff, like she was trying to find herself too. Then she settled in and everything's been good. I grew to love her, and yet I betrayed her and Harry. Despite that, they didn't kick me to the curb or call social services or anything like that. I was shocked to be loved and accepted. I never experienced that before. Now I don't ever want to let it…them…go."

"I'm positive you don't have to worry about that."

"I've got plans."

Dr. Stein smiled. "What plans?"

"I want to be a nurse like Nurse Lynn. But I have to finish high school first. I think I can take a test. Then college and nursing school…I mean a nursing degree."

"Those are very solid plans."

"I'm going to do it."

"I'm sure you'll succeed."

Dr. Stein's face turned serious.

Wha? Was nursing not a realistic plan?

"Let's talk about Margo and her upcoming trial. Must be scary to even think about seeing her?"

Joanna leaned back in her chair, as if that would protect her.

Dr. Stein paused.

There wasn't any running away. Like Kaylee convinced her—this wasn't just going to go away. Margo was the last living link to the horrors of their past.

"I beat her with my fists, in Greece. I wanted to kill her. But she lived, and she lives in my head. I need to evict her forever. I don't know how I'll react when I see her in court, or how she'll react when she sees me." Joanna swallowed past her dry mouth. "I decided to go. I need to go."

"I agree. Here's my advice. Breathe deeply. Know that you are the one in control. You don't have to look at her immediately. Count to ten slowly in your head. Then face her. She can't hurt you. Don't let her hurt you. Release her from your conscious mind. What happened to you will be with you forever, but file it way—fence it off. Don't let her and the others rule the rest of your life. You are the queen of your destiny."

Hot years spilled down Joanna's cheeks as she got to her feet. "Can I hug you? Is that wrong?"

"No."

Dr. Stein stood and walked round her desk, where Joanna waited for her.

Dr. Stein embraced her with nonclinical arms.

"You're going to do well. You're going to have a bright future. Know that I'm available to you any time."

"Thank you for helping me."

"You're welcome."

It was so worth it.

The scary part was not so scary after all.

Joanna returned to the waiting room with her face relaxed, and even with a little more than a half-smile.

The doctor must have given her softball questions, because any tough questions would surely have made her flee with deer-in-the-headlight eyes.

Good call on the doctor.

Process of elimination, she was next.

She'd have to entertain the doctor for what? Thirty minutes max?

Then they could all go to lunch. Man, she was starved.

Kaylee stood at attention.

Let's get this thing over with.

"Kaylee?" Dr. Stein inquired.

Well, duh!

"Yes, that's me," she replied cheerfully.

The doctor grinned. "Come with me," she said.

"Okay."

Kaylee almost skipped behind Dr. Stein.

She followed the doctor to her office and plopped into the tan leather chair, wiggling into it until she hit the sweet spot of comfort.

"Nice chair."

"Thank you. I'm glad you find it comfortable."

"Am I your last patient of the day?"

"Yes, you are."

"Great. We'll both be free after this. So what do you want to know? Shoot!"

"I see that you're a no-nonsense type of person."

"Nothing personal but I don't want to waste your time or mine. I imagine I was sent here to talk about Margo's upcoming trial. I'm sure you're up to speed with that."

Dr. Stein arched her well-groomed brows at Kaylee.

"I appreciate your bluntness. I imagine it took a lot of courage to deal with your captors."

"I did what I could to survive. Some of it worked, and some didn't. I wasn't going to die there without a fight."

"You are a fighter, Kaylee."

"I'm sure you'd do the same."

"I'm not sure, but I imagine I would because I wouldn't have anything to lose."

"But your life," Kaylee added.

"Yes."

"I'm ready to move on and give that bitch, Margo, the heave-ho to prison for the rest of her days and nights just like she took my days and nights away from me…and Joanna. And others before us."

Kaylee balled her fists. She hadn't done that since she waited to smack Margo over the head with that dinner tray. Stabbing Otto in the eye with that plastic fork was so easy. She jammed it right in there and his yelps were music to her ears. Otto was done for but Newell and Margo were like zombies from a grave full of stench. Newell now shares a grave with Otto. And Margo? May she live out the rest of her days captured—ha— with no place to go.

Kaylee had automatically gone to the hell she worked so hard to avoid. And it was all the doctor's fault.

Kaylee loosened her fists and grabbed the chair's armrests.

"I understand you and Joanna are scheduled to testify at Margo's trial in Miami in three weeks."

"Yes."

"How do feel about going back to Miami?"

"I lived there all my life. And although I ended up being kidnapped from where my parents lay dead in a car, and went through hell, after that, ironically the Greek man I was sold to was my salvation. Demetrios admitted he made a huge mistake getting involved with Newell and Margo and the deceased Otto. His refusal to pay for me got him killed."

Tears burned Kaylee's eyes.

Damn it. She made me go there!

"He loved me. I loved him." Kaylee clutched the armrests. "Everyone I loved, died."

Dr. Stein plucked a tissue out of the tissue box on her desk, walked around it, and knelt in front of Kaylee.

Every muscle in Kaylee's body revolted, the muscles contracting until she lost complete control of her body.

Kaylee grabbed the tissue and bolted out of the chair, causing Dr. Stein to step back.

And then Kaylee ran out the door.

Except this door had no locks.

The locks were in her head. Permanently.

"Kaylee!" Dr. Stein called.

Kaylee burst into the waiting room and leaped into Harry's arms.

What the hell happened in there?

Harry held Kaylee tight. Every muscle in her body shook so hard that his arms vibrated.

"It's all right. I'm here."

Harry pulled Kaylee's head to his chest.

Dr. Stein stood there apologetically…and leave it to Kaylee to knock a psychiatrist off balance.

"I'm sorry," he said to Dr. Stein.

"It's okay. Don't be. It happens. Some breakthroughs can be traumatic."

"I had no idea this would happen," Lou Ann said.

Damn, he felt sorry for Lou Ann too, since Kaylee instinctively sought comfort with him instead of her. That had to hurt, bad.

Joanna grabbed Lou Ann's hand.

"Is she gonna be okay?"

"It'll probably take time to calm her down," Lou Ann said.

How long would it take to calm Lou Ann?

And here he thought Joanna would be the one who fell apart. He was sure Lou Ann felt the same. They'd prepared for Joanna, and not Kaylee.

It was always "not Kaylee." Kaylee was the warrior. Kaylee pushed upstream when downstream was the better…easier…choice.

Kaylee sniffled in Harry's arms. Her tears soaked his shirt. Good thing he was wearing a cotton one.

Dr. Stein returned with a stack of tissues and handed them to Harry.

"Thanks."

"You're welcome."

Kaylee pushed against Harry's arms, signaling she was ready to disengage from his hug. He let her slowly go, giving her the option of returning to him.

She swallowed audibly a few times and pressed the remaining tears into submission, leaving ruddy cheeks in their wake.

"Are you ready to go?" he asked.

Kaylee nodded.

"Okay. Let's go."

Harry walked Kaylee to the car while Lou Ann came behind with Joanna.

It was only 1:30 pm, and it was going to be a long day, not to mention the dark hours ahead.

23

Kaylee slid into the back seat next to Joanna while Lou Ann got into the passenger seat. Her body sank into the leather.

It was true. She did favor Joanna over her own blood.

She owned leaving Miami and abandoning Kaylee. This was the price to be paid. And it was steep, not matter how much she tried to convince herself that it wasn't.

Mending broken hearts was draining—between Harry and her—between her and Kaylee—between her and her brother, because she could only ask his forgiveness post mortem.

She'd failed at all of it.

Lou Ann stared out the windshield while Harry got in and started the car.

"I'll bring you all home, and I'll order takeout from the diner. I think it's best we eat lunch at home."

"That's fine with me," Joanna said.

Kaylee didn't answer.

"It's a good plan," Lou Ann said.

Kaylee might not eat, but they all needed to stick together. That's all Lou Ann could offer at the moment—basics. They had to start from the beginning and not in the muddled middle. In the novel of life, there were no shortcuts.

24

Kaylee sat on the edge of her bed and twisted her ruby ring. The ring's presence always comforted her. Why did she allow that psychiatrist to trigger her? It was all Joanna's fault. It was her doctor in that hospital that decreed Joanna should follow up with a psychiatrist, and not her. She should've drawn the line and said no. After all, it was she who convinced Joanna to testify at Margo's trial. She was the brave one, not Joanna. Joanna was the weak one.

Joanna apparently was given softball questions. Meanwhile, Stein picked at her head like she was really the problem all along.

Just exactly what did Lou Ann and Harry say about her?

It must have been negative, as usual.

God. She was all alone again. But after the trial was over she'd be free. Deep down, no one really wanted her to stay.

Fine with her.

Joanna entered the bedroom without knocking. Well it was her bedroom initially until Kaylee came along.

"I brought you lunch from the diner—a fat cheeseburgers and the world's the best fries."

Kaylee shrugged. She was hungry but she refused to appear needy.

Joanna sat next to Kaylee and handed her the full plate. The cheesy, thick burger begged her to pick it up and stuff it in her mouth while the fries sizzled.

"I dare you to eat just one."

It would be a waste to refuse it.

Kaylee succumbed to her starving id, grabbed the burger with both hands, and bit into the savory meat, its warm juice dribbling down her chin.

Damn, this is good!

She set down the burger, dabbed her mouth and chin with the napkin, and then tackled a fry. The salty potato flavor burst on her tongue. "Mondo" was an understatement.

"It's good, isn't it?" Joanna asked.

"Mmmm," Kaylee muttered with her mouth still full.

Joanna sat silent while Kaylee emptied her plate.

Kaylee sighed. Her tummy was way full.

Joanna took Kaylee's plate.

"I'll be right back," Joanna said.

But she didn't want Joanna to return. She wanted to be left alone. She'd had enough of people intruding in her life, and that included family.

Nevertheless, Joanna returned as promised.

"Do you want to talk about it?" Joanna asked.

"Not really."

"Okay."

Pesky Joanna remained sitting next to her. Kaylee wanted to say "Get lost," but couldn't do it.

Who's the weak one now?

"Did you not like Dr. Stein?"

"She was okay."

Which was partly true. She wasn't awful or rude to her.

Kaylee looked at Joanna, who was already staring at her.

"She brought up Miami, and Demetrios, and my ring. I lost everything except this ring. I don't want to be reminded of that constantly." Here came the tears again. "I know I should, but I don't fit in here no matter how hard you, Lou Ann, and Harry try. And it hurts."

"It's not true. You've just convinced yourself that it is. I know losing Demetrios remains traumatic. It's not something you'll ever forget. I wish I could fall in love with someone who cares and protects me. But I doubt it'll ever happen to me. I can't help feeling jealous."

"You will find that someone. I had that someone. Now I'm done."

Joanna hugged Kaylee. "No, don't say that."

Kaylee rested her head on Joanna's shoulder. And she called her "pesky."

As much as she tried to push everyone aside, Joanna and she were, for better or for worse, forever linked.

Maybe she'd take Joanna with her to Greece where Joanna, too could find someone to love.

Harry hesitated in the hallway. The sessions at Dr. Stein's office ended so abruptly. He and Lou Ann needed to reassess whether Kaylee would be able to testify at Margo's trial.

"Ironically, he felt that Joanna could. How could they give Kaylee an out without making her feel guilty, or worse, cause her to cast them out of her life. Could he and Lou Ann risk that?

There'd be others to testify at Margo's trial.

Whoever did or did not testify, Margo was going down for a long time.

Harry nodded to himself and proceeded to the thankfully open door.

"Hey," he said.

"Hey," Joanna and Kaylee answered.

He focused on Kaylee.

"How was lunch?"

"It was good, thanks," Kaylee said.

"Fab as always," Joanna said. "Best mondo fries on the planet!"

Harry and Joanna chuckled, and Kaylee even grinned.

"Anybody up for a walk on the beach to burn off those calories?"

Kaylee's eyes lit up, and Joanna popped to her feet.

"Me!" Joanna called.

"That'd be nice," Kaylee said.

"Great."

"We'll get our swimsuits on."

Lou Ann peeked into the bedroom.

"Great idea, Harry. We haven't been to the beach in ages."

Lou Ann looked at Kaylee first, and then Joanna.

Then Harry took Lou Ann's hand.

"Let's hop to it," he whooped.

Are they overdoing it?

But the beach calmed the soul, and they could all use that.

Besides, Lou Ann in a bikini was a golden plus.

25

Lou Ann gathered four beach chairs and dusted them off. She bought two new ones a while back thinking she and Harry would use them, but they never did. She stored them away after the break up. Finally, the chairs were worth it. But she'd let Kaylee and Joanna use the newer ones while she and Harry settled into their sturdy still-good and ones.

She grinned. Their relationship wasn't new and no new chairs were needed. They were building on years of past happiness that was now happily full circle.

Lou Ann grabbed a beach umbrella, and along with the chairs trudged toward Harry's car.

Harry ran up and grabbed the chairs.

"I'll get these and the umbrella too."

She was perfectly able to carry them but it boosted Harry's protective instincts so she let him. What was he going to do? Stand there and watch her?

Harry loaded the chairs and umbrella into the trunk.

"I'll go and get the rest of necessities."

Harry propped his hands on his hips and shot her a smile.

"I'll wait here."

Lou Ann trotted to the front door.

She and Harry had spent many days at the beach when they first started dating and then beyond. As they got more and more busy with their careers, and spent less time with each other, the beach became only a memory.

Harry appeared as thrilled as she to rekindle what was, except now they'd share it with Kaylee and Joanna. It was as if those four beach chairs were meant to be.

Lou Ann hummed while stuffing towels and plenty of sunscreen in a tote.

"We're ready to go," Kaylee said.

Kaylee and Joanna bounced from one foot to another in their flip-flops while wearing cover-ups over their suits.

Letting them pick out their summer wardrobe paid off. And it made her happy because she could do that for them.

Harry's spontaneous suggestion to go to the beach was an obvious hit. It pulled Kaylee out of her anxiety better than a cheeseburger and fries and that was saying a lot.

"Okay, let's head out. Harry's waiting for us."

"What about Isabelle?" Joanna asked.

"Unfortunately, dogs aren't allowed on the beach."

Isabelle turned and walked away, as if she understood that she wasn't allowed to go.

Joanna pouted."Awwww."

"She'll be all right. She has plenty of water and kibble to snack on, and we won't be gone forever."

Joanna caught up with Isabelle while Kaylee petted her.

Lou Ann leaned over and Isabelle gave her a nose bump.

"I promise we'll find you a dog beach next time."

Isabelle trotted into Lou Ann's bedroom.

"I'm sure she'll be comfortable on my bed. Plus, she'll have the whole house to herself."

Something Lou Ann admittedly missed herself, especially after a long shift.

Harry had been gone out of her life for a while, and she had no idea Kaylee and Joanna existed. It was just her and Isabelle. Wow. Glad she didn't confess that to Dr. Stein.

But Harry was back, and Joanna and then Kaylee appeared, and going to the beach with everyone, except of course Isabelle, was worth giving up some solitude. Besides, for the most part, they all backed off when she needed downtime, and she hoped Kaylee and Joanna could too, and that she didn't need to hover over them.

But it was so hard to let go. She wanted to protect them—shield them. They were physically safe, but on the inside it would take a long time for them to feel safe, and maybe even never. She had to understand that she couldn't control that, and most important that Kaylee and Joanna knew it too.

"Hey, we arrived at just the right time," Harry said.

Many of the morning beachgoers had already left making plenty of spaces available at the pay lot close to Clearwater Beach.

"Here's a perfect spot."

Harry pulled the car into the space and everyone climbed out.

Bright-eyed, Joanna inhaled the ocean breeze.

While hitchhiking in Miami—where she ultimately landed from a New Jersey trailer park—and not the retirement or happy kind, but the outskirts kind that belonged in the outskirts—she saw the blue of Biscayne Bay and the lapping shores from the causeway above and most breathtaking of all were the cruises ships all lined up, and ready to go or returning with equally happy passengers.

Joanna considered stowing away and cruising to exotic lands, but never had the courage. Plus it would be hard to get away with it. One day, when she became a nurse, she would vacation properly, like everyone else. She wouldn't have to stand there and watch others board. While on board she would wave to others who, like her before, hadn't the means.

She blinked back to the present.

Harry took out his cell.

"I'll pay for three hours, more if we need it."

"That should be plenty," Lou Ann said.

Harry tapped his phone.

"Done," he said.

"What's done?" Joanna asked.

"You can pay for parking using a cell phone."

Harry showed Joanna the parking app.

"Wow. I didn't know you can do that."

"Yep."

"Cool."

Harry and Lou Ann began to unload the beach booty.

"I'll carry the tote," Kaylee offered.

"I can carry a chair," Joanna said.

"Here you go." Harry handed them each their preferred chore.

Joanna strapped the beach chair on her shoulder like a badge of honor.

Lou Ann strapped on two chairs, one each shoulder, while Harry hoisted the fourth chair and grabbed the umbrella.

"This is why we don't go to the beach that often," he teased.

Often? This was Joanna's initiation to a real beach—not one in the background, or a picture of one.

She was really here, a genuine beach only a short walk away.

Her heart beat in her chest and the hot sun kissed the top of her head.

The beach chair tapped her side while she walked across the road to the beach entrance, her flip- flops smacking her heels.

And then her flip-flops sank into the white sand, and soon gritty granules pushed between her toes and under her feet. Sand! A new discovery. Her flip-flops got heavier while she trudged next to Lou Ann and Kaylee, and then fell farther behind.

Harry approached her. "Are you all right? I can take the chair."

"No. It's fine. It's just so beautiful here."

"I forgot how beautiful it is. This beach is consistently in the nation's top ten."

"I can see why!"

Joanna shuffled along, passing a rainbow of beach umbrellas sticking out of the sand.

Skins glistened and smelled of coconut.

A frisbee whisked in the air between two guys, and kids dug their shovels in the sand to add to a sand castle. Joanna veered to inspect the growing structure.

"Wow!" she said to the boy and girl.

"Wanna help?" the girl asked.

"Maybe later."

"Okay. See ya."

Joanna waved to the kids and hurried to catch up with Harry.

"They're building a castle," she said. "Can we make one?"

Harry paused.

Is that too childish?

Then he looked over at the kids' castle.

"Eh. We can do better."

"Awesome!"

Lou Ann and Kaylee stopped.

"How about this spot over here?" Lou Ann called.

"Perfect, hon!"

Harry and Joanna joined Lou Ann and Kaylee and Harry set down the umbrella.

Joanna looked around. It was the perfect spot. Not too crowded. It was their own oasis!

While Harry set up the umbrella, Lou Ann, Kaylee, and Joanna unfolded the beach chairs.

Kaylee pulled off her cover-up, revealing her bikini while Joanna slowly peeled off hers, revealing a one-piece suit. Kaylee looked awesome in that bikini, but Joanna had picked out a one piece so no one gawked at her body.

Lou Ann pulled two tubes of sunscreen from the tote and and tossed one to Harry.

Joanna slogged through the sand toward Lou Ann. Although she considered Harry the father she never had, and he was never inappropriate with her, but she still couldn't bear to have a man's hand touch her skin, and Harry was a man—a decent man—but it was all about the trigger.

Harry didn't seem offended.

"I could do it myself," Kaylee said to Lou Ann.

Joanna positioned in front of Lou Ann, who rubbed sunscreen on her back and shoulders, then handed it to Joanna so she could apply it to areas well within her reach.

"Thanks."

"No problem."

Kaylee contorted to apply sunscreen on her back and shoulders.

Lou Ann and Harry happily rubbed sunscreen on each other.

"Come on, Joanna. Let's get in the water," Kaylee said.

"Ummm. I'd rather wait here."

"Have it your way."

"Race you to the water," Lou Ann challenged Kaylee.

Kaylee and Lou Ann raced to the water and leaped right in.

Joanna watched them frolic in the waves.

They they disappeared under the water.

"Harry! Harry!"

"What?!"

Just then Kaylee and Lou Ann surfaced.

"Uh…nothing."

Joanna took baby steps toward the water, but stopped well before the water's edge.

Lou Ann and Kaylee beckoned for her to join them.

"The water's great!" Kaylee called.

Even the kids who were building the castle were taking a break in the water.

Families, and even babies, squealed in the water.

"Come on, Joanna. Let's jump in," Harry said.

Joanna curled her toes in the sand.

Kaylee and Lou Ann trudged out of the water.

"What's wrong, Joanna?" Lou Ann asked, concern wrinkling her forehead.

Kaylee waited, and Harry walked up next to her.

Joanna's lips trembled.

"I can't swim."

Lou Ann and Kaylee took Joanna's hands.

"It's okay," Lou Ann said gently.

"We've got you," Kaylee reassured her.

Joanna shook her head.

"No. No."

"Just wet your feet. You can do that. We'll be right there with you. I promise we won't let go of your hands...just your feet," Kaylee reiterated.

"I'll look stupid."

"No. No one's looking," Lou Ann reassured her. "We'll go slow."

Kaylee took one of Joanna's hands and Lou Ann took the other one and they led her toward the water.

They stopped right before the water and stayed there for a while, and then a wave lapped over Joanna's toes.

Her shoulders stiffened.

"Feel the water spill over your toes," Lou Ann said quietly.

The gentle wave covered Joanna's toes and the next one enveloped her ankles.

"Water's nice, isn't it?" Kaylee asked.

"Yes, it is."

Joanna continued farther into the water.

"Don't let go," she pleaded.

"We promise," Lou Ann said, while squeezing Joanna's hand. "You're doing great."

"I'm so embarrassed."

"No one cares. We're just having fun," Kaylee said.

Harry entered the water and positioned himself in front of Lou Ann, Joanna, and Kaylee.

He beckoned her with both hands. "Keep coming, Joanna."

She'd made it to above her knees. Nothing had had happened. The water didn't swallow her up.

"Do you want to go back?" Lou Ann asked.

Joanna shook her head. "No, not yet."

"Okay," Lou Ann said.

Joanna inched farther into the water until the it sloshed around her lower tummy.

"Ooh!"

"Are you okay," Lou Ann asked.

Joanna giggled. "Kind of tickles."

Harry held out his hands.

"Do you trust me?"

"Yeah."

Lou Ann and Kaylee slowly let go of Joanna's hands.

Joanna reached for Harry, and he gradually backed up through the water while holding her.

"Put your arms around my neck. Is it all right if I rest my hands at your waist?"

"Yes."

"I'm going to take you out a little farther. Not deep. Not over your head. I want you to relax and float along with me. I promise not to let you go."

Joanna let her feet float up from the bottom, tightening her grip around Harry's neck.

"I'm sorry."

"You're not hurting me."

"Okay."

She once learned to ride a neighbor's bicycle. Roy was his name. He ran alongside her and then let her go. This was that same feeling.

She and Harry were bobbing when someone called out,."A boat. A boat!"

"They're far out. Trust me, no boat's going to get too close, although we might get waves from it."

Harry tightened his grip.

The waves from the passing boat undulated toward them.

"Oh, no!"

"It's all right."

A wave smacked her face.

Joanna sputtered.

Salty water dripped into her mouth.

Harry lifted her higher.

"That happens."

"It caught me by surprise."

"I'll take you back."

"No, I want to stay in a bit longer. Is that okay?"

"It sure is."

"Here comes another boat," Joanna said. "I'll be ready for this one."

A series of waves came.

Up, down. Up, down.

"See. Now you've got it!"

"It's fun. But don't let me go."

"I won't."

There was a pause. Then Harry asked, "Do you want to touch the bottom?"

"I'm not going to go under?"

"No, you won't."

Joanna lowered her feet and readily touched the sandy bottom.

"I thought it was deeper!"

"You're standing by yourself."

"I am!"

"Ready to get out?"

"Yeah."

"Okay. Water taxi, here!"

Joanna giggled.

She walked almost all the way to the shore and let go of Harry's hand, knowing it would readily be there for her.

Joanna pushed past a few more waves and reached the shore.

She hurried to their umbrella where Lou Ann and Kaylee sat in chairs, waiting for her and Harry.

"I did it!" Joanna squealed.

Lou Ann wrapped a towel around her.

"I saw."

Harry walked up to the umbrella and shook his wet hair.

"Hey, don't I get towel service?"

Lou Ann tossed him a towel. "Here you go."

"Thanks."

The four of them sat in the beach chairs, drying off while watching others splash each other.

Joanna leaned back in her chair.

Her heartbeat settled into a relaxed rhythm, and she closed her eyes, listening to the crash of waves and breathing in the salty air.

Three hours was way too short for her.

Lou Ann, Harry and Kaylee breaths weaved in and out in a sweet symphony.

"Joanna," Harry nudged her. "Castle time?"he asked.

Who said today couldn't get any better!

"Sure."

"Where's my construction crew?"

Lou Ann and Kaylee raised their hands.

This was going to be an awesome castle!

The four settled near the shore to get the maximum damp sand necessary.

Then they went to work.

Joanna dug her hands into the sand bringing up fistfuls.

They patted. They dug. Piled piles upon piles. Packing here. Packing there. Their castle began to take shape, higher and higher.

Finally they stepped back, marveling at their construction.

Theirs was the best castle!

"We need to dig a moat to keep our castle safe from invaders!" Kaylee called.

"I'm on it…with you," Joanna collared back.

She and Kaylee pushed and dug through the sand until they built a deep barrier.

Just then a wave came in and filled the moat, but their castle still stood tall.

Barriers. She and Kaylee knew all about barriers.

Kaylee and Joanna high-fived each other.

"Job well done," Kaylee said.

"Couldn't have done it without you." Then Joanna looked at Lou Ann and Harry. "And without you guys."

They sat around their castle.

Harry's cell phone went off.

"Are we ready to go?" he asked.

Joanna nodded.

"Yeah,' Kaylee said softly.

"We'll come again," Lou Ann said.

"Absolutely," Harry added.

They folded up the beach chairs while Lou Ann filled up the tote, and Harry lowered the umbrella.

Then they packed everything else and headed to the car.

Home.

Joanna looked back at the castle. It wouldn't last forever. It would eventually crumble if someone stomped on it or if the tide got high enough.

But for the day it was their very own castle, and that was enough for her.

26

Lou Ann nudged closer to the shower spray to blast away the sand and sunblock. She'd purposely left the master bathroom door open as an open invitation, and Harry accepted it, and joined her in the shower.

Lou Ann smiled, her lips damp.

"What took you so long?" she teased.

"I mulled it over for about thirty seconds before hopping in."

"I'm glad you joined me."

Although their relationship was beginning to right itself, Harry let her set the pace.

Lou Ann soaped Harry's back.

"Today was good, the calm before the storm."

Everyone, but especially Kaylee and Joanna, had needed to the release —to wander away from the inevitable pain of twenty-four hours from now to enter the courtroom where Margo would sit awaiting her judgement.

Harry turned around and embraced Lou Ann while water sprayed over them.

"I know."

"Are we doing the right thing?" she asked.

"Yes. Bogeymen or women don't go away unless you face them. Margo is also the lock on Joanna and Kaylee's minds and that lock needs to be blown to bits. No way around it for them."

"I was thinking about how Joanna was so scared of the water, unable to swim. I don't want her to drown."

"She has us to hold her hands and keep her afloat."

It was Harry who kept her afloat, and Lou Ann wished it was her. She could've done it, but then Harry was there.

Joanna and Kaylee gravitated to him. He was like the cool parent, and she was the disciplinarian.

They need both, but hell, she'd really like to be the "cool one" for just one day.

Joanna sat on the the edge of her bed holding her Barbie doll while her wet hair cooled the hot skin of her back.

No one was watching her.

Lou Ann and Harry were in their bedroom and Kaylee was still in the shower.

She was all alone with Barbie.

Joanna stroked Barbie's long blond hair and then set the doll next to her.

"I'm scared," she addressed Barbie.

Barbie sat silent but she need not or could not speak.

It was crazy to be talking to a doll, but Barbie represented the innocence Joanna never had, and that she sought it now even though it would never be possible. She couldn't undo everything that had happened to her, from a drug-addicted mother to Newell, Otto, and Margo, who she stupidly once believed was a kind nurse—and the mother she never had—but Margo was a monster only dressed as a daydream.

The spraying sound of the shower stopped.

Kaylee would be out any minute.

Joanna picked up Barbie, kissed her, and then gently tucked her away in a drawer.

Even though Kaylee bought her that doll without judging her, the last thing Joanna wanted was for Kaylee or anyone else to know about her childish need for a doll to hold and to talk to. They'd send her right back to Dr. Stein.

Kaylee stepped out of the shower and wrapped herself in the fluffy white towel.

Margo would give her a threadbare excuse of a towel—long past any claim to being white.

They were hospital towels, Margo her. Lying as usual.

She should have known right away that no hospital would offer those rags to patients.

But she was not a patient.

Kaylee dropped the towel and stared at her naked body in the mirror.

Margo used to gawk at her body, make her turn around in front of her so could examine every inch. She was a commodity to be sold.

Unlike Joanna's horrifying experience, Newell and Margo kept her away from sleazy Otto and his gang of rapists.

But Newell and Margo reveled in humiliating her.

She groomed herself now, but every swipe of a razor pulled her back to when Margo shaved her privates and then made her dress without one bit of remorse.

And it was a razor Margo inadvertently left behind that allowed her to fashion a weapon to slash Otto's face before she plunged that fork in his eye. Too bad she didn't do that to Margo. But that hit on Margo's head with the same platter that she used to bring gruel to her daily, gave her enough of a head start to run for her life. But they still caught her and punished her.

Does Margo remember that? Doubtful because it was no big deal to her. The bitch actually enjoyed it.

Now Kaylee would actually enjoy retelling it.

Kaylee placed the towel in the hamper and strutted out of the bathroom, naked and in control.

"That shower was refreshing," Kaylee said.

"I thought so too," Joanna said while looking away.

Shit! They'd made Joanna ashamed of her body—any woman's body.

Kaylee quickly dressed and then bounced on her bed. "You were really brave today," she said.

"Thanks to you, Lou Ann, and Harry."

"Remember that."

"I will."

Kaylee grabbed her cell and scrolled through her email.

So far no reply from Peter.

She scrolled and scrolled.

And then it hit her.

Peter's prior email had gone to her junk mail.

And there it was!

She'd keep this one secret from Joanna.

Regrettably he was unable to come up with enough money for her trip, but Demetrios's sister, Daphne, arrived and she wanted to meet Kaylee. Daphne's private jet would be available at the same airport. Kaylee just needed to give her a date.

Kaylee emailed Peter back.

16 August.

27

Lou Ann lay back on her and Harry's hotel bed.

After a five-hour trip from Clearwater to Miami, she was exhausted… even though Harry drove the whole way.

They all had a light dinner after their afternoon beach jaunt, and then retired early, knowing they'd have to get an early morning start.

But no one slept. Just a lot of silence. They'd already said everything beforehand, and there wasn't anything more to add.

Besides, constantly reviewing and preparing for tomorrow morning was counterproductive, and would make Joanna and Kaylee even more nervous.

Joanna and Kaylee would just have to go on the stand and take a deep breath, recalling horrors they both wanted to forget.

The most gut-wrenching part for both of them would be coming face-to-face with Margo.

Harry lay quietly next to her.

"I'm not going to be able to sleep, and I fear Kaylee and Joanna won't be able to either."

"Count me in," Harry said. "But our sleeplessness is because you and I have to watch Joanna and Kaylee recount their nightmares. Joanna and Kaylee's sleeplessness is the same sleeplessness they've endured for months, and will recur from time to time for months and years to come. That's the unfortunate reality."

Lou Ann rested her head on Harry's shoulder.

"I had no idea, when I first saw Joanna and thought she was Kaylee, that Joanna had endured torture. I wanted to throw up when we went into that house with Joanna, but I swallowed the sting in the back of my throat because I needed to hold Joanna's hair back while she vomited in the bushes. Then came all the revelations about Kaylee and where she was. And here we are."

"We have Joanna and Kaylee back. Others have not had that chance and are still looking for their children."

"I'm grateful every day and that they're in the next room."

Harry tightened his embrace.

"So am I."

He wanted to jump out of his courtroom seat and throttle that monster until she turned to blue in the face before collapsing in his grip.

It was his running fantasy.

As a Special Agent, he was trained to extract the truth from the sociopaths. It wasn't personal. It was his job and he excelled in it.

But this was gut-punching. Plus, he couldn't use his methods here. He had to sit on his hands.

A jury would decide, and the judge would render a sentence.

Florida still had the death penalty. Although Margo didn't physically kill any girls…that he was aware of…instead she murdered their souls.

Kaylee…well, she killed to survive.

But he'd go to the grave with that secret, because it was justice, pure and simple.

Joanna shivered under the covers and clenched her jaw tight to keep her teeth from chattering.

"Are you awake?" she asked Kaylee.

"Yes."

"What if I freeze up there on the stand?"

"Everyone knows it's going to be hard to talk about unspeakable things. If you can't do it, it's okay. They'll go on. No one will blame you. No one will think less of you."

"I can't look at her. She let Otto bring in all those men in. I bet she made a shitload of money so she could buy expensive clothes, makeup, and haircuts. I bet she's not really blonde."

Kaylee laughed, which made Joanna laugh so hard that she stopped shivering.

"Do you think she and Newell did it?" Joanna asked.

"Nah. I think Newell made her skin crawl—not as much as Otto did, but I bet even Otto's own dick revolted at his touch."

Laughter filled the room.

Joanna rolled to her side and hunched over.

"I'm going to bust a gut!"

"Shit, that was funny!"

"I can't even picture that!"

Joanna's and Kaylee's eyes met.

"Thank you," Joanna said. "I'll just picture Otto's dick calling out SOS when I'm on that stand."

Kaylee smiled. "You do that."

She not only made herself laugh, but most important, she made Joanna laugh.

Joanna would either do fine or run away.

Kaylee bet on "fine."

The dick thing was genius, and it was pretty hilarious, better than picturing everyone naked, including Margo. Yuck!

Margo had this hot and lukewarm personality.

She did give Kaylee an antiquated boom box, and she let her shower in Newell's own shower at the house that last day before leaving for Greece. It satisfied her to invade his personal space. It was definitely a control thing.

And she was okay with makeup application.

Margo knew she had to do a good job, because she was presenting Kaylee to the billionaire Demetrios, and not some other "John."

But in the end, the joke was on them.

Kaylee kissed the ruby ring. Demetrios was physically gone, but not spiritually.

This last one is for you my darling Demetrios. I'll visit you soon.

28

Lou Ann and Harry walked behind Kaylee and Joanna as they entered the Miami-Dade courtroom.

They'd all discussed how to enter, and Harry and Lou Ann agreed to take the position behind Kaylee and Joanna.

The benches were filling fast, courtesy of the intense media surrounding Margo's trial.

Both she and Harry discussed the expected media crowd with Joanna and Kaylee, but the network of reporters piling out of media trucks was bigger than Lou Ann expected.

The media spilled into the courtroom and rushed past them.

Joanna froze.

Lou Ann and Harry had experienced media scrutiny in the past, but Joanna and Kaylee were virgins.

Cameras clicked and whirred. The crowd of observers tumbled in and jockeyed for the best view to see the woman who'd ruined lives to appear.

Lou Ann rested her hand on Joanna's shoulder and leaned to whisper in her ear.

"You can do this. One step at a time. We're here."

Joanna began to move, and tailed just behind Kaylee, who slowed down.

The right three front benches were reserved for those testifying.

"Go," Lou Ann said softly to Joanna. "Follow Kaylee."

Lou Ann and Harry took their seats two rows behind.

The reserved seating for testifying witness filled with girls, some younger than Kaylee and Joanna.

"Look at them all," Lou Ann whispered in Harry's ear.

Harry took her hand and squeezed it.

He, along with Brad Jarret, their shared colleague, who travelled with them to Greece to find Kaylee, were further instrumental, along with a sex trafficking force, in rescuing girls, domestically and internationally. But there were more girls missing, captive, or dead. Far more than those victims who sat crowded hip-to-hip deep in those long courtroom benches.

Lou Ann scanned the families sitting among them.

Sobs echoed. Tears streamed down both women's and men's faces.

Lou Ann sucked back her own emotions.

She glanced at Harry, who sat with shoulders back and his mouth tight.

They had to keep it together for Joanna and Kaylee.

The crowd's murmurs halted.

Margo entered the courtroom, handcuffed, but instead of her orange jumpsuit she was wearing navy blue pants and a white, button-down cotton blouse. Her blonde hair hung limp down her back with dried split ends and badly in need of a haircut.

Lou Ann got a peek at Margo while she sat in the car Newell drove to Demetrios's mansion to confront him. Even though Lou Ann's glance into the car was quick, this woman, although wearing court clothes, appeared haggard and disheveled in comparison.

But the next time she saw Margo's face, it was raw and swollen. Bubbles of blood spewed from her nostrils. Joanna had beat the woman's face with unleashed rage until it was unrecognizable. Had Harry and Brad not pulled Joanna off Margo, Margo wouldn't be sitting in that defendant's chair today.

Margo's team of lawyers—a thirty-ish woman in a matching beige pencil skirt and blazer, and sporting a string of pearls around her white chiffon blouse, and a well-groomed man about ten years her senior, with a strands of gray in his hair and wearing his navy courtroom suit complete with a narrow, pinstriped tie—surrounded her. She looked worn and extra dull in comparison to these public defenders. They needed to look extra suave, because they were the only thing their appointed client had going for her.

A male bailiff followed the black-robed woman judge as they entered the courtroom.

The judge walked to behind her sprawling mahogany desk and stood.

"All rise for the honorable Judge Mavis Reiner," the bailiff announced.

The entire courtroom rose, including Margo, her attorney tag-team, and the woman state prosecutor, whose navy suit matched Margo's attorney's attire and, ironically, Margo's navy pants, that no doubt her woman attorney purchased for her for this solemn occasion.

The judge sat and the rest of the courtroom followed.

Lou Ann spied Kaylee's and Joanna's backs.

There was no turning back now.

The brown- haired girl seated on Kaylee's right offered her hand.

"Hi. I'm Alexis."

Kaylee shook Alexis's hand.

"Kaylee. And this is Joanna next to me."

Joanna leaned over Kaylee and toward Alexis and nodded.

A thin girl with her blonde hair secured in a ponytail, half-raised her hand and announced softly, "I'm Cara."

Cara looked about her and Joanna's age but thinner.

Cara pointed to a bony sprite of a red-haired girl with with her green eyes wide like a cornered animal. She couldn't have been more than ten.

"She says her name is Jill. At least that's what I got out of her earlier," Cara whispered.

Shit!

Tiny Jill stared straight ahead.

"I heard Newell was shot dead in some takedown," Cara said in Kaylee's ear.

"That's what I heard too."

It wasn't a lie. It was, however, not even one tenth of the complete truth.

"You knew Otto, right?" Cara continued.

"I believe we all did."

"I heard he shot himself. Committed suicide. Easy way out for that bastard."

That was true, except after she carved him up and stabbed him in the eye, it was Newell who "pity" shot him. Newell couldn't take Otto's moans anymore, and it was the only way to shut him up.

Kaylee heard the shot and never saw Otto again. It was just like Newell to stage it as a suicide. But that wasn't on Margo completely. She only assisted Newell to get rid of Otto. It would be stupid to leave the house stinking of death rot and attracting attention while they were in Greece. It was a last-minute effort and a decent plan.

"Ladies, please," the judge admonished.

Joanna, Kaylee, Alexis, and Cara joined Jill in silently facing straight forward.

Then Kaylee veered her eyes to the left, and as if receiving some kind of extrasensory cue, Margo turned her head and glared right back at her.

* * *

Joanna shut her eyes and pressed her spine against the bench back, staying out of the line of fire between Kaylee and Margo.

She promised herself to never look at Margo's face again, not even when she was on the stand.

Joanna preferred to see Margo's face only after her fists were done with it.

Would Margo look like she used to look, or had she left Margo's face permanently altered?

She hoped so.

Joanna also hoped that Margo would never mention that beating. Kaylee reassured her Margo was too vain to admit that Joanna bested her. She'd go with that, because Kaylee was always right about things like that.

The woman in the beige suit next to Margo stood to present the opening case in Margo's defense. That woman lawyer was paid to do it. Joanna knew that much.

But how could she do that?

The lawyer lady walked straight over to the jury.

"Margo Marie Weston," the lawyer lady began.

Marie?

Kaylee's and the other girls' eyes went huge.

They all knew her as Margo. Not even a last name much less "Marie." It made her sound like a saint, or at least a normal woman.

Puke!

The lady lawyer went on to describe Margo as "misguided." Poor judgement. Newell as some sort of Svengali. That Margo once worked in the fashion industry as a makeup artist to models, and that she didn't recruit any of those models for trafficking. Then she met Newell.

Joanna and the rest of the girls on that bench leaned forward. None of them knew how Margo got involved with Newell and shockingly, sleazy Otto.

Margo detested him.

From her locked cell in that house of horrors, Joanna recalled yelling and name-calling.

But yet she allowed Otto and his band of cretins to pound away at her. Margo took no pity on her. Even Newell took a turn too. But he jumped off of her lightening-fast and zipped up his pants as if he'd crossed the line. He seemed caring at first. Said he rescued her from a parking lot after she passed out, and brought her to a fake hospital. Margo the "nurse" turned out to be anything but. And then as soon as Joanna caught on, her situation worsened.

Joanna rubbed her sweaty palms against her skirt, and could feel the soles of her feet sweating in her ballet flats. She curled her toes to lift the bottom of her feet up off the inside of her shoes.

Pop.

She sat on the end the bench, nearest the exit. All she had to do was get up and run out of that courtroom.

But then she'd be on the news as the girl who fled.

No.

Breathe in. Breathe out. Just like Lou Ann told me.

Kaylee put her hand just above Joanna's knee.

"Are you okay?" she whispered.

Joanna exhaled past her pursed lips and sucked the breath back in. "Yes."

The lawyer lady finished painting Margo as a victim.

Please, don't call me first. Please.

Why did she end up on the aisle seat?

She'd convinced herself it didn't matter until the the prosecutor lady, who sat on their side of the courtroom and opposite of Margo, called, "Joanna Stemple."

Lou Ann balled her fists.

Oh, shit! Not Joanna.

She pressed her lips tight.

This was bad. Real bad.

Joanna sat there.

Maybe Lou Ann should go up there and rescue her.

She'd do it quietly. Simply walk up quietly and take her hand.

"She can't do it," she whispered to Harry.

Harry pressed his hand against her thigh, making it impossible for her to stand.

"Let go. I have to get her."

But then Joanna stood.

Harry's "insurance policy" hand remained in place, but he let up on the pressure.

"Let her go."

Joanna eased out into the aisle and waited, unsure where to move next.

Ms. Miller, the prosecutor, smiled and beckoned Joanna toward her.

She began to walk toward the woman and suddenly her steps felt extra light, like she was floating.

Elizabeth Miller led her to the stand.

Joanna walked up two wooden steps to the designated deep red leather chair.

She was about to sit when the bailiff gestured for her to remaining standing.

"Please raise your right hand."

Joanna did as he instructed.

"Do you swear to tell the whole truth and nothing but the truth, so help you God?"

"I do," came out of her mouth.

"You may now sit."

The judge smiled down at her.

"Are you all right?"

"Yes ma'am…I mean Judge."

"That's fine. Thank you, Miss Stemple."

Nobody ever called her Miss Stemple. It was nice to be addressed that way, respectful.

She liked and trusted this judge.

"How did you become acquainted with Margo Weston?" Ms. Miller asked.

"Umm. I didn't know her last name. I just knew her as Margo."

"Can you point to the woman you knew as Margo?"

Joanna looked straight into Margo's face. Her nose was indeed a bit crooked. Joanna smiled inwardly. She did a good job on her. Joanna aimed her index finger directly at Margo.

"That's her," Joanna said.

Joanna continued. "I met Dr. Newell first. I was selling flowers on US 1 in Miami—West Kendall—to make some money so I could eat. I'd hitchhiked from New Jersey to Miami because it was too cold in New Jersey, and I could sleep outside if I needed to in Miami. It was supposed to be a dream place. Anyway it was a hot day, and I started to get dizzy, and I having another super-heavy period, so I needed to get out of the traffic. I crossed over to the parking lot of a building. It happened to be the building where Dr. Newell had his office.

"I felt lightheaded, and started seeing stars, so I ducked into the air-conditioned building. In the lobby I saw a bulletin board and among the postings I saw that Dr. Gerald Newell was a gynecologist who specialized in treating women's bleeding, and that if you were uninsured, he could help. I went to the office and got an appointment that day. I thought I was real lucky.

"I was escorted to an exam room and Dr. Newell came in without a nurse. He told me how terrible it was that I was homeless, and that he'd fix my problem for free. He left and came back, alone. He jammed some kind of clamp inside me, and I cramped hard. Then he said he was all done.

"I felt shaky so he escorted me out a back door—not the one I came in —and then my knees went weak. I remember him cradling me, and when I woke up I was in a windowless room.

"Dr. Newell told me it was windowless because it was an intensive care unit.

I had an IV in my arm, and I could barely keep my eyes open. He told me I was having seizures and that the medicine I needed made me sleepy."

"Have you ever had seizures before or ever been in a hospital or on medication for seizures?" Ms. Miller asked.

"No ma'am."

"Please continue."

The judge nodded.

"Then Margo came in and introduced herself as my nurse. She was pleasant at first and even said she was sorry about my condition and that Dr. Newell was the best doctor. I asked why there were locks on the door on the outside and she told it was for my protection because there was a crazy guy wandering around in this hospital."

Kaylee and the other girls nodded in unison.

"But I'd seen hospital rooms on TV, and where I was wasn't anything like that."

"So you realized that you were being held captive in a fake hospital?" the prosecutor asked.

Margo's lawyer lady stood. "Objection," she called. "Leading the witness."

Had she said too much?

Judge Mavis sighed. "Objection sustained. Please continue, Ms. Miller."

The prosecutor paced and then halted in front of Joanna.

"While you were in this room, what was Margo's role? How many times a day did you see her or engage with her?"

"Mmm. There was no calendar, clock, or windows, so I had no idea how long I'd been there, and the only hint I had was when Margo brought me three meals consisting of breakfast-type stuff, a sandwich, and then later some kind of meat. The food appeared runny, but I was so hungry, I basically shoved it in my mouth and swallowed so I wouldn't have to taste it."

"So you saw her about three times a day?"

"Mostly, unless I protested and then I saw her more. She would rant that I was ungrateful." Joanna paused and then added, "I don't think she lived at the house."

"Why do you think that?"

"I heard a car engine, and then it faded, and that happened after she left me a dinner platter. Plus I no longer heard her voice or heard her arguing with Otto, which happened every day."

"Otto Pearson," Elizabeth clarified.

"What did happen was that Otto would unlock the door with a series of keys and rape me, and then he started bringing other men. Then Margo yelled at him, yet but she didn't stop him or take away his keys."

"One day Newell and Margo came into my room and Newell injected something in my IV that made me dizzy. Then Margo and Newell took me to another room that had like an exam table. They put my legs up and apart. I got sick and vomited all over Margo's shoes. She slapped me and yelled for Newell to put me out. I didn't remember anything after that. I woke in that locked room. My belly and privates hurt."

"After that man after man climbed on top of me and you know…"

Joanna paused.

"I remember I started feeling hotter and hotter. I could no longer lift my head, and my vision blurred to the point I could no longer see. Then my body gave out, and my last thought was that I was relieved to be dead."

Oooh's and ahhh's filled the courtroom. Cameras whirred closer.

"I can't remember what happened after that. I eventually woke up in a Naples hospital. Everyone started to call me Kaylee, and said I'd survived a car accident where my parents died.

"None of that made sense, but I was so scared Newell, Otto, and Margo would find out I was alive, so I played along. Then a woman came, Lou Ann Jasinski, Sergeant Jasinski, and I went home with her because she thought I was her niece. But meeting Lou Ann Jasinski was the best thing that happened to me."

"You live with Lou Ann now?"

Joanna searched for Lou Ann's face.

"Yes."

Joanna looked at Kaylee.

"Kaylee Jasinski can tell you more because we're connected for life now"

All of it just came out. Most all of it.

Judge Mavis Reiner looked down at Joanna, her eyes rounded and soft. Then the judge turned her focus to Margo's team. "Any cross examination?"

Joanna's heart banged against her breastbone.

Lady lawyer stood.

"Not at this time, your honor."

Judge Reiner gave Joanna a closed-lip smile with a "good job" look.

"You may step down, Ms. Stemple."

She could go. She could really go. She did it!

Joanna stood and planted her feet.

Please don't trip.

One step, and the next step down. She just needed to make it back to the bench.

Camera lenses spied on her.

Keep walking.

Joanna picked up her pace, and when she'd reached the bench she slid quickly into her place and drew a deep breath. It was over.

Kaylee hugged her.

Cameras clicked louder.

"You did great."

"I can breathe now. I'm done."

Lou Ann clutched Harry's hand.

"She did it."

Harry squeezed her hand back.

Lou Ann's chest rose and fell, and her eyes began to burn, warning of tears.

She sniffed to stem what was inevitably to happen.

The tears spilled over her lower lids and rolled down her cheeks.

Lou Ann grabbed her handbag and stuffed her hand inside, rummaging for a tissue. She clutched a soft wad and pulled it out, and pressed the wad on one cheek and then the other.

She swore she wasn't going to do that.

Harry nudged her.

She glanced at him. And then again—because his eyes glistened.

Harry sneaked his hand low to Lou Ann.

She peeled back the still-dry outer tissues from her wad and placed them in his palm.

Harry squeezed the tissue and then swiped it across his eyelids.

He hid the crumpled tissue in his hand and lowered his fist to hide his pain from others, because that was what Harry did best.

They knew Joanna for months. She lived with them. They knew about her horror, but they hadn't absorbed the full rawness—the sordid details both Harry and she unconsciously pushed away—deciding it was in Joanna's best interest to not dig into the unspeakable torture she endured —but they skirted it—damn well avoided it—but it was painfully and finally clear—it was she and Harry who'd served their best own interests. And it took Joanna's brave testimony to show them that.

"I'd like to call Kaylee Jasinski to the stand," Ms. Miller announced.

Joanna pumped her fist.

"Go get her," she murmured to Kaylee.

Kaylee gave a quick nod and eased her way past Joanna and into the courtroom aisle.

She strode toward the red leather chair and stood with her shoulders pinned back, ready to take the oath.

Kaylee raised her right hand and said, "I do,"when prompted.

She sat in the chair and tossed Margo a narrow-eyed stare.

Margo returned with a smirk.

Ms. Miller walked in front of Kaylee to block the revenge tête-à-tête .

"Ms Jasinski, can you please point to the woman you knew as Margo?"

Kaylee aimed her finger at Margo. If she could, it would've been her middle finger.

Margo slow-blinked and grinned.

Grin all you want, bitch. You're going down.

"Tell us how came to know Margo."

"I was on a college road trip with my parents, and we were heading back to our home in Miami. My dad decided to take the Tamiami Trail instead of Alligator Alley because he thought it would be quicker and less congested. There was a summer downpour, and after my mother and I begged him to pull over, he did. When went he went back on the road once the rain stopped, he lost control on the slick road, and the car swerved off the road and crashed. I was stunned, but my parents were unresponsive."

Kaylee's throat shriveled and the words pasted on her tongue. She smacked her lips.

"It's all right Ms. Jasinski. Take your time," the judge said.

The courtroom grew silent. Even the cameras stopped whirring.

Margo's eyes flickered with delight.

Kaylee cleared her throat.

"I can only imagine how hard it is for you to talk about that day," Ms. Miller said.

But that was not the end of that terrible day. It was only the beginning.

"I struggled to get out of the swamp water because I had twisted my left foot. I'd called 911 before my cell sank into the murky water. I hobbled to the roadside to flag down the ambulance. We were closer to Naples than Miami, so I knew it could take a while for an ambulance to reach us.

"Then a car pulled up, a black one. Newell popped out and identified himself as a doctor. I told him about my parents, and he said he'd go down to help them. He told me to stay in his car since I was soaked and injured. He wrapped me in a towel and put me in the back seat. I wanted to go with Newell but Otto, who was in the driver's seat, ordered me to stay put.

"I knew there was something wrong about him, and I decided to get out anyway. But when I opened the door, Newell was already blocking it. He told me he couldn't help my parents because they were dead and since it would be a long time before the ambulance came, it would be quicker if he took me directly to the hospital. I wanted to stay with my parents and get out. And then I saw a syringe. He and Otto pinned me down, and then came the jab, and I went blank.

"I woke up the room described at the same false hospital with fake Nurse Margo. At first I thought it was an old, decrepit hospital and that my parents were alive and in another hospital. I finally gave up when I realized the truth of my situation.

"Yes, I was taken to the same procedure with the lie that Newell was going to fix my ankle. I woke up cramping and bleeding from having an IUD inserted like what happened to Joanna and probably all the others taken prisoner to be sold. No pregnancies to worry about for him, besides menstrual bleeding to nearly or almost nothing. No down time for "his girls."

The courtroom crowd oohed and some woman yelled, "Oh, my God!"

"Please, I know these brave testimonies are shocking, but please keep silent. If you find these testimonies disturbing, you may quietly leave the courtroom at any time," Judge Reiner announced.

The observers hushed—compelled to hear more.

"I had no concept of time, but I knew when Margo came and went. After the procedure, I didn't see Newell, but I did hear his voice on occasion. I began to exercise and gain strength and plot my escape. I crouched at the door, and when it opened, I hit Margo over the head with a dinner tray, and ran past her, and locked her in the room. I disabled Otto, stabbing him with a plastic fork I had hoarded. I found keys that opened a back kitchen door, and I was out, running barefoot in the woods. I had no idea where I was. I found an empty cabin and nursed my foot where I impaled it on a twig. That slowed me, but I kept going until I heard cars on a road and yelled. Newell and Margo heard me and tracked me down. They forced me down on my belly, and Margo stomped on my fingers, crushing them as revenge.

"Newell dragged me to a car, drugged me, and put me in the trunk. I ended up back at the house, this time bound to the bed as punishment, with the impaled twig which Newell took pleasure ripping it out without any pain medicine or anesthesia. He then ordered Margo to watch over me like a warden in his absence.

"From my cell I heard a gunshot, and then no longer heard Otto moaning. They locked me in, and I heard Newell order Margo to help him dispose of Otto's body. They came back after an hour or so with Newell ranting about how he needed to return to his office and to prepare me to go to Greece, where I was to be sold to a Greek billionaire.

"Eventually she loosened me from the bed, but kept my hands and feet bound. Neither Newell or Margo trusted me.

"She led me to the cell's filthy bathroom shower, but thought better of it and actually then led me to Newell's bathroom shower. He had his own room at the house, and apparently stayed there on occasion. I hadn't seen that part of the house before.

"Newell had nice clothes for me wear to while on Demetrios' private jet where I would meet him when we arrived in Greece."

"When we arrived in Athens Greece, Demetrios was there. I was whisked away with him in his limo. He had a separate limo for Newell , Margo, and Newell's girlfriend, Sophia, because he provided a beautiful property of his where they could stay in luxury. Apparently part of the deal was that Demetrios would sponsor an office for Newell to set up a practice. I learned Newell wasn't going to go back to the US, especially after Otto's body was discovered. He wasn't going to take any chances.

"My parents were dead, and I felt I had no more home left to go to in Miami. Demetrios Sakalis turned out to be the best part of my life. He treated me like a princess, and never touched me with sexual intent. He was sorry he ever dealt with Newell, and he was expecting Joanna. I ultimately admitted who I was. It didn't matter. I loved him. He loved me. He put a hold on the money he forwarded to Newell, which enraged Newell, who drove to Demetrios's mansion and, coward that he was, he shot Demetrios in the back, killing him."

Kaylee twisted the ruby ring on her finger and squeezed her eyes shut. But that was no barrier to the torrent of tears spilling down her cheeks and down her neck.

Ms. Miller grabbed a box of tissues and handed one after the other to Kaylee.

"We're going to take a break," the judge said. "We'll reconvene in thirty minutes."

Lou Ann popped up from her bench seat.

"Come on, Harry. We need to get to Kaylee."

She pushed Harry toward the aisle, nudging him along while they climbed over the couple next to them, who sat wide eyed.

"Excuse, us, " she said to them.

They spilled into the aisle.

Lou Ann sprinted toward Kaylee.

"Kaylee!"

And to think Lou Ann expected Joanna to have a meltdown on the stand.

Harry's breath was right behind her.

Kaylee shook her head and before Lou Ann could reach her, the prosecutor and the judge whisked Kaylee to a side door.

Judge Reiner held up her hand, aiming a warning shot at the media vultures.

"Hold it right there, folks, or I'll ban all of you."

The gaggle of reporters slunk back.

Margo was escorted to the opposite door, craning her neck and managing a victorious, narrow-eyed poke at Kaylee before disappearing behind the door.

"They need to rein in that monster," Lou Ann hissed.

Harry grabbed Lou Ann's hand and pulled her along with him.

"Let's just ride out the pandemonium."

Joanna ran up to Lou Ann and Harry.

"She's not okay."

"We'll wait at that door. The judge and the prosecutor are surely giving her direction.

Yet again, Lou Ann lost out. Kaylee dismissed her *direction*, her gut-wrenching concern for her.

Harry wrapped his arm around Lou Ann's shoulders.

She was tired of being runner-up.

Elizabeth Miller emerged from the mysterious door.

"We need about ten minutes more with Kaylee, and she then wants all of you to come in."

"Kaylee said that?" Lou Ann pressed.

Elizabeth cocked her head.

"Yes, that's what she wants. Have a seat on that bench over there, and I'll come out and get you."

Harry let Lou Ann and Joanna slide in first, and then he sat down.

They breathed in unison.

Lou Ann looked at her watch. She'd time the ten minutes.

Harry massaged his head and raked his hair back.

Joanna sat on Lou Ann's other side and bounced her knees.

"What's taking so long?" Joanna asked.

"It's only been about three minutes," Harry said.

Lou Ann glanced at her watch. "Actually it's been four and half minutes."

"What are they doing back there?" Joanna asked.

"Probably talking about her testimony," Lou Ann replied.

"She was doing okay until she got to the part about Demetrios. Kaylee's still so sensitive about him."

Lou Ann turned to Joanna. "Does Kaylee talk to you about him?"

"Umm. Yeah."

Joanna's and Lou Ann's gazes collided.

Lou Ann was so hell-bent on banishing Demetrios from Kaylee's life and replacing him with her, that she'd stymied not only that important conversation with her, but also set any relationship with the niece she'd missed all those years farther back.

Can love be so instantaneous?

For Kaylee and Demetrios it was, and it was past time for Lou Ann admit it.

The judge leaned against her desk in her chamber while Kaylee and Elizabeth Miller sat in high back chairs facing the desk.

"Kaylee, you were brave on that stand, but I can see that it took a deep toll on you. I sincerely want to know if you want to continue testifying, and it's perfectly fine if you decide to end here. You've described in such heartbreaking detail of what you've endured."

Elizabeth Miller nodded."Your testimony was key."

They're giving her an out, but did she want to take it?

It was her that was sitting here and not Joanna. If she caved, she'd walk away the loser. She could hear Margo clapping—*brava, Kaylee!*

And what about Alexis, Cara, and tiny Jill? She couldn't disappoint them.

Most important, she couldn't disappoint herself.

"No, I can't and won't end here. I want to, need to, finish."

"All right," the judge said.

Elizabeth reached out and patted Kaylee's hand. "I'll be with you all the way."

"Thank you, and thank you, judge."

"And thank you, Ms. Jasinski."

"May I let your family in?" Elizabeth asked.

"Yes."

The door squeaked open.

Lou Ann popped up from her seat, and then Harry and Joanna rose.

Elizabeth walked in. "Kaylee wants to see you."

"We're coming," Lou Ann replied, her words quick and needy.

From the get-go, all she wanted was for her and Kaylee to share what connected them—family. And she promised she wouldn't insist on that bond since it only drove them farther apart. She'd hold back and let Kaylee set the pace.

Lou Ann took a deep breath while following Elizabeth Miller.

She, Harry, and Joanna entered the judge's chamber, where Kaylee was standing, waiting for them.

Lou Ann reached to hug her tight but stopped.

"Kaylee," she said softly. "I didn't know," she gulped.

Kaylee approached her.

"My fault too," she cried.

Lou Ann opened her arms and Kaylee slid into them.

Lou Ann held her, holding back the squeeze she craved to give.

"It was never your fault. I just never knew how to approach you. I didn't want to cause you pain by reliving it all again. I was wrong."

"I needed to hear that. I decided to continue."

"I'm listening. We're all listening."

Lou Ann released Kaylee, who hugged Harry.

"Take care of her," she whispered in his ear.

"I will," he whispered back.

Kaylee slowly pushed out of his arms and hugged Joanna tight.

"I'll finish for you and all of them."

"You should," Joanna replied.

"It's time to go," Elizabeth said.

"You know where we'll be," Lou Ann said.

Kaylee nodded and smiled.

"Absolutely."

"The court may come to order," Judge Reiner announced.

Silence prevailed.

Kaylee retook the stand.

Elizabeth approached.

"So let me recap. Gerald Newell shot Demetrios Sakalis, the man you were staying with?"

"Yes. As I stated earlier, I was originally sold to Demetrios under another identity, Joanna."

Kaylee pointed to Joanna.

"You look strikingly alike," Elizabeth said.

"Yes."

Joanna nodded.

Observers ping-ponged their heads between Kaylee and Joanna while cameras panned between the two.

"Then Special Agent Boxer and Sheriffs Brad Jarrett and Lou Ann Jasinski took Newell down."

Kaylee left out that she took the first shot, killing Newell. Lou Ann, Harry, and Brad kept that secret. It didn't matter, because Newell had everyone's bullet holes in him and he deserved them all.

"And was Margo present at that time?"

"She was waiting in Newell's car."

"Lou Ann Jasinski? Is that your aunt?"

"Yes, she was also a deputy with the Pinellas County Sheriff's department at the time." Kaylee smiled. "She's now a sergeant."

"You seem proud of her."

"I am. And also Harry Boxer. They're together and he's at the house a lot."

"You're living with your aunt now?"

"Yes, that's where I'm staying, along with Joanna." Kaylee paused. "They traced me to Greece—to Ekali specifically, where Demetrios lived —and brought me back to the US—Clearwater instead of Miami, since my parents are dead. Lou Ann is the only relative I have left, and that's how that happened."

"Thank you, Ms. Jasinski."

"Any cross?" the judge inquired.

Margo's male lawyer stood.

"Yes, your honor."

Judge Reiner arched her brows.

Shit! What just happened?

Elizabeth blinked at the surprise attack and then nodded to Kaylee.

"Proceed," the judge said.

The slick-haired man in his Sunday's best navy suit approached.

Why wasn't it lawyer woman? But she knew why. They chose a man to intimidate her. To trigger her.

"Good morning, Ms. Jasinski—Kaylee."

"Good morning," she firmly responded firmly .

"That was a compelling testimony."

"Please move on, Mr. Hart," the judge warned.

"You said Margo brought you food."

"If you can call it that."

"But you weren't starved."

"If I disobeyed, I was denied food as punishment."

"And who decided that?"

"Newell was the boss. Margo mostly did what he said, but she had an independent temper too. She was vengeful at times."

"But you just said Gerald Newell called the shots."

"I also said that not all the time."

"It was Gerald Newell who brought you to this house, right?"

"Yes."

"Margo was not in that car at that roadside."

"That's right. Otto was."

"She commiserated with your situation when you arrived. Your friend had said the same. But like Joanna, you did find Margo empathetic."

"Commiserated? She was an accomplice. She didn't call the police. She lied. She was in on it all the way the whole time! Her fake empathy was short-lived."

"I understand your animus toward her. She has admitted to her part in trafficking. But just like you and all the other girls, Margo fell under Newell's spell."

"She's no victim! That's laughable!"

"Ms. Jasinski, please maintain your composure," Judge Reiner said calmly.

"Given her faults, she was instrumental in placing you with Demetrios Sakalis, a man you professed to have loved."

"She did it for the money because he was extremely wealthy. I was just a vehicle."

"A transaction that you admit that he cancelled."

"Because he had a conscience."

"A conscience? He paid for Joanna…actually you."

Kaylee raised her palms and shrugged. This guy was trying to shave off Margo's sentence. She could be out again—look up her and Joanna. No way! She'd do even more damage. She wasn't going to change. Find the Lord in prison—Ha!

"Mr. Hart, I'm warning you. Demetrios Sakalis is not on trial here."

"I'm pointing out that my client attempted to give Kaylee the best option in the admittedly seedy world of trafficking."

The judge sighed.

"Kaylee. May I call you Kaylee?"

"That is my first name."

"Did Margo at one point give you a "boom box" with her private CDs? Although antiquated, it worked, right?"

"Yes."

"And you were dancer, a ballet dancer to be correct."

"That's right."

"So she provided a much-needed outlet for you."

"I questioned her motive, but it was a momentary pleasure for me…a distraction from an awful existence."

"An existence orchestrated by Gerald Newell."

"Yes, I said he was the head of the operation."

"Did you know that Margo was once a makeup artist for models?"

"Not until today. But I guess she loved it so much that she gave it up to traffic young girls."

Slick lawyer man set her up. His trigger was working. She'd have to be mindful before responding. Not to answer so quickly.

"Dr. Newell bound you. Correct?"

"As punishment after I attempted to run away."

"And I understand he left Margo in charge of you in his absence."

"Yes."

"And one point she loosened your bonds and led you to a shower, and after that she applied antiseptic cream to the abrasions as a result of the bonds."

"Yes. But that was because we were about to leave for Greece, and she didn't want anyone to notice the wounds while we boarded the private jet, and definitely wanted to conceal them from Demetrios. It was all about the presentation—not caring."

"That was your perspective. It wasn't Margo's. She was remorseful about what happened to you. However, she did treat your wounds."

"I already addressed her motive."

"But you confirm that she applied antibiotic cream and bandaged your wounds so they could heal."

"Yes, there was the cream and the bandages. And a long-sleeved blouse to cover it all up so no one would ask questions."

"You then you left for Greece with Newell and Margo, on Demetrios's private jet ."

"Newell's girlfriend, the woman he was dating, was on board too."

Kaylee noticed Sophia sitting in the back of the courtroom with her hands folded in her lap, and their gazes met.

"Newell could be very charming, and he'd charmed Sophia all the way from her tiny Miami apartment to Greece. And then he turned on her. But she just didn't see it until the bullets flew. Newell was dead and the only known link to him was Margo. Sophia shared their revenge, because she was Newell's victim, but in in a very different, very costly way."

"While in that trip in a luxury jet, you slept in the same cabin with Margo, ate in the jet's dining room next to her. She kept you away from Newell."

"Yes, because he was privately busy with Sophia."

Sophia bowed her head.

"And during those meals when Newell and Sophia went away, Margo and you joked about Newell and his machismo. Yes?"

Apparently Margo cherry-picked the times she wasn't a complete bitch to Kaylee.

Margo grinned.

"Yes."

"Did Margo ever encourage either Newell, or Otto, or other men to sexually assault you?"

"Newell wasn't interested because he apparently was infatuated with Sophia, and Margo hid the keys to my cell from Otto."

"So she was protective."

"No. Because neither Margo nor Newell wanted a repeat of what happened to Joanna. They needed me alive and, in the end *well* enough to turn me over to Demetrios."

"So Margo treated your wounds, ate and slept near you to keep you from further harm, and she even applied makeup in a professional way, which you yourself were very happy with."

Cherry pick! Cherry pick! Cherry pick! Damn her!

"Minor self-serving deeds."

"Self-serving? Really? Doesn't sound self-serving to me."

Of course. You're her fricken' self-serving lawyer.

Kaylee shook her head. Her testimony was useless, and countered by what Margo must've fed her lawyers.

"That's all, your honor."

Slick lawyer man took his seat next to Margo, who was now grinning.

"You may step down, Ms. Jasinski," Judge Reiner said with an apologetic tone.

Margo's slick lawyer man had done his damndest to discredit her testimony—to twist her words—and Margo was loving every minute of it.

Kaylee had strutted up the two stars to the stand ready to nail Margo. But between Lawyer Man and smirking Margo, her fireworks testimony fizzled to nothing more than a kid's sparkler.

She'd failed them all.

Kaylee descended the steps with a muted thumps.

Margo jumped up and screamed, "She's lying! They're all lying."

The media pounced.

Guards cuffed Margo's hands behind her back and rushed her out the side door with her lawyers right behind them.

The crowd's shock pitched to a roar, and a throng of observers began to flood the aisle.

Now was Kaylee's chance to escape.

She did what she came to do.

It was done.

They wouldn't need her anymore.

Lou Ann and Harry were submerged somewhere in the throng, and she wouldn't get to say goodbye to Joanna.

It was better that way.

Kaylee weaved through the crowd and reached the building's lobby.

She reached for the glass double doors when someone one grabbed her shoulder.

No!

They couldn't keep her here against her will.

Kaylee whipped around to find Sophia.

"I want to thank you," she said.

Kaylee looked past Sophia for Lou Ann and Harry.

She needed to leave right now.

"You don't have to thank me. He fooled you too. I wish you peace. I've got go."

Kaylee bolted out the doors and sprinted through the parking lot, then turned right at the first street. She grabbed her cell and tapped her UBER app, pinning in her location.

Then she traced the UBER on its way.

ETA, five minutes.

29

"Opa-Locka Executive Airport," Kaylee told the UBER driver.

The driver was waved through, and halted his vehicle at the private jet.

"You don't have any baggage," he commented.

"Nope. I don't need any."

Kaylee reached into her purse and paid the driver, including a handsome tip.

She tapped her cell.

"I'm giving you five stars."

"Hey, thanks! Have a great trip, wherever you're going."

"Greece."

"Lucky lady."

"I am."

Kaylee jumped out of the UBER and waved to the driver, who returned with a wave, and then a thumbs-up.

Her stomach flipped at the jet's tail sporting the same blue and white Greek flag with the initials, DS. Was it the same jet that brought her to Demetrios?

Her knees trembled while she walked up the same blue-carpeted steps to the jet's entrance.

A woman in a blue uniform and matching captain's hat greeted her.

"Welcome, Miss Kaylee."

"Uh, thank you. Where's Michael? And, uh, Adam?"

Michael was Demetrios's private captain and Adam, Demetrios's handsome yet totally skeevy nephew was co-pilot during her last trip.

"I am Daphne Sakalis's private captain, Angeliki, and this is my co-pilot, Katerina. It's a pleasure to serve you today. Please, make yourself comfortable. Takeoff will be in about twenty minutes."

"Wow. An all-woman crew and passenger! She couldn't wait to meet Daphne. She had no idea Demetrios had a sister. But everything happened so fast. What she wouldn't give to be with Demetrios *and* his sister.

Kaylee showed Angeliki her passport.

"Thank you."

Captain Angeliki waved Kaylee into the jet.

Kaylee blinked.

The carpet. The anteroom-cabin sofa. The leather seats. All whiter than white. It was if she was in the middle of a blizzard.

With her teal sheet dress and matching flats, she was a peacock in the snow.

Kaylee squinted toward the back of the first cabin.

Ah, nice contrast.

A light oak desk and chair stood at the precipice to what was surely only the end of the cabin, and if Daphne's jet was anything like Demetrios's then this cabin was only a prelude.

Daphne and Demetrios clearly had similar taste in jet decor. But Demetrios's was now going to be Kaylee's own private jet, however, she'd plan to leave it just as he left it, and she'd hire her own staff— perhaps Michael, but not creepy Adam.

Kaylee approached the desk and ran her fingers across its polished top. Then she walked around and sat in the beige leather cushioned chair and reclined it, her hands behind her head.

She was positive this was Daphne's desk.

Kaylee had no idea what Daphne did for a living, but whatever it was, it was important.

Kaylee pulled out the long drawer beneath the desk and located a silver laptop. She slid it on the desktop and let her fingertips rest on the keyboard.

Whoa!

Kaylee glanced at her watch.

Uh-oh. Ten more minutes to takeoff.

No time to break into the laptop.

She put the laptop back in its place, jumped out of the desk's chair, not wanting to be caught sneaking around, and hurried across the cloud-soft white carpet, plopped into a leather chair, and buckled her seat belt.

Just in time, because Katerina emerged from the cockpit.

"I see you're ready for takeoff, Miss Kaylee."

"Absolutely."

Captain Angeliki will let you know when you can freely move around the jet. Meanwhile, relax."

How could she not relax while in this buttery chair?

She touched the panel on the right armrest and the window shade automatically lifted.

Margo showed her that little trick while they were on Demetrios's jet.

Margo was *useful* for some things.

Kaylee looked at her watch.

Twenty-two minutes had passed.

"I apologize, Miss Kaylee, but we haven't been cleared for takeoff yet. Busy summer travel. I'm sure we'll be off, shortly," Angeliki announced over the speaker.

Lou Ann pounded her fist on the dashboard.

"I can't believe she took off like that!"

She turned from the passenger seat and glared at Joanna, who sat church-mouse quiet in the back seat.

"You knew about this, didn't you?!"

Joanna shook her head. "No."

"Damn it! She's going back. I can't believe it. I knew I shouldn't have given her the life insurance money. I should've kept it safely away from her until she was mature enough to handle it."

Harry shook his head.

"Kaylee turned eighteen. It's rightfully her money," Harry said.

"What?!"

"Lou Ann, take a deep breath. I'll drive around and maybe we'll find her walking around."

"I don't think so," Joanna ventured.

"Why do you say that?" Harry asked.

"She received an email from Peter, like three weeks ago."

"Peter. Peter," Lou thought out loud. "Peter, Demetrios's Peter, who hid Kaylee under a bush to protect her from Newell that day. He didn't know who I was. He shot me and only grazed my leg, and I fired back at him. I didn't know. Glad I didn't kill him and that he's alive. But he has no right to beg Kaylee to return. Demetrios is gone, and she never belonged there."

"Aunt Lou Ann, ummm, you don't understand her. You said you would try to talk about Demetrios. She's still connected to him. Before he died, Kaylee told me that he told her that all he had was hers now. She inherited his estate."

"Why didn't she tell me?"

"Because you wouldn't have let her go."

Lou Ann clasped her hand over her mouth.

"I know where she is," Harry said. "Opa Locka Executive Airport where private jets take off. She wouldn't be able to fly as readily on a commercial flight."

"Where and when did she get her passport?"

"Same place she got her driver's license. It was in her stuff that I packed away when we were at the house in Miami for the funeral. I'm sorry," Joanna said.

Lou Ann rubbed her forehead to combat the explosion festering in her head.

"It's not your fault, Joanna. Hurry, Harry. We need to stop her."

"I'm going as fast as I can. At least we don't have to fight rush hour traffic."

"Unfortunately, we're going to be delayed for another thirty minutes," Captain Angeliki announced.

Kaylee drummed her fingers on the chair's armrests.

By now Lou Ann and Harry would know she was missing.

They were probably driving around the streets surrounding the courthouse, or at the house in Miami. The estate hadn't been settled yet…at least that's what Lou Ann said. Kaylee didn't trust her. She had to fight for the life insurance money that was rightfully hers. After all, she was eighteen now.

No matter. The house was pennies compared to Demetrios's estate. And it meant nothing to her now that her parents were dead. Lou Ann could have it for all she cared.

She wasn't ever coming back. She'd apply for Greek citizenship. Joanna could come and visit any time. Harry too. And when Lou Ann came to her senses, she could also come. That way she could have both families.

Kaylee sniffled. Also she'd be able to take care of Demetrios's grave.

"We'll be there in fifteen minutes," Harry said.

"What are we going to say to her? How should we handle this?" Lou Ann asked.

She'd tossed back two Ibuprofen and the pain medicine was starting to dull her headache.

With the Kaylee's and Joanna's testimonies complete, they should've been back on the road to Clearwater. Ironically, she was going to rest while Harry drove, because—damn—she had that sheriff's department meeting in the morning.

Even if they got to Kaylee in time, Lou Ann was now a bucketful of nerves, and that bucket was about to overflow.

"Perhaps we could get her to think about it a bit more, not rush away without thinking. Kaylee's bright."

"She is. And impulsive. Like me."

The very thought that she and Kaylee shared those qualities took the rest of her headache away.

Attacking Kaylee wasn't the way to go.

Harry turned into the airport's entrance.

"There's the jet with the Greek flag, and the initials DS."

Could Kaylee have really inherited Demetrios's property, including that luxury jet?

Harry stopped the car but left the engine running.

He ran into the main building and bobbed back in the car five minutes later.

"We have approval to approach the jet."

Harry drove toward the jet, but a man in a neon vest halted him.

Harry rolled down his window.

"I'm sorry, sir I can't allow you to go any farther because the jet's stairs are now closed, and the doors are secure. The jet is ready for takeoff."

The jet reversed and began to pull out onto the runaway.

Lou Ann bowed her head.

"We missed her."

They'd been cleared for takeoff ten minutes early.

Kaylee looked out the window.

"Damn! There was Harry's car. They'd traced her here.

She told Joanna nothing about her plans today.

Harry must've figured it out or questioned Joanna, or both.

Kaylee's heart pumped extra-hard in her chest, forcing her to take deeper breaths. The seatbelt suddenly felt tighter.

She disappointed Harry. Surprised Joanna. But worst of all, she betrayed Lou Ann. There was no way to patch things up with her now.

Lou Ann had to have known that Kaylee wouldn't stay with her forever. And neither would Joanna, bless her. She was going to be a nurse. Maybe meet someone someday. Lou Ann would eventually have to let go of her too.

She had Harry. They needed to, should, work things out. It would be easier for them to do that without her, because yes, she could be a real bitch.

But she'd be better off in Greece, and they'd all be better off without her. It would take some time.

Kaylee watched Harry's car turn from her vantage point in the air. She blew them a kiss.

Goodbye, and I love you.

30

Harry exited the airport.

The firestorm dwindled to a thin smoke.

Harry looked over at Lou Ann.

She sat silent with her head cocked and pressed against the window.

He hadn't heard a peep from Joanna.

They'd been betrayed and it stung.

He'd tried connecting with Kaylee—sparing Lou Ann the emotional exhaustion.

They were all flawed and Kaylee capitalized on that.

But now they were all wounded, and this time there really wasn't a way back.

Kaylee made a choice, and they had to let her go.

Deep hurt oozed from Lou Ann's eyes.

He would take all her pain away if he could, inhale her pained breaths.

Harry shook his head.

Lou Ann was in shock, and he couldn't do anything about it except be present.

Pain was a lonely experience.

Then he gripped the steering wheel.

It was going to be one hell of a long ride home.

How could she have missed that?

She and Kaylee talked all the time.

Kaylee even read the email from Peter to her.

But that's where that stopped.

Kaylee must have had further contact with him.

Joanna rubbed her palm across her forehead.

After everything. All the nightly chats. The shared bed. Kaylee didn't trust her.

And why would she?

She thought Kaylee going back to Greece was a fantasy. Dang! She even encouraged it.

She should've seen that coming when Kaylee got that life insurance money.

She thought Kaylee would put that money aside to go to college, where she should've been in the first place, had she not had the life-changing misfortune to meet Newell.

Joanna had no such plans. Her plan was to survive on the streets.

But both her and Kaylee's plans changed—once again in a life-altering way.

Lou Ann climbed out of Harry's car and into the humid summer dusk.

Harry stood at her open passenger door with his palms raised.

"It's okay, Harry. I got it."

But Joanna slid toward him and he opened her door.

She hugged him and said nothing. She didn't have to say a word.

Harry had his own house key, and Lou Ann needed a moment to herself.

"I'm going next door to fetch Isabelle."

Her neighbor, Suzy, was more than happy to watch over Isabelle and Isabelle really liked her.

Lou Ann trudged down the driveway and onto the sidewalk, her steps on automatic pilot.

She walked up Suzy's porch and rapped on the door.

Suzy opened the door wide.

"Come in," she beckoned.

Suzy hugged Lou Ann, who fought her shoulders stiffening.

Suzy backed away.

"How did everything go?" Suzy asked quietly, apparently afraid of the answer.

And she would be right.

Lou Ann sniffled.

Suzy took Lou Ann's hand. "Oh, no. It must have been so hard on you and the girls. I know you were particularly concerned about Joanna, and Kaylee too."

Suzy's eyes went huge.

"Something's wrong."

"Kaylee took off from the courthouse."

"Give her and Joanna some time to process the whole thing."

"Kaylee didn't just take off. She left for Greece."

"Oh, my God. I'm shocked. I can't begin to imagine how you must feel."

Lou Ann hung her head.

"Suzy, I love you but I can't talk right now."

"I understand."

Isabelle barked and bolted toward Lou Ann, but then the dog skidded to a halt, her doggy nails scraping against the floor.

Lou Ann could never hide from Isabelle.

"Let's go, girl."

Isabelle stood next to Lou Ann.

"Thanks again, Suzy."

"Any time. Call if you need anything. I can pick up groceries. You know, anything."

"I appreciate it, and I'll let you know."

"You look exhausted. Try and get some rest."

"I will. Good night."

"Good night."

Suzy slowly shut her door, but Lou Ann was sure Suzy was watching her from her window.

Suzy was a good neighbor and a better friend.

Isabelle clicked along beside Lou Ann, and she opened the unlocked front door and both walked in.

Joanna hugged Isabelle.

Isabelle gave Harry a slow tail wag.

Then she roamed her doggy eyes.

She was looking for Kaylee, the only missing family member.

"Kaylee's not here, Isabelle," Lou Ann said.

Isabelle went to the front door and lay against it.

"Isabelle," Lou Ann called.

But Isabelle didn't budge.

"Leave her," Harry said. "Let her mourn."

Joanna went up to the dog.

"I know it hurts. I miss her too."

Isabelle tucked her snout under her paws.

Lou Ann wanted to do the same.

Harry turned the water on in the shower and tested it. Warm, but not overly hot, just like Lou Ann liked it.

"I put a towel there for you."

Lou Ann gave him an abbreviated kiss. It was more than he expected.

"Thank you, Harry."

"You're welcome."

He closed the bathroom door on the way out.

Then he headed for Joanna's...and Kaylee's...room.

Joanna lay back on her bed and stared at the ceiling.

She then gazed at Kaylee's empty bed.

Kaylee made her bed before they left for Miami.

Her pink and white polka dot comforter lay empty and unwrinkled.

But Kaylee's purse that Joanna haphazardly tossed in one of the many boxes she packed away as her own booty before leaving Kaylee's Miami house, belonged to Kaylee. She didn't know the contents beforehand.

If she wasn't in such a rush to grab what wasn't hers, including that comforter on Kaylee's bed and that little stuffed white bear siting lonely on it, she wouldn't have that purse and Kaylee wouldn't have her passport and wouldn't be on that jet.

But Kaylee had long ago decided to escape back to Greece. She would've sneaked out and gotten another passport.

Kaylee was a warrior. She mortally wounded Otto, smacked Margo over the head, and ultimately shot Newell.

She ran way then and now.

Except this time she was leaving for Greece as a free woman, and not a captive one.

Please, God. Watch over Kaylee.

Harry peeked into Joanna's and formerly, Kaylee's room.

If she happened to return as the prodigal "daughter", her bed waited for her.

"Hey," he said, allowing Joanna to invite him.

"Hey," she returned softly.

Harry took Joanna's response as an okay to enter further.

Harry walked around Kaylee's bed and sat on the edge of Joanna's bed.

"How are you doing?"

"Okay. It's strange to be here alone. I don't think I'll be able to sleep much."

"Yeah, none of us will."

"I just want today to end, but I had no idea it would end this way. Honest."

"We're all in shock. But we know you had no idea about Kaylee's plans."

"She acted so normal the night before. For Kaylee, that is. We talked about the testimony, and she told me I'd do fine. It's not fair. They left me alone, and they went after Kaylee. I was broken, but Margo's lawyer guy kept at her, trying to break her and make Margo the victim."

Joanna punched her fist into the mattress.

"You should've let me beat her to death."

"You almost did. But that wouldn't solve anything. You'd be arrested and stuck in jail in a foreign country."

Joanna popped up from the bed and bear-hugged Harry.

"Thank you for saving me."

"Get some rest. I'll see you in the morning."

"Can you leave my door open?"

"Sure thing."

Just after Harry left, Isabelle pit-pattered into the bedroom.

Because of her short legs and long back, she wasn't able to jump onto Kaylee's bed. Instead she curled up at the foot of Joanna's bed.

"Good night, Isabelle," Joanna said.

Isabelle looked up at her and then resumed her position.

Joanna wouldn't be alone tonight.

31

Lou Ann rolled over and grabbed her cell.

She'd set it for 6 am to give her plenty of time to get ready and leave for headquarters for the department meeting.

She'd planned to sleep in the car on the way home from Miami so she'd be awake and refreshed for her first departmental meeting, and to get Dan Mathews out of her hair for the rest of the day.

She'd seen 12:01 am, 1:30 am, 2:13 , 3:31 , 4:30, and now 5:30.

Lou Ann turned off the cell alarm and sat on the side of the bed with hunched shoulders. She gave up. Thirty more minutes' sleep would be worthless.

Harry had rolled over so many times that between the two, the bed sheets lay in a crumpled wad at the foot of the bed.

Harry groaned.

"I'm up…again. I'll make breakfast while you dress."

"Not hungry."

"You have to eat. You'll have one hell of a headache if you don't."

"Too late," she grumbled.

"A worse headache," Harry clarified. "At least coffee and some toast."

Lou Ann shrugged and rocked out of bed not bothering about the tangled sheets.

She heard the door close while on the way to the bathroom.

The hell with breakfast. What she needed was ibuprofen. She reached for the medicine cabinet and caught her refection in its mirror.

"Damn."

Angry streaks invaded what used to be the whites of her eyes, and the swelling extending from her her lids to her upper cheeks made her like she'd gone several rounds and lost.

How was she going to show up looking like this?

First she opened the bottle of ibuprofen which took her three tries and swallowed two with a swig of water from a bathroom paper cup. But the pills jabbed her in the back of her throat before landing in her empty stomach.

She put the cap back on the pills on the first try, and then got out a bottle of eyedrops. She tilted her head back and the drops landed in her eyes, while the excess rolled down er cheeks. She blotted it with a hand towel before the drops rolled any farther. She must've squeezed that bottle too hard.

Lou Ann blinked. Her eyes burned, but then they settled into a dull roar. The eyedrops were working, but now she needed to tackle her face.

She'd have to pan her normal minimalist look.

Lou Ann pulled out the bathroom vanity drawer and rummaged through makeup she'd completely forgotten about.

She grabbed the under-eye concealer and smoothed it over the bags under her eyes. She looked in the mirror. It wasn't foolproof, but it was an improvement. Lou Ann smoothed on an extra layer of foundation and patted powder over it to complete the intended disguise. She went light on the blush to distract from the zombie she was.

Lou Ann dressed in her uniform and her gunbelt tipped her sleepy body to the side. She jolted awake and forced herself to straighten.

How was she going to make it through this day?

She had no choice.

While she slept fitfully and struggled to get up and dress, Kaylee had yet to arrive in Greece.

Wasn't that a kicker!

Lou Ann trudged down the hallway in her work boots.

She passed Joanna's and what used to be Kaylee's open bedroom door.

Joanna was a lump under the covers, and she wasn't moving— understandably exhausted.

Fortunately, Harry was still on his leave of absence, and it comforted her to know Joanna wouldn't be alone today.

Isabelle shook her head, rattling her collar.

"Kind girl."

Isabelle stretched and walked toward Lou Ann.

"Ready for breakfast?"

Isabelle blinked her tired eyes.

"Yeah, me neither. But we have to try."

Isabelle walked by Lou Ann's side to the kitchen, where Harry had finished brewing coffee.

"I'm going to get mine to go while you stay here with Harry and Joanna."

Isabelle hesitated, pattered toward her dog bowls, and looked at Harry.

"Let me take care of Lou Ann, and then we can eat."

Isabelle sat.

Harry filled Lou Ann's coffee thermos.

"You sure you don't want to sit?"

"No. I had to spend extra time putting on this face mask, and I don't want to be late."

Harry wrapped two buttered slices of toast stacked facing one another in a napkin.

"Here. At least take this."

"Thanks."

"Promise me you'll grab some lunch."

"Okay."

He kissed her.

"I'll be here all day. Text me when you can."

"Will do."

Lou Ann sipped her coffee and managed to take several bites of the toast while stopped at red lights to douse the ibuprofen's gastric dawdle.

At least her headache was manageable, but dealing with Dan could bring it back.

She pulled her cruiser into the lot and cut the engine.

Traffic was light, and she'd arrived ten minutes early.

Lou Ann looked at her watch.

Kaylee had already arrived in Athens.

Lou Ann rested her forehead against her palm.

Who would pick up her up from the airport? A young woman alone and in a foreign country was vulnerable.

Peter. Peter. Please make it Peter. She repeated to herself. Peter always protected Kaylee. Sadly, she couldn't anymore.

Lou Ann climbed out of her cruiser. If she stayed there any longer, she'd lose it. She needed to keep her mind and her body occupied.

The morning sun poked her in her eyes. She squinted, shielding the burn until she could get inside.

She passed through security, her head down.

"Are you all right, Sergeant? the security officer asked.

"I'm fine. Just a little tired this morning."

Lou Ann hurried to the elevator bank, hoping to catch an empty elevator.

The arriving elevator dinged and as soon as the metal doors parted, she rushed inside and pressed the elevator close button.

She'd managed to have an elevator car to herself.

Lou Ann fixed her gunbelt and sucked in a deep breath.

Please, don't make this too painful, she prayed.

Just as she exited the elevator, Dan walked out of the adjacent elevator at the same time.

Thank God he wasn't in the same elevator car.

"Morning," Dan said in his annoying monotone voice.

"Morning," she replied briefly, and headed for the conference room with his footsteps right behind her.

Dan was her superior, and she should have deferred to him.

Screw him. She was in no mood for decorum.

Lou Ann entered the conference room and went straight for the coffee dispenser. She needed the extra jolt. Then she bypassed the tray of breakfast bagels and sat.

Dan sat across from her.

She wished he'd sit on the same side, as except not next to her. That way she wouldn't have to look at his face.

More ranking deputies filed in and helped themselves to coffee and the assorted bagels.

Lou Ann could feel the chill from Dan's prying eyes while keeping her own downcast toward her coffee cup.

Everyone stood when Glenda and Sheriff Carson entered the room, and conference chairs rustled while they all sat back down.

Lou Ann concentrated on her coffee cup.

Voices garbled and the lights went off for the slide presentation.

Lou Ann eased her hand to her mouth, stifling a yawn.

Sheriff Carson continued the slide presentation on crime stats.

Lou Ann swayed and jolted awake, the dark room lulling her to fall asleep.

Luckily, no one seemed to notice, not even Dan. And he would've gleefully glared at her.

Lou Ann sipped her coffee and struggled to catch up with the sheriff's details, but she'd missed several slides and wouldn't be able to add to the discussion afterward. But she was a newbie, and hopefully her comments wouldn't be necessary or welcome. She was more than happy to be a proverbial fly on the wall.

More babble and arguing followed, and no one seemed to care that she was present. The roll call established that she dutifully attended the mandatory meeting.

As soon as Glenda and Sheriff Carson departed, the room emptied.

Lou Ann pressed passed the others, escaping Dan, only to land next to Glenda.

"Good morning, Lou Ann… Sergeant Jasinski," she said, correcting herself.

"Good morning, Chief Martinez."

Glenda winked. "Baptism by fire. You'll get used to it."

"I'm counting on it."

"Good."

Glenda leaned forward and took a closer look at Lou Ann.

"Are you all right?"

"Yes, I didn't sleep well. First meeting and all," Lou Ann spun the half-truth.

She'd already been granted an extended and more than gracious leave of absence for her previous search for Kaylee. Ironically, Kaylee was right back there, and there was no rescue mission planned or requested. She'd not rehash her private dilemma.

Glenda peeked over Lou Ann's shoulder.

"Have a good and peaceful day."

Dan busted through the crowd.

That's what Glenda meant!

"There you are," he huffed. "What's with you? Don't you *ever* yawn during a meting ever again."

Damn, the bulldog noticed.

"I'm sorry, sir. Restless night. Won't happen again."

"Damn straight it won't."

Lou Ann nodded.

Anything to get rid of him, especially today.

"I'll be in my office."

"I left a list of files requiring your review on your desk."

By 4:30 pm.

Dan always wanted to be out by 4:30 pm.

"Send them to my email by 4:30 pm," he added.

"Yes, sir.

Lou Ann hurried to the stairwell.

Dan always took the cheap elevator trip one floor down to their third floor offices.

Lou Ann beat him and fast-walked to her office and shut the door.

Then she sat down at the only furnishing in her office: a formica desk, an office chair, and a laptop. Which was more than she needed today.

32

Kaylee sat at the luxury jet's dining table, where Katerina joined her. Kaylee inspected the luscious plate of assorted fruit, a puffy omelet, and fresh squeezed orange juice.

Their server was outfitted in a black and white uniform just like the one who served them on Demetrios's jet. But like the pilot and co-pilot, he wasn't the same guy, and the lone guy on this trip.

She'd slept fitfully on a king-sized bed in the jet's private suite, the same kind of bed Newell and Sophia shared on Kaylee's first journey to be turned over to Demetrios.

Michael was the pilot and kind. She couldn't say same about Adam Sakalis, co-pilot and Demetrios's nephew.

He'd leered at her and then when she'd lost her way in Demetrios's massive jet, Adam took great pleasure in steering her straight to Newell's and Sophia's suite where Newell was pumping away on Sophia to her delighted squeals.

It wasn't the same king bed, but the memories of the moment and Newell's bare ass remained seared in her brain .

But she was positive that Sophia never forgot and eventually regretted that moment, shocked at the Newell she didn't know existed.

Did he or could he have loved Sophia?

Yes.

He'd plucked her from being a car wash girl to the fantasy of a Greek vacation. Except he lied. Even though he intended to keep her in Grecian luxury—emphasize on keep, as in control—deep down he was too far gone to change. Perhaps he was a good doctor at one time, but Kaylee could only guess at that, and she doubted Sophia found him any different. He was such a suave talker. But he talked no more.

Kaylee had just finished her breakfast when Captain Angeliki made the announcement that they were about to approach Athens airport and to return to her seat and buckle her seat belt for landing.

Landing! She made it!

The jet bumped and skidded until Angeliki maneuvered it into a smooth ride along the landing strip, slowing it to a stop.

"Welcome to Athens," Angeliki cheered. "You may unbuckle your seat belt."

Kaylee hesitated.

Her heart thrummed in her ears, popping them fully open after the long flight.

She stood, panicked at what she'd done.

Now what?

Angeliki and Katerina emerged from the cockpit.

"Daphne Sakalis is waiting for you at customs and arrivals," Angeliki said.

Daphne Sakalis?

This was her private jet, but Kaylee expected Peter or one of Demetrios's drivers to meet her.

She was going back to Demetrios's, and now her mansion, right?

Kaylee would make that clear to Daphne.

Angeliki and Katerina bid a good bye, both kissing her cheeks, one and then the other.

Kaylee descended down the blue-carpeted stairs in the private jet area.

She crossed over to the same customs and border area as before.

A statuesque woman in a teal suit with a silver-sequined tank peeking out just right from her open jacket, approved Kaylee from the other side of customs. Her high-heeled silver jeweled sandals clacked in a staccato rhythm, and her honey-blonde shoulder-length hair bobbed with every step.

The woman smiled with pink lipstick lips.

Kaylee widened her eyes.

Unbelievable.

The woman had Demetrios's same characteristics. It was like looking at Demetrios, except in a softer tone.

One could not deny that this was Demetrios's sister, Daphne Sakalis.

Daphne opened her arms.

"Kaylee, we finally meet."

Kaylee presented her passport to the customs agent.

He looked at the passport and then back at her.

Newell was in charge of her paperwork before.

Now she was by herself.

Did she not do everything correctly?

Kaylee's palms moistened.

"Miss Jasinski is with me."

"Very well, Madame Sakalis."

The agent gestured Kaylee through.

"Minor issues resolved," Daphne arched her perfectly groomed brows, "the Greek way."

"Welcome, Kaylee," she continued.

The two-kiss greeting again.

"I am Demetrios's sister—older," she clarified.

Wow! One couldn't tell.

Daphne was beauty perfected.

"You have no baggage?" she asked.

"No, my…uh…departure was rather impromptu."

"Ah, spontaneous. My kind of young lady. You remind me of me."

Kaylee grinned. She liked Daphne from the beginning.

She'd been afraid of Demetrios. That he was some rich perverted old man who would lock her away.

But soon found that her fears were completely unfounded.

Exploring Athens with Demetrios that day turned out to be the best day of her life. Meeting Daphne was distant second, and that was saying a lot.

"Demetrios said such wonderful things about you. He was so taken with you."

Kaylee's heart cracked.

"I was in Zurich at the time, and I couldn't get back in time to meet you and attend my brother's funeral. I'll never forgive myself for both absences."

"I wasn't there either."

Lou Ann had hijacked her back to the states.

"We'll have our own ceremony. But enough of this talk. We need to get you settled."

A white limo pulled up.

This was so Daphne.

A muscular young chauffeur popped out of the vehicle and shot Daphne and Kaylee a smile while he opened the back limo door.

Daphne gestured for Kaylee to enter first, just as Demetrios had done.

"Where to?" the thick, black curly-haired and mega-buffed chauffeur asked.

Kaylee's breath hitched while waiting for Daphne.

She hadn't considered going anywhere than her inherited home.
"Demetrios's."

"Very well," the hunky chauffeur announced over the speaker.

Kaylee settled back against the butter-soft leather.

The limo weaved in and out of Athens' congested roads.

Daphne pulled out the backseat bar, but instead of offering her champagne, she poured Kaylee and herself a carbonated seltzers into crystal glasses and with her French manicure, she picked up lemon wedges with shiny, mini tongs and dropped a lemon wedge into their drinks.

She lifted her bubbling glass, and Kaylee did the same.

"Salut!"

"Salut," Kaylee responded.

They clinked their glasses and Kaylee brought the seltzer to her mouth where the bubbles tickled her lips, just like champagne.

"While on your jet I noticed a stunning desk."

Kaylee left off that she'd played around with it.

"Yes, I always work during my necessary travels."

"May I ask you what you do?"

"Sure. I own a fashion company."

Fashion? No wonder that besides being Demetrios's sister, she looked familiar.

Then it hit her. She'd seen Daphne's picture before.

DS? Ds? Dee-Ess! The Greek version of Anna Wintaur!"

"Oh, my God! You're Dee-Ess!"

Daphne chuckled softly. "Yes, that's me."

"I can't believe it!"

What else had Demetrios not been able to tell her before he died?

The limo slowed around a curve. They'd reached Ekali.

"Do you live in Ekali?"

"Part-time. But I spend most of my time on the island of Crete, where Demetrios, my other brother, Kosmos, and I were raised."

Another revelation.

"There are many family details I have to tell you during your stay."

Stay?

33

Joanna kicked the covers from her hot, sweaty body despite the AC running all night. She hid from the empty bed next to her—Kaylee's.

But she couldn't hide from the emptiness of the morning.

She peeked at the foot of Kaylee's bed.

Even Isabelle had left.

Joanna scratched her cheek and grabbed her cell from the nightstand she shared with Kaylee.

Ten a.m.

She googled the time difference between Clearwater or Eastern Standard Time and Greece.

It was 5 pm there.

While she ate breakfast, Kaylee was having dinner.

They were worlds apart. It was bound to happen, but she'd hoped it wouldn't be so soon.

Joanna rocked out of bed and shuffled barefoot to the hallway bathroom.

Kaylee's towel lay in a dry, crumpled wad in the corner.

Humph. She's such a slob.

Joanna picked up the towel and tossed it in the hamper.

Maybe Kaylee was completely different in that mansion.

Nah. She probably had maids to pick up after her.

No maids here.

Joanna rinsed off the heat under the cool shower.

She grabbed a towel and, when done with it, tossed it in the hamper on top of Kaylee's.

She'd do laundry. Run the dishwasher. Dust. Anything to keep busy.

Once dressed, she walked into the kitchen and found Harry sitting at the kitchen table and staring at the wall.

"Uhum."

Harry turned toward her.

"Oh! You're up."

"Yeah, I overslept."

"Breakfast?" Harry asked.

"Um. I can make my own. I'll have cereal."

"I'll get us bowls."

"You haven't eaten?"

"Nope. I brewed coffee for Lou Ann and forced her to eat toast on the way to work."

Joanna opened the fridge and reached for milk.

"How was she this morning?" Joanna asked while her head was still in the fridge so she could hide from the pain on Harry's face.

"Exhausted."

"I guessed that."

Joanna grabbed the milk and closed the refrigerator door.

Harry set the bowls on the table and Joanna brought the carton of milk.

"Cornflakes?" he asked.

"Sounds good."

Joanna and Harry ate in silence except for the flakes crackling in the milk.

"I forgot the orange juice," Harry said.

Joanna pushed back in her chair. "I'll get it."

Harry went back into the cupboard for glasses while Joanna dove back into the fridge.

They sat back down.

Joanna poured the juice.

Breakfast continued.

Joanna stared at Harry's bloodshot eyes.

"I didn't sleep well either," she said.

Harry sighed. "That makes three of us then."

"Four, counting Isabelle."

"Are you thinking about what she's doing now? It's like dinner time there."

Harry pushed back in his chair.

"I hope she's enjoying it."

He gulped the orange juice, picked up his bowl, spoon, and glass and shoved them in the dishwasher.

"I'll run it," she said.

"Okay. I'll be out mowing the lawn."

Harry went through the side kitchen door and into the garage, then shoved the door shut.

Joanna heard clanking behind the door while she loaded the dishwasher.

Kaylee's favorite glass stood in the top rack.

More clanking and then Harry yelled, "Shit!"

Joanna let Harry be while she loaded what remained of their painful breakfast.

She closed the dishwasher door and pressed the start button.

Have a pleasant dinner, Kaylee.

Damn it! He'd stubbed his toe while getting to the lawnmower.

Lou Ann and her boxes.

Actually, most of them were his.

Humph. She didn't throw them all away or leave them on the driveway for him.

They'd come a long way.

Now they used the garage for storage.

One day he'd get rid of his possessions that were no longer relevant. But not today.

Harry wiggled the lawnmower free.

Worst of all, this was his fault. He put it here after he last used it.

He traded his flip-flops for his grass-stained lawn shoes and pressed the garage door opener, maneuvering the mower around his and Lou Ann's cars parked in the drive. Lou Ann had the cruiser—one less vehicle to work around.

The grass didn't need to be cut for another three days, but he had the time off, so he might as well do it now.

Harry yanked the throttle and the mower's engine roared.

He gave it a shove and mowed strip after strip whether it needed it or not.

He shoved harder and harder, but the loud roar of the engine couldn't drown out the noise in his head.

They lost Kaylee among the crowd in the courtroom during Margo's planned outburst and the guards swarming her.

The chaos gave Kaylee the right moment to escape, and Margo handed it to her.

Harry mowed the grass down to the quick, and when he finished he cut the throttle and rolled the mower back into its spot in the garage.

Then he swiped the sweat off his face and flapped his wet tee away from his body..

After trading his lawn shoes for his flip-flops, he closed the garage door and re-entered the kitchen.

"Lawn's done."

34

The limo's dark-tinted windows obstructed Kaylee's view, but the familiar winding roads to Demetrios's mansion pacified her. Plus, she took an instinctive like to Daphne and trusted her.

The limo eased to a stop.

Kaylee started to reach for the door handle but thought better of it.

It wouldn't be becoming for her status as the lady of the estate.

Demetrios would've wanted her to exit with dignity.

The hunky chauffeur opened her door.

Kaylee grinned. He'd be perfect for Joanna.

He held out his hand. "Lady Kaylee."

She'd forgotten how sweet that sounded.

Kaylee stepped out of the limo.

Her heart paused.

The fountains leading to the entrance stood dry in the heat and the flowers surrounding them limp. But the grass remained a manicured green.

She had a lot work to do...or *have* done.

Daphne must've misspoken.

Kaylee wasn't here to stay. She was here permanently. She'd have to make that perfectly, but politely clear.

Peter rushed to greet her.

"Peter!"

She was home!

Vasiliki trailed behind him, wearing her standard black dress and white pinafore, and with her hair still slicked into a tight bun. But that constipated look when Kaylee first arrived as Joanna was gone, and replaced with a pleasant smile. The acerbic woman who Kaylee had begged Demetrios to replace was the same woman who'd wept over

Demetrios's dead body and embraced Kaylee while both shook in each other's arms.

Kaylee waved.

"Vasiliki!"

Vasiliki curtly bowed her head.

"Laydee Kaylee," she called in her thick accent.

She spoke broken English, but words didn't matter, because they understood each other.

Kaylee would enlist Peter and Vasilki, and of course Daphne, to teach her Greek.

She'd not only need to have command of the language for citizenship, but also for her daily conversations at the mansion and beyond.

The buffed chauffeur assisted Daphne out of the limo.

"Madame Daphne, a pleasure to see you. I'll have your room prepared and a plate set for dinner," Peter said in English—for Kaylee's sake.

"That would be wonderful, thank you, Peter," Daphne returned in fluent English.

Daphne, being a renowned global traveler, was surely proficient in numerous languages.

Maybe Daphne would take her along for one of her fashion tours. Dare to dream!

Then Kaylee's starstruck attachment to Daphne skidded to a halt, and the reality of Demetrios's permanent absence smacked her in the chest.

"Miss Kaylee?" Peter prompted her. "No luggage?"

"No. Just me and my purse."

She'd made Peter aware ahead of time of her planned departure on August 16th, the day of her testimony at Margo's trial, and luckily she kept to that date and didn't need to reschedule another secret rendezvous.

"Not a problem. Vasiliki will accompany you to your room. Everything you need is there, just as when you…left," Peter said, his voice trailing off.

"Thank you, Peter."

Vasiliki led her up the familiar staircase to her room while Peter escorted Daphne up the staircase where Demetrios would disappear. Although Kaylee had never gone there, she assumed it was his private wing.

Now that the mansion belonged to her, she'd explore every part of it.

Vasiliki removed a key from her pinafore pocket and unlocked Kaylee's suite.

"No one been here. I open windows and door to balcony."

Kaylee lay on the super-sized, cushy bed where she slept—where she and Demetrios made love—where she lost her virginity. He was large man, but still Demetrios treated her as gently as dove in his palm. It was she who approached him, assured him. He never touched her in that way before she begged him to.

He rued the day he'd contacted Newell. But then they would've never met.

Kaylee buried her face in her hands and wept.

Vasiliki sat at the edge of the massive bed.

"Oh, do not cry. He gone. You here in his place. He be happy."

Kaylee swallowed her tears and nodded.

She was responsible for his death. If he'd never met her, he'd still be alive. and she probably wouldn't.

"I leave now. Clothes in closet. Towels in bathroom. I come back to you for deener."

"Okay." Kaylee managed a smile. "I'll wait for you."

"Very good."

Vasiliki bowed her head and left the room.

The breeze from the windows and the open balcony door swished away the bit of stale air.

Vasilki must've locked it after Kaylee left.

Kaylee slid to the end of the boat of a bed and pushed off of it.

She walked onto the balcony and braced her arms across the railing, taking a deep breath, relishing fragrances of the various blossoms in the garden below.

Instead of the nightmare of Peter hiding her in the garden that day, and then the gunshots, she'd chosen the same garden as her refuge. Demetrios loved walking in that garden. She'd go there tomorrow and pick fresh flowers, making bouquets for her room and Demetrios's room when she found it in the other wing, and then she and Daphne would place the largest bunch at his grave.

Kaylee had promised herself that she'd return to Demetrios.

"I'm here, Demetrios," she called.

A hint of petal-soft rose scent wafted to the balcony.

"I love you too."

Kaylee leaned her head forward, under the double golden shower heads, letting the warm water massage her neck, shoulders, and down her back.

She'd worn the same court clothes for more than a day, and she felt like a schoolgirl next to Daphne, who met her in polished perfection.

She had no extra clothes to change into while on Daphne's jet and decided to skip a shower then, because putting stale clothes back on afterward was useless and gross.

Kaylee pushed the code on the waterproof panel mounted on the marble tiled shower wall and cut the shower heads off.

That first night she giggled while playing with every code: hot, warm, cool, one shower head, two shower heads, rain forest, jet.

She'd tried them all that first time.

And she remembered all the settings like she'd never left, until Lou Ann whisked her away.

But she won. She'd returned to Greece on her terms, and Lou Ann had no more claim on her.

She was eighteen now, and could do as she pleased, and she pleased to live in her own home, Demetrios's mansion.

Kaylee stepped out of the shower, which was the size of her and Joanna's bedroom.

Joanna would get a kick out of that.

When things settled, she'd invite Joanna to visit. Then she could introduce her to the thick-haired, hunky chauffeur.

She'd invite Lou Ann, but she was sure Lou Ann would decline. Harry might convince her, but Kaylee doubted that he'd succeed.

Kaylee stepped into the equally massive vanity, picked up the white fluffy towel Vasiliki set out for her, and patted her skin dry.

So much better.

She stood naked in front of the mirror that spanned one entire wall and stared at her womanly body. Now that Margo was to be tucked away, rotting in prison, Kaylee was finally free to accept her body instead of slink away from Margo's leers.

Kaylee blow-dried and styled her hair while smiling at her reflection.

Looking good!

She spread the rose-scented lotion over her body in honor of Demetrios since roses were his favorite flower and scent.

Makeup was next.

Kaylee opened the vanity drawers where the top-notch cosmetic still remained. And why wouldn't they since her suite had been under lock and key during her absence?

They all knew she was returning. Her family, less Demetrios.

Kaylee picked up a tissue and dabbed at the tears swimming in her eyes before they could spill down her cheeks.

She couldn't show up for dinner with her face ruddy from crying.

Kaylee artfully covered up her pain, reminiscent of Margo's makeup artistry, her only redeeming quality. If Margo had only stuck to that profession, then she wouldn't be locked up. Choices.

What to wear for her first dinner since her return?

Choices.

Kaylee grinned as she remembered the rose printed sundress she wore during their day trip to Athens.

No rose print dress tonight.

Kaylee walked into the colossal closet.

Rows and rows of every type of shoe took up one side, while gowns, dresses, skirts, pants and blouses hung military-straight on silk hangers, organized by category, and including scads of apparel Kaylee had never worn much less seen.

She could spend days in there, but now she needed to choose something.

Pants.

She rummaged through the racks of pants, arranged by color, and went for white. She picked the third pair to be quick about it—classic, white linen.

Next, a matching top.

She selected a silk tank. It slid right off the hanger.

Kaylee turned around in the closet and a pair of gold sandals caught her eye.

Mine!

Belts of all styles, thicknesses, and color hung for her perusal in the handbag and belt section.

She skipped the handbags and chose a gold belt to match the sandals.

Then she opened the white chest of drawers and selected a white silk bra and matching panties.

Done!

She quickly dressed in the closet and checked herself over in, yes, the tallest gold-framed chevalier mirror probably in the whole world. Demetrios was never a tardy man, and Daphne, a fashion workaholic, would surely share the timely mannerism.

Kaylee would strive to be the same.

A Grecian goddess stared back.

She waved at her reflection and strode out of the wardrobe wonderland.

Vasiliki stood waiting for her ninja-style as only Vasiliki could.

As always, she didn't hear the woman sneak in.

Vasiliki grinned, a sight Kaylee still needed to get used to.

The woman nodded with approval.

"I take you to deener now, Ladee Kaylee."

Kaylee followed Vasiliki out of the bedroom suite and down the separate, and familiar staircase that led to the dining room.

There were more secret passages for her to discover…later.

Daphne stood next to the table that could easily sit twenty-five, but tonight it was just the two of them.

Daphne wore a diaphanous, pale pink chiffon dress with matching lipstick. Since she was Demetrios's older sister, she had to be at least fifty or something, yet she looked thirty at the most. How much of her youthful look was because of powerful genes, and how much was paid for, wasn't clear. But what was unmistakable was Daphne was beyond gorgeous. And she had to be in her business.

Daphne clapped.

"That ensemble is completely stunning!"

"Thank you."

"It's one my best designs."

Kaylee brought her hands to her chest.

"You designed this?"

"Yes, I designed everything in your closet."

Kaylee's jaw dropped.

Another revelation. How many more?

She took a break and paused and decided to take the grateful route.

"It feels as awesome as it looks."

"Good. It was intended to." Daphne gestured toward the chair next to hers. "Please sit. I hate to shout across a table. This way we can just talk."

Kaylee waited for Daphne to sit and then she sat.

A fine china plate inscribed with the initials, DS, sat in front of her, flanked by a plethora of silverware.

Demetrios would chuckle at the formal place settings and admit he only needed a fork, knife, and spoon, and a good glass of wine to keep him happy and fed. He'd wave away the extraneous silverware and the butler would remove them and then Kaylee would request that hers to be taken away as well.

But Daphne clearly enjoyed the rows of utensils on each side of her plate.

Kaylee said nothing.

Use outside to inside. Or was it inside to outside? No. Definitely, mmm maybe, outside to inside. She decided to do whatever Daphne did.

The butler wheeled his silver cart into the dining room.

"George!"

The butler nodded smiled.

George, Demetrios's favorite butler, was still here, and pray the same kitchen staff, including the chef.

George lifted the huge, silver dome by its handle revealing a platter of sliced roast beef, rosemary potatoes, and….

Kaylee stifled a grimace.

Green beans. Yuck! No matter how exotically prepared they were still green beans, even when disguised.

Kaylee couldn't pinpoint the day she declared war on green beans, but the smell, color, and that stringy texture made her look away…until tonight. Balking at Lou Ann's or her own mother's cooking was expected. How to handle the situation?

She could push them under her meat, hiding the green suckers, but that would be childish.

Better childish, she decided rather than retching at the dinner table.

Or better yet, to make sure green beans would be banished from any further menu, she'd confess she was allergic to the vegetable.

Yes, a polite way out.

George filled Daphne's plate and then began to lay out thick slices of roast beef, and the perfectly-angled cut potatoes on her plate.

Kaylee gently raised her hand before George could land the green beans on her plate.

"Allergic," she softly said, politely declining the beans.

"I'll notify the chef. What shall he prepare for you?"

"Nothing for tonight. This meal is more than satisfying for me. Jet lag, you know."

That last addition was true.

George filled their wine glasses.

"Beaujolais 2019," George announced.

"Excellent," Daphne lauded the vintage.

Daphne raised her glass, and Kaylee followed the prompt.

"Here's to your arrival."

Daphne and Kaylee clinked their crystal glasses.

Kaylee sipped her wine.

It trailed velvet-smooth down her throat and settled warm in her stomach.

She set the wine glass down and started on her entree, silverware from the outside in.

She was right the first time about proper utensil selection.

Between her outfit, surprisingly one of Daphne's designs, the wine, and a gastronomic entree— less green beans—her return was even better than she'd dreamed.

George stood tall while a young uniformed man collected their plates and then he disappeared into the kitchen.

Kaylee hadn't seen him before, but perhaps he'd come on board in her absence.

The young man was swift and polite.

She'd keep him on.

George clapped, and porcelain bowls of mixed greens arrived.

She'd forgotten that salad was served after the entree, European style, but she missed the kitchen table fun at home…or used to be…sort of.

Kaylee grinned, remembering how Joanna struggled with those chopsticks. But she got the hang of it.

"What are you thinking about?" Daphne asked. "Must be nice."

"It was. But tonight is nicer."

"I'm glad."

Daphne lifted her salad fork.

"How do you find your quarters?"

Kaylee needed to adjust to Daphne's terms.

She meant her bedroom.

"I find it just as I had left it."

"Let me know if you need anything else."

"I don't believe I'd ever need anything more…" Kaylee paused. "There actually is something."

Daphne arched her penciled eyebrows.

"Fresh flowers from the garden. I'm going there tomorrow morning to collect not only a fresh bouquet for my room, but also for Demetrios's quarters, and the largest to place at his grave. Can you take me to him tomorrow?"

Daphne's vivid blues clouded.

Kaylee raised her hands and waved them like she was erasing what she just said. "I'm so sorry. I didn't intend to upset you."

"You didn't. We'll go to the garden together. I'll have Peter unlock Demetrios's quarters, and then we'll go to Demetrios's place of rest."

"Thank you."

After the salad came the four-layer slices of chocolate cake.

Kaylee patted her belly. Her formfitting pants were clearly not expandable.

Dinner was beyond excellent.

"I'm happy I wore this dress. It has some give." She smiled at Kaylee. "You may loosened that belt if you wish."

Kaylee loosened the belt two notches.

"Thank God."

Daphne and Kaylee giggled, just like she used to with Shawna, her high school best friend in Miami. And then with Joanna. She even had a spontaneous laugh with Lou Ann, and she couldn't begin to list the times she had a belly-buster with Harry.

"Let's retire to the parlor, shall we?" Daphne said.

"That's fine."

She followed Daphne into the roomful of beige upholstered sofas and peppered with matching wingback chairs.

Daphne pointed to an oversized loveseat.

They sat, and Kaylee turned toward Daphne.

"I know you arrived here impromptu. Peter let me know that the two of you agreed on a date of your departure. That being said, I'm sure you've left your family shocked and hurt. I'm more than happy you arrived safely, and that I was able to greet you."

"And I'm more than grateful," Kaylee said.

Daphne raised her finger. "But I beg you to call them and tell them you're safe and that you are sorry that things evolved as they have. Put their hearts and fears, and perhaps disappointment, to a rest. You may use my phone, but they won't recognize my number. Nevertheless, you're welcome to use it. Alternatively, you can use your cell phone and I'll pay for the international charges. You choose."

"I have money. I'll pay. It's something I need to do."

Daphne stood. "I'll give you privacy."

"Thank you."

Daphne left the room.

She was right.

Kaylee needed to make the call.

It would be easier to call Joanna because she'd not hang up on her.

And Harry shouldn't be her first call either.

Kaylee took a deep breath and called Lou Ann.

Lou Ann hid behind her closed office door, and so far she'd made it to lunchtime without Dan busting in.

He must be ill, she mused.

She saved her files and then shut down her laptop.

She managed to power through three files, with a pileup waiting for her review.

Dan would have to deal with whatever she sent to him, and yes, at 4:30 pm.

He'd probably have one foot out the door as usual, so she had that going for her.

She'd wait until he drove away and then she'd do the same—Joanna and Harry paramount on her mind.

Kaylee had made her decision not to be part of the family.

Lou Ann shoved Kaylee to the back of her brain, knowing full well Kaylee would spring right back the way she always did.

And they were all just starting to meld as a family.

Was Kaylee acting, waiting out her time until she could run away?

But run away to what?

Demetrios was dead.

She shouldn't have taken Kaylee away. That was her first mistake among many.

But at the time Lou Ann still thought of Demetrios as Kaylee's buyer, and she made the decision to ferry Kaylee out of the whole bloody mess.

She'd denied Kaylee the opportunity to grieve, and to process the catastrophe.

Ironically, Lou Ann had run away too after her father committed suicide. He couldn't live without the woman he spent fifty years with, the woman he lay beside every night, the woman whose opinion he sought in every matter.

Their love was as spontaneous as that of Kaylee's and Demetrios's.

She was wrong.

Lou Ann propped her elbow on her desk and rested her chin in her palm.

Huge regret.

Her forehead throbbed.

The toast and coffee, including two more cups after she drank the thermos-full Harry sent her off with, hadn't gotten her far. They only gave her a colossal headache. No more coffee. Only water and a sandwich from the cafeteria.

She pushed back her chair, stood, and was about to head out the door when her cell rang.

Probably Harry. She did promise to call or text him back at the first chance she had.

She picked up cell and fumbled, nearly dropping it.

It wasn't Harry.

The call was from Greece.

"Kaylee?"she muttered past her pasty mouth.

"Aunt Lou Ann? Are you there?"

Was she about to hang up?

She had every right to.

Kaylee clutched her cell and pressed it to her ear so she could hear better.

"I'm right here. Are you okay?"

"Yes. I made the flight okay traveling on Daphne's jet, Demetrios's sister," she quickly clarified.

"Oh, I didn't meet her. She wasn't there that day, was she?"

"No. And I hadn't met her either before earlier today. She met me at the airport and drove me to Ekali...to Demetrios's mansion. She's very nice. Gracious. Ummm."

Kaylee hadn't told Lou Ann about the will.

She needed to tell her so Lou Ann and Joanna and Harry would understand her secrecy and her actions.

"I'm here because before Demetrios died, he told me everything he had was now mine. I've inherited his estate."

Silence.

"Lou Ann?"

"Wha...Wha...What?"

Lou Ann's mind circled, speeding faster and faster.

She grasped for a thought—any brass ring her brain could catch.

This was absolutely insane.

Lou Ann sucked in the longest breath she ever held, and then blew out an equally long exhale.

"Kaylee."

"I'm here. I know you're shocked. I couldn't tell you until now. I'm going to stay here permanently."

Lou Ann's headache exploded to DEFCON 2.

"Do you have the will?"

"No. But it's here somewhere. I trust Demetrios. He wouldn't have lied to me. I'm positive he locked it in his office. I'll have to get the key since I only got here today."

Lou Ann's heart squeezed in her chest.

She'd known Demetrios a short time. He was a billionaire. He had a sister and God knows how many other relatives.

A pain beyond words awaited Kaylee.

But she'd have to be careful with Kaylee's heart.

There was no way to begin to convince her this wasn't true.

She desperately wanted to speak with Daphne.

But she'd wait, because if she probed Kaylee, she risked having Kaylee shut her out.

"I'm relieved you called. I was so worried about you."

"I saw Harry's car from the jet."

"Yes, we were there. We just missed you."

"I know. I'm sorry things happened this way but now you understand…I hope."

She'd never understand this.

And when Kaylee's fantasy world imploded, Lou Ann would be on a plane to Greece to pick up the pieces of Kaylee's shattered life.

Right now, though, she had to resist the urge to fetch Kaylee because it ended badly last time.

Lou Ann wouldn't repeat the mistake.

"Can you call me again? I miss you. We all do. Even Isabelle. We'd all like to share your adventure."

Lou Ann needed to leave the open invitation in Kaylee's court.

"I'll do that. Send everyone one my love."

"I promise. I love you, Kaylee, and I want you to be happy."

The words stabbed Lou Ann in the heart.

"I honestly love you too. Goodbye for now."

Kaylee ended the call.

Lou Ann hugged her cell against her heart to soak up every word said between them.

Kaylee stared at the cell in her hand.

She did as Daphne recommended.

Daphne was right.

It was a relief to speak with Lou Ann, who surprisingly didn't go ballistic over the call.

Their conversation began awkwardly, but in the end Lou Ann wasn't planning to hop on a plane.

Kaylee now hoped that, instead of Lou Ann bursting onto the property, she'd arrive as a much-welcome guest.

Lou Ann, Harry and Joanna could visit all they wanted. Isabelle too! She'd make them comfortable with their own rooms. They could take a dip in the pool, rest under a cabana. Endless food and drinks.

Chef would whip up anything they wanted.

She'd take them to Athens's Syntagma Square where she and Demetrios spent an unforgettable afternoon.

Meanwhile, perhaps she could busy herself by joining Daphne in her fashion empire—a Sakalis family business.

Daphne entered the parlor.

"How did it go? Did you speak with your aunt?"

"Yes, and I have to thank you, because our conversation went smoothly. Well, it was awkward at first. She didn't expect me to call. But

I'm glad I did. I'm going to call her frequently. And I think…I hope… she'll visit along with her boyfriend, Harry, who really should be her husband, because like Demetrios and I, they belong together. And then there's Joanna, who looks spookily like me even though we're not related. And Isabelle, the cutest dachshund you could ever meet."

Daphne blinked.

"I'm sorry to have babbled on."

"No, that's quite all right. You have quite a family."

"They'll always be my family, but my place is here with my other family. You know…Peter, Vasiliki, you!" Kaylee rubbed the corner of her eye. "And I'll be close to Demetrios too, and take care of his grave, where I'll be one day."

"Kaylee, you're young. You're eighteen. So much life ahead of you."

"And I'll do it all here."

"Kaylee, I'm tired, and I'm sure you are too, with the long flight and the stress of your sudden departure. Let's get some sleep. There's a lot to be done tomorrow."

Kaylee stood. "I agree. I'll see you tomorrow at breakfast?"

"See you then. Goodnight, Kaylee."

"Goodnight, Daphne."

Kaylee watched Daphne climb the mysterious stairwell.

She couldn't wait to enter Demetrios's quarters, which Daphne referred to as bedroom suites.

Daphne would take her to Demetrios tomorrow.

Kaylee yawned.

It had been a long and complicated day.

Kaylee climbed the stairwell to her third floor suite and, when she entered it, she saw Vasilki had already turned down the bed.

What would she do without Vasiliki? Demetrios was right about her.

Too bad they never had a chance to discuss Daphne. She came as a complete surprise. His nephew, Adam, was the only relative of Demterios's that she'd met. He was copilot on Demetrios's jet, and he'd given her the shivers. He was mischievous and, she could tell, mean-spirited. He wasn't anything like Daphne or Demetrios. Daphne had mentioned that Demetrios's and Daphne's younger brother was Adam's father. What about his mother? Where did she fit into this family?

Demetrios, if only you could tell me.

Daphne would surely fill her in.

Kaylee had forever to find out about family secrets.

Kaylee stretched and was about to change into nightclothes when a knock came at the door.

Daphne?

"Kaylee, it's Peter. May I enter?"

"Sure," she called. "I'll be right there."

She walked to the bedroom door and opened it.

Peter's face looked very serious. They only time she hadn't seen him smiling was when he hid her in the garden, and when he and Lou Ann traded friendly fire. And his absolute pallor when he learned Demetrios was murdered.

"Come in, Peter. What's wrong?"

Peter entered and closed the door.

Then he tilted his head toward the door, surely listening for footsteps. But why?

"I have to warn you," he said, barely above a whisper.

"Warn me about what?"

"About Daphne."

Kaylee's mind stuttered.

"Uh, what about her?"

"Be careful around her. Don't trust her. She can seem very kind, but she's a shrewd businesswoman. She has her eyes on you and this property. Demetrios originally willed this house and the surrounding property to be divided between her, their younger brother Kosmos, and his nephew Adam since Demetrios had no children. But he changed the will when he met you. You should know that."

"Do you know where Demetrios hid that will?"

"He moved it out of his office to somewhere in his quarters before Newell showed up that day. He told me about that will that before he gave me the pistol and instructed me to hide you in the garden. He knew what was coming."

Kaylee covered her mouth and gasped.

"No, no! Don't be frightened. But be on guard. George, Vasiliki, and I will watch over you. It's okay. I had to tell you. I've to go. Otherwise, suspicious eyes, you know."

Peter left, leaving Kaylee to a sleepless night.

<h1 style="text-align:center">35</h1>

Lou Ann picked up her cell and called Harry.

He answered on the first ring.

"Hey, how're you doing? I've been thinking about you. You need to get lunch."

"Harry, stop."

He paused.

She could hear him breathing on the other end.

"Kaylee called," she blurted.

More breathing.

"What'd she say?"

"That she'd made it safely to Greece on Daphne's jet."

"Daphne?"

"Apparently Demetrios's sister."

"I saw no sister."

"Neither did I, and neither did Kaylee, because until today, she had no idea the woman existed."

"So she's staying with a complete stranger."

"She says that Daphne has been more than gracious to her, and I believe her."

"Well, that's great. The woman sends her jet to fetch Kaylee."

"Kaylee has been in contact with Peter, and he would never have put her in danger. Admittedly, she did this of her own free will. Nobody kidnapped her."

They both went silent at those spine-crushing words.

"I'm sorry. I didn't mean that," Lou Ann softly said.

"I know you didn't. We're both frightened for her."

"But there's more," Lou Ann added. "Kaylee said that Demetrios willed his entire estate to her. She's under the impression that she's inherited the whole shebang."

"That's preposterous!"

"I know. But we can't lose contact with her. We have to pretend to be interested in her daily life. She'll cut us off if we flinch."

Harry sighed "You're right."

"She sends you and Joanna her love."

"That makes it all better," he snarked.

"As harrowing as this, we have to be smart about it. Prep Joanna so she's fully informed by the time Kaylee eventually calls her. And I bet that she will."

"Maybe Joanna knows more than she admits."

"Find out. I'll be home around 5:30. Text me or call if anything explosive happens before I get home."

"Explosive, huh?"

"Yeah."

"My recommendation stands. Get lunch before they have to peel you off the floor."

"Okay."

She'd just hung up when someone started pounding on her door.

"Hey, you still in there?" Dan yelled. "I gotta give you mandatory lunchtime. Get a move on. I don't want to take the fall. You hear me?"

"Yes, I hear you. I'm coming."

Another appetite ruined.

Harry paced in the kitchen.

"Unbelievable," he muttered.

"What's unbelievable?" Joanna asked.

Harry rubbed his head.

"Kaylee called Lou Ann."

"She did?!"

"Yeah. I just got off the phone with Lou Ann."

He widened his eyes at Joanna.

"Has Kaylee called or texted you?"

"No."

"Have a seat. I'll make us sandwiches."

Joanna pulled out a kitchen chair.

"Seems we just had breakfast."

Harry chuckled. "We did. But since then we've done some morning chores."

And the morning still lagged.

"I told Lou Ann to eat lunch too."

"How was she after Kaylee called?"

"Shocked, but relieved to hear that she's okay."

"She's at the mansion?"

Harry looked her.

"Where else?"

"I wanted to make sure she isn't roaming aimlessly around Athens."

"I thought she'd been in contact Peter."

"Only once that I heard. Kaylee didn't tell me anything more about Peter or her plans. I thought she'd go back in the future. She wanted to. She did say it would be fun if I went with her, but I said I couldn't. We didn't talk about Greece again. We were focused on our testimony at Margo's trial, and then amid all the chaos, she slipped away. I lost her in the crowd."

"We all did."

"I see the way you're looking at me. I didn't believe she'd actually leave. I thought she was all talk and that leaving wasn't really possible. I mean, how would she manage it? But knowing Kaylee, I gotta hand it to her. She found a way."

"Who knows what cogs turn in her head?"

Damn. Kaylee would make one hell of a Special Agent.

And as a Special Agent, he knew when someone was lying. Joanna was telling the truth.

"Turkey and Swiss?" he asked.

"Sounds good."

36

Kaylee and Daphne strolled past olive trees.

Dewdrops dotting flower petals glistened in the morning sun.

Kaylee gazed up at the cloudless blue sky. It was the perfect day to collect for bouquets.

She swung her basket ready to fill it to the brim with the assorted fragrant flowers all at her fingertips and bursting with every color. So many to choose from! A flower shop from the heavens!

Kaylee meandered through the path that Demetrios and she walked those few precious mornings.

The meditative stroll set the tone for his endless phone calls, pending contracts and victorious deals.

She *was* one of those deals.

But how that all changed.

She didn't hold it against him.

What unfolded between them altered their lives forever, cut horribly short.

The afternoons and evenings they spent together were worth a lifetime.

Kaylee grabbed her garden shears and snapped away.

Roses. Oleanders. Hyacinths. Freesias. Blood red peonies. Velvet lilies. And there it was—Passion Flower. All overfilling her basket. All overfilling her lungs.

"Look, Daphne!"

Kaylee turned with her flower-filled basket.

Daphne wasn't behind her. She wasn't even in sight.

"Daphne!" she called. "Daphne!"

Kaylee stood alone in the garden, flowers and bushes surrounding her. Had she wandered off too far? She was so busy collecting flowers that she must have lost her way.

She looked around in every direction in the garden maze.

Which way out?

Kaylee craned her neck. Not an olive tree in sight.

The bushes rustled.

Her heart pounded in her ears.

She dropped her basket.

Flowers lay strewn on the dirt path.

Peter stepped out of the bushes.

"I did not mean to frighten you."

"You startled me."

Peter squatted and began to pick up the flowers.

Kaylee bent over and grabbed a handful.

Whew. The flowers survived the fall.

"I'm so sorry," Peter said.

"What are you doing here? Where's Daphne? Have you seen her?"

"Watching over you."

"Peter, stop."

"No one is after me. I wandered off, that's all."

"You're like some Ninja." Kaylee laughed. "Have you been taking lessons from Vasiliki?"

"She told me where you and Daphne went into the garden."

"Did you see Daphne?"

"I came through the back way into the garden." Peter pointed. "Go straight, then right and immediate left. She sit on bench."

"Why are you so spooked by her?"

"Spooked?"

"Afraid."

"I am not afraid of Daphne. My concern is for you. She no tell you about the attorney meeting?"

"No. What meeting"

"Tomorrow. You ask her. You make sure you be there. I get driver for you."

"I don't need a driver. If this is the case, I'll go with Daphne."

"If you go with her, you have to come back with her."

"Of course."

Peter shook his head.

"Guard your heart. We guard you."

"Kaylee!" Daphne called.

"I'm over here," Kaylee called. "I'm coming your way."

Kaylee turned around.

Peter was gone.

Daphne met Kaylee along the same path Peter had directed.

"I was so focused on picking flowers that I must have wandered off."

"I know this garden well so, I knew you where you were. But I grew tired and over warm." Daphne chuckled and winked. "Consequence of my age," she joked. "And jet lag too."

"I'd go with the just jet lag since you're fit, beautifully so, and it's already hot out here. I'm done and ready to go inside."

Daphne peeked into Kaylee's basket.

"You definitely are done. What a beautiful array."

"I could've cut more, but they wouldn't have fit in my basket."

"Paul is an excellent gardener."

"I'll have to keep him on."

"Hmmm. Yes. Let's be on our way."

Kaylee searched for Peter while following Daphne, but there was no sign of him.

Did Daphne see him?

Better not ask until Peter and Vasilki could explain their unfounded suspicions. From what she'd gathered, Daphne and Demetrios were close, at least according to Daphne. Plus Peter wouldn't have let Daphne greet her at the airport and leave with her if he didn't trust her. And allow her to stay at the mansion. Kaylee hadn't detected any friction between them. Daphne had a room there—in the same wing as Demetrios's. She probably lived here at least part-time, except when Kaylee had been present.

Had she moved in after Kaylee left?

Did Daphne know Peter and she were communicating? That she was coming back? She didn't seem surprised or annoyed at the airport. Her greeting was more than cordial. Kaylee took to Daphne right away, and she considered the feelings mutual. So what was all the grumbling about? More family secrets?

But what Peter and Vasiliki didn't take into account was that Kaylee specialized in family secrets.

Kaylee set her basket on the counter next to the kitchen sink.

Vasiliki clapped. "So beautiful!"

Kaylee grinned. "There are, aren't they? Can you please fetch me two large vases and large…" Kaylee gestured with her arms wide…clear wrap…for Demetrios."

"I get it right away."

She and Vasiliki arranged a composite of cut flowers in two bouquets —one for her room, and one for Demetrios's chamber. Then Vasiliki rolled out a sheet of clear cellophane and made a perfectly even cut.

"Good?" she asked.

"Very good!" Kaylee answered.

"We put for Demetrios's place cool paper towels. You carry one vase. I carry other."

"Peter!" Vasiliki called.

Peter arrived in the kitchen.

"We go to Laydee Kaylee chambers first and then we will cross to Master Demetrios's. You have key, right?"

"I have key. Where is Daphne?"

"She said she was tired and hot and she was going to rest in her room before we go to the cemetery in Athens this afternoon."

Peter glanced at Vasilki and then acknowledged Kaylee.

"Very well. We go."

Peter held out his hand.

"I take flowers from you. I will carry vase."

"No, I have it, because this one is for Demetrios's room."

"Okay."

Vasiliki and Kaylee followed Peter to her room.

Peter opened the door and Vasiliki set Kaylee's bouquet on her dresser.

"Look beautiful. Smell even better. You sleep good tonight."

Kaylee rested her hand on Vasiliki's shoulder.

"We did well."

"Oh, no. You picked well."

Kaylee clutched her vase of flowers.

"Take me to his room."

Peter gestured for Kaylee and Vasliki to step out of Kaylee's suite, closed her door, and then locked it.

"You keep key."

She'd never locked her door before. She was all by herself on the third floor wing.

Peter led them along a hallway and unlocked another door.

Kaylee had seen the door before, but thought it was a linen closet. It was just a simple door.

But when Peter unlocked and opened it, Kaylee widened her eyes.

This was no closet.

A steep, winding stairwell lay beyond it.

That's how Demetrios had entered her room, and that's how he must've left.

"Be careful. Watch your step," Peter warned.

"Yes, it steep," Vasiliki added.

No wonder Demetrios was in such good shape.

Going down required little effort, other than balance. But climbing up would wind anyone—anyone other than Demetrios.

But his muscles weren't able to repel a bullet to the back—a coward's bullet.

Kaylee hugged the vase and grabbed onto the railing to steady herself.

"Are you all right, Lady Kaylee?"

"Just got a little dizzy."

"I'll take the flowers. We stop."

"No. I need to hold onto them. I'm okay now. Let's keep going."

They exited on the second floor through a door exactly like the one where they entered.

Plain door.

Kaylee's heart hammered. She hadn't ventured to this wing.

Her feet sank into the thick blue carpeting.

So typical of Demetrios!

They stopped at a set of white double doors with gold trim and gold handles.

"This is Demetrios's suite."

What exquisite furnishings lay behind those doors?

Peter removed two keys and unlocked both doors.

Kaylee clutched Demetrios's vase full of flowers with his favorite, roses, in the center of the arrangement and along the periphery, with white lilies and pink and white oleanders.

He would've loved it.

Peter opened the doors to a shockingly plain bedroom that was smaller than hers. A bright blue bedspread stood in contrast to pale blue walls where oil paintings hung. An icon of Jesus hung angled in one corner and beneath it another gold-framed one.

"That is Saint Demetrios, his patron saint."

"I had no idea. When Demetrios brought me from the airport, he pointed to blue-domed churches. He said they were Orthodox Churches, and that he would take me there one day. Of course we never had time to go."

"He, of course, was baptized Greek Orthodox, and his funeral was in an Athens's cathedral."

"I missed it all."

All because of Lou Ann!

"You had no choice," Peter said.

"Yes, I did. I could've fought. I always fight. But all Lou Ann saw was massive damage. So much blood. And then Joanna beat Margo. It was too much for her. She took me away. Away from Demetrios. She was my guardian—my ruler."

"No, don't say that. She is a good woman."

"She shot you, Peter."

"I deserved it, because I make mistake and shoot her first. Think she is Margo. She make mistake. I make mistake. We both live. Although you here, you honor her. She love you. We love you."

Kaylee rubbed her runny nose.

"No, you don't cry now," Peter said. "You be strong."

Vasiki nodded. "That's right."

Kaylee set the bouquet on Demetrios's nightstand, which was as large as an ordinary table, like the kitchen table at home…um…Lou Ann's home.

She turned toward Peter.

"Where would he hide the addended will?"

"Away from Daphne," Vasiliki said.

That was clear. How awkward was it going to be at Demetrios's attorney's office in Athens when Daphne finds out she's no longer the beneficiary, and neither are Adam and his father. Kaylee would face them all tomorrow. But she would be gracious and not leave them completely empty-handed. That was only fair.

Peter pointed to Demetrios's closet.

"Why would he put it there?"

"Where would Demetrios hide what? Daphne asked while standing at the open doorway.

"The bills for the mansion," Pete quickly replied .

"I've talked with the family accountant. We're not behind on any payments. Plus, Demetrios's golden life insurance policy should cover any debts and then some."

"Okay, that is good news," Peter said.

"That's a lovely bouquet you've arranged for him, Kaylee. He would be very happy."

"I know he's happy. I can feel it in my bones."

"So let's go make him happier by visiting him."

Daphne waited in the doorway for them to leave.

What timing.

Daphne watched them leave the room, and saw Peter lock Demetrios's bedroom doors.

While Daphne strode ahead, Peter slipped the keys to the secret entrance and to Demetrios's room into Kaylee's sundress pocket.

37

Kaylee took the keys to the passageway and to Demetrios's room out of her sundress pocket and stashed them under her mattress.

"Are you ready to go to Demetrios's resting place in Athens?" Daphne called from behind Kaylee's closed door.

"Yes. I'll be right out."

She smoothed her hair in the mirror and straightened her rose print sundress, the same one she wore the last time she and Demetrios were in Athens. But she was here and he was already there, forever.

Kaylee drew a long inhale, held it, and then exhaled the pent-up anxiety about seeing him tucked away.

What would his forever place look like?

Kaylee pressed her lips tight.

Would it look like her parents' grave?

Everyone who mattered deep in her heart was dead.

Kaylee pressed her fingers against the corners of her eyes, stemming the fallout.

She promised herself she'd remain composed in Daphne's presence and would request private time with Demetrios without Daphne. And she would let Daphne do the same.

Daphne and she knew him differently.

I'm coming, Demetrios. Kaylee grinned. *I'll be the one in the rose print dress,* she joked.

The levity cleared her sorrow.

Kaylee opened her door.

"I'm ready. Let's go."

Daphne and Kaylee descended the marble staircase to the grand foyer —the same foyer where Newell's bullet-ridden body lay under the smashed chandelier. The foyer since had been completely renovated, physically wiping out the stain of that day. But nothing could ever wipe out the stain out of her memory. That day was imprinted not only in her brain, but also in her heart.

They stood outside the steps of the mansion until the hunky chauffeur drove Daphne's white limo around the circular drive to the front.

He got out and escorted Kaylee and Daphne into the same back seat where they both sat after Kaylee arrived in Greece, for the second and permanent time.

Vasiliki brought out the cellophane-wrapped bouquet Kaylee had arranged to place at Demetrios's grave and handed it to her.

"I place extra wet paper around it to make last longer."

Kaylee rested the flowers on her lap.

"Thank you, Vasilki."

"You most welcome. You give him…how you say…my regards."

Kaylee leaned over and smiled.

"I will."

"To Athens's Garden Cemetery."

"Very well, Madame Sakalis."

There would've been two Madame Sakalis's had Demetrios lived.

But she'd make sure she lived in his place, overseeing it the way he clearly wanted her to do.

Daphne wore the same turquoise outfit from the airport, clashing with Kaylee's rose sundress.

They sat silent until they exited Ekali.

"You did a good job arranging the flowers from that basketful."

"Thank you. It came rather effortlessly. They're all his favorite flowers." Kaylee looked down at her dress. "Especially the roses."

"Prickly things, though."

"It's a matter of how you handle them to avoid pricking yourself. Or anyone else," she added.

Daphne seemed to be concentrating on traffic out the window and didn't offer a response.

Perhaps silence was Daphne's way of grieving, whereas Kaylee wanted to talk about Demetrios. What Daphne saw was an end, Kaylee saw was just the beginning.

"We've encountered a bit of traffic," the hunky chauffeur announced.

The limo's swerves and the honking horns already told Kaylee they'd arrived in Athens.

After stopping and starting, the limo merged to the right and slowed.

He must've taken an exit, so the cemetery shouldn't be far.

Then the limo halted.

"We've arrived, Madame and Lady."

The chauffeur exited the vehicle.

Kaylee's heart pounded in her ears and the wrapped bouquet quivered on her lap.

"A moment, please," Kaylee said.

Daphne and her chauffeur waited.

Kaylee nodded. It was time to visit Demetrios.

"All right. I'm ready."

Kaylee squinted while she stepped out of the cool dim and into the hot sun. She blinked to adjust her eyes to find a cloudless blue sky and a stone pathway with planted flowers flanking it. Monuments popped up from manicured green. Which one belonged to Demetrios?

"Come this way," Daphne said.

Kaylee followed Daphne along the stone path where at the end loomed a black and white marble mausoleum complete with Grecian white marble columns.

SAKALIS was carved in front of the mausoleum in gold letters, signaling that this was probably a family crypt especially since it was much too large for a single person, and Demetrios's name was not there.

Kaylee clutched the flowers to her chest while Daphne unlocked the door to the ornate expansive funerary structure.

The heavy door creaked open.

Demetrios's granite-covered tomb lay in the far center of the mausoleum, his full name engraved on the front, Demetrios Stephanos Sakalis, no date of birth and, thank God, no date of death. He was as he was in life.

Instead of his resting place being mired in darkness, two golden light stands burned an incandescent, soft white.

Kaylee roamed her eyes up to the arch-shaped stained glass window, where a rainbow of light shone through onto Demetrios's tomb.

Demetrios would never rest in complete darkness at night, and during the day, full color bathed his final home.

Daphne sat the on the mausoleum's marble bench.

A quarry somewhere must have been completely emptied.

Kaylee approached and sat next to Daphne while still clutching the flowers. She wanted to be alone with Demetrios—to lay her flowers on his tomb—to talk to him—to ask him for advice.

She couldn't and wouldn't do that in front of Daphne.

"Do you want to go first? Because I'll be awhile?" Kaylee said.

"All right."

Daphne and Kaylee stood and Kaylee began to walk toward the door. "You don't need to leave."

Kaylee stopped, returned to the bench, and sat.

Now it would be that much more awkward, if perhaps even insulting, to ask that Daphne leave her alone with Demetrios.

But she had to do it. Just as she would have to stand up for herself at that attorney's office. She would be even more outnumbered tomorrow. She might as well start today in continued congeniality with Daphne.

Daphne crossed herself and mumbled something in Greek at Demetrios's tomb.

Kaylee's parents had dragged her to a Protestant church more Sundays than not. She had no connection there other than to gossip with Shawna, who likewise was a "captive"attendee. God, to her, was a secondary character.

Where was He when she needed Him most?

She prayed that her parents survived that car crash. She prayed she'd be freed from captivity. She prayed Newell wouldn't find her when she escaped. She prayed for her own death at times. She prayed Otto, Margo, and Newell would die. She prayed her Aunt Lou Ann might find her.

Some of those prayers were answered. Ultimately she gained her freedom. Newell and Otto died. Margo might die in prison. And Lou Ann did find her, but not in the way she hoped.

And she was finally free with Demetrios. Ironic justice. Their time has been sweet and tragically cut short.

Kaylee clung to the bouquet. Meeting him was the only thing that had gone right in her life.

Daphne returned.

"Go ahead," she said.

"May I be alone with him?" she asked, politely.

Daphne paused.

Kaylee didn't want to complicate matters, especially with tomorrow's meeting lingering over her. She needed Daphne to be on her side, despite Peter's suspicious warning about her.

It didn't make sense.

Both she and Daphne loved Demetrios, and both wanted to fulfill his wishes.

They had that in common.

"All right. I'll be outside. Take whatever time you need."

Kaylee slowly approached Demetrios's tomb, her knees suddenly weak.

"I brought these for you. I know how much you loved roses, so I put them in the center. The garden is still well-tended."

Kaylee lay over the tomb, the granite cool to her skin.

"My heart has this massive hole. I came too late. But I saw to you justice. I'm not here to rehash what happened because I can't change it. I wish to God I could—we could—go back in time and change everything." Kaylee's tears dripped onto Demetrios's tomb. "But that's not possible."

"But our memories are sealed forever. No one or nothing can ever remove them. We are forever together, and that's what helps me move forward."

"I want you to know that I will care for the house and everyone there. I know you'd find it amusing that Vasiliki and I are as close as I am to Peter. You were right about her. She misses you greatly and she wanted me to tell you that. You never told me about Daphne."

A light flickered.

"She's been gracious. I flew to you on her jet. Not as exquisite as yours of course."

Two flickers.

Kaylee lifted her head and glanced at the door. It was closed, and Daphne hadn't returned.

She whispered, just in case, "Peter warned me about Daphne, and he told me that he and Vasiki are watching over me. I don't understand."

No flicker.

"Tomorrow, Daphne and I have an appointment at the attorney's office to go over the will. I know your brother and Adam will be there. I need your help. I need the will you told me about—that all that you have is mine. You know I'm not here as a gold-digger. I believe what you said was true. Is it?"

A strobe.

"Then I will go armed. I'll search your room." Kaylee winked. "Now I know where it is. Smaller than mine. You gave me everything. It was a dream come true."

Another strobe.

"I wish you could tell me where it is."

Slow flicker-flicker-flicker.

"Three? What does three mean?"

A rainbow of light enveloped them.

Then the door groaned open.

"Are you okay?" Daphne asked.

"Yes. Thank you for my time."

Kaylee kissed the granite tomb.

"Not ever goodbye," she whispered.

<h1 style="text-align:center">38</h1>

Lou Ann managed a cup of soup for lunch and then ducked back into her office, taking the stairwell instead of the elevator so she could dodge Dan.

No more coffee for her because she was jittery enough.

She tried to maintain her focus on the review of files for her electronic signature, but she kept glancing at her cell, hoping for another call from Kaylee, but it had only been an hour since she spoke with her.

It seemed so long ago.

Her head spun trying to reconcile Kaylee surprising her about the mysterious will.

Lou Ann grinned.

Kaylee always loved surprises. A cookie. A new book. She'd been such a voracious reader starting at age three. Lyle built a bookshelf to house Kaylee's books. Much to Lyle's chagrin, she helped Kaylee paint it pink, Kaylee's favorite color at the time.

Kaylee didn't own anything pink anymore, but then she wasn't three anymore either. And even if pink wasn't her favorite color now, it didn't matter because her youth was stolen.

If it hadn't poured rain that Sunday, causing the roads to be slick, Kaylee would be going to college in the fall.

Instead she was chasing after a fantasy life in Greece.

Although Lou Ann's chest ached, and her eyes failed to close at night, she would absolutely not interfere with Kaylee's life lessons. Even a book couldn't teach that, and neither could she. It was only for Kaylee to experience on her own. And that was a sad fact.

Lou Ann powered through more files than she expected.

Dan would never admit it, but he'd be satisfied.

Lou Ann's cell alarm went off. Four-thirty pm, the bewitching hour.

She pressed send on her computer and tossed her hands up in victory.
"Ta-da!"
Dan acknowledged the email files she sent him.
Then she sat back in her chair and blinked.
Did she read that right?
He replied, "Thanks and have a good night."
Okay, what alien abducted the real Dan?
Who cared? She'd beat him to the parking lot.

Lou Ann screeched her cruiser to a stop in the driveway. The guy across the street quit trimming his hedges and Suzy popped out onto her porch.
"Sorry," Lou Ann called.
The guy continued with his yard work, but Suzy ran over.
Then Harry and Joanna bolted out the door.
The three surrounded her.
"Are you okay?" Suzy asked.
"I'm so sorry. I was in hurry to get home."
Joanna stood next to Harry, her eyes as wide as his.
It was so unlike her.
"I heard from Kaylee today," she said to Suzy.
"I know it's so hard for you, but I know you must be relieved."
"I am."
"Hi, Harry. Hi, Joanna."
They returned Suzy's hi.
"I'll let you guys be. Always next door if you need."
"I know that. Thanks, Suzy."
Suzy returned to her house and went inside.
"That was quite an entrance," Harry said.
"Have you heard from Kaylee?"
Harry and Joanna shook their heads.
"Oh."
She had hoped that Kaylee would've called Joanna too, but with the cost of international calls or texts, she understood why the two of them hadn't heard from her.
Lou Ann, Harry, and Joanna went inside the house.
Lou Ann unfastened her gunbelt and then her uniform.
"I'll be right back."
She changed into shorts and a tee, and when she returned to the kitchen, Harry had already placed a bowl of mixed greens on the table and Isabelle was lapping up her dinner.
She sat at the kitchen table with Harry and Joanna.

Just the three of them.

"I have a surprise!" Joanna exclaimed.

Lou Ann grinned.

Surprises were the order of the day.

Harry smiled wide.

Something was up.

"Harry downloaded the study guide for me to get my learner's permit!"

"That's awesome," Lou Ann congratulated her.

"And when I get the permit, both you and Harry can teach me to drive, whoever of you is available."

"We'll work it out," Lou Ann said. "Now that I work days and the summer days are long, I can teach you, and I'm sure Harry will too when he's available. Between the two of us, you'll be driving, *safely*, in no time."

Joanna clapped. "Yay! And, I have another announcement. When I get my driver's license, I can go to one of those night classes to get a high school diploma." Joanna took a breath. "And there's more."

"More?"

"Yes. I'm going to find a job. A day job, so I can pay for my room, help with the food, and save up for a car...a used one."

"One step at at a time," Lou Ann said.

Lou Ann looked around the table.

What started out to be a day of struggle turned out to be not such a bad day after all.

Lou Ann raised her glass of iced tea.

"Cheers."

"Cheers," Harry and Joanna replied.

Her appetite was back.

39

Kaylee lay on her bed and glanced at the vase of fresh flowers on her nightstand.

Demetrios was definitely communicating with her from beyond. He answered through those flickers.

Three slow flickers. That was the clue to where he hid the addendum to his will—for his eyes only.

But now the addendum was for her eyes only until tomorrow. She had to find it before the attorney meeting.

Daphne and she went their separate ways after the cemetery—both admitting they needed a rest, from not only the intense summer heat, but more so after the emotional toll of their visit with Demetrios.

Kaylee pushed out of the bed. Dinner was in one hour—one hour that she could use to search Demetrios's room for the will. But Daphne was resting in the same wing as Demetrios's room complicated her plan.

She'd better hurry before Daphne woke.

Kaylee stuck her hand under the mattress and pulled out the keys Peter had sneaked to her.

Then she went to her bedroom door and grimaced while easing it open.

Although she had the third floor to herself, anyone could be around.

She poked her head out and looked both ways.

No one.

She closed the door, and the click of it echoed in the long empty corridor.

Kaylee tiptoed to the secret door and tried the first key.

Nothing. It was the wrong one.

She tried the second.

Success. The door unlocked.

She opened it wide enough for her to slip through, and then secured it again.

She maneuvered the winding stairwell with unexpected ease since this time her arms were empty.

Kaylee approached the door that led to the second wing and pressed her ear against it and listened.

No footsteps. No conversations.

Now.

She opened the door and left it unlocked for a quick getaway.

She remembered Demetrios's room was the third one on the right.

But she had no idea which one belonged to Daphne.

Kaylee reached in her pocket and removed the two keys, both with the letter "D" engraved.

It could stand for Daphne, but no, she could swear she counted the all the rooms with double doors correctly.

She took a deep breath and inserted both keys.

Each turned easily, and Kaylee opened them.

Kaylee sighed in relief when she saw Demetrios's blue bedspread, the same pale blue walls, and the same icons in the corner.

She eased the double doors shut and went to his closet, where Peter was before Daphne sneaked up on them.

Did she know about the addended will? Did Demetrios confide in her?

Maybe, but Daphne hadn't told her about it.

So Kaylee needed to find it on her own.

Kaylee entered Demetrios's closet and closed herself in.

Three long flickers, she repeated to herself.

She searched three drawers but came up empty.

Three. Three. Three.

She scanned the huge closet.

Three bins sat on a top shelf way, out of her reach.

Kaylee looked around.

No step stool.

Demetrios wouldn't need a lift but she did.

She went to the chest of drawers and climbed on top of it.

Although it was the right height, her extended arms could not reach the shelf with the bins.

Now what?

She needed to hurry.

But she refused to leave before she inspected the bins.

Kaylee climbed down from the chest.

If she could only move the chest closer.

She proceeded to the side of the chest, braced her hands against it, and shoved.

Her feet slid. The chest of drawers didn't budge.

Shoot!

She tried again.

No go.

If she emptied the contents, it would be lighter.

Kaylee removed drawers full of Demetrios's underwear, T-shirts, socks—enough for a year without doing laundry—and set them on the closet floor.

She walked the empty chest toward the shelf.

Yes!

Kaylee climbed back on top of it and reached the bins.

Three. The third.

She removed the third bin and looked inside of it.

Wow!

It was full of sealed envelopes.

But which one had the addended will?

Kaylee went through the stack and at the very bottom was one with her name on it!

Oh, my God! Something went right!

She put the remaining files back in the bin. She'd return later to find out what the rest contained, but now she needed to get out of here—fast!

Kaylee walked the chest back to its place and was about to slide the drawers in when she heard the bedroom doors open.

Kaylee froze and held her breath.

"Peter!" Daphne yelled. "Come right now!"

Kaylee then remembered seeing a cordless phone on Demetrios's nightstand when she placed the vase of flowers there.

Daphne was just outside the closet.

Kaylee exhaled slowly.

"How may I assist you?" she heard Peter ask.

"Why is Demetrios's chamber unlocked?"

"Vasiliki was cleaning in here."

Damn. Peter is good on the fly.

"Why on earth would she need to clean in here?"

"She wants to pick up any errant flower petals and to change the water in the vase."

"I didn't see her, and the door was unlocked. Speak to her that these doors are to remain locked at all times."

"I will speak with her, Madame."

"I'm off to the dining room. Please make sure that Kaylee is on time."

"I will."

Demetrios's doors closed.

Peter opened the closet door.

"You better hurry."

"I found it, Peter. The will."

"Go quick. I'll straighten up here before Daphne wanders back in."

"Is she after the will?"

Peter only cocked his head.

Kaylee held the envelope to her chest.

"I gave you spare keys. I have all the masters. Go, now!"

She rushed out and down the hall and past the secret door she left unlocked. Up the winding stairs and to the third floor.

Kaylee locked the door and ran into her room.

Sucking air into her lungs, she locked her door.

Then she shoved the keys and the envelope under her mattress.

Done!

She dodged into the bathroom and straightened her hair.

The rose print sundress wasn't appropriate for dinner.

She popped into her mega-closet and yanked down a black satin dress with diamond-encrusted straps—positive that it was another Daphne creation—and traded the sundress for it.

Shoes? Quick.

She scanned the racks of shoes, and chose black satin stilettos with diamond flowers. Then she grabbed a clutch.

Kaylee hurried out of the closet, stumbling in the sky-high heels, and then waved her arms to catch her balance.

No more soccer shoes for her.

But the tradeoff was well worth it, now that she was an heiress.

She teetered out her room, locked it, and deposited the key in her clutch.

Kaylee held her head up and looked straight ahead.

If she looked down, she'd wobble and fall over.

She reached the marble stairway leading to the dining room.

You can do it. One step at a time.

Kaylee finally made the last step and she was still standing.

She gathered her clutch and her dignity and strode into the dining room, even beating Daphne.

Daphne entered the dining room.

"Don't you look absolutely exquisite!"

"Thank you, and may I say the same about you."

"Thank you, dear."

Daphne twirled in her strapless silver satin gown without a wobble in her matching spike-heeled sandals.

Kaylee and Daphne took their places at the oversized table.

George entered the room and announced, "Dinner is served."

George wheeled in the silver dinner cart.

"What has chef created for us this evening?" Daphne asked.

"Swordfish with mushroom rice pilaf."

Daphne nodded. "Well done."

Kaylee had never eaten swordfish, but whatever the chef prepared was always delicious.

George unveiled the swordfish entree.

The chef's artful presentation made it almost criminal to disrupt.

Daphne tight-lipped smiled when George filled Kaylee's plate first.

Kaylee glanced at her plate and hesitated.

The order of dinner was violated.

For now Daphne was the madame of the house.

Did George know that, after tomorrow, Kaylee was to wear the "crown."? Had Peter and George spoken?

George should've served Daphne first tonight for the last time, because now it was blatantly obvious that Kaylee was about to supersede Daphne.

Why would Daphne want Demetrios's estate, since hers was surely as decadent and probably even more so—given her fashion sense?

Kaylee was sure Daphne was sent to greet her at the airport and escort her to the estate. And once Daphne was satisfied that Kaylee was comfortable, she would return to her own mansion. But now Daphne planned to stay until the will was read and official.

However, Kaylee had the addended will, and the rest would be finalized tomorrow.

Kaylee brought a forkful of swordfish to her mouth.

Mmmm. Delectable. Just how she expected it to be.

"My compliments to the chef," Daphne announced.

Perhaps Kaylee misunderstood Daphne's odd demeanor because, now she was clearly pleasant and, maybe a little over the top, ebullient.

Whatever it was, dinner returned to smooth wit and conversation.

"I've never tasted swordfish before, but I'll let the chef know to make a permanent place for it on the menu."

Daphne lowly chuckled. "It already is my dear."

Kaylee nodded. "Good to know."

Was that a dig, or only informative?

She chose to see it as informative.

"Besides swordfish and the roast beef from last night's dinner, you should get together with George in regard to future entrees."

Ah! Daphne said *future,* acknowledging me.

"Yes, I'll do that!"

"Good."

"I'm positive you and chef who are just as talented."

"I do. You'll have to visit me to find out that and more," Daphne said, practically beaming.

Everything was going to go just fine. Daphne would soon return to her home, and Kaylee would assume responsibility for the estate and the staff. And of course keep fresh flowers on Demetrios's tomb.

"Where is she?!"

Kaylee's fork clattered on her plate.

His voice was permanently embedded in her head.

Her heartbeat blasted an octave.

Adam Sakalis, Demetrios's co-pilot nephew who she collided with on the jet stomped into the dining room.

He shot his finger at Kaylee.

"What are you doing here?!" he bellowed, his voicing ricocheting off the dining room walls.

George and Peter rushed into the dining room.

George raised his arms.

"Master Adam, stop," he warned.

Peter planted himself protectively next to Kaylee.

Daphne stood.

"Adam! Leave this dining room, now!"

Adam fired his next arrow.

"You're telling me to leave my home, and for her to stay?"

Home? His home?

Adam lowered his voice to a bark.

He pushed out a chair next to Daphne and opposite Kaylee.

"Bring me dinner, George, please."

George looked at Daphne while Peter continued to stand guard over Kaylee.

"Sit and behave," Daphne ordered.

Kaylee was brushed aside as the undeniable head of the estate.

Adam sat, his surly demeanor aimed at Kaylee.

But she wasn't about to duck.

"It's all right," she said to Peter, and then nodded at George.

Peter slowly retreated, ready to reinstate his protective stance at the first sign of Adam's aggression.

George rocked a plate in front of Adam in another warning shot.

Adam devoured his swordfish. His silverware scraped against the china like fingernails scratching on a chalkboard.

Kaylee didn't back away from her dinner. No way would she satisfy Adam. He would not be the victor in this surprising evening. He had no idea who his real opponent was.

Adam smacked his lips and tossed his utensils on his plate, signifying he was finished.

Daphne sighed.

"Adam, please! A bit of decorum."

"Humph," he grumbled. "And having a prostitute at this table—oh, sorry, former prostitute—isn't it?"

Daphne pounded her fist against the table.

"Enough! Leave!"

"I'd be more than happy to depart from this debauchery."

Adam pushed back his chair and tossed his white cloth napkin in his plate. "I'll be in my room for the remainder of the evening."

Peter wagged his finger. "No, no!"

"What 'no, no'? You don't get to tell me anything." Adam pointed to himself. "You have and always will be my servant."

Peter seethed past his gritted teeth.

Adam laughed. "Don't take it so personally, old man."

Daphne apologetically shook her head at Peter.

"I'll see you early tomorrow," Adam said to Daphne. "Father will meet us at the attorney's office."

"You'll be taking the Bentley?"

"Yes, of course. I can't waste time waiting for a limo either way."

He grimaced at Kaylee and then nodded to Daphne.

"Goodnight."

Adam had shot another arrow at Kaylee. He apparently had many arrows in his quiver, but she had more, and she was a better shot.

"Goodnight, Adam," Kaylee called to his back. "Sleep tight."

Kaylee brushed her teeth harder and harder, still seething about Adam's surprise visit and his nasty, rude volatility at the dinner table directed at her.

What a scum! Calling her a prostitute!

Yes, Demetrios regretted ever getting involved with Newell. He paid for her out of loneliness. Even when he thought he was getting Joanna, and Kaylee knew Newell talked up Joanna as sexually available for his pleasure. Demetrios was never going to control Joanna. He promised to give her a good life on the estate, fearing for her safety. It wasn't about the control. Newell planned to talk Demetrios into being the master, hoping to seal another deal with him for another girl.

Money. Money. Money.

But Demetrios fell in love with someone he wasn't supposed to—and that someone was her.

Kaylee spat into the sink.

And don't you forget it, buddy boy!

She'd showered and brushed her teeth. Now she crawled into bed, needing to be well rested for tomorrow. She needed to stay on point. Not waiver. Adam had knocked her off balance, temporarily. She'd be steady as a bull tomorrow, ready to charge!

Kaylee sat on the bed just as a soft knock came at her door.

Now what?

She pushed out of bed and approached the door.

"Who's there?"

"It's me, Peter."

Peter, her perpetual protector.

The dinner from hell was over, and they'd all gone to their separate corners.

She'd reassure Peter that she was fine and just needed to sleep.

Kaylee unlocked her bedroom door. Even though Peter had a master key, he would never enter her room without her consent.

"What's up? Dinner was exhausting, and not to insult you, but I need to get to bed."

Peter closed the door and brought his index finger to his mouth.

"I get it," she whispered.

"Adam two doors down."

"What!"

"Shhhhh."

"What is he doing on the third floor where I am?" Kaylee whispered.

"Before you came, Adam was aways on third floor, since he was a boy."

"Boy?"

Could Peter be anymore cryptic?

Peter gestured for them to get away from the door.

"Okay, I sit on bed?"

"Okay."

Peter and Kaylee sat on the edge of the bed at a respectable distance.

"Demetrios raise Adam after Adam's mother, Maria, died. Kosmos, his father, go crazy. Unable to take care of boy. Adam come live with Demetrios. He difficult boy. Throw toys. Wreck every car. Drink. Bring women here. Demetrios tell him no more. Straighten up or get out. Adam beg not. Demetrios soft heart. Put Adam in pilot school. Not trust him as captain so make him co-pilot of jet. But Adam he no change—how you say?—stripes."

She and Adam were like oil and water from the beginning. She even slapped him on the jet when he purposely misled her to Newell's and Sofia's suite, where they were in the middle of humping and pumping, a sight she had never been able to unsee to this day. He admitted he was Demetrios's nephew and took great pleasure that Demetriosis liked "them young." She had no idea what awaited her, fearing Demetrios would lock her away, but she was wrong. Yes, Adam never "changed his stripes."

The story of Adam was another tale Demetrios never shared.

"Why didn't Demetrios tell me about Adam, and why would he put me on the third floor with Adam doors away?"

"Because Adam have rich apartment in Athens. Before today, he not come for long time. Daphne told him you here. He come after you because you are threat to him. He want estate. You no give. I make sure he no get. Daphne interfere where she don't need. I need to tell you before too late, not to cause you poor sleep."

"That's okay. Thank you for warning me. I'll sleep with one eye open."

"You be safe. Door lock. You and I have only key. He no bother you."

Peter stood and grazed Kaylee's head with a kiss.

"Goodnight."

"Goodnight, Peter."

Peter walked out her door and locked it.

She was safe until morning, at least.

40

Lou Ann blinked awake. Her sweaty back had soaked through her nightie. She flipped off the sheet, sat on the edge of the bed, and pressed her palm against her moist forehead.

She slowly pushed out of bed, not wanting to disturb Harry, who continued snoring.

He would only tell her to lie down.

She was better off on her own right now.

Kaylee was in trouble. She could feel it. It was the same intuition she'd honed over the years as a deputy sheriff that had kept her alive.

Did Kaylee inherit that ability? But her niece was just as stubborn and as crafty and that kept her alive.

Ironically, Lou Ann had fought Kaylee, seeking to rid or at least mute those qualities—to reel in her behavior—to make her more pliable and more respectful—and thank God she had failed.

It would soon be dawn in Greece.

Lou Ann grabbed her cell off the nightstand and pattered barefoot into the den and out of Harry's or Joanna's earshot.

She sat on the sofa and looked at the clock.

Lou Ann clutched her cell and decided to text Kaylee.

How are you? Been thinking about you and so have Harry and Joanna. Saw weather in Greece. Hot, huh? Just want to stay in touch. Get a chance, text back. Love you. (heart emoji)

Sent.

She didn't expect a text right way, if ever. But she left open a line of communication she prayed Kaylee would maintain.

The sweat had evaporated, leaving her chilled.

Lou Ann snuck back into bed and under the covers.

Harry shifted, sleepily hugged her, and returned to sleep with a gasp and then rhythmic snoring.

If only she could do the same.

Kaylee and Daphne stood at the portico while waiting for the hunky chauffeur to arrive.

Kaylee stifled a yawn. After Peter's visit, and knowing Adam was only two doors away from her bedroom, she slept poorly. And today's appointment with the lawyer added to her insomnia.

She'd set her alarm extra early to get ready, but she'd risen well before then and turned it off.

Presentation was everything. She needed to look powerful, to feel powerful. So she stood next to Daphne— feminine yet bold—after choosing a deep purple fitted jacket and creased matching trousers. No dress today. Not even a skirt. A string of pearls rested under the collar of her white silk blouse. Her pumps with a modest two inch heels afforded her enough height without screaming legginess.

Daphne, on the other hand, wore a stark white suit, also with trousers, and a gold pendant with the initials, DS, hung from her neck.

The contrast between them couldn't have been more striking.

Kaylee wondered what Adam would show up wearing.

Like she cared!

Meeting Kosmos was what really piqued her interest.

His impaired psychological state should make him a weak opponent.

Daphne's white limo pulled up.

Hunky chauffeur popped out and opened the door to the rear seating.

Kaylee entered after Daphne while clutching the black briefcase with DS centered in gold between the gold latches that Peter brought to her early this morning. Peter had a key to every place in the mansion, including Demetrios's office.

She slid the envelope with Demetrios's will into the briefcase and while she was finishing getting ready for the appointment, she heard the the latches open and click shut. And when she returned from the bathroom, Peter instructed her not to open the briefcase until the meeting with the attorney. He didn't tell her why, but only asked her to trust him. Then he dropped the key to the briefcase into her jacket pocket.

Another pocket for keys!

Daphne gave the briefcase a lingering once-over while they waited under the portico, and a second, extended look in the limo. But she didn't comment while they waited for the limo, and she didn't offer one now.

Kaylee hadn't seen Adam since last night, and he must have left for the attorney's office before dawn in his black Bentley—that probably belonged to Demetrios.

She had no use for it anyway. He could have it.

They'd bypassed breakfast, but as in Demetrios's limo, Daphne pressed a button and a tray containing croissants on china plates with pats of butter on the side and two porcelain cups of coffee on saucers, complete with cream and sugar appeared.

"Eat well," Daphne said. "It will be a long morning."

And a longer ride home—her home.

The limo's stop and start progress told Kaylee that they'd entered Athens. But instead of visiting Demetrios in death, she would be representing him in *life*.

Kaylee ran her fingers over his initials on the briefcase.

"We've arrived," the hunky chauffeur announced.

The chauffeur opened the rear door and escorted Daphne and Kaylee out the limo.

Kaylee held out one hand while clinging to the briefcase with her other hand.

"I'll park along the street waiting for you," he said.

"I'll be awhile, possibly all morning," Daphne warned. "You're free to get coffee and perhaps something to eat. There's a cafe across the street."

"I may go."

"You decide. Come, Kaylee let's go inside."

Kaylee searched for a black Bentley, but didn't see one. Adam must be planning another surprise appearance.

Kaylee walked with her head high and shoulders down next to Daphne, who strolled without abandon up to an iron gate.

Daphne swung it open.

A car squeaked to the curb.

Kaylee turned.

Adam had arrived.

She needed to beat Adam to that office and secure prime seating in front of the lawyer. No back seat for her. She was here to honor Demetrios's wishes, and wherever and whomever those landed on.

A placard on the door read, Thelonious Chaconas, Dikigoros.

Kaylee blinked. "Which one is his name and how should I address him? Does he speak English?"

She prayed he did, because otherwise she wouldn't understand a word he said. She'd have to trust Daphne to translate, and then they could speak Greek among themselves. This was going to be a disaster.

"His full name is Thelonious Chaconas, and Dikigoros means lawyer. You may address him as Mr. Chaconas, and he speaks English," Daphne said.

"Okay."

Kaylee clutched the briefcase's handle until her knuckles tingled.

Walk straight. Relax. You've come prepared.

They'd entered the lawyer's air-conditioned office where a young secretary with her dark hair in a perfectly plaited braid down her back stood to greet them.

She looked about Kaylee's age, and was wearing a beige cotton button-down blouse, a tan skirt, and a coral lipstick smile.

"Welcome," she said in perfect English. "One minute, please."

She picked up the phone and said something in Greek.

A man in a blue suit and tie came out of an office. His full head of black hair looked freshly cut, half inch above his collar, and his face clean-shaven. He smelled of shaving cream. He must've just stepped out of the barbershop. He curved his lips into a welcoming smile.

She was sure Demetrios had chosen an old, wise lawyer, but Thelonious couldn't be more than thirty—Adam's age.

Shit! Maybe they knew each other. Shared the same circle of friends. Maybe went to school together.

She was in trouble.

Mr. Chaconas led them to his office.

"Come in, please. Kosmos is already here."

Two chairs were positioned on one side of Thelonious's long, carved mahogany desk and two on the other side. He was clearly waiting for four people.

A man in a black suit that matched his dark demeanor sat in the far left chair while staring ahead and not acknowledging Daphne, his own sister.

What the hell happened between them?

Then she thought of the rift between her father and Lou Ann.

Kosmos with bags under his eyes and a receding hairline with slivers of gray, was the youngest of the three Sakalis siblings, but looked the oldest.

Daphne sat in the chair on the right side closest to the desk leaving a seat farther away for Kaylee.

The last seat on the left was for Adam.

At least she didn't have to sit next to him.

Kaylee set the briefcase in front of her feet and reached into her left jacket pocket. The key to the briefcase was still there. Then she reached for her cell in the right and took it out.

Shit! A text from Lou Ann.

Kaylee had been so preoccupied this morning that she failed to look at her cell until now.

She read the text and thumbed a response.

Sorry missed text. Yes, hot as the devil's backyard. Found will. In lawyer's office. Love to all and can't wait for all of you to visit.

Kaylee just hit send when Adam strolled in wearing jeans and a red shirt, tucked in and with the top two buttons open.

He poked his finger at Daphne.

"Don't even..." she shot back. "She has every right to be here. Surely Demetrios left something for her."

Something?! Wow! They're in for a shock!

Kosmos stood and embraced Adam.

"You came!" Kosmos cried.

"Of course. I wouldn't miss this."

They spoke in English on purpose so she'd understand her place.

Kosmos and Adam parted and both sat.

Adam crossed his legs, showing off brown Italian leather shoes.

He turned his head and smirked at Kaylee in his red Matador shirt.

Little did he know that she was the bull.

Mr. Chaconas sat behind his desk on which sat two folders.

"Shall we start?"

Everyone nodded except Adam who grumbled.

"I will proceed in English," Thelonious said.

Kosmos stood up and yelled, "I object!"

"Sit down down, Kosmos, and shut up!" Daphne yelled back.

Thelonious rose. "Stop! I will not continue in this chaos!"

Daphne folded her hands in her lap and Kosmos collapsed in his chair.

"For God's sake, Father, sit up," Adam said.

Kosmos shifted in his chair and sat erect and, most important, quiet.

Thelonious sighed. "To continue."

He opened an envelope from one folder that was thicker than the one she had in the briefcase.

"This is Demetrios's original will notarized two years ago and leaving his complete estate and management of it to be divided two thirds to his sister, Daphne Sakalis and one third to his nephew, Adam Sakalis. To his brother, Kosmos, he leaves the three apartments in Athens, his black limousine, and stable of horses outside of Ekali."

Kosmos popped out of his chair and spat.

He yelled something in Greek and Thelonious jumped up and yelled something back in Greek right back.

A huge bald man with muscles straining at his shirt burst into the office.

What the…..

The Greek muscle man picked up Kosmos like a twig and began to cart him away.

"Stop," Adam said. "I'll take care of him. He's not quite right. And I'll pay to clean the carpet."

Muscle man dumped Kosmos back in his chair and left.

"Behave papa. You'll stay with me."

"Wait a minute. I own two thirds of the estate, and since all the Athens apartments, which are huge and ornate, belong to Kosmos, I will buy Adams's lesser share of the estate."

Talk about a Greek tragedy!

Adam raised his fist. "The hell you will!"

Kaylee grabbed her briefcase, set it in her lap, and guarded it with her arms.

Mr. Chaconas looked straight at her while the Sakalises declared war on each other.

He nodded to her. And pointed to the other envelope.

He *was* on her side.

While Daphne and Adam faced off, and while Kosmos grinned devilishly watching the spat, Kaylee pulled the key out of her jacket pocket and unlocked the briefcase, and when she opened it, her eyes went huge. Not only was the will in the briefcase, but also a memory stick. That's what Peter sneaked in there. But what was on the memory stick?

Kaylee approached Mr. Chaconas without the bickering siblings noticing, and set the contents of the briefcase on his desk.

"I have Demetrios's addended will."

The lawyer smiled. "I know."

"There's a memory stick too, but I have no idea what is on it."

"I have a clue."

This was no time to be cryptic.

"Quiet!" Thelonious yelled.

Daphne and Adam froze. Then retreated and sat, scowling.

Kosmos laughed.

Adam elbowed him, and Kosmos scaled it down to a snicker.

Daphne sighed. "Can we just finalize this?"

"No," Mr. Chaconas said.

"No?" Daphne asked, wanting clarification. "Oh, what did Demetrios leave to Kaylee?" she added.

Adam scoffed. "Nothing. Nada."

"Not so," Thelonious said. "I have Demetrios's addended will to discuss."

"Addended? That's more like it," Adam said.

He had no idea.

Adam straightened in his chair, positive he had won the lion's share of the estate, while Daphne blinked. Even Kosmos stopped giggling.

Mr. Chaconas picked up the second envelope and opened it.

Kaylee shifted in her chair. After the lawyer read the addended will making her sole heiress to the estate, complete pandemonium would make their bickering child's play. And after Daphne heard the second reading, Kaylee would have to find another way home.

Peter would help her.

Kaylee focused on Mr. Chaconas.

And if they attacked her, there was always the muscle man.

Thelonious cleared his throat.

He tapped the bottom of a stack of papers against his desk.

"Demetrios and I spoke before his death...murder.... because he wished to modify the existing will to make Kaylee Marie Jasinski as the sole inheritor to his estate, his private jet, and including management of all staff of her selection. And set aside fifty million dollars for Kaylee's lifetime living expenses."

Adam laughed. "No fucking way! She knew him for a millisecond. That's not a valid document. He was infatuated with her. This is a joke."

Daphne stuttered a breath.

"What happened?" Kosmos asked.

"Nothing, Papa."

Adam stood and reached for the original will on Chaconas's desk, but the lawyer slammed his hand over the it.

"Sit down," he warned Adam.

"I will not sit. You're fired! I'm going to seek a competent lawyer."

"As you wish, but along with the sealed document, Demetrios left his intent and instructions in a video."

Adam halted.

"What video?"

That's what was on the memory stick. Peter knew where it was and contacted Mr. Chaconas. She had the clear advantage now.

The bull wins!

Thelonious picked up his phone and said something.

The secretary walked in with cords and adapters.

Thelonious attached his laptop to a flat screen. Then he inserted the memory stick, and Demetrios appeared on-screen.

Kaylee raised her hands to touch the screen—to touch Demetrios—but then slowly lowered them.

Demetrios folded his hands on his desk in his study.

"I only dreamed of love, but my wealth was also my Achilles heel. Countless women only wanted me for my riches and the exorbitant lifestyle it would provide them. I gave up. Yes, I am guilty of paying for the company of a young lady from an unscrupulous person. I am not proud of that. But then Kaylee arrived, through no fault of her own. I knew, from the moment I saw her, that she was different from the others. Today I returned the money, and I wish to make her my wife when she is of age chronologically. But her real age is wiser. Kaylee, you are a wonder. Your smile lights my soul. You are as intelligent as you are humorous, and everyone else says the same. So, I give you everything I have. We share it now. Should something happen to me, I've instructed my attorney, Thelonious Chaconas, to see to it that, in accordance with my wishes, you are the rightful heiress to my estate."

"Now, Daphne, you know my true feelings about Kaylee. You are set for life through your own hard work, and I've always applauded that. Do not feel slighted about this change. You, my sunshine sister, are above that."

"Adam, I know you will be crushed, but do not be. The apartments are all yours. Take care of Kosmos. He needs you. He will be comfortable in Athens. Have the Bentley. Work just as hard as I have and you and Daphne will have your own success."

"Kosmos. Kosmos. My dear baby brother. Do not keep mourning Maria. She's waiting for you. I know that."

"To all of you, if I'm not around one day, Kaylee is kind, and I leave it up to her to disperse only what she sees just and fit. She is not your enemy."

"So this will supersedes the other. Although our family has had its challenges, I love you all, and wish for all your happiness and success."

Demetrios grinned.

"Now I have to go, because Kaylee is waiting for me in the dining room. Breakfast and stroll in the garden. Life could not be sweeter!"

Demetrios disappeared from the screen.

Tears tracked down Kaylee's cheeks and dripped onto her jacket.

"What? She's crying? Boo-hoo. I'll give her something to cry about— all the way back to the US, where she belongs!" Adam bellowed.

Kaylee stood.

"I'm not going anywhere but to my home in Ekali."

"Don't come near my *home*, except to pack your bags! I'll even give you a ride to the airport and buy you a ticket home."

"That won't be necessary, because I can drive myself home."

"We'll see about that!"

Muscle man burst into the office.

"I'm going. I'm going."

Adam held out his hand to his father.

"Let's leave."

Kosmos shook his head.

"Everyone's gone crazy here. So find your own way home, old man!"

Adam stomped past muscle man and exited the office.

The secretary ran in.

"What?"

"It's all right. It's over."

But it wasn't.

Adam wasn't going to budge out of the house.

Kaylee gathered the briefcase, and Thelonious gave her Demetrios's memory stick.

"Thank you."

"You're welcome. I'll arrange for a ride back to Ekali."

"That won't be necessary," Daphne said. "Come on, Kaylee. Let's go home…to your home."

Kaylee hesitated. Did she hear right? This had been the most bizarre morning.

Daphne nodded. "It's fine."

"What about Adam?"

"If we leave now we'll arrive before him. I'll take care of the rest."

"I don't understand. I saw and heard what was going on after Mr. Chaconas read the addended will. Aren't you angry with me? Maybe hate me? I can take it."

As dysfunctional and threatening of a family, they were nowhere near as scary as Newell and his cretins.

"We'll talk in the limo."

Kaylee looked at Thelonious for an opinion on the hot matter.

"Offer still stands, but I know Daphne. She could've left you here."

"Adam has a lead foot," she cautioned. "But my chauffeur knows every shortcut, and he can drive like the devil. Time is running out."

"All right. Let's fly."

She had no choice, but to trust Daphne. At least for the moment.

Sadly, after that, perhaps never.

41

Daphne chattered on her cell in Greek.

When Daphne and Kaylee exited the attorney's office, hunky chauffeur already had the limo's engine purring in front of the office.

Daphne waved him off, and she and Kaylee hopped into the back seat, forgoing formality.

"To Ekali—quick," Daphne ordered.

The limo lurched forward, pushing her and Daphne against the the seat back.

The chauffeur maneuvered in and out of traffic lanes with the skill of a race car driver.

What route did Adam take?

Either way, a confrontation was brewing.

"I'm not angry with you," Daphne said while they swayed in the back of the limo. "It was all an act on my part."

"An act?"

And Kaylee thought the morning couldn't hold any more surprises. But this was a shocker.

Daphne's shoulder pressed against Kaylee's.

"I told him to speed." Daphne continued. "Demetrios told me about the will and his intentions toward you. I told him I thought he was acting rash, since his and your relationship was newborn, and I recommended he wait and see how things would unfold. I did know in advance that you were coming and after Demetrios described how Newell described you, physically, I outfitted the closet and even decorated your room, even though I did not approve of you. I tried to dissuade him from this deal, but he insisted on having you come. No one saw the tragedy coming."

"I'm so sorry."

"No, wait. Demetrios knew from the moment he saw you, that you were the one for him. I have to give him that. Adam, on the other hand, despises you. I needed to pretend that I was on his side to protect you. I will handle Adam. Actually as much, as a fuck up he is, he made out well. And Kosmos, I'll protect him too. Adam only pretends that he loves his papa, and that he'll care for him. None of that is true."

"I'll help take care of Kosmos. Demetrios would've wanted me to, and it's only right."

Daphne set her hand on Kaylee's knee. "Kosmos can be very volatile, and he can get very strong when he's agitated. He's too much for you to handle. I can calm him down, but my work often keeps me away from Athens. I'll get a professional to watch over him. Although Kosmos distrusts strangers. We'll deal with that later. Adam is the one we need to worry about."

The chauffeur skidded the limo to a stop at the portico and Kaylee followed Daphne out of the vehicle.

Kaylee scanned for Adam's car.

No sign of the Bentley.

The hunky chauffeur should get a trophy!

Peter and Vasiliki applauded when Kaylee entered the grand foyer.

She was careful to not say she'd won because Demetrios was gone and there were no clear victors.

Instead she said, "Demetrios's addended will was recognized."

"I knew it!" Peter cheered. "Demetrios spoke."

Her heart squeezed as she replayed his face and voice on that screen.

"Yes, and I thank you beyond words for slipping that memory stick into the briefcase. But why the secrecy?"

"You needed to make your case first, and for Demetrios to seal the document."

A wave of warmth spread through her body. "He did!"

"Hurry upstairs and lock your door. Vasiliki will bring you lunch."

"I won't hide from Adam."

"For sure. It is not your personality. But he'll be on fire when he comes through here. No good will come if you collide with him. You must stay away until he wears his anger down. That is how Adam has always been —screaming until he goes hoarse. Let him stomp around until he fall on bed and sleep. Trust me. He like child."

"Peter is right," Daphne agreed. "Go now. He'll arrive soon. Peter and I will detain him."

"All right...for now. He and I won't be able to avoid each other forever. But we both need a cooling-off period."

A car screeched to the curb and a car door slammed.

Peter nodded toward to the staircase.

"Go, Lady Kaylee!"

Kaylee clutched the briefcase and trotted up the marble stairs.

She made it to the third floor and peeked down from the top.

"I'm not done with her!" Adam yelled.

"Stop, Adam!" Daphne called.

"Master Adam, you need move car. Food delivery truck coming."

"Food service goes to the rear."

"No, back is blocked for repair. They come front."

"Then you move it."

Adam tossed Peter the car keys.

Peter shook his head. "I don't drive."

"Drive! Park it," Adam insisted.

"You wanted the Bentley, you got, or…" Daphne countered.

"The Bentley is mine as is everything else. I'll do it myself."

Adam stomped away.

Peter strikes again!

Kaylee eased her pace and strolled to her bedroom where she locked the door, walked over to the bed, set the briefcase on it, and then lay next to it, with Demetrios's image close by.

She ran her fingers over his gold initials.

"We did it."

42

Lou Ann stretched in bed.

A thunderbolt pierced her calf.

"Ow-ow-ow!"

Harry bolted up in bed. "What's wrong?!"

"Leg cramp!"

Harry jumped out of bed and rushed to Lou Ann.

"Which side?"

"My right."

Harry braced Lou Ann's calf, placed his hand under her sole, and sharply flexed her foot.

The gripping pain crumbled.

Lou Ann exhaled. "Thanks."

"Don't mention it. I needed to get up anyway," he teased.

"I stretched too hard."

Harry climbed up to her and set his warm, thick lips on hers, and then the curve of his smile took over her mouth. And she once kicked him to the curb. Harry had his faults, but persistence wasn't one of them.

He eased his mouth away from hers and held out his hand.

"You shouldn't shower alone after an injury. You might fall over, so you need someone there to catch you."

"And that someone might be you?"

"Yeah. I volunteer."

Lou Ann laughed.

His humor reeled her in every time.

"I think that would prudent."

"Perfect. You wait here and rest those gams while I crank up the shower to a sizzling warm."

While Harry trotted to the bathroom, Lou Ann slipped out of yet another sweaty nightie.

Her cell pinged, announcing a text.

Damn Dan! His arrogance had no sense of timing. What was her punishment today?

Jasinski. Out in field today. Report HQ 1600.

Thank God.

She tossed her cell on the bed and slowly rose, her right calf still in tender retreat.

The phone pinged again.

What else, Dan? He'll have to wait, because Harry was here first!

Lou Ann gingerly hobbled into the bathroom where Harry stood naked while wearing a smile that creased into his cheeks.

Harry waggled his brows. "Wow! Lady Godiva would be green with envy."

"I have no horse."

"That's good because it wouldn't fit in here. Two's the limit."

"Okay, shower for two, then."

Harry gestured for her to join him.

"Reservation, please," he joked.

"I believe we called to confirm."

Harry looked at his palm. "Ah, there you are. Party of two."

Lou Ann took Harry's hand, and he escorted her into the shower stall. Harry closed the shower door and opened his arms.

Ordinarily, Lou Ann took quick, military showers—in, out, and on the job. But her leg cramp woke her and then Harry, early, so this morning's shower provided them with some extra time together.

Harry hugged her, and then twirled her, under the spraying water.

"I forgot what a terrific dancer you are," Lou Ann said over the water drumming the tiles.

"Having a terrific partner is key."

Lou Ann yanked Harry to her body.

"I request a slow dance."

"Okay. Ladies' choice."

Lou Ann wrapped her arms around Harry's neck, and he enveloped her waist, then slipped his hands slowly down to her lower back.

"Thank you," she murmured.

"A little early, because I'm not done yet. Then you can thank me, and I can thank you."

Shampoo and suds. Wet and slick. Inside and out. He lifted her ballerina-gently—the tile warm on her back. She clasped her arms around his neck and legs around his waist—locked and steady—the water pelting them. She tightened her grip. He pushed hard.

Three-two-one. The release overtaking her. Harry's sweet persistence —his ultimate reward.

He lowered her as gently as he'd lifted her.

"Thank you," she repeated.

"And thank you."

They rinsed off, and Lou Ann cut the shower off.

She winked.

"It's the least I could do."

They toweled off, and while Harry shaved at his vanity sink, Lou Ann blow-dried her hair.

Harry sneaked over and kissed Lou Ann, leaving a trail of white foam on her face.

"Oops!"

"Yeah, oops!"

She wiped off her face with a towel.

"You're dangerous," she said while leaving the bathroom.

"007 dangerous?" he called.

"No. Just dangerous," she called back.

Lou Ann sat naked on the bed.

She hated to spoil a perfect morning, but she'd text Dan back because he'd keep texting until she replied. It was a game she had to play.

She picked up the cell.

Her heart skipped.

It wasn't Dan. It was Kaylee.

"Harry!"

Harry hurried from the bathroom, clean shaven and with a towel wrapped around his waist.

"What happened? Another cramp?"

"No."

Lou Ann held up her cell.

"Kaylee."

Harry sat next to Lou Ann.

"She won. She inherited Demetrios's estate."

"That's our Kaylee," Harry said.

Lou Ann looked at Harry.

"Was our Kaylee."

Kaylee had enough.

She had dinner and breakfast in her room.

Her cell chimed an incoming message.

Kaylee inspected her cell.

Lou Ann had responded to her text.

Congratulations and I love you.

What did she expect after she took off? At least Lou Ann responded.

She deserved to be congratulated.

This was her home and she wasn't going to be a prisoner in it.

Kaylee reached for the doorknob, but a knock on the door beat her to it.

"Who's there?" she droned.

"Peter."

This was out of control, and she'd be firm with him about that since Peter was now her employee.

Kaylee opened the door and walked into the hall.

"Peter…"

"The estate is safely yours. Adam left this morning, and Daphne is packing and getting ready for a business trip to Rome."

"Rome, huh?"

She ached to go with Daphne, but her place was here for right now. Rome would have to wait.

"I'll go wish her a Bon Voyage. Dinner for one this evening, then, in the dining room,"she added.

Peter bowed his head. "As you wish, Lady Kaylee."

She walked past him and didn't look back.

Why did I do that?

Peter was her employee, but he was also her friend and family. She needed to rethink this.

"Peter, make that dinner for three. You and Vasaliki will join me."

"Oh, no."

"Oh, yes. I say so."

Kaylee grinned and walked to the marble staircase.

My family. My Greek family.

First on her list was to redecorate all the bedrooms on the third floor, even hers. Those would be ready for Lou Ann, Harry, and Joanna when they decided, if decided, to visit. She would move into Demetrios's room. Maybe she would change it, or maybe not.

She'd begin with Adam's room first. She'd have his belongings packed and delivered to his choice of address. She needed to make it clear she was in charge.

Kaylee trotted down the staircase and headed toward the kitchen where Peter kept the master keys.

George and the chef were already preparing for dinner.

Kaylee sniffed. "That smells delicious."

While George looked over the chef's boiling pot, Kaylee surveyed the kitchen for the keys.

Several rings of keys hung on hooks anchored in a far wall.

Kaylee sidled over to the wall and noted the hooks were arranged by floor and wings.

Kaylee popped off the ones for the third floor.

The keys jangled, but George and the chef continued arguing about the pot.

She dropped the keys in her jeans pocket and waved to George and the chef on her way-out, and they waved back.

"See you at dinner."

"Yes," George responded and then opened one of the ovens.

Kaylee dodged out of the kitchen and hurried up the stairs to the third floor.

She stopped outside Adam's room, two doors from her room.

He won't be needing this room anymore.

The first key worked.

Kaylee pushed the door open.

Dark green walls came at her from all sides.

A king-size bed stood in the middle of the room. Black satin sheets lay crumpled upon it. Adam hadn't even bothered to at least make his bed partially. Certainly, Vasaliki hadn't been in there, if ever. Whoever was in charge of cleaning up this mess was derelict.

Kaylee grimaced at Adam's clothes strewn across the floor, including socks and yuck, underwear.

She should've worn a HAZMAT suit and brought tongs.

He'd left in a hurry and shoved his mess in her face.

It was just like Adam to be passive aggressive.

Good riddance!

The whole room would need to be fumigated.

And Lou Ann thought she was sloppy.

But now that the estate was hers, it was time to make tidiness and order priorities. Lou Ann would be proud.

Kaylee high-stepped over the underwear, and over to a black lacquered chest of drawers. A model jet spanned the top of it.

Why would he leave that here?

But then she knew why. He wasn't ever going to co-pilot Demetrios's jet, and now her jet, ever again, and she was positive Daphne would never allow him to set foot on her jet. Besides, she had the best women's crew. Kaylee decided to investigate having an all-woman crew for her jet too.

Kaylee reached for the model jet and grabbed it with two hands.

Damn, it was big and heavy, and it spilled into her arms. Hidden behind the supersized model, Kaylee stepped back and onto one of Adam's shoes. Her foot slid off the shoe. She wobbled back, and the jet flew out of her arms and crash-landed on the hardwood floor, smashing in two.

Shit!

The wings of the jet sagged and the tail was completely gone.

Kaylee gathered the damaged jet and tossed the pieces onto Adam's unkempt bed.

That's that.

She'd have it all bagged and removed.

"What the fuck!" Adam yelled from the open door.

Kaylee whipped around.

She could bark back the same, but nothing came out of her open mouth.

Why did he return, and who let him in?

Kaylee peered over Adam's shoulder.

He wasn't alone. Kosmos lurked behind him.

Kosmos stepped forward.

He shot his finger at Kaylee. "You!"

"It was an accident," Kaylee explained.

"My jet! Not Demetrios's!" Kosmos bellowed.

Kosmos kicked the door shut.

His hand shook while he groped into his jacket.

"No you don't!" Adam screamed.

Kosmos flung out a gun with his finger in the trigger. He swung the barrel haphazardly.

Kaylee hit the floor.

Pow-pow-pow!

Adam collapsed. Blood oozed from his chest and puddled around his body.

"What have you done?!" Kaylee screamed.

Kosmos tossed the gun on the floor at Kaylee's feet, and he bolted out of the bloody scene, screaming, "Fight! Fight! She killed my son! Policia! Policia!"

Kaylee leaned over Adam's body and listened for him breathing. Nothing. She then pressed her fingers against his neck, her own heart pounding. She couldn't feel a pulse.

Kaylee ran to the door and yelled, "Help! I need help! Call an ambulance!"

Kosmos dashed back into the room, laughing, and lurched at Kaylee.

She grabbed the gun, her hands slippery from Adam's blood, and pointed it at Kosmos.

"Back away!" she ordered him.

Daphne and Peter bolted into the room.

Daphne grabbed Kosmos.

"Drop the gun, now!" she ordered Kaylee.

The gun slid from Kaylee's hand.

With his eyes bulging, Peter grabbed Kaylee.

"What happened?!"

"I…I…no…I didn't kill him." Kaylee pointed at Kosmos. "He did. He missed me and shot Adam."

"You have the gun. Kosmos is disabled. He couldn't do this." Daphne kept shaking her head. "You hated Adam. He hated you. But to shoot him…"

"I did not."

"I can't believe this happened. Kaylee not do this," Peter pleaded.

"She's killed before."

"Different. No. Daphne, no."

"This is now a matter for the police. And no one touch that gun."

Kaylee's heart pounded to the back of her throat.

She was in a foreign country. Didn't speak or understand Greek. And now was accused of murder.

43

Kaylee sat on a bare, raged mattress and stared through the iron bars that caged her inside an Athens prison cell. They stripped her and searched her in ways Newell hadn't. Her bloody clothes were removed, bagged, and carried away. While Kaylee stood handcuffed, a woman guard hosed her down in a tiled shower room that reeked of bleach. Her "murder" clothes were replaced with a washed-out gray top and pants with no underwear or bra beneath the prison garb. She looked like some zombie doctor. Newell was surely smiling from his grave while Margo, who sat confined in whatever US prison they sent her, would be rolling on the floor, laughing.

What started out as a day of victory, ended up a mere twenty-four hours later in a resounding defeat. Worse, Kosmos was free.

Kaylee bent her head down, her chin to her chest. How could Daphne accuse her of murdering Adam?

Her head throbbed and her heart slammed against her ribs, like someone squeezing her so hard that she couldn't breathe.

Kaylee bolted to the steel commode, knelt on the cold concrete, and vomited what remained of her lunch. She never did have dinner with Peter and Vasaliki. Instead, she forced down some diluted mystery soup that they brought to her cell.

Kaylee laughed. It was actually worse than whatever Margo fed her—that is when Newell demanded Margo starve her as punishment.

The soup spewed from her mouth mixed with stomach acid, a concoction worthy of a laboratory experiment. When her insides filled the commode, she retched some more, releasing spoonfuls of yellow bile, and then collapsed on the concrete, which was absurdly cooling.

Kaylee rolled to her side, pulled her knees to her chest, and finally cried. Her tears dripped onto the concrete slab.

She was utterly alone.

She should never have gone into that kitchen, stolen those master keys, and invaded Adam's room when it hadn't even grown cold from the heat of his body. Now it was stone-cold and surely sealed off as a crime scene—a crime she didn't commit.

But no one was listening.

A rippling clanking across the iron bars assailed her ears and threatened her head to explode.

"You, there. Get off the floor," the woman yelled within accent.

Kaylee squinted up at the woman guard.

Her first instinct was to yell at the woman to go to hell, but she didn't. That would only make matters a thousand times worse, if not unsurmountable.

Kaylee pushed to a stand as ordered.

A lock clicked.

Her heartbeat rocketed. The clicking locks on her cell at the Miami house of horrors resurfaced.

The woman guard and another behind her stepped inside the cell with guns drawn.

"Hands on your head," the head guard commanded.

Kaylee complied.

Everyone she had contact with, including the arresting officer, the driver on the other side of the wire netting in the prison transport van, and the guards, spoke English. How many times had they arrested US citizens? Didn't matter. She'd only fantasized that she was one of them— a Greek.

The guard positioned Kaylee's hands to behind her back, handcuffed them, and then shackled her ankles while the other one pointed her gun at Kaylee as a warning to not resist.

They flanked her out of her cell and led her down a long hallway with cracked and peeling paint that used to be yellow.

She passed women in cells sitting on the same dingy mattresses, some still as statues, and others rocking back and forth. Women screamed Greek profanities while gripping the iron bars and some cackled. Kaylee shuffled forward in the most bizarre catwalk.

They halted in front of a wood door that had been clearly updated to this century.

The guard pressed a buzzer attached to the wall next to the door.

A click.

One guard opened the door while the other escorted Kaylee into the stark room where the same arresting officer and, man she'd never seen, in a black robe, his face stern below his black bushy brows, sat on the same side of a dark wood table with a single chair which sat opposite them, meant for her.

The guard lowered Kaylee into the chair.

"Good evening, Miss Jasinski,"the arresting officer said.

"Good evening," Kaylee responded.

The more polite and cooperative she was, the sooner they would realize that she was innocent, and then she could go back to the mansion after the charge was dropped.

"This is Judge Markou. He is the investigating judge assigned to your case."

"I don't understand. Is this a trial?"

"No, it is not. Our system provides for a judge to begin the investigation and then, when the case is prepared, it is passed to a judge who will hear the case and render a decision along with a jury."

"Do you understand the charge made against you?" the judge asked.

"My apologies, Judge Markou, but I do not feel comfortable responding to your inquiry without an attorney present."

She knew that much. But that was in the US, and might not be the same in Greece.

Judge Markou nodded, stood, and left the room.

Shit. Had she angered him?

The officer pushed a document across the table and in front of Kaylee. It was in Greek.

"I request a translator."

"No need." He turned over the paper to reveal the English version." Please sign this attestation."

Kaylee shook her head. "I won't sign anything without an attorney."

"You don't understand. Please read it. It states that you understand that you have been read all rights accorded to you under Greek law. As you may recall, I read you those rights upon my arrival to the Sakalis domicile."

"I was in shock."

"Understandably so. Please read."

Kaylee reviewed the one page document. It was as the officer said.

"I'll sign, but I need at least one hand, my right hand. I'm right-handed."

The officer nodded to the guard who loosened Kaylee's handcuffs.

She looked at her wrists. Although they weren't excoriated from the the zip ties Newell ordered, her wrists still ached from the handcuffs.

Under the watchful eye of the guard and the officer, Kaylee signed the document.

"May I call my attorney now?"

"Yes," the officer answered. "I'll bring you to the telephone."

The guard re-secured her handcuffs, and she and the officer led her to another room where a telephone sat on a desk.

"Ummm. I don't know how to use this."

She'd heard of landlines, but she'd never seen one. Apparently they weren't obsolete here.

"We will dial it for you. Local calls only."

"My attorney's name is Thelonious Chaconas. His practice is in Athens, but I don't have his telephone number."

She'd left his business card in her bedroom. So far, she hadn't been allowed visitors.

A bead of sweat trailed down her spine.

The officer took out a directory.

They still had directories?

He pointed to Thelonious Chaconas, Dikigoros.

"Yes, that's him."

The officer dialed the number.

Kaylee forgot it was evening and Mr. Chaconas's office was certainly closed.

She could hear the phone ringing on the other side of the receiver. A message in Greek followed.

Figures.

The officer hung up the phone, but then he picked it back up and dialed another number.

A man answered in Greek, but she recognized Mr. Chaconas's voice!

The officer held the receiver to Kaylee's ear.

"Mr. Chaconas, I desperately need your help. I've been accused of killing Adam. I didn't do it! Please help me!"

"I'm on my way. Please give the telephone back to the officer so he can tell me where you are being held."

Oh, my God. She had no idea where she was, only that it was some prison in Athens.

"Okay," the officer said and hung up the phone again.

Mr. Chaconas would explain everything. She was saved!

The guard removed Kaylee's handcuffs and shackles after her return to her solitary cell, the guard slammed and locked the bars that separated her from the outside.

Kaylee lay on the saggy mattress.

The chaos surrounding the other prisoners was eerily quiet, and it wasn't even lights out.

Kaylee stared where the gray ceiling intersected with the paler walls.

At least she had a window in this cell, a tall rectangle no wider than both her hands and covered with black bars.

Summer evening sunlight beamed into her cell.

The lock released and the cell's bars slid open.

"Mr. Chaconas! You've come!"

"Of course."

"I didn't do it!"

Thelonious held up his hands.

"I don't know the details of what occurred, but what I do know is that you're not capable of murder."

Kaylee swallowed past her dry throat.

What if they found out that the fork she stabbed into Otto's eye didn't kill him, but contributed to his ultimate demise? And then she shot Newell. But that was to avenge Demetrios's murder at Newell's hands. Besides, Newell's body was riddled with gunshots from Harry, Brad Jarrett, and Lou Ann. They covered for her, but she shot him first. She wasn't going to admit to any of this. She landed here accused of killing Adam, and that was what she was going to defend. If they wanted her for Newell, they would've already have come after her.

Kaylee blurted the catastrophic events that occurred in Adam's room.

Thelonious slowed her several times to digest the details.

"Where's Kosmos?"

"I don't know. After he came back to attack me, I picked up his gun in self-defense. Then he ran away and the police arrived and arrested me."

"You picked up the gun with Adam dead on the floor?" Thelonious clarified.

"Yes."

"Okay. Did you speak with the police or with a judge?"

"No, I politely declined until I could consult my attorney, you."

"Did you sign any documents?"

"Yes."

Thelonious winced.

"I signed what the arresting officer read to me regarding my rights before taking me away."

"All right."

"What's our next step?" Kaylee asked.

Thelonious shifted on the mattress.

"Kaylee, I do not specialize in criminal defense."

Her hope deflated before it could rise off the floor.

Thelonious put his arm around Kaylee's shoulder. "Wait. I'll contact the US embassy for legal aid. Plus, I know a colleague who does specialize in criminal defense. I'll help you."

"I need to get out of here, Mr. Chaconas."

"You'll need to stay here while we mount your defense."

"How long is that?"

Thelonious shrugged.

"Can you please call my Aunt Lou Ann? I don't have my cell, and they would've taken it away anyway. They only let me make a local call with the phone in the the office…and I called you."

"Absolutely."

Kaylee ticked off the number and Thelonious entered in his cell and then gave Kaylee the phone.

Her heart pounded with every ring.

Please, please, pick up!

44

Lou Ann 's cell rang. She pulled her cruiser into a lot and grabbed her cell.

She smiled. Probably Harry calling her about this morning.

Lou Ann glanced at the caller ID. It was from Greece, but it wasn't Kaylee's number.

What the….

"Hello?"

Snotty blubbering.

"Hello?"

"Aunt Lou Ann," Kaylee squeaked out in between gasps.

Lou Ann's stomach knotted.

"What's wrong? Where are you?"

"I'm in a prison in Athens."

Lou Ann cut the cruiser's engine.

Her breathing echoed in her ears. She clasped her hand over her mouth.

"Aunt Lou Ann!" Kaylee cried.

Lou Ann clutched her phone.

"I'm right here. Why are you there? What happened?"

"I've been accused of murder."

Lou Ann's heart seized in her chest.

"Don't say anything. I'll get an attorney. Where…where…are you? What prison?"

"I don't know! A big one," she sobbed.

"Here," Lou Ann heard Kaylee say.

"Hello, Ms. Jasinski. I'm Thleonious Chaconas, Demetrios's lawyer. This is my cell number. Kaylee is understandably distressed so she handed me the phone."

"Thank you,"Lou Ann breathed.

"I know this is as big a shock for you as it is for me, and most important for Kaylee."

"I'm unfamiliar with the justice system there. I'll be on my way to Athens, shortly, and I have your number. Can you text me where she is?"

"I'll do that."

"Thank God you're with her."

"Yes. Unfortunately, I don't do criminal defense, but I have a colleague who does. I'll contact US Embassy. We will begin to mount a defense for her."

Lou Ann swallowed. "It will take me one or two days to get there."

"Call me or text with your arrival information and I will meet you at the airport. I'm so sorry all this happened."

"I'm in shock myself."

"I know it is beyond difficult, but breathe and be safe. This will be a long process."

"All right." Lou Ann paused. "May I speak with Kaylee again?"

"Aunt Lou Ann," Kaylee blurted.

"I'm coming. It's going to take time. I know how strong you are. We're all going to pull together."

"Okay."

"Okay," Lou Ann responded.

But it was far from okay.

Lou Ann parked the cruiser into her driveway, and Jake parked his cherry red Porsche behind it.

Harry's car was gone.

Jake followed Lou Ann to the front door.

He placed his hand on Lou Ann's shoulder.

"We'll make a plan."

She didn't flinch or swat off his hand. She well remembered Jake's sexual overture's, but his gesture was clearly comforting.

She unlocked and opened the door.

"Come in."

Jake stepped inside.

"You're home," Joanna called.

She rushed to the living room and skidded to stop.

She pointed at Jake.

"Who's that?"

"This is my friend, Jake. He's an attorney."

"Jake, this Joanna, who is lives here and is part of my family."

Jake nodded and extended his hand, but Joanna rebuffed his offer.

"Why is he here, and why do you need a lawyer?" Joanna demanded.

"I don't need a lawyer, but Kaylee does."

The faster she revealed the gut-wrenching reason, the faster she and Jake could move to free Kaylee.

Joanna's eyes popped huge.

"What?"

"We have to sit down and talk."

Joanna backed down, but her glare directed at Jake didn't.

"Let's go into the den."

Joanna gathered her papers from the coffee table.

"I was studying in here."

"What are you studying?" Jake asked.

"I'm planning to obtain a high school degree so I can study nursing. The other stuff is from the DMV to get my driver's license."

"Looks like you've been very busy. That's terrific."

"Yeah."

"Here's what needs to happen," Lou Ann said. "First, I need to finish my shift. I can't abandon my duties. I'll need to contact my superiors and let them know that I'll require a leave of absence."

Again.

She was prepared to accept the consequences.

Jake looked at Joanna. "Only if it's all right with you, I'll stay here and get the ball rolling to leave for Greece."

Lou Ann looked at Joanna.

"Your opinion matters. I can vouch for him.

Joanna studied Jake.

"Okay. I'll be in my *locked* room."

"I wouldn't put you in danger," Lou Ann reassured Joanna.

"I know. But I prefer to be alone. I have a lot of studying to do."

"I'll stay in here and wait for your return," Jake said. "But, before you leave, I'll need a laptop. I'll log in as a guest."

"No need."

Lou Ann grabbed her laptop and logged into it. "Here you go. I should be back around five."

She stopped by Joanna's and *Kaylee's* room and knocked on the door.

"Are you okay?"

Joanna didn't come to the door, but called from beyond it, "Yeah. Do what you need to do."

"I'll be back soon."

Probably sooner.

* * *

Joanna put her ear against the bedroom door.

Silence.

Where was this guy?

She hadn't heard any footsteps going toward the hall bathroom—the one she and Kaylee shared, and now only her bathroom.

No toilet flushing. No water running in the sink.

Joanna tucked Kaylee's laptop under her arm and eased the door open.

This guy, Jake, had Lou Ann's best interests in mind and, most important, Kaylee's. And it was in her best interest and Kaylee's to work with him.

Joanna entered the den to find Jake engrossed in a laptop.

"Ahem."

Jake looked up.

"Hi, Joanna."

"Hello."

She sat on the couch opposite Jake, who sat in a chair with the computer across his lap.

"What are you searching?"

"Greek law.

"Ummm. That is key."

"I agree."

"I can help you with important information on Kaylee's laptop. She gave me the password so I"m not doing anything wrong, just to let you know."

"All right, especially since you revealed that she willingly gave you the password."

"Kaylee and I shared a room, and since I didn't have a laptop of my own, we shared this one."

Joanna clicked her fingertips over the keyboard.

"Here are Kaylee's emails. She'd been in contact with Peter, Demetrios's right hand man."

Joanna hadn't accessed the emails since Kaylee disappeared from that courtroom.

She entered the emails.

"Oh, my."

"What, oh, my?"

"Umm. Here's Peter's email."

Jake entered Peter's email into his cell.

"What's bothering you?" he asked.

Joanna shrugged. "It's personal, and I can't do anything about it now."

"Anything I can help you with?"

"Nope."

She was so busy searching for drivers' licenses and high school equivalency courses that she hadn't even looked at Kaylee's emails. Besides, Kaylee was already gone, and she thought Kaylee would be happier in Greece. She couldn't fathom how this venture would turn so dangerous. Kaylee didn't let her know about her plan to escape to Greece that day…or that Peter was instrumental in providing a jet for her. Kaylee had betrayed her.

But what was done was done. Now she needed to focus on extricating Kaylee from a situation of her own making. But murder? No.

Joanna closed the laptop.

"So you and Lou Ann will be going to Greece?"

Jake nodded. "I have a friend in Greece who specializes in criminal defense, such as murder."

"She didn't do it."

"That's exactly what your Aunt Lou Ann and I are convinced of, too."

"Is your friend good?"

Jake grinned. "She is. She's a fighter."

"That's a perfect match, because so is Kaylee."

<h1 style="text-align:center">45</h1>

Lou Ann drove around in her cruiser, her mind circling. She desperately needed Harry, but he apparently was on a secret mission and temporarily unavailable, and she had no clue how long "temporary" would last.

He'd been away for weeks in the past.

Forgive me, Harry. I can't wait. I know you'll understand.

Four o'clock sharp had arrived, Dan's bewitching hour.

But today four o'clock couldn't come fast enough.

She hurried back to headquarters. Fortunately, she'd received no calls. God was certainly looking out for her, and she prayed He was watching over Kaylee.

She shuddered when she imagined Kaylee's wretched prison conditions.

She smacked the steering wheel. How much more? Kaylee survived Newell' captivity, and now she was a prisoner again.

Lou Ann parked the cruiser and strode into headquarters.

She'd go straight to Glenda's office.

Dan was a roadblock waiting to happen.

Lou Ann passed through security and took the elevator to Glenda's fourth floor office.

She drew a deep breath and entered the reception area.

"I urgently need to speak with Deputy Chief Martinez," she said to Glenda's assistant.

"One second, please."

Why do they always say one second?

The assistant looked sideways at Lou Ann and went into Glenda's private office.

"She'll see you now."

Lou Ann entered Glenda's domain.

Glenda looked up from her desk. "Oh, hi, Lou Ann."

Glenda's smile melted.

"You look pale. Are you unwell?"

"You could say that. I received devastating news that my niece, Kaylee, is presently detained in an Athens prison and accused of murder."

Glenda's eyebrows shot up to her forehead.

"I thought she was living with you."

"She was. But she returned to Greece. I can't go into details right now, but I need my shifts and duties covered."

"How much time do you need?"

"I don't know right now. Undetermined. That's the best I can offer."

Dan burst into Glenda's office "The best you can offer?" he barked.

The assistant ran into the office. "I tried to stop him, ma'am."

Glenda raised her hands. "Everybody, quiet."

"There's a chain of command here," Dan seethed.

Glenda drew a deep breath.

"Sergeant Jasinski, Lieutenant Mathews is correct."

"I can't hold held her position. She has no further leave of absence available. I can empathize with her niece's troubles, but foreign trials are a hundred times slower than the ones here, and you how long those take."

"My niece's troubles?" Lou Ann shot back.

"That's enough," Glenda warned.

"Lou Ann, unfortunately I can't grant an unknown leave. We have to continue to function. If you leave now…" Glenda massaged her forehead,"then you leave me no choice but to suspend you."

Dan nodded.

"Okay. I'll take the suspension."

"I'll need your firearm, and keys to your cruiser."

Lou Ann removed her gunbelt, and set the keys to her cruiser on Glenda's desk.

"I'm so sorry. But at this time, this is a suspension and not a termination."

"I understand. You have to do what have to do, and I have to do what I have to do."

Lou Ann faced Dan. "I emailed the reviews by 1630."

Then she walked past him and out the door.

Lou Ann exited the building.

She wasn't their problem anymore.

She pulled her cell out of the pocket of a uniform that soon would go stale, and called Jake.

"Can you pick me up at headquarters?"

"Uh, yeah. What's up?"

"I've been suspended."

"I'm on my way."

Lou Ann stared straight ahead in Jake's Porsche.

"I can't believe you still have this. But you've kept it in mint condition."

"Somethings are meant to last."

Jake stopped at a red light.

"I'm sorry about how we ended. I'm not the best at relationships."

Lou Ann turned to look at Jake, but he was already looking at her.

"Really?"

They laughed.

"I missed you, but I respect that you and Harry have reconciled. I'm not in this to cause any trouble. But I've experienced when someone you love is unjustly accused and the devastation surrounding a seemingly never-ending process. I…uh…went into law because of that."

"You never told me."

"You only gave me three months." Jake hesitated. "And that was on me."

Lou Ann chuckled. "So true."

"Yeah, I was an asshole, and still tend to be one. But I'm working on it. See? I've stayed within the speed limit."

"If you hadn't sped by me that day, I'd be floundering to help someone I love." Lou Ann eyes. searched into Jake's eyes. "You floundered, too."

"Still do."

The light turned green.

Jake parked where Lou Ann's cruiser used to stand.

"Are you okay?"

"I will be."

"All right. It's time to hit the ground running."

Joanna opened the door, waiting for them.

"Jake told me."

Jake shrugged. "I had to explain why I was leaving. Plus, Joanna and I were working together when you called. She heard the gist of the conversation. I had to be straight with her."

"I'm sorry, Aunt Lou Ann."

"Don't be. I'm not."

On the upside, she'd dreamed of sticking it to Dan.

"Okay. I'm going to change out of this uniform and into another set of "working " clothes. Then I can see what you two have accomplished."

"We'll be waiting for you," Joanna said.

"Then I certainly don't want to be late."

Lou Ann shut her and Harry's bedroom door.

She took off her uniform and hung it far back in her closet where she couldn't see it. She'd made her decision, and she'd have to accept the consequences that her seven-year career was over.

Glenda was always on her side, but suspensions never ended well. They were only terminations in disguise.

She couldn't allow what happened, or what she might happen, to detract from the real priority, Kaylee's future.

Lou Ann returned to the den. Dressed in jeans and a tee, she was ready for business.

Lou Ann, Joanna, and Jake gathered around a coffee table covered with laptops, legal pads, and pens. Even Isabelle attended the meeting. Harry was the only one absent.

Lou Ann had called his personal cell and left a message for him to call her about a critical matter involving Kaylee. That's all his voicemail could hold, and that's all she wanted to reveal.

He'd call back the second he listened to it, but his cell was probably locked up somewhere. He was most likely involved in some highly classified sting operation, which required that there be no personal cell calls to distract or to be hacked.

Otherwise, Harry would be here in a heartbeat.

"How far did you guys get?" Lou Ann asked.

"I accessed Kaylee's email and was able to get Peter's email address."

For reasons she never understood, Peter didn't own a cell, and he couldn't drive. His communications were either via in person or email. Email would have to do at the moment.

It was midnight in Greece, but Lou Ann fired off an email to Peter to get critical details on the circumstances surrounding Kaylee's arrest. She didn't know when or how often he checked his email, but she could only hope that he'd answer back before she and Jake departed for Greece.

"Email to Peter done," she announced.

Joanna checked it off on their to-do list.

"I've booked airfare for two to Athens. We leave Tampa International at 2 pm tomorrow, but we need to get there at least by eleven. I was lucky to get those in lightning-short notice. Coach."

"I don't care if they strap me to the wing. Thank you, Jake."

Lou Ann looked at Joanna.

"It's fine. It's important that you and Jake go. I can't help Kaylee, but you can. I'll stay here with Isabelle and wait for Harry."

"I love you, Joanna."

"I love you too, and Kaylee, despite our tiffs. I'd give anything to argue with her again."

"And I'd be overjoyed to referee."

Jake stood. "I'm leaving to get ready. I'll pick you up at ten tomorrow."

"See you then, Jake."

46

Kaylee lay on her mattress in the quiet dark, the full moon her muted nightlight.

Thelonious promised to return with his colleague in the morning, and who knows when anyone would arrive from the embassy.

But the more lawyers on her side, the better chance she stood of getting out of this hellhole.

Plus, they could search for Kosmos, the real perpetrator.

Daphne had to know where he was. She was probably hiding him.

And she thought Daphne was her friend—her family.

Peter was right about her.

She rolled to her side.

How many more nights would she have to stay in this prison?

Kaylee covered her face with her hands.

What if they falsely convicted her?

She might never get out of here.

The bang and thrum of a baton across the iron bars was meant to wake her. But the joke was on the guard because Kaylee was already awake.

She half-nodded off a few times, but never approached REM.

Kaylee sat up to shut up the guard's Neanderthal alarm.

The guard shoved their version of clean prison garb through the bars.

A gap-toothed comb followed.

"You get ready. You have visitors waiting. You have five minutes."

Humph. Five minutes to get presentable by prison standards.

The guard stood on the other side of the bars.

There was nowhere to undress. Nowhere to hide. Margo all over again.

"Can you please turn around?"

"No."

Kaylee sighed.

"Now you have four minutes," the guard announced.

"May I have underwear? Panties at least?"

"You must get credits to purchase or lawyer to bring."

Kaylee pulled off her prison pants, using the top to cover her privates. Then she yanked on the stiff bleached pants. She tore off her top and ducked into the equally stiff new one. At least they were sanitized.

She inspected what remained of a black comb and stuttered it through her tangled hair.

"Time is up. Back against the wall."

Two guards marched in. She hadn't seen these two before. Change of shift, she supposed.

"Hands on head."

She knew the drill.

On went the handcuffs. On went the shackles. Out of the cell. Past the same rowdy inmates.

But they led her past the inquisition door, down another hallway devoid of cells and buzzed her into a room with the same wood table and chairs.

Mr. Chaconas stood, and so did a blond-haired man who looked more like the lawyer's son. Despite wearing a well-fitted suit and a polite smile, this couldn't be a man of experience. Crap. He probably just graduated from law school. This wasn't good.

But she trusted Thelonious.

"Good morning, Mr. Chaconas. Pardon my appearance."

"You slept poorly, yes?"

"Yes."

"But today, progress."

Her heart singed. "You found Kosmos?!

"No"

Scratched vinyl.

"Progress meaning the beginning of your defense."

"Kaylee, may I introduce you to my colleague, Constantine Galatas."

"I'd shake your hand, but you know…."

Constantine chuckled. "I like her."

The guard lowered Kaylee into the chair and position herself in a corner.

"Does she need to be here?"

"Yes. This is an old prison, and they've only now started to upgrade with cameras."

Kaylee sagged in the chair.

Constantine took a folder out of his briefcase.

"I reviewed the police report, but I'm here to represent you, so I want you to tell me exactly what happened before, during, and, after."

"I was trafficked from Miami to Demetrios Sakalis, but circumstances radically changed. We fell in love. He regretted ever getting involved with the traffickers. He reneged and refused to pay them. He was murdered for that.

"Before all that, as Mr. Chaconas can verify, that Demetrios amended a will naming me as his beneficiary. Pandemonium happened after. Adam and Kosmos were very angry. An argument ensued involving them and Daphne too. I thought Daphne, although a little sour, accepted the will. I mean she has own large estate. Adam left for good, I believed, and Daphne said she would arrange for custodial care given that Kosmos is mentally challenged."

Constantine grinned.

"What is so amusing, Mr. Galatas?"

"Go on. I'll tell you later."

"All right. I decided to redecorate the third floor bedrooms, where my and Adam's's bedrooms are located. I wanted to turn them into a place where my US family can stay. I obtained a master key, entered Adams's ex-room, and in the process I picked up a large model airplane. I tripped on scattered clothes and shoes on the floor and the model airplane broke.

"Then Adam and Kosmos walked in…and strangely, Kosmos appeared more upset than Adam about the broken jet. Kosmos' hands were shaking. He reached into his jacket, and I was convinced he was aiming at me, so I hit the floor and the bullets hit Adam. I tried to save Adam, but there was too much blood. Kosmos dumped the gun at my feet and ran out screaming for police and yelling that I shot Adam. He then came back and he was lunging at me. I picked up the gun in self-defense. Peter and Daphne arrived. Daphne accused me of shooting Adam. Kosmos disappeared. The police arrested me for a murder I didn't commit, and here I am."

Thelonious Chaconas nodded. "The part about the addendum in the office is correct. Kaylee's description matches exactly what she relayed to me. There are no inconsistencies."

"I see you signed only one document, and that was the one you attested that were read your rights. That's standard. Nothing incriminating. Mr. Chaconas told me you didn't sign any other papers or discuss the nature of your allegation to anyone else."

"That's not exactly true."

Thelonious's and Constantine's faces soured.

"Mr. Chaconas, remember I used your cell to tell my aunt."

"Oh. That's not what he or I meant. No one else? No one here?"

"No."

"I'm going to show a photo that may shock you," Constantine said.

"At this point, nothing can shock me."

"This will."

47

Lou Ann dialed Harry.

Voicemail again.

"Come on, Lou Ann. They're boarding. We can't miss this flight."

She caught up with Jake.

They slow walked along the jet's long aisles, stopping and starting while passengers stuffed their roller bags into the overhead bins.

She wanted to get off the jet without having to claim bags and then stand in line at international arrivals.

Then there was the threat of lost luggage between their stop in New York and the final destination, Athens. She'd leave nothing to chance.

They made it to their seats two thirds in, and managed to push their small bags into the bin behind their assigned seats.

Let this be an omen.

There was still time to make a call before they took off.

"We're on board," she said to Joanna.

"I'll take care of everything here."

"Thanks, sweetie."

"And yes, I'll keep trying to reach Harry and let him know."

"You read my mind. I have to go now. I'll call you when we land."

"Stay safe, and tell Kaylee to keep strong."

"I will."

Lou Ann pushed back in her seat, set her phone in airplane mode, and plugged it into the charger.

Jake plugged his in next to hers.

She'd try Harry again, and Joanna, when they got to New York.

"Here's some good news. My Greek attorney friend is on her way to see Kaylee."

"Her?"

"Yeah, she's a kick-ass criminal defense attorney, and no we've never dated."

"Kick-ass is exactly what Kaylee needs."

Kaylee studied the photo Constantine slid in front of her.

He warned her it would be shocking, but it was more of a fantastical disbelief.

Behind the mustache and curly black wig, she could tell by his eyes and his angular features, that it was Kosmos.

"That's Kosmos ,and why the disguise? When was this photo taken?" she demanded.

"Last week," Constantine replied.

"Last week? Where? How? Does Daphne know? Did Adam know?"

"A lot of questions. Excellent questions. And I'm going to answer them."

"Like you, I am a meticulous observer. I went with friends to a nightclub just on the fringe of Athens that I'd never been to before. We heard all this whooping and hollering and that made us look to see what was going on. So we heard that this guy, Tobias, was celebrating a windfall coming his way. He was buying drinks for everyone. He was a standout, so we took our phones out and snapped some photos. I didn't think any more of it until Thelonious called me to represent you and handed me photos of the Sakalis family, and of you. There was something about Kosmos. I knew I'd seen him somewhere , and then it occurred to me to look at my cellphone photos. I expanded the images and both Thelonious and you identified him as Kosmos. I believe it is. And based on the dancing, drinking, and conversations, it's easy to conclude that Kosmos is not an idiot, and he's not disabled. As far as Daphne and Adam are concerned, I don't believe they know he's been faking his illness all these years, or that he's been living a double life. We're going to question Daphne."

Kaylee shook her head. This was mind-blowing. And it was going to exonerate her! Then she had second thoughts about her celebration.

"Adam is dead, and Daphne is out of the country by now. Where does that leave me?"

"Temporarily here."

"How temporarily?"

"Let's focus on your defense."

"Answer me."

"The murder allegation, although false, is serious. The system takes time."

"What am I looking at?

"Twelve to eighteen months before your trial."

Kaylee's muscles seized and Constantine's reassuring words scrambled in her head.

She rattled her handcuffs and shook her leg irons.

"No!"

The guard called for another guard.

Constantine stood. "Wait please. Give her a moment."

"Kaylee, you'll be free sooner. Trust me. That is the standard, but I swear to you that you are anything but standard." Constantine leaned forward and softly added, "You have to stay calm because they can add time for disobedience."

Kaylee drew a painful breath and apologized for her outburst.

The other guard left, but the head one nodded and resumed her position in the corner.

"Good," Constantine remarked.

Thelonious's cell rang.

"Hello. Yes she's doing as well as possible. Good, I'll meet you at the airport."

"Was that Daphne?

"No, it was your aunt. She's in New York, and she should arrive this evening."

Kaylee sniffled.

That was a million times better than Daphne.

Aunt Lou Ann and Harry would know exactly what to do. They did before.

"How's Kaylee holding up?"

"Chaconas says she's doing the best she can. But she was psychologically damaged before any of this happened. If I only could've gotten to her before that jet took off."

"She would've gone that day or another day." Jake paused. "I have to be completely honest with you. If she wins her case and is exonerated, Kaylee will still be the beneficiary of the estate, so be prepared that she may not leave Greece."

"But she's not a Greek citizen?"

"I'll bet you she's investigated the process."

Lou Ann's heart hammered hard against her ribs.

Jake only sought to soften the fall coming.

"We need to step it up if we're gonna make our connection," Jake said.

Their roller bags' wheels whirred behind them while they rushed to the last leg of their journey.

48

The buzzer announced another request to enter to the prisoner conference room.

"Who could that be?" Kaylee asked.

It couldn't be Lou Ann because she was en route to Greece. Plus, Lou Ann wouldn't be allowed into the room that was strictly for attorneys and their client prisoners. Kaylee hadn't been allowed any other visitors…yet.

The guard proceeded to the door and peered through the tiny, netted window.

Then she opened the door and a woman in a gray suit, her brown hair in a bun, entered.

"Hello. I'm Anelle Florakis-Dikigoros, criminal defense attorney," she clarified.

Kaylee shrugged, and Thelonious and Constantine widened their eyes.

They too had no idea who this statuesque woman carrying a gray briefcase was.

"Are you from the US Embassy?" Thelonious asked while Constantine was checking her out.

"No. I have a US colleague who knows Miss Jasinski's aunt, and I've been asked to represent Miss Jasinski."

"We could use an excellent attorney to join, although it is up to Kaylee."

"I need all the help I can get," said Kaylee, "but I can't afford you, Ms. Florakis."

"No retainer is needed, because my services are already paid for."

"My aunt?"

Kaylee wasn't willing to bankrupt Lou Ann.

"No."

Anelle Florakis stood waiting.

"You know about me through a colleague who knows my Aunt Lou Ann Jasinski?" Kaylee asked.

"That's correct."

Thelonious stood.

"Please have my seat and you two counsel Ms. Jasinski. I'll be outside."

"Mr. Chaconas," Kaylee called.

"It's all right. You are in excellent hands, and I will always be available for you."

"Thank you, for everything."

"Demetrios wanted me to look out for you, but after meeting you, I would have done it anyway."

Kaylee and Thelonious waved, and he left the room.

Constantine stood and shook Anelle's hand.

"Constantine Galatas."

"Anelle Florakis."

"I'd stand, but as Mr. Galatas can attest, I couldn't greet him properly either," Kaylee said.

Anelle smiled. "That's all right. I get it."

Anelle and Constantine sat opposite Kaylee.

"I'm really popular this morning," Kaylee joked.

"You're popular everywhere today."

"Is that good or bad?"

"Mostly good. Okay, let's get down to business. Mr. Galatas will bring me up to speed. Basically this a circumstantial case. The only witnesses are you and Kosmos. But it was his gun. And we're waiting for the medical examiner's autopsy report on Adam."

Constantine showed Anelle the photo of Kosmos he so fortuitously took, along with the explanation.

"So our suspect likes to play masquerade. And I love masquerade. Lots of fun."

Anelle reviewed the arrest document and the assigned investigating judge.

"I know this judge. He's as reasonable as he is fair. We have that going for us."

"I've presented to him too, and I agree."

"Nothing about this has been fair," Kaylee said.

Anelle nodded. "I know. I can understand how frightening this has been."

Kaylee leaned forward as much as she could. "I've been frightened before."

Kaylee sat on the saggy mattress and rubbed her wrists. She'd been handcuffed all morning. But it was worth it because she had a crackerjack legal team, now including the super-nice Embassy lawyer, who was on standby.

They were all on her side, dedicated to see her through this. Lou Ann and Harry were the only ones missing from her team, but hopefully not for long.

Kaylee stuttered a breath.

What if despite Anelle's and Constantine's experience with the investigating judge, the judge remanded her case to the next judge and then to a jury? Tears smudged her cheeks. What if after up to two years in this prison cell she'd be found guilty? It happened to foreigners all the time.

The same guard overseeing her attorney meeting unlocked and slid open the cell's bars.

Her gun remained holstered, and she entered alone.

"Lunch," she announced, her voice lacking its usual brusqueness, even bordering on polite.

The guard set the tray with chunks of lamb, boiled potatoes—and, yes, Kaylee's nemesis vegetable, green beans, on the mattress next to Kaylee.

"Eat."

The guard turned and left without looking back, unprecedented and trustworthy.

She'd heard everything, and made up her own mind.

The guard secured the bars.

"Thank you, "Kaylee said.

"You're welcome."

Hmmm. She'd even eat the green beans.

49

Lou Ann and Jake sailed through customs. Another good omen.

Jake waved to a leggy woman in a gray suit and with her hair in a loose bun. Her pearl necklace bobbed while she strode with purpose toward them.

"Anelle!" Jake called.

She hugged him.

"So happy to see you again."

Again?

"Anelle Florakis, this is Lou Ann Jasinski, Kaylee's aunt. Lou Ann, meet Anelle, Kaylee's kick-ass lawyer," Jake introduced them.

"One of Kaylee's kick-ass lawyers," Anelle clarified with a smile.

She held out her hand to Lou Ann, and the women shook.

"I can't thank you enough for representing Kaylee," Lou Ann said.

"She's a strong and brave young lady, and innocent."

Lou Ann struggled against the tears stinging her eyes. The sleepless flight added to the burn.

"I can't believe this is happening."

Anelle's eyes softened. "A circumstantial and very defendable case."

"My sentiments exactly," Jake added.

A white-bearded man tottered toward them.

Lou Ann raised her arm.

"Peter!" she called.

Peter waved with his hands criss-crossing.

Lou Ann ran to him and they collided with a hug.

"I have a driver. I didn't want to miss you."

"I'm so glad to see you."

"I told the police Kaylee not do this. They no let me see her."

A dark-haired, clean-shaven young man eased to the group.

"Thelonious Chaconas," he introduced himself.

Wow. He looked her age. Or maybe even younger. But he spoke eloquently, and with perfect English. Lou Ann instinctively trusted him.

"Yes, we spoke the other day, and you let me speak with Kaylee for the first time since she left, and I am eternally grateful to you."

"What happened is a tragedy, and it is not right."

Lou Ann gazed at the overwhelming greeters surrounding her.

"I didn't anticipate all this outpouring, and I'm thrilled to find she has so many supporters."

"Let's get you settled. You two must be exhausted. Are those all your bags?" Anelle asked.

"Yes, we limited to carried-on to avoid any delays."

"Smart. You're welcome to stay in my apartment in Athens."

"We'll stay at a hotel."

"I have limited room, but I'll be happy to share," Thelonious said.

Peter interrupted. "Nonsense. They'll come with me. I have a driver dedicated to Lou Ann and her friend, and there are ample rooms ready and waiting at the mansion."

Lou Ann hesitated. Demetrios's estate meant nothing but murder to her.

"You'll be nowhere near the tragic incident. Kaylee and Demetrios would've wanted you to stay."

Jake shrugged. "Totally up to you. Don't do anything you're uncomfortable with."

Despite Anelle's and Thelonious's genuine offers, Lou Ann walked up to Peter.

"Let's go."

The chauffeur stowed Lou Ann's and Jake's bags in the limo's trunk and escorted Peter, Lou Ann, and Jake into the more than roomy rear seating.

Horns beeped while the limo maneuvered in and out of busy lanes to the airport's exit.

"We'll be in Ekali in about thirty minutes," the driver announced over the speaker.

Lou Ann touched Peter's right arm where she mistakenly shot him last time in Demetrios's garden.

"It's good. Heal well." Peter grinned. "How is your leg?"

"It's good. Healed well," she parodied him.

She and Peter and chuckled.

"Friendly fire?" Jake asked.

"Very," Lou Ann replied.

Lou Ann took out her cell and called Joanna, who answered on the fourth ring.

"Hi, Joanna. We're in Athens and on the way to the mansion."

"Mmm," Joanna sleepily said.

"I'm sorry. I forgot about the time difference."

"It's okay. I'm awake. How are you and Jake?"

"All right."

"So are you in a taxi?"

"No. I'm calling from a limo."

"Limo? Wow."

"You remember Peter?"

"Vaguely. I know him from his emails."

"I'm here with Peter and Jake. Two of Kaylee's lawyers also met us. They're top-flight."

"That's awesome. Kaylee needs them, and you."

"She needs you and Harry, too."

Lou Ann held her breath.

"Aunt Lou Ann?"

She exhaled. "Yes, I'm here."

"I haven't heard from Harry."

"We'll keep trying to reach him, and I'll keep you in the loop."

"I love you."

"I love you too. Give Isabelle a hug, and hopefully I'll be back with Kaylee. Goodnight."

"Good night, and call me no matter the time zones."

Lou Ann ended the call and called Harry.

Her heartbeat buzzed in her ears.

Voicemail again.

She'd keep trying until he finally answered.

"No go, huh?" Jake asked.

"No."

"Sorry."

"So am I."

They arrived at the estate ten minutes early.

"He has, how you say? Lead foot," Peter said.

"With bricks on top," she joked.

Peter shook his head, perplexed.

"I don't think he got it," Jake said.

"Got what?" Peter asked.

"Never mind," Lou Ann said.

The chauffeur assisted them out of the back seat.

"Damn! This place is huge!"

It was as colossal as Lou Ann remembered, but more welcoming from the perspective of scaling a fence and crawling on her belly.

Now she just walked up to the place.

A gentleman in a black suit and tie came out of the mansion's double doors and walked down the rounded marble stairs of the portico.

"George, please take these bags to the two suites I've prepared on the east wing of the second floor."

George easily handled the two small bags.

"Follow me," Peter said to Lou Ann and Jake. "You each have your own separate suite. He isn't Harry. He not be new Harry?"

"No, Jake is my friend, and not new Harry."

It was too complicated to explain that she and Jake once were more than friends.

"Oh, good." Peter looked at Jake. "Nothing personal."

"Didn't take it at that way. And thanks for putting us up."

"You 're welcome, Jake." Peter leaned over and whispered in Lou Ann's ear. "And 'not Harry'."

Lou Ann squeezed Peter's hand. "Harry couldn't come. He's on a secret assignment."

"He come later, then."

"Um…maybe. But I'm here."

"Thank God."

"Yes, thank God."

Peter, Lou Ann, and Jake followed George up the staircase to the second floor, and along a hallway.

George stopped at one room.

"Jake, this is your room."

"Thanks."

George delivered Jake's bag.

Jake reached for his wallet.

"No, you're welcome guest of Lady Kaylee."

Jake nodded and closed his door.

Peter and Lou Ann followed George to two doors down.

"Lou Ann, this your suite."

Lou Ann stared at a room the size of hers and Harry's and Joanna's bedrooms combined.

"I'll get lost in here."

"You get accustomed to it."

"I don't know."

"Lie down. Rest. Long flight. Different hours. I don't want you to fall over. Kaylee needs you be awake. Nothing you can do now but rest. Tomorrow come soon enough."

"No tomorrow. Today. I need to see Kaylee today."

"So, she see you with red eyes? No good. Difficult, but you must be strong. Nothing change today."

"I'll rest, but I'm meeting with Anelle and the other attorney and probably Thelonious."

"Okay. They come here for dinner and meeting."

"I don't have time to make those arrangements."

"I call Thelonious and he make arrangements. You no worry. Close eyes. Rest."

Peter went to the door.

"I wake you in time."

"Okay."

"Okay."

Peter left and quietly closed her door.

Lou Ann went into the mega-bathroom and splashed cold water on her face.

She walked out of the bathroom and was about to lie down when the door squeaked ajar.

"Hello?" a woman said.

"Uh...hello."

"May I enter?"

Lou Ann planted her feet firmly on the floor in her familiar deputy stance.

An older woman in a black and white pinafore, and with her silver hair in a tight bun, stepped inside Lou Ann's guest quarters while carrying a stack of puffy white towels.

"I am Vasiliki. Sorry to interrupt, but I bring fresh towels."

"Vasilki, I remember you."

Vasiliki bowed her head. "Not good memory."

"No. But Kaylee speaks so highly of you."

"She no like me so much at first, but people and things change. We good friends. She like daughter I never have. I pray for her every day."

"I do too."

Vasiliki blinked away tears, and if she stayed any longer, the two of them would end up blubbering.

Vasiliki cleared her throat, proceeded into the the bathroom, and then returned.

"I go now," she said. "You sleep. I wake you for dinner."

"Thank you, Vasiliki."

"You most welcome."

The door closed for the second time.

Lou Ann lay on the bed and stared at the high, scalloped ceiling.

Her eyes burned and her shoulders ached from the long flight and the stress, but her mind kept ticking.

She rolled to one side and then the other.

Someone shook her shoulder.

"What?!"

Lou Ann blinked and Vasiliki's face went from fuzzy to clear.

She must have dozed off.

Lou Ann sat up.

"Thank you for waking me."

"I come back soon to get you for dinner."

"I'll be ready."

Lou Ann plopped her bag on the bed and unzipped it. She unrolled her clothes that she carefully packed to budget space. Thank goodness they'd survived unscathed and wearable.

She hadn't been out to dinner much if one didn't count going to the local diner. What she wouldn't give to be at that diner with Kaylee, Joanna, and Harry.

Lou Ann dressed in a black nylon pants and a white stretchy wrap blouse that revealed only modest cleavage. She brushed her hair and reapplied makeup. Then she slid into black pumps and sat on the bed waiting for Vasiliki to arrive.

But she answered the knock on the door to find Peter.

"Where's Vasiliki?"

"She help in kitchen. I come. I disappoint you?"

"No, not at all."

Peter held out his hand.

"Escort you to dinner?"

"You may, and I'm hungry."

"Good. I take care of both."

Peter led her down an unfamiliar marble staircase and into a dining room filled with the longest dining table she'd ever seen outside of a documentary highlighting homes of the rich.

Anelle, Constantine, Thelonious, and even Jake were already seated, the massive table dwarfing them.

"Sorry, I'm late," Lou Ann said with a sheepish grin.

Anelle smiled. "We're actually early, and you're the one who's on time."

It didn't feel that way.

The chair at the distant head of the table lay empty, and the chair next to it ,too.

She was positive the vacant chairs belonged to Demetrios, who was never going to sit there again, and to Kaylee, who was going to once again dine there.

Lou Ann sat next to Jake, and opposite Kaylee's legal team.

George entered the dining room along with the chef.

"For this evening, we present you with Pastitsio, a traditional type of Greek lasagna."

Surely the description was meant for her and Jake, the only non-Greeks at the expansive table.

"You'll adore this," Thelonious said.

"I'm a bad Greek woman who doesn't cook, but dines out a lot. But this, you can't even get at the best restaurant. My compliments to the chef,"Anelle enthused.

Fresh-cut cucumbers and tomatoes surrounded the Greek lasagna from heaven.

"I have to move here," Jake said.

"Pass the Greek bar. I'm in need of a thirsty associate."

"I may take you up on that."

Lou Ann smiled, but offered no such relocation fantasy. Her sole purpose in Greece was to make sure Kaylee had a choice.

The Greek lasagna melted in her growling stomach.

She swallowed and put her fork down. While she savored this dinner, Kaylee was alone, chomping through prison food.

"Everything to your satisfaction?" George asked. "I can have the chef bring you something else."

"No, it's delicious."

Lou Ann picked up her fork and decided she'd eat so she wouldn't insult her hosts, but to also keep up her strength.

After finishing their meals, everyone moved to the parlor for coffee and dessert, and to discuss their action plan.

Lou Ann and Kaylee's legal team settled on the sofas in the sitting room.

George brought out coffee and baklava and then departed, sliding the French doors shut.

"Let's begin," Constantine said.

"I'll be following up on Adam's autopsy report, which should be completed within the week," Anelle said.

Thelonious sipped his coffee. "I'm an extra, but I'll do whatever you need."

"Thelonious, you can find Daphne, because we not only need to interview her beyond the police report, but even most important, we need her regarding the whereabouts of Kosmos. So far he's evaded the police, but they are searching all the apartments Demetrios had owned, which are many."

Lou Ann ping-ponged between the conversation, not being in the game.

But she'd change that. Her seven years in law enforcement kicked in.

"I've investigated countless homicides as a US deputy, so I've dealt with evidence gathering and have experience testifying regarding the crime scene and the suspect."

Lou Ann pressed her lips tight. Kaylee *was* the suspect.

"I had no idea of your background," Anelle said.

"Neither did I," Constantine added.

"Surprised me too. A good surprise," Thelonious added.

"I didn't disclose that earlier because I was…am…focused on Kaylee as family. That hasn't changed. But I can't sit on my hands."

"Of course not, and we wouldn't want you to," Anelle declared.

"I knew she would step into gear, and now you have the best of the best," Jake declared.

"He's biased," Lou Ann said.

"Biased? The woman ticketed me."

"You were speeding."

"Precisely. But I do a lot more than pull over speedsters."

"You're invaluable to us," Anelle said. "Because you don't have Greek credentials, you can come with me to inspect the evidence collected, clearly one of your strengths."

"I'm there!"

"This is my plan for tomorrow night, "Constantine began. "It will be Saturday, peak club night."

Anelle grinned. "I know where you're going with this. Brilliant."

Lou Ann refused to be the odd woman out. "Bring me up to speed about *brilliant*."

"Oh, our fault. Constantine recognized Kosmos , who before this all went down, in an Athens nightclub, even though Kosmos was wearing a disguise and using the alias of Tobias."

"Even Kaylee recognized him when I showed her this photo."

Constantine tossed the photo on the table.

"I've never seen Kosmos before, so I can't comment on this photo," Lou Ann said.

Thelonious took out another photo. "This is what Kosmos really looks like."

Lou Ann and Jake studied the photos side by side.

"I see it now," Jake said.

"He's not disabled!" Lou Ann shouted. She lowered her voice. "Sorry."

"Don't be. We were as shocked and angry as you about his deceit." Constantine said. "So, I'm hoping he'll be at that club and once we spot him, we can quietly notify the authorities, and have them nab that cowardly bastard who framed Kaylee.

"I'll go with you," Lou Ann announced

"I'm going too," Jake said.

Lou Ann narrowed her eyes. "We'll make it a night for him to remember forever."

50

The parlor meeting concluded, and Anelle, Constantine, and Thelonious bid everyone a good evening.

"I'm beat. I'm out for the night," Jake said.

Lou Ann yawned. "I'm fading too."

"There are many stairs and passages, and is easy to get lost," Peter said. "I will lead you to rooms."

Lou Ann and Jake followed Peter to the second floor.

Jake waved. "Good night. Peter." He winked at Lou Ann. "Until tomorrow."

She nodded. "Until tomorrow."

Lou Ann waited until Jake closed his door and gestured to Peter to walk farther.

"I need to see Adam's room."

Peter shook his head.

"Is it still closed as a crime scene?" she asked.

"No. Police got all they need. Door locked."

"Please," she begged. "I need to arm myself with everything I can to help Kaylee. You want to help Kaylee, don't you?"

Peter hesitated and then agreed.

"We go to third floor, where Adam room is, two rooms away from Kaylee's."

"They were that close!?"

"When Demetrios here, he put Kaylee safe in very wonderful room. Adam not been here in two years and never planned to return. After Demetrios die and Kaylee inherit , Adam and Kosmos very angry. Daphne unhappy too. Adam come back for fight." Peter bowed his head. "I should have protected her, move her to close to me, even though in staff wing. But she stubborn…but strong."

"She is both, and it wasn't your fault. Kaylee would never blame you."

"Come with me."

Lou Ann followed Peter to the third floor.

Her heart pounded harder with every step.

Peter stopped. "Here is room."

He reached into his pocket, removed a key, and unlocked the door. He pushed it open, releasing the stink of rancid bloody remains, the kind that sticks to tires running over roadkill. But this wasn't an animal fatefully surprised before its demise. Adam might not have been embraced, and perhaps had been morally challenged, but he was a person—a murdered son.

"Vasiliki was ordered to stay out, but now okay. She come in morning, and she and I clean."

It was the same in the US when the owner was stuck with the ultimate emotional and financial burden to restore order once the scene was cleared.

Lou Ann stepped inside.

Adam's bedding had been removed, his mattress left bare. Blood spatter covered one wall. Lou Ann took out her cell and snapped photos of what remained after the scene was processed—positive that the crime scene unit had taken their own photos.

She widened her eyes at the smashed model jet. They didn't take that?

Lou Ann didn't touch the jet parts for fear of contaminating part of a scene they might have missed or not considered relevant. She stepped over dried, caked blood smears and took photos of the blood smears and the broken model.

She proceeded into the bathroom. A razor and shaving cream sat on the vanity counter, and an electric toothbrush sat fully charged in is cradle.

Lou Ann walked back to Peter, who waited for her at the open door.

"I'm finished. You can lock it up."

Peter secured Adam's room.

"I want to see Kaylee's room."

Peter's eyes sagged.

"I show you."

Peter stopped two doors away and unlocked Kaylee's door.

Because of the colossal rooms, two doors down was more like a pedestrian hike.

Peter unlocked Kaylee's paradise.

Demertrios indeed loved her. He could have kept her well within his grasp, but instead he gave her own heaven on earth. Lou Ann was convinced Demetrios did indeed regret getting involved with Newell. Kaylee was right. They were meant for each other, despite how they were brought together.

Her palatial suite was completely in order. Although Vasiliki cared for Kaylee's suite, surely Kaylee ditched her sloppiness. She had gained pride and a much-needed maturity from her brief time with Demetrios.

An undigested dinner rolled around in her stomach, and its remnants crawled up to the back of her throat.

"Please, I need to get back to my room."

"You sick?"

"No, I'm just tired. I didn't rest enough."

"Okay, we go now."

Peter locked Kaylee's suite and led Lou Ann back to her second floor room.

"Can I get you anything?" Peter asked.

"No, thank you. I have water."

"You call me anytime, even in middle of night and I come."

"I know you would. Goodnight."

Lou Ann started to close the door.

She didn't want to rush Peter along, but her dinner was about to come up.

Lou Ann ran into the suite's bathroom, leaned over the toilet, and let loose her dinner and dessert.

Her stomach muscles cramped, but nothing more came up.

She was absolutely positive this wasn't food poisoning, but due to stress.

Lou Ann was convinced she just ate too fast.

All she needed was rest.

Peter was right. Nothing was going to change about Kaylee's detention tonight no matter how much she wished it were so.

Tomorrow she'd see Kaylee and let her know she had an army of attorneys and herself, Harry, and Joanna, as well as Peter, Vasiliki , and all the others of Demetrios's staff who were also pulling for her.

Lou Ann rinsed her mouth and forced herself to take a quick shower.

Clean but exhausted, she crawled onto the blessedly cushy bed and had just closed her eyes when her cell rang.

She sleepily grabbed it, because it might be a crucial change involving Kaylee.

"Hello? she muttered.

"Lou Ann?"

She blinked awake.

It was Harry!

"Lou Ann, babe, are you all right?"

"I'm okay," she sniffled.

"I completed my assignment and got my personal cell back. I just read all your messages and texts. I can't believe what's happening."

"I can't either."

"I'm in Denver and waiting for my flight to Tampa. When I get home I'll book a flight to Athens."

Stab in the heart.

"No, Harry. Stay home because you might be called back out. It's not like last time, when it was a trafficking assignment." Lou Ann swallowed and paused. "I need you to work because…I've been suspended, which is code for termination."

"Lou Ann…."

"It's okay. I did what I had to, and they did what they had to, given I've already gone way past a leave of absence. They'll need to fill my position, because I may be here a while."

" A while,' Harry repeated softly.

"But Jake's colleague, Anelle, who's licensed to practice in the US and Greece, is kick-ass and Demetrios's attorney, who oversaw the will, enlisted a colleague, Constantine, who's also very sharp. So Kaylee is well represented, and we hope and pray we can free her.'

"Jake?"

"Yes. He came with me because of Anelle. He and I are staying at the mansion in separate suites. I just needed to talk with you—to be with me and Kaylee."

"You know I am and always will be."

"I know. But I need to hear your voice."

"And I need to hear you."

"Save my spot in the bed."

"I'll keep it warm. I love you. My plane is boarding."

"I love you too. And I'll call you every day."

"And I'll answer no matter what time it is."

Lou Ann ended the call and pressed her cell to her heart.

51

Lou Ann eased out of the bed. Her mind fluttered and her knees failed. She held onto the bed to quell her lightheadedness.

After several deep breaths, she straightened, her momentary morning condition abated.

Dehydration collided with jet lag.

Lou Ann winced and tiptoed to the bathroom to find something that would keep away the lurking beast of a headache.

Nothing that fluids and an aspirin wouldn't fix.

And nothing was going to keep her from seeing Kaylee today.

She brushed her teeth and gargled the sour taste out of her mouth, and then dressed in pressed beige slacks and a creme-colored blouse, both fitting but a bit snug.

Lou Ann kept her usual makeup light and professional.

She slipped her feet into her shoes and rushed out of her room.

She'd memorized the maze to the dining room, and took off not waiting for anyone.

She'd meet Jake at breakfast and then she'd be off to the prison.

"Good morning, Peter," she said, startling him.

"I was going up to escort you."

"Thank you, but I'm here."

Peter gazed at her.

"You need strong coffee."

"I do. And do you have any aspirin?"

"I do. I get you."

"Jet lag catching up with me," she qualified.

Lou Ann sat at the ridiculously long table.

George brought her coffee and two aspirin.

"Thank you. Light breakfast. Maybe just a Danish."

"Very well."

Jake tottered into the dining room. "Damn, my head is revolting. Is that aspirin?"

"Yes."

George entered carrying a plate topped with a cheese Danish.

"I'll have what she's having, including the aspirin."

"Popular breakfast today," George said.

"On the bright side, I passed out last night," Jake said.

"I slept okay," she said, stretching the truth.

"You do look a bit peaked."

"Just nervous about going to that prison and seeing Kaylee."

"I'm sure she'll be happy to see you too. I'm going to work with Anelle today, and tonight we'll go *clubbing*."

"Looks like my day and night is filled."

The chauffeur let Lou Ann off at the secured entrance, and because he wasn't allowed to stay for security reasons, she'd call for him to return.

"Be well and strong," he said. "I'll be around close, and you call when ready, okay?"

"Okay, thank you!"

Lou Ann entered the visitors' door and immediately searched.

"I'm here to visit with Kaylee Jasinski. I am her aunt, Lou Ann Jasinski."

A woman guard led her to a bare room with long tables and chairs, and a wooden barrier separating them.

Three visitors sat quietly chatting with the women inmates.

Lou Ann clasped her hands while waiting for Kaylee to be ushered in. She was prepared to see Kaylee not looking like her usual self, and promised herself she wouldn't look shocked or even surprised.

Handcuffs and leg irons rattled.

A guard ushered Kaylee into the visiting room.

Kaylee's blonde hair sagged, oily and flat on her shoulders. Her thin lips curved into a smile.

Lou Ann held out her hands.

"Sit. No touch," the guard warned Lou Ann.

Lou Ann complied. She'd visited prisoners before, but not family.

Kaylee sat opposite Lou Ann.

"I'm so sorry, " Kaylee blurted.

Tears streaked down both their faces.

"I'm here for you, and you have an army of lawyers and me working on this day and night. Just hold on. You'll be free soon."

"I know how it goes," Aunt Lou Ann. "I might be here for one to two years. I love you, but go home."

"Nope. I'm not leaving until you do. We're going to get to Kosmos," LouAnn whispered.

"Okay," Kaylee droned.

"We have a plan."

"Okay."

Lou Ann stared at Kaylee's wan face.

"It's not in your nature or mine to give up. Genetics, you know."

Kaylee smiled.

Lou Ann grinned back. "See?"

Kaylee changed the subject.

"Don't lose too much sleep over me. Weirdly, I'm getting used to my cell. They actually brought me sheets and a pillow this morning. And I have the place to myself. No roommates. And after my attorney meeting, my meals got edible. And I have a calendar."

"I still won't be able to sleep soundly."

"Is Harry here?"

"No. He called last night as soon as he got all my calls and messages. He was on a secret assignment and didn't have his personal cell." She'd carefully let Kaylee down. "He's not on assignment here this time, and he may be unpredictably called out, so we discussed everything that's going on and, although he's heartbroken, he'll call you and me at least every day. I'm sorry."

Lou Ann didn't plan to divulge that her career was on CPR.

"I understand. I wouldn't want him to get him in trouble…or you."

"No worries. I'm good."

"Please let Harry, and Joanna, and Isabelle know I'm thinking about them."

"They know, sweetie."

"Time's up," the guard announced.

"I put money in your account so you can buy something at the commissary. I'll keep replenishing it."

"Thank you."

"You'll be shopping at the mall soon."

"The mall's not important anymore."

"Gotcha!"

"Bye, Aunt Lou Ann."

"Bye for now."

Lou Ann watched Kaylee trudge away, and then called for the chauffeur.

52

With her stomach still processing the abbreviated breakfast, Lou Ann bypassed lunch. Instead she lay on the bed, recalling Kaylee's drawn face and her stooped shoulders.

She needed to get her out of that prison—and fast.

And tonight was a make or break night.

Kosmos better be there tonight.

The last time Lou Ann went clubbing was ten years ago and that was in the states.

She doubted nightclubs changed, but then she'd never been to one in Greece.

She only packed conservative and moderately dressy clothes, but not anything to wear at a nightclub without sticking out.

Jake always looked sporty, and men could pass easier at a club. But a woman? No.

Perhaps Kaylee had some club-worthy clothes in that mega-closet that Lou Ann could squeeze into.

She called Peter, but he sent Vasiliki, the woman who, admittedly, wasn't fashion forward.

But to Lou Ann's surprise, Vasiliki led her to Kaylee's never-ending closet and went straight to a flattering A-line retro black, sequined dress with matching sandals.

"Look good," Vasiliki said. "I used to pick out for Kaylee."

"Thanks."

"You are welcome. Go get Kosmos. And put on lipstick."

Lou Ann and Jake followed Anelle and Constantine into the dim, smoky Athens nightclub, nearly blinded by the kaleidoscope of disco lights illuminating their path to a far empty table.

Jake pulled out her chair.

"Thanks," she shouted above the pulsating Greek techno music.

Anelle and Constantine sat too.

Kosmos wouldn't recognize them, but he'd peg Thelonious, and they couldn't risk him fleeing, so Thelonious stayed behind, choosing to work on Kaylee's defense.

A waitress approached and took their orders in Greek.

Constantine ordered their prearranged drinks—seltzer for her.

And then they saw him.

Kosmos swayed to the music while meandering through the crowd to the bar, where he slid onto a barstool.

Bingo.

The waitress brought Anelle and Constantine their cocktails, plus a beer for Jake, and Lou Ann's seltzer.

"That's all what you're going to have?" Jake shouted in her ear.

"Yep."

Hard liquor, or even a beer, would not play nice with her stomach, and she couldn't chance having to heave in a ladies' room and lose sight of Kosmos. Kaylee's future depended on nabbing him.

"Dance?" Jake asked.

The last thing she wanted to do was to twirl about, but she had to blend in.

Jake took her hand.

He grinned ear to ear.

"Bet you never thought you'd be in a place like this with me," he shouted above the music.

Lou Ann smiled back. "Not in my wildest dreams!"

Lou Ann kept an eye on Kosmos, who was leaning against a lady who was clearly out of his league.

The woman tossed her perfectly trimmed black hair off her shoulder. But she didn't walk away. What was it about Kosmos?

Then he slipped the woman a rolled paper.

Ah, so that was the attraction.

Wow. A disabled drug dealer.

Lou Ann kept dancing and nodded meaningfully in Kosmos's direction.

"I saw," Jake acknowledged.

"And?"

"And what? It's a nightclub."

"I raided these kinds of places."

"Yeah, well, you're in one of these kinds of places."

Jake had a point.

"Enjoy yourself on that seltzer."

"I will."

Kosmos pushed off the barstool.

Shit! He was heading toward the door.

Then Constantine jumped up and yelled something in Greek.

The bar patrons began to cheer, and Kosmos returned to the bar.

The bartender sloshed drinks everywhere.

"Damn! He just bought drinks for everyone. That's a hell of a bar tab!" Jake yelled.

"He's apparently as wealthy as he is smart," Lou Ann replied.

Lou Ann took out her cell and documented the free-for-all.

Constantine and Anelle caught up with them.

"Outside, now, and watch out for the stampede when the police arrive. I just called them about Kosmos's location. I'll stay."

Anelle ushered Lou Ann and Jake to an alley. "Stand against the wall. We'll be okay."

Adrenaline pumped through Lou Ann's veins. She was going to miss the excitement of raids and arrests, but not the paperwork! And definitely not Dan!

Throngs of partygoers thundered out of the club.

Kosmos could escape in the crowd.

Sirens blared and blue lights pulsed.

Lou Ann, Jake, and Anelle crept out of their hiding spot, and just in time to see Kosmos in handcuffs and Constantine following behind with a satisfied grin.

Mission accomplished!

After celebrating the first item in a strong defense for Kaylee, Lou Ann bounced on the bed in her room while still wearing in Kaylee's sequined outfit, now a lucky one. She'd keep it on a bit longer while she savored the successful evening.

The police were detaining Kosmos until Monday, when he'd go before a judge.

Lou Ann picked up her cell and called Harry with the encouraging news.

"Hey, babe."

"Great news. We cornered Kosmos in a nightclub where he was using an alias and peddling drugs. They've detained him until Monday for the drug charge and to question him about Adam's murder. I can't wait to tell Kaylee the news."

"Whoa. That's a positive finding and already the hill is less of a climb."

"I know, but I'm not going to quit until Kaylee's vindicated."

"And you shouldn't. I'm itching to be there, but I've thought hard about it and you're right."

"It's not a punishment."

"I know. Joanna and I are praying for you and Kaylee to come home."

"She may be free. But I have to let her decide about whether to go home."

"True. Love you, and it's night there. Get some rest. Nightclubs can be draining," he teased.

"We'll have to go to one when I get back."

"I'll root through my disco clothes!"

"Ewww."

Lou Ann and Harry chuckled at the same time.

"Good night, babe. While you sleep, I'm going to mow the lawn."

"Goodnight."

53

Lou Ann woke early Sunday morning grateful for last night's arrest of Kosmos. Plus, as bonus, she finally slept managing an uninterrupted sleep, and started the day with renewed vigor.

She showered, dressed in her own conservative clothes, and walked alongside Peter and Vasiliki, who'd invited her to attend church services.

The minute she stepped into the Greek Orthodox Church, incense and a grand mysticism overwhelmed her soul.

She'd been raised Protestant, but her attendance after her mother died and her father committed suicide waned to a nonexistence.

Vasiliki gave her a candle.

"For Kaylee," she said.

Lou Ann followed Vasiliki to the gold candle stand, lit the candle from the others offered, and planted it for Kaylee.

The service, which was called Divine Liturgy, brought tears to her eyes.

She thanked God for the justice being served, and prayed for Kaylee to be declared innocent and cleared of all charges.

The flickers of candles and the chanting returned a resounding "Believe."

They'd returned from church planning a day of rest.

Lou Ann's cell rang.

Anelle was calling her.

Lou Ann's heart rocketed.

Something good. She'd already prayed.

"Lou Ann, Daphne was rushed to the hospital this morning. She's in intensive care and on a ventilator."

Lou Ann sat with Peter, Thelonious, and Anelle in the hospital waiting room.

A doctor entered and searched the room.

"Family for Daphne?"

She purposely left off Sakalis, but they were the only ones present.

Thelonious raised his hand.

Since Daphne had no relatives or children to address, and with Demetrios and Adam dead and Kosmos in jail, Thelonious, as the Sakalis attorney, was Daphne's closest de facto representative.

"We're all here for Daphne," Thelonious clarified.

The doctor sat across from them.

"Miss Sakalis was transported to our hospital after collapsing outside an Athens apartment belonging to her brother, who was not present. She was barely breathing. She is now in intensive care and on a ventilator. Her heart is strong, but she's unresponsive. The brain scan is normal, but she is severely anemic, and it appears to be a chronic condition, something called aplastic anemia, and her blood work is suspicious for leukemia."

They all leaned forward as if they were listening to some macabre tale.

"Her blood is being screened for toxins."

Peter shook his head. "She hasn't been sick."

"I saw her in my office just last week and she seemed perfectly healthy," Thelonious added. "It doesn't make sense."

A chill crept up Lou Ann's spine and goose bumps freckled her forearms."Wait! What did Kosmos's wife die from?"

"Leukemia," Thelonious and Peter said at the same time.

"Doctor, does her toxicology screen heavy metals like arsenic?" Lou Ann asked.

The doctor stood. "I'll add it. Excuse me." She hurried away.

"Come with me," Lou Ann said to Thelonious. "Daphne has to have a key to the apartment somewhere in her belongings."

Lou Ann and Thelonious rushed to the the intensive care, and Thelonious convinced the nurse to let him go through Daphne's belongings, where he discovered the key to the apartment in her purse.

"Let's go," Lou Ann said.

Lou Ann and Thelonious jumped into Anelle's car and, directed her to Kosmos's apartment.

With Sunday traffic light, they arrived within ten minutes.

God was on her side.

Anelle parked outside the apartment, and they scrambled out of the car and up to the apartment door.

Thelonious jammed the key into the door and shoved it open.

"What are we looking for?" he asked.

"Anything and everything." Lou Ann said. "This is where Daphne collapsed last, and she was surely here searching for Kosmos."

The apartment was orderly, and then Lou Ann spied a a half-eaten pear on a plate on the kitchen table.

"Find me a plastic bag—or any bag."

Anelle and Thelonious rummaged through cabinets and drawers.

"Here! Plastic bags," Anelle shouted.

"Bring one here."

Lou Ann grabbed a paper towel and picked up the half-eaten pear, dumped it into the bag, and sealed it.

"We need to go back to the hospital."

They rushed out of Kosmos's apartment and climbed into Anelle's car.

She jammed on the accelerator while Lou Ann clutched the plastic bag.

"I'll drop you off in front of the hospital, and then I'll go park the car."

Lou Ann and Thelonious rushed back to the intensive care.

"I need to speak with Daphne Sakalis's doctor," Lou Ann announced, breathless.

The doctor came out of Daphne's ICU cubicle.

Daphne's choking echoed into the hall.

"You got me thinking, and I couldn't wait. Daphne responded after we injected an activated charcoal and magnesium mix into her nasogastric tube. We were just able to take out her breathing tube. We're repeating her blood work now, and I should have her toxicology report by tomorrow. I've also called the police to report a highly suspicious poisoning."

"When they show up, give them this. This pear was the last thing she half ate."

One candle had worked many miracles!

54

Lou Ann tossed back coffee and her standard cheese Danish.

Anelle was waiting for her.

"I don't know when I'll be back," she yelled to Peter on her way out the door.

She climbed into Anelle's car.

"Excellent news," Anelle reported.

"I can use excellent news."

"Daphne is awake and recovering. Still waiting for the toxicology. Better yet, Adam's autopsy report is ready. We'll pick up a copy. I was able to secure the evidence from the scene including the blood spatter analysis. And hold on." Anelle beamed. "I got us an emergency hearing with the investigating judge in Kaylee's case because of the titanic shift regarding Kosmos's arrest. But we have to dot all our i's and cross all our t's, and let the facts do the rest."

God is definitely pulling the strings.

Lou Ann and Anelle grabbed the autopsy report and proceeded to the police station only to discover that Thelonious and Constantine had already arrived and combed through the evidence gathered from Adam's room.

"While you were all at the club last night, I made extensive notes, reviewed them on Sunday, and called Constantine early this morning. We can prove Kaylee couldn't have shot Adam, and physics doesn't lie," Thelonious explained, his voice rising with excitement, and his words spilling over.

"And we have Adam's autopsy to prove it too."

"I just have to kiss you, Thelonious!"

Lou Ann planted a kiss on each of Thelonious's cheeks.

"Kaylee should be on the way for the 10 am hearing," Anelle warned.

"Let's roll!" Constantine called."I'll ride with Thelinious and, Anelle and Lou Ann will meet us at the court."

Lou Ann jumped into Anelle's vehicle and buckled her seat belt.

This could be it.

The guard unlocked Kaylee's cell door.

Kaylee held up the empty breakfast plate.

"I'm finished."

But the guard approached her and not the plate.

"Please. I didn't do anything wrong."

"Hands," the guard ordered.

Something bad happened. She was never going to get out of here.

Her heart grew heavy in her chest and Kaylee turned and put her hands behind her back. The handcuffs clicked.

She waited for the leg irons that did not come.

Another guard joined them.

"Court today."

Court? She was about to be convicted already? On a Monday? Did Lou Ann know? Where was her army of attorneys?

"I want to speak to my attorneys," Kaylee announced.

"You'll see your attorneys in court."

A lot of good that'll do. They couldn't help her.

The guards shuffled her to the prison transport van, loaded her inside, and then got in.

The driver pulled away.

Kaylee looked out the window at the Athens bright morning, shades of her and Demetrios promenading the streets she'd never see again.

The van stopped and the guards unloaded Kaylee.

"Face the judge. You'll be fine."

"Keep the van running," she called to the driver over her shoulder.

The guards escorted her up the court steps and past the heavy doors.

Kaylee's heart lifted.

"Lou Ann!"

Her aunt bowed her head.

This was bad. Lou Ann had come to see her for the last time, to be with her before they locked her away.

Kaylee scanned the room. No jury. They didn't even accord her that.

Her attorneys nodded, and Kaylee was seated to the right of the same investigating judge who came before her that first day when she declined to answer all his inquiries. Now she had no choice but to answer.

* * *

"I understand you have new evidence which emerged this weekend. So I have agreed to this emergency hearing," the judge declared from his bench.

Anelle stood. "We have, your honor."

"Bring it forward."

The judge peered over his papers at Lou Ann.

"And who is this?"

Lou Ann stood.

"I'm Lou Ann Jasinski, Kaylee Jasinski's aunt."

The stoic-faced judge nodded.

"I have the autopsy results for Adam Michael Sakalis."

The judge gestured for Anelle to approach.

Anelle handed the envelope from the medical examiner's office to the judge.

"You may sit."

Anelle returned to her seat.

The judge opened the envelope and skimmed over its contents.

"Mmmm," was his only comment.

"He didn't even read it," Lou Ann whispered in Anelle's ear.

"Just wait," Anelle whispered back.

The judge eyed them, and Lou Ann and Anelle folded their hands in their laps doing their best to appear well-behaved.

"Anything else?"

Kaylee 's jaw dropped.

Constantine stood.

"Along with the autopsy result, we have reviewed the collected evidence including blood spatter on the walls and on the clothes our client, Kaylee Jasinski, was wearing. There is no gun residue on her clothes nor is there any spatter or blowback from her alleged discharge of the firearm. She picked up the gun belonging to Kosmos Sakalis only after he shot his son, left the scene, and then returned and lunged at Kaylee Jasinski. However, she did not discharge the firearm in self-defense. Peter Halaris, and Kosmos's sister, Daphne Sakalis, arrived after the fact. Kosmos fled and was arrested Saturday night on drug trafficking charge in an Athens night club. He is presently being detained."

The judge nodded, and said, "I will review the evidence you have submitted. Mr. Kosmos Sakalis remains to be interviewed. And where is Daphne Sakalis?"

"She is presently in a hospital intensive care unit after being poisoned. She was found outside an apartment belonging to Kosmos Sakalis, who also goes by the alias of Tobias. No last name."

The judge shifted in his chair while he apparently mulled over the newly disclosed details.

"You may remand Miss Kaylee Jasinski. I will render my decision whether to pass this case forward within the week."

"Within the week?" Lou Ann whispered .

"That's actually expedited."

"Is there an issue you wish to discuss further?" the judge asked.

"No, your Honor."

"This hearing is over."

Lou Ann rushed over to Kaylee, but the guards blocked her.

"Kaylee!"

Kaylee sent her a forced half smile.

Lou Ann watched, helpless, while the guards escorted Kaylee out of the courtroom. Kaylee didn't look back.

"This isn't right!" Lou Ann protested after the judge left.

Anelle wrapped her arm around Lou Ann's shoulders.

"Time is on our side."

Time. That was all she and Kaylee had left.

Kaylee rolled to face the cell's lifeless gray wall. She was trapped again.

"Lunch," the guard announced.

Kaylee continued staring at what would be her forever home—which ironically was in Greece.

The lunch tray landed with a thud on the foot of the bed.

At least her cold shoulder to the guard didn't end with the tray dropped on the floor.

Her appetite was as lost as she was.

Kaylee rolled into a ball and away from the lunch tray.

Even her dream team of attorneys couldn't get her out of here.

The judge wasn't impressed even with every piece of evidence clearly in her favor.

But that's how the law worked or didn't work here.

Kaylee closed her eyes.

Demetrios ,what am I to do?

The smell of his cigar and his cologne permeated her cell.

Kaylee laughed.

It was all in her imagination.

Monday dragged on.

Anelle, Constantine, and Thelonious left the courtroom to meet and discuss contingency plans.

Lou Ann declined the meeting. There were no contingency plans. They'd presented hard evidence.

For God's sake, they had Kosmos in custody.

And it was still not enough for this judge. If he sent Kaylee's case to a trial judge, they'd have to start all over again.

And Kaylee knew it when she was led out of the so-called emergency hearing.

But no matter how long it took, she'd see to it that Kaylee was declared innocent.

55

Lou Ann did without Monday night's dinner, having slept right through it.

Vasiliki brought up a late-night plate of moussaka, so Lou Ann picked at it, not wanting to insult Vasiliki and the chef.

Everyone had been warm and welcoming to her. They truly loved Kaylee.

She hadn't the heart or the courage to call and disappoint Harry or Joanna. Instead she texted them about Kaylee's emergency hearing and said she was waiting for a decision from the judge.

Vasiliki came to remove her plate and kissed Lou Ann on the head.

"Everything will be good. Kaylee be back soon."

She woke to horns blaring.

Footsteps ran to her door.

"Get up! Get up!" Peter yelled.

He stirred Jake awake too.

"Come downstairs now!"

Lou Ann had fallen asleep in her clothes. She hurried down the marble stairs to the dining room.

"Champagne for breakfast!" Anelle cheered.

Constantine swooped Lou Ann up in his arms, plunked her on a sofa, and Anelle handed her a glass of champagne.

Jake raised his arms. "Yeehaw!"

Lou Ann's head swirled.

This was the funkiest dream.

"Hey, Miss Deer in the Headlights. It's true. The investigating judge ruled. Kaylee is free. Kosmos is going to take her place. And thanks to you, Daphne is awake and has been transferred to a regular room."

"Oh, my God. I'm *not* dreaming."

"Nope," Jake said. "If you were dreaming, I wouldn't be in it!" he joked.

Every muscle in her body shook.

"Give me a phone! Give me a phone!"

"Hello," Harry answered on the first ring even though it was the middle of the night there.

Lou Ann's heart pounded to almost out of her chest.

"We did it! Kaylee's free."

"Oh my God. Joanna!" he yelled

Harry put the phone on speaker.

"Joanna, baby! Kaylee's free!"

"I want to talk to her!"

"It's a process. They're getting her ready to be released."

"Hallelujah, baby!"

"Hallelujah! I'm going to go get her. We're coming home!"

Lou Ann shifted in Anelle's car.

"I'm going to have to peel you off the roof of this car!"

"You might have to pull over," Lou Ann teased.

"This is strictly a nonstop trip."

Lou Ann clutched the bag of clothes and undergarments Vasiliki had packed for Kaylee to change into before her release.

Her bloodstained clothes would forever be stowed away in an evidence box. Kaylee would soon ditch the drab gray prison garb for something fresh from her closet.

Anelle pulled into the women's section of the prison.

"You know I can't stay here. I'll park down the road and return for you and Kaylee."

Lou Ann couldn't quit smiling.

"Don't go far!"

Lou Ann passed through security, and there stood Kaylee, quaking in her prison garb.

Lou Ann surrendered the bag to the guard.

"I'll bring her right back," the guard said.

Kaylee brightened and waved.

Lou Ann blew her a kiss.

"See you on the other side," Kaylee called.

56

Nine Months Later

Kaylee's chauffeur glided to a stop in front of the hospital lobby.

Joanna texted Kaylee, while Kaylee's jet landed, that Lou Ann's labor continued to crawl along.

Kaylee jumped out of the limo and rushed into the hospital and to the front desk.

"My aunt is in labor! Where's the maternity unit?!"

"Third floor," the woman at the desk said.

"Thanks!

"Wait! I need an ID."

Kaylee whipped her wallet out of her Daphne designer handbag. She pulled out her Greek driver's license.

"Oops. Wrong ID." She presented the Florida license.

The woman handed her a hospital pass and Kaylee smacked the adhesive badge on her blouse and dashed to the elevator bank.

She arrived on the maternity unit to find Jake and Anelle holding hands while sitting in the waiting room and next to a woman she didn't recognize.

"You're finally here!" Anelle cheered. "And given the nail-biting situation, I'm going to give you a pass from studying. We'll be in the states for the next week..." Anelle smiled and wagged her finger at Kaylee, "then back to your law courses."

"That's a promise."

The woman sitting next to Anelle and Jake, stood and offered her hand.

"Hello, Kaylee. I've heard all about you. I'm Glenda Martinez, from the sheriff's office. I rushed your aunt to the hospital when her water broke, despite her insistence that she needed to continue working on a homicide case. She's the hardest and sharpest homicide investigator we've ever had."

Kaylee shook Glenda's hand.

"I'm really proud of her."

Because of Lou Ann, Kaylee was now free and Kosmos was convicted, not only for Adam's murder, but also for the poisoning death of his wife Maria, confirmed after her exhumation, and his attempted insecticide poisoning of Daphne using the same insecticide. He failed to frame her, too. But in the end, Kaylee and Daphne won.

Lou Ann's groan echoed into the maternity hallway.

"I better get in there!" Kaylee said.

Lou Ann grabbed Harry's hand.

Her contractions increased exponentially, squeezing harder and faster.

Harry winced.

"Take it like a man," Kaylee quipped. "And hurry up, Aunt Lou Ann. First I had to come back for your wedding, and now you pull me back for this marathon!" she teased.

"Yeah. What she said," Harry begged.

"Shut up! I'm working here!" Lou Ann yelled.

"And you're doing an awesome job," Harry soothed.

Joanna inspected the fetal monitor. "The baby's looking good and your contractions are a minute apart. Should be anytime time."

Dr. Lindley, Lou Ann's OB, strode into the room. "Your niece is right!"

Joanna grinned. "Just practicing before I officially become a nurse."

"I'll be happy to hire you."

Kaylee rolled her eyes. "Show-off," she said to Joanna.

"Rich…you-know-what!"

Kaylee and Joanna cracked up and hugged.

"It's nice to know *someone's* having a good time!" Lou Ann shouted.

Dr. Lindley examined Lou Ann.

"You're completely dilated, and the baby's head is right here."

Nurses entered the room and heated an infant warmer.

Dr. Lindley dressed out in her delivery garb.

"The baby's coming now?" Harry asked.

"Yeah. I don't dress like this all the time," the doctor teased.

Dr. Lindley sat on her stool.

"Okay, Lou Ann, time to bring it home!"

Three pushes later, Lou Ann and Harry's baby squirmed into Dr. Lindley's arms.

"Here's your girl."

"Oh my, God. She's beautiful! Joanna cheered.

"Yeah, she's a bit wet but not hopeless," Kaylee said. "I'm kidding!" she added. "She's priceless!"

"Want to cut the cord, Harry?"

"Yeah!"

Harry cut his baby daughter's umbilical cord.

"I'm officially remaining outnumbered in this household. But I wouldn't have it any other way."

Lou Ann hugged her wet and squalling daughter to her chest.

"She'll fit right in with the rest of us," Kaylee added

Lou Ann stroked her baby daughter's hair.

She gazed at Kaylee and Joanna.

"Please meet Joley Kay Boxer."

Kaylee smiled and cooed at her and Joanna's namesake.

"This trip was definitely worth it!"

The End